"Trollope knows how to build suspense of the heart . . . It's a breeze to slip into the world of *A Spanish Lover* and once the novel is over, it's hard to leave behind the world that Trollope has so artfully constructed."

—*USA Today*

"Like much of her fiction, [*A Spanish Lover*] balances precariously on a thin line between serious fiction and soap opera, yet it never falls on the wrong side . . . All of her characters are at once vexing and endearing, which is to say fully human, and her prose is supple and smooth."

—*The Washington Post*

"This book is a marvel—for its crystal clear prose, skillful construction with flashbacks seamlessly woven in, and wonderful full-bodied and fallible characters. A rich, mature novel dealing with growth, change, loss, and survival, this is as entertaining as it ought to be enduring."

—*Booklist*

"With sparkling dialogue, Trollope brings all of her characters, adults and children, to full life while managing to bestow unforgettable glimpses of Spain in all its melancholy and magnificence. She makes her readers want to drop everything in order to keep on reading."

—*Publishers Weekly*

"Trollope turns conventional terrains and rural idylls into complex battlefields . . . This is a novel about people steering their own lives, but equally about other people's selfish, entirely human attempts to control them."

—*Newsday*

"Trollope constructs a beautiful plot, and her descriptions of Spain will have you itching to call your travel agent."

—*Library Journal*

"Like her illustrious ancestor, Trollope is a clear-eyed recorder of the sudden domestic tempests fueled by the ties of family affection and habit . . . A wonderfully wise and bracingly honest novel that celebrates happiness and the good, quiet things that sustain the human spirit."

—*Kirkus Reviews*

A SPANISH LOVER

JOANNA TROLLOPE

BERKLEY BOOKS, NEW YORK

A SPANISH LOVER

A Berkley Book / published by arrangement with
Random House, Inc.

PRINTING HISTORY
This book was originally published in Great Britain
by Bloomsbury Publishing Ltd., London, in 1993.
Random House edition / February 1997
Berkley edition / March 1998

The Penguin Putnam Inc. World Wide Web site address is
http://www.penguinputnam.com

ISBN: 0-425-16234-6

BERKLEY®
Berkley Books are published by The Berkley Publishing Group,
a member of Penguin Putnam Inc.,
200 Madison Avenue, New York, New York 10016.
BERKLEY and the "B" design
are trademarks belonging to Berkley Publishing Corporation.

PRINTED IN THE UNITED STATES OF AMERICA

10 9 8 7 6 5 4 3 2 1

For Liz C.

A SPANISH
LOVER

Joanna Trollope

PART
ONE

DECEMBER

ONE

Someone—probably one of the children; Robert would never have dared—had stuck a poster on the kitchen noticeboard. It was a small poster, printed in black and bright pink and yellow, and it showed a scatty drawing of a wild-haired woman hand in wing with a goggle-eyed turkey. Underneath the drawing it said, in wayward lettering, "Women and turkeys against Christmas."

"I think it had better be at least twenty-two pounds," Lizzie said into the telephone receiver. "No, not before it's drawn, after it's drawn. Will it be a free-range turkey?"

She looked across the kitchen at the poster and involuntarily touched her hair. It felt all right.

"Heavens," she said to the butcher. "That much more!" She screwed up her face. Was she going to be responsible about turkey liberation, or was she going to have another ten pounds to pour into the greedy maw of Christmas? "OK," she said. "Free-range." She thought of a whole lot of happy turkeys gobbling about together in an orchard somewhere like an illustration in a nursery book. "Free-range, twenty-two pounds, and either I or Mr. Middleton will collect it on Monday. Yes," she said, "yes, I know it's a late order, Mr. Moaby, but if you had this house and four children and Christmas and a business and three extra people coming to cope with, you'd be late too."

She put the telephone down. She should not have spoken like that. Mr. Moaby had run his butcher's shop in Langworth for a quarter of a century, like his father before him, and had a mentally handicapped child and was finding supermarket competition increasingly threatening. In his heart of hearts, Mr. Moaby probably felt about Christmas as women and turkeys did.

Lizzie went across the kitchen and peered at the poster. It wasn't hand-drawn; it was printed. No doubt Harriet had bought it, thin, clever, sarcastic thirteen-year-old Harriet, who would have spotted that Christmas had come to be a menace for her mother and not a marvel any more. Lizzie and Harriet had quarrelled at breakfast. They quarrelled most breakfasts and the quarrels usually ended with Harriet skipping off to school wearing her private and maddening smile, the one she wore to convey to her three younger brothers how much she pitied them for being mere boys, poor mutts.

Harriet had asked Lizzie if she was going into the Gallery that day, the Gallery that she and Robert had opened when they first came to Langworth sixteen years before. Lizzie said no, she wasn't.

"Why not?"

"Because of Christmas."

"Why on *earth*—" Harriet had lain back in her chair and rolled her eyes at the amazing, the impossible thought that anybody could put a minor domestic hiccup, like Christmas, before their real work in life.

Lizzie had lost her temper in an instant. She had heard herself, in horror, screeching about her exhausting multiple responsibilities and Harriet's unspeakable ingratitude. Harriet watched her, calmly. Davy, who was only five, began to cry, and large round tears slid down his unhappy face and diluted the milk in his bowl of Cocopops.

"Look," Harriet said with satisfaction. "Now you've made Davy cry."

Lizzie stopped screaming and stooped to put her arms round Davy.

"Oh darling—"

"You'll frighten Christmas away!" Davy wailed. "If you aren't careful!"

Harriet slid off her chair.

"I'm going to see Heather," she said. "I'll call in at the Gallery and tell Daddy you won't be in."

Lizzie set her teeth. "Please stay in the house, Harriet. I need you. There's so much to be done—"

Harriet gave a vast, deep, gusting sigh and dragged herself elaborately from the room, slamming the door shudderingly behind her.

Lizzie had fed Davy his cereal then, as if he were a baby, to comfort him, and afterwards she had set him and Sam to wind red festive ribbons round the banisters. Sam, who was eight, thought it would be more amusing to wind the ribbons round himself and Davy, and to attempt to wind them round the protesting cat. Lizzie had left them to it, to go upstairs and make beds and pull lavatory plugs and find, for herself, a hairbrush and some earrings and the list she had made last night, for today, and lost somewhere. Then she came downstairs again, to telephone the butcher, and found the poster. Harriet must have pinned it up in the fifteen minutes Lizzie was upstairs. Was it a sorry? Was it a gesture of solidarity? Lizzie longed for solidarity between herself and Harriet, for the conspiratorial closeness of being together in the same sex. That was what being a twin did to you, Lizzie thought, turning back to the table and the wreck of breakfast; it made you want to bind yourself tightly to someone else when your other half wasn't there. And Frances wouldn't be there until Christmas Eve.

Robert and Lizzie had started the Middleton Gallery in a tiny shop in one of Langworth's rambling side streets. They had met at art college—Lizzie a sculptor, Robert a graphic designer—and become inseparable. There was a photograph of them in those far-off days pinned up in the Gal-

lery office, Robert wearing a frown of seriousness and
bell-bottomed trousers and Lizzie—an extraordinary, almost skinny, Lizzie—in a skimpy jersey and platform-
soled shoes, her hair pushed up into a huge, floppy peaked
velvet cap. They weren't much older than that when they
opened the Gallery, renting the shop and the damp, rickety
flat above it, furnished with ill-assorted items their parents
had given them. Frances had had her first job in London
then. She telephoned Lizzie three times a week and came
down to Langworth with exotic urban treasures like silver-
mesh tights, or an avocado pear in a paper bag.

Robert went to evening classes in Bath, and learned to
make picture frames. Lizzie reluctantly abandoned her clay
for patchwork making, flower drying and the patient bees-
waxing of indifferent but fashionable pieces of pine furniture. They both discovered that they had a commercial eye.
By the time that Harriet was born, in 1978, the original
shop, which by now resembled the perfect seventies' fantasy
of an Anglo-Saxon rural idyll, all sprigged cottons, naive
water-colours, spongeware mugs and wooden spoons, was
both highly successful, and bursting at the seams. With a
loan from Lizzie's father, William, and another from the
bank, the Middleton Gallery moved into a former florist's
shop, in Langworth High Street, where the front windows
were shaded by a pretty pillared portico of white-painted
Victorian wrought iron.

Frances had wanted to see it immediately. Lizzie had
chugged off to Bath station to meet her in the emerald-
green Citroën Deux Chevaux that was now such a familiar
sight in the streets of Langworth, and had taken her back
to the Gallery with a mixture of rapturous pride and anguish. Watching Frances's face as she looked at the Gallery,
at the pale, newly sanded and waxed floors, at the pools of
romantic light cast by uplighters and downlighters, at the
freshly stained and painted shelves waiting for casseroles
and cushions and candlesticks and pottery jugs, Lizzie
could feel a surge of unstoppable exultation at what she
and Robert were achieving. But at the same time, chained
as she was to Frances's innermost self, she felt a simulta-

neous surge of pain; pain for Frances, toiling away in a mediocre travel company and returning at night to a gaunt flat in Battersea which she shared with a girl she quite liked, but not very much. And then there was Nicholas, quiet, self-contained, undemonstrative Nicholas, so unlike Robert, so wrong, Lizzie thought, for Frances.

"We're going to import kelims," Lizzie said. "And hang them here, on wooden rods. Rob's got a friend who can supply us with marvellous dried things from Africa, seed-heads and pods and stuff."

"What are kelims?" Frances said. She was standing gazing at the whitewashed brick wall against which the rugs would hang.

"Rugs," Lizzie said. She watched Frances. Could she, on top of all else, all this richness and promise of her and Robert's life, tell her the other thing?

Frances turned from the wall to face her.

"Rugs," she said. "Hanging up. How lovely. You're pregnant again, aren't you?"

"Yes," Lizzie said, thinking she might cry. "Yes, I am."

Frances put her arms round her.

"I love that," she said. "I love it that you're pregnant again."

That pregnancy was Alistair. He should have been twins—Lizzie longed for twins—but his brother died at birth. Frances came at once, she came almost before she knew there was any reason to come, and stayed for three weeks, using up all her remaining annual holiday. She was hopeless with Alistair, Lizzie remembered, awkward and gauche, as if a baby was absolutely alien to her, but she was wonderful with everything else, with the house, with relentless, small Harriet ("*Why* does there have to be a baby?"), with Rob, with the Gallery. Lizzie had broken down when Frances went back to London, had felt incompetent and incomplete.

"Perhaps I should have married both of you," Robert had said, gazing down at her as she lay in bed, feeding an insatiable Alistair. "Except that I couldn't be in love with

Frances in a million years. Isn't it odd? So like you in so many ways, but no factor X."

Soon after that, quiet Nicholas had also decided that there was no factor X to Frances, and drifted off.

"Of course I'm sad," Frances said, "but mostly disappointed. In myself, I mean."

Lizzie prayed urgently, to no one in particular, for the right man for Frances. He would have to be tall (like Rob) and attractive (like Rob) but not as gentle or as artistic as Rob or else she, Lizzie, might begin to make comparisons between Frances's man and Rob, and she had an instinct that this would do none of them any good. Frances solved the problem, in the short term, by falling in love with an architect and then with an actor and then, disastrously, with the boyfriend of the girl with whom she shared a flat. In the meantime the Middleton Gallery prospered, held three exhibitions a year, opened a health food café on the top floor, repaid all its loans and went into profit. Lizzie, in between giving birth to Sam and then to Davy, did the buying for the Gallery and moved house. They moved four times in sixteen years, from their original flat to an eighteenth-century cottage that had once been a tea-room and had never lost the smell of toasted teacakes, to a Victorian villa, and finally to the Grange.

The Grange had been one of Langworth's best houses in the late eighteenth century, with a calm and handsome stone façade and a pedimented porch. It had sat then in appropriate gardens, with a gravel sweep between the front door and the street, and lawns behind it, rolling smoothly away to a walled vegetable garden. Now, fussed about with by the Victorians who had added a warren of leaking rooms to the back, and pressed in upon on all sides by the modern urgency for new building, the Grange was like a battered old liner crammed into a very small port. New executive dwellings with pictorial nameplates and fancy stonework filled the vegetable garden, and half the lawns had vanished long ago under a street called Tannery Lane, in memory of the nineteenth-century tannery that had, for fifty years, filled the streets of Langworth with a gagging stench. What was left of the Grange garden was plenty big enough, Lizzie and Rob considered, for cricket, bicycles, camps and fighting. The inside of the house was big enough for anything. Surveying the light and beautifully proportioned original rooms, the sweeping staircase, the Victorian muddle at the back that could be knocked through to make a magnificent kitchen-living room, and visualising the whole painted terracotta and deep blue and Chinese yellow, with polished floors and sharp white paintwork, Robert and Lizzie reckoned that the Grange would set the seal upon their success. An expanding business, an appropriate house (large but not boastful), four clever and strong-minded children, a rising local profile—what a considerable thing to reflect upon! Because he did reflect upon it a good deal, with a kind of astonished pride, Robert pinned up, in his newly decorated office in the Gallery, the photograph of himself and Lizzie as students, just to remind himself of exactly how far they had come.

It was just before Davy's christening that Frances had first surprised them. They had been in the Grange for a year, and half the house was painted in just the rich, strong colours that Lizzie so loved. The stairwell was yellow and white, the sitting room deep green, the newly extended kitchen blue and russet and cream.

"Why is Davy being christened?" Frances said. "You've never christened the others."

"I just feel I want him to be. So does Rob. We wish we had christened the others, now. It seems—it seems more traditional, somehow—"

Frances looked at her sister. Then she looked at the kitchen, its back door open to the sunny garden, its windowsills charmingly crowded with scented geraniums and pygmy amphorae of parsley, the trug of lettuces on the table, the rag rugs on the wooden floor, the shining new Aga, the rustic Spanish candelabra of greenish metal. She winked at Lizzie.

"Watch it, Liz. You're getting to be such a solid citizen."

"Am I?"

Frances waved an arm.

"Look at all this!"

Lizzie said, slightly defensively, "It's what we want."

"I know. And now you want Davy christened."

"People change," Lizzie said stoutly. "We're bound to change. It would be affected to stay rigidly as we were at twenty-five."

Frances went to the mirror hanging by the garden door and opened her mouth.

"What are you doing?"

"Looking at my teeth."

"Why?"

"Because they look the same as they always have. The thing is, I don't feel so different, I don't feel I've changed—"

"No. Well—"

"But then," said Frances comfortably, coming away from the mirror, "I haven't had a husband and four children, have I?"

"I didn't want to say—"

"Let's go up and look at Davy, shall we?"

Davy lay in his wicker Moses basket in the centre of Lizzie and Robert's bed, shrouded in a muslin cat net, like a joint in a larder. They peered down at him. He was fast asleep, snuffling faintly, his shrimp-sized fingers balled into tiny fists. Lizzie breathed down through the net at him with helpless yearning. Frances wondered how he would react if he opened his eyes. Would he yell?

"Lizzie," she said.

"Yes," Lizzie said, adoring Davy.

Frances straightened up and walked over to the huge wardrobe that held Lizzie's clothes. It had a long oval mirror set into the door, a mirror that gave back the moony, soft reflection of old glass.

"I want to tell you something."

Lizzie came to join her sister. They stood side by side and gazed at their reflections, two tall, big-boned English girls, broad-shouldered, long-legged, with thick tawny hair cut in longish bobs. Lizzie's had a fringe; Frances's was cut to fall forward in a heavy swathe on one side, like a bird's wing, when she bent her head.

"We aren't glamorous, are we——"

"No, but I think we're quite attractive. I think we look interesting."

"To whom?" Frances said.

Lizzie looked at her.

"What were you going to tell me?"

Frances leaned towards her reflection. She licked her forefinger and ran it along first one dark eyebrow and then the other.

"I'm starting my own business."

Lizzie gaped at her.

"You aren't!"

"Why aren't I?"

"Frances," Lizzie said, seizing her sister's arm. "Frances, please think carefully. What do you know about running a business? You've always been employed, an employee——"

"Exactly," Frances said, "and now I've had enough." Gently, she took her arm away.

"Where's the money coming from?"

"Where it usually comes from," Frances said. She turned up her shirt collar and pushed up her cardigan sleeves and turned to look at herself in the mirror, over her shoulder. "Some from the bank and some from Dad."

"From Dad!"

"Yes. He lent you and Rob some, didn't he?"

"Yes, but that was——"

"No," said Frances, interrupting. "It wasn't different. It's just the same, except that I am doing it later, and on my own."

Lizzie swallowed. "Of course."

"Why don't you want me to?"

Lizzie went back to her bed, and sat beside Davy's wicker basket, on the patchwork counterpane, one of the range made by a local farmer's wife, that had proved one of the Gallery's best sellers. Frances stayed where she was, by the wardrobe, leaning her back against the smooth, cold mirror-glass.

"We're twins," Lizzie said.

Frances bent her head and studied her feet, her too-big feet encased in good, dull, dark-blue leather loafers. She knew exactly what Lizzie meant. We are twins, Lizzie had said, leaving the subtext unspoken. We are twins, so we are a unit, we have a kind of joint wholeness, together we make up a rich, rounded person, but we are like two pieces of a jigsaw, we have to fit together, and to do that properly we can't be exactly the same shape.

"You have the domestic life," Frances said. "I like that. I love it here, this house is home to me, your children are very satisfying to me. I don't want any of that, that's your part of our deal. But I must be allowed to expand myself a little if I need to. And I do. It won't touch your business if I have a business, it won't touch us, how we are, together."

"Why do you want to do it?" Lizzie said.

"Because I'm thirty-two and I know enough about travel now to know I'm better than a lot of people I work for. You want to have Davy christened, you've come to a point. I've just come to another one."

Lizzie looked at her. She remembered their first day at Moira Cresswell's nursery school together, in green drill overalls, with "E. Shore" and "F. Shore" embroidered on them, for painting classes, and their hair held back by tight Alice bands made of green ribbon and elastic. "We won't have to stay if we don't want to," Frances had said to Lizzie, but Lizzie had sensed that wasn't true. School had an inexorable feeling about it. She had hated watching Frances realise this.

"What kind of business will it be?"

Frances smiled. She put her hands under her hair, lifted it off her neck and then let it fall back.

"Secret holidays. Staying in tiny towns and hidden hotels and even people's houses. I shall start with Italy, because all the English have this passion for Italy."

"And what will you call it?"

Frances began to laugh. She did a dance step or two, holding out the sides of her skirt.

"Shore to Shore, of course!"

Like Davy, Shore to Shore had grown out of all recognition in five years. It began in the sitting room of the Battersea flat, and its beginnings were very shaky, with too few customers and too many mistakes. Then Frances realised that she would have to look at every single bed and table at which she expected her clients to sleep and eat, so she went to Italy for four months, driving herself along the minor roads of Tuscany and Umbria in a hired Fiat she used as an office and a wardrobe and, sometimes, as a bedroom. Before she went, she was apprehensive that she would find it all a cliché, done to death by the remorseless English mania for a civilised release from the shackles of a chilly Puritanism into an acceptable sensuality. But she needn't have worried. You could read about it in a thousand novels and newspaper articles, you could see it as the richly romantic backdrop to a thousand films, yet still, Frances thought, no sensitive heart could fail to lift, every time, at the sight of that landscape, the lines of the olive-dun and grape-blue hills punctuated by saffron walls, russet roofs and the casually, perfectly placed charcoal-dark spires of the cypress trees.

She set up little journeys for her clients. Some were through vineyards, some were for painters, or photographers, some were like small investigations, in search of the Etruscans, or Piero della Francesca, or a once mighty, now decayed family, like the Medicis. She sold her share of the flat in Battersea to a brisk girl specialising in venture capital, and moved north, across the river, to a narrow house just off the Fulham Road. She couldn't afford to buy it, so she rented it, using the ground floor as offices, and living on the first floor with a view, at the back, of someone else's cherry tree. She hired an assistant, a girl to work the switchboard and run errands, and invested the last of her borrowings in computers. Before the company was four years old, three larger, well-established and better-known businesses had tried to buy her out.

Lizzie was proud of her. At Frances's request, Lizzie came up to London, and planned the décor of the ground-floor office, covering the floor with seagrass matting, and the walls with immense, seductive photographs of Italy—bread and wine on an iron table on a loggia, with a distant view of a towered hill-town beyond, Piero's infinitely moving pregnant Virgin from the cemetery chapel at Monterchi, a gleaming modern girl swinging carelessly down a timeless, mouldering medieval street. They installed an Italian coffee machine, and a baby fridge to hold pale-green bottles of Frascati, to offer customers.

"You see," Frances said. "You see? I told you it wouldn't change us. I *told* you."

"I was afraid," Lizzie said.

"I know."

"I'm very ashamed of that now, it seems so selfish, but I couldn't help feeling it."

"I know."

"And now I'm just proud. It's wonderful. How are bookings?"

Frances held out both hands, fingers crossed.

"Solid," she said.

That, Lizzie thought now, had been their only hiccup, the only time when their parallel progress together through life had faltered even a step. Looking back, Lizzie felt not only a twinge of residual shame at her lack of generosity but a puzzlement. Why had she been afraid? Knowing Frances as she did, what was there to fear in a personality that was almost her own, twined about her own as it was? Frances was, after all, the least greedy of people. Lizzie hoped, with a sudden, small, urgent pang, that she wasn't greedy. Had she, she asked herself sternly, ever envied Frances those trips to Italy while she stayed in Langworth attending Sam's measles or Alistair's cello practice or weary late-night sessions with Robert and the Gallery accounts? Only for a second, she told herself, only for a fleeting second, when beside herself with exhaustion and demands, would she ever have willingly exchanged her richly domestic and effective life for Frances's free but lonely one. There was no doubt about it, Lizzie reflected with a sigh, sitting down at the kitchen table and pulling towards her one of her endless pads of paper, to make a menu list for Christmas, that Frances was lonely.

Someone—an egregious customer at the Gallery who was trying very hard to turn herself into Lizzie's friend— had given her an American cookery book called *Good Food for Bad Times*. It was written by a person called Enid R. Starbird. Lizzie opened it idly, thinking that it might provide a few economical ideas for feeding a household of nine—the six Middletons, Frances, the Shore parents—for four days. Robert had said last night, in the careful voice he kept for breaking disagreeable news, that the Gallery takings so far, in the run-up to Christmas, looked as if, instead of being twenty per cent up as usual, would be ten per cent down. They had both suspected that this might be so and had had, during the course of the year, a number of superficially philosophical conversations about the possibility of an economic recession. Last night, they had had another one.

"So," Lizzie had said. "It means a careful Christmas."

" 'Fraid so."

Lizzie looked down at the open page of Mrs. Starbird's book. "Never forget," Mrs. Starbird said brightly, "the cabbage soups of south-west France. A pig's head, that vital ingredient, is not, as you will find, so very hard to come by."

Lizzie shut the book with a slam, to banish the image of a reproachful pig's head. She seized her pad. "Sausages," she wrote rapidly. "Gold spray-paint, dried chestnuts, things for stockings, cat food, sticking plasters, big jar of mincemeat, second-class stamps, collect dress from cleaner's, walnuts." She stopped, tore off the sheet, and began again on a fresh one. "Make up spare beds, check wine, finish wrapping presents, ice cake, make stuffings, check mince pies (enough?), remind Rob about wine, clean silver (Alistair), Hoover sitting room (Sam), pick holly and ivy (Harriet and Davy), decorate tree (everyone), make garland for front door (me) and quiches for Gallery staff party (me) and brandy butter (me), and clean the whole house from top to bottom before Mum sees it (me, me, me)."

"Help," Lizzie wrote at the foot of her list. "Help, help, help."

The kitchen door opened. Davy, who at breakfast had been fully and properly dressed and was now wearing only socks, underpants and a plastic policeman's helmet, sidled in. He looked guilty. He came up to Lizzie and leaned against her knee. Lizzie touched him.

"You're frozen!" Lizzie said. "What have you been doing?"

"Nothing," Davy said, trained by Sam.

"Then where are your clothes?"

"In the bath."

"In the *bath*?"

"They needed a wash, you know," Davy said confidingly.

"They were clean, clean this morning—"

Davy said, almost dreamily, "They got a bit pastey."

"What kind of pastey?"

"Toothpastey," Davy said. "Toothpaste writing—"

Lizzie stood up.

"Where's Sam?"

"Pimlott's come," Davy said. "Pimlott and Sam are making a Superman camp—"

"Pimlott?"

Pimlott was Sam's dearest friend, a frail, mauve-pale boy with watchful light eyes and a slippery disposition.

"Don't you have a Christian name?" Liz had asked him on his first visit. He stared at her.

"'Course he doesn't," Sam said. "He's just called Pimmers."

"Where are they making the camp?"

"It's quite all right," Davy said, adjusting the helmet so that only his chin showed beneath it. "It's not in your room, it's only in the spare room—"

Lizzie shot out of the kitchen and up the stairs. A spaghetti trail of red ribbon lay tangled at the bottom; the banisters were bare.

"Sam!" yelled Lizzie.

Thumps came distantly from somewhere, like the sound of road-mending machinery heard through closed windows.

"Sam!" Lizzie roared. She flung open the spare-bedroom door. The floor was strewn with bedclothes and on the beds, Lizzie's cherished Edwardian brass beds for which she had so lovingly collected linen of a similar age, Sam and Pimlott were trampolining, grunting with effort.

"Sam!" Lizzie bellowed.

He froze, floating down from his last leap as if transfixed in mid-air, landing rigid and upright on the mattress. Pimlott simply vanished, sliding snakelike from on top of the bed to underneath it.

"What are you doing?" Lizzie shouted. "I've given you a job to do and you haven't done it and I said you weren't to have Pimlott here today, or at least until you had done everything I asked you to do, and this room is out of bounds, as well you know, and I have to make it nice for Granny and Grandpa and I have a million things to do and you are a naughty, disobedient, beastly little boy—"

Sam subsided into a sulky heap.

"Sorry—"

"Mum," a voice said.

Breathlessly, Lizzie turned. Alistair stood there, a tube of glue in one hand and a minute grey-plastic piece of model aeroplane in the other. Across one lens of his spectacles was a smear of something chalky.

"Dad's on the phone," Alistair said. "And then could you come and hold this bit because my clamp isn't small enough to hold it while I stick the last piece of fuselage—"

Lizzie fled across the landing to the telephone beside her and Rob's bed.

"Rob?"

"Lizzie, I know you're up to your eyes, but could you come? Jenny's gone home, feeling ghastly, looking ghastly, poor thing, and the shop's suddenly terribly busy—"

"No."

"But Liz—"

"I'm sorry, I mean, I'll try, but it's complete chaos here and there's so much to do—"

"I know, I know. I'll help you tonight. Just leave things."

"I can't come for half an hour. And I'll have to bring Sam and Davy."

"OK," Robert said. "Soon as you can."

Lizzie put the telephone down and went back on to the landing. Through the open door of the spare room, she could see Sam and Pimlott, watched by Davy, incompetently piling bedclothes back on to the beds. Alistair still waited.

"Could you—?"

"No, I couldn't," Lizzie said. "I have so much to do I feel quite frantic. I want you to clean the silver."

Behind his spectacles Alistair's eyes widened in amazement.

"Clean the silver?"

"Yes," Lizzie said. She went into the spare room, pushed out the three children and slammed the door. "Men do clean silver. They also cook and change nappies and go shopping. What women don't do is waste time making something as utterly pointless as a model aeroplane."

"Heavens, you *are* cross," Alistair said.

"Go home," Lizzie said to Pimlott. "Please go home and stay there till after Christmas."

He regarded her with his light, shifting eyes. He had no intention of obeying her. He had never—unless it suited him anyway—obeyed an adult in his life.

"And you," she said to Sam, "are going to Hoover the sitting room, and, Davy, go and put some clothes on and then go and find Harriet. I need her."

"I'm hungry," Sam said.

"I really don't care—"

"Telephone!" Davy said excitedly. "Telephone! Telephone!"

Alistair slipped past his mother and into her bedroom,

to answer it. He said, "Hello?" and not, "Langworth, 4004," as she and Robert had told him to, and then, in a warmer voice, "Hi, Frances."

Frances! Salvation! Lizzie hurried into her bedroom, holding out her hand for the receiver.

"Frances? Oh Frances, thank God it's you, it's so awful here this morning, you can't imagine, a complete madhouse. I'd like to murder Prince Albert and Charles Dickens and anyone else responsible for making Christmas such a nightmare—"

"Oh poor Lizzie," Frances said. Her voice was, as usual, light and warm.

"And now Rob wants me to go and help in the Gallery and I only got round to ordering the wretched turkey this morning—"

"Does that matter?"

"Not really, except that I don't feel in charge, I don't feel in control, which is madness really as I've done Christmas for years and years—"

"I know. Too many years, probably. Next year I'll set you up for an anti-Christmas holiday."

"Too likely. What about my horrible children?"

"I'll look after them."

"Oh Frances," Lizzie said, beaming into the receiver. "Oh Frances. Praise be for you. I can't wait to see you!"

"Lizzie—"

"When are you coming? I know you said Christmas Eve, but couldn't you just shut up shop tomorrow, at the weekend, and come down on Sunday?"

"Yes," Frances said. "That's why I rang. I *am* coming down on Sunday. To bring your presents."

"What?"

There was a small pause on the far end of the telephone line, and then Frances said quite easily, "Lizzie, I also rang to tell you that, this year, I won't be coming down to Langworth for Christmas. That's why I'm coming on Sunday. I'm coming to bring your presents, but then I'm going away again. I'm going—away for Christmas."

TWO

When Barbara Shore had been told she was going to have twins, she had said nothing at all. Her doctor, an old-fashioned, comfortable country general practitioner, who still did his rounds in a baggy suit with interior pockets ingeniously tailored to hold all the tools of his trade, believed her to be struck dumb with delight. That, after all, was the proper response. But Barbara had only said, after a while, "How perfectly preposterous," and had then gone home to do what she did best in times of crisis, which was to rest in bed.

Her husband, William, came home from a day's history teaching at a local minor public school, and found her resting.

"It's twins," she said. She sounded accusing.

He sat, with some difficulty, on the slippery, satin-covered quilt beside her.

"How wonderful."

"For whom?"

"For both of us." He thought a bit, and beamed at her. "Shakespeare had twins. Hamnet and Judith."

"I don't want twins," Barbara said distinctly, as if speaking to someone hard of hearing. "I only just want one baby and I certainly don't want two. It's awful being a twin."

"Is it?"

"Awful," Barbara said.

"How do you know?"

"Because I have an imagination," Barbara said. "Because you can never be quite your own person, if you're a twin, because it stunts your relationships with anyone else, because you can't ever be quite free of the other person."

William got up and went over to the window. Outside, the autumn fields lay pleasingly striped with stubble and speckled with partridges. He was full of an utterable delight at the thought of twins, at the completeness that a brace of babies suggested.

"The Americans love twins," he said irrelevantly. "There's somewhere called Twinsburgh, in Ohio, where they—"

"Shut up," Barbara said.

"We'll get a nanny, a mother's help. I'll buy a washing machine." His eyes suddenly filled with tears at the thought of his pair of babies existing there, inside Barbara's body, only feet away from him, the size, perhaps, of hazelnuts. "I'm—I'm so happy."

"It's all very well for you," Barbara said.

William turned away from the window and came back to the bed. He looked at Barbara. She had been his headmaster's daughter and now she was his wife. He wasn't altogether clear how the transition had come about, nor how he had felt about it, but he knew now, gazing down at Barbara, shoeless and resentful on the satin bedspread in her autumn jersey and skirt, that he loved her deeply and gratefully for being pregnant. He wanted, rather, to put his hand on the heathery-coloured tweed where it lay, flatly as yet, on her stomach, but he refrained. It was 1952, after all, and the New Man, who participates in both pregnancy and his child's arrival, was still a creature of the future. Instead William kissed Barbara's forehead.

"You shall have anything you want," William said.

"Anything to make things easier for you. I shall make you a cup of tea."

He went downstairs to the kitchen, blowing his nose because his eyes again seemed to be full of tears. The kitchen, cream-painted and orderly, was a monument to Barbara's fearsome domestic competence: nothing out of place, nothing smeared or grimy or sticky, not even a single intrepid fly buzzing against the speckless windows. He took the kettle over to the sink and filled it, and then lit the gas and set the kettle to boil on the hissing ring of blue-and-orange flames.

"Twins," he said to himself. The luck of it, the sheer blessed good fortune of the prospect of twins filled him with awe. What had he done to deserve this? What, indeed, had he ever done to deserve anything, except stumble amiably through life falling obligingly into events and circumstances as if led ever onwards by some unseen and guiding hand? He had been just too young even for the war, still safe at school, and had only learned about its true and terrible nature from the men he had found himself at university with, men whose own education had been interrupted by six years of fighting. William had felt humbled then. He felt humbled now.

"I am twenty-five," he said to the empty kitchen. "I am twenty-five, and quite soon after my twenty-sixth birthday, I shall be the father of twins." He paused and straightened his shoulders, as if for the National Anthem. "The father of twins."

Barbara did not want to tell the nursing home in Bath, where she went for the twins' birth, her age. She did not want the nurses to know that she was older than William, and she had also convinced herself that thirty was an embarrassingly late age at which to start having babies. So she simply stared at them all, when they asked her how old she was, and in the end had to write it down for them in silence, daring them, with a furious glance, to read the date aloud.

The twins were born steadily, slowly and painfully. William, tiptoeing in afterwards with a bunch of lilies of the valley, was alarmed at Barbara's gaunt, grey face and air of being drained of every drop of energy.

"I'm so glad they're girls," William said in a whisper. He kissed Barbara's hand. She gripped him with her free one.

"Don't make me do it again."

"But—"

"Never," Barbara said. "You don't know, you can't know. I thought it would never stop."

"Of course," William said. He badly wanted to go and look in the pair of grim little hospital cradles at the foot of Barbara's bed, but Barbara still held him. If she never wanted another baby, did that mean that she would never again allow ... ? Help, thought William, and swallowed. Mustn't think of it, quite the wrong moment, terribly self-ish, poor Barbara, worn out completely, quite justified in saying it's all very well for him ...

"It's all very well for you," Barbara said. "But I'm simply not even going to contemplate—"

"No," William said. "Of course not. Just as you like."

She relaxed her grip a little.

"Lovely flowers," she said, in a more normal voice. "Mother sent horrors. Look over there. Mauve chrysanths, only fit for a funeral. How could she find such a thing in May?"

"I'm going to look at the girls," William said.

"They look quite intelligent," Barbara said. "Luckily."

To William, they looked vulnerable, beautiful, and heart-stoppingly his. He couldn't believe them. He couldn't believe that they were so tiny, so complete, that they were there in the world at all and not in some confused and obscurely imagined arrangement upside down inside Barbara.

"Oh," William said. He touched each cheek with a rapturous forefinger. "Oh, thank you!"

Barbara almost smiled.

"They're going to be called Helena and Charlotte."

William touched his daughters again. One of them stirred and sucked briefly at the air with a miniature mouth.

"No they're not."

Barbara, unable to sit up on account of inches of postnatal stitchery, raised her head commandingly.

"Yes they are. I've decided. Charlotte and Helena."

"No," William said. He straightened up and looked at Barbara, glaring at him from her blank white pillows. "On the day you told me you were going to have twins, I called them, in my mind, Frances and Elizabeth. I knew they wouldn't be boys—don't ask me how, I just knew. They have been Frances and Elizabeth for months."

"But I don't like Frances."

"I don't like Barbara much, either," William said, adding after a pause, but without any urgency, "as a name, that is."

Barbara opened her mouth, and then shut it again. William waited. Gradually, she subsided back on to her pillows, and closed her eyes.

"As you wish."

"This one is Frances," William said. "The one with the bigger nose."

"Neither of them have any nose to speak of. Elizabeth is the older. Frances gave me far more trouble, I thought I—"

The door opened. A nurse put her head in.

"Bottle time!" she said.

William thought improbably of black bottles of stout, amber bottles of cider, green bottles of gin . . .

"I'm not feeding them," Barbara said. "I mean—" She gestured at the blue frills of her nylon nightgown. "I mean, I'm not feeding them myself. I refuse."

"I see," William said, never having given any previous thought to how babies were sustained.

"And another thing—"

"Yes?"

"The moment I can get out of bed, I'm going up to

London. I'm going to the Marie Stopes Clinic. To arrange,"
said Barbara loudly, "for really effective contraception."

The twins were exhausting babies, colicky and fretful. William and Barbara took it in turns to get up in the night
for them, and in the afternoons the daughter of the school's
head groundsman, who was waiting for a place at a training college for nursery nurses, came up so that Barbara
could get a couple of hours' sleep.

It was a peculiar existence for a year. William forgot
what ordinary life was like, life where adult priorities really
could be priorities, where one wasn't dazed and fuddle-headed from lack of sleep, where conversations with Barbara weren't exclusively about how many ounces Frances
had taken and how often Elizabeth had been sick. He
wasn't in the least resentful of the twins' tyranny over their
lives, merely accepting it as he had accepted so many
changes previously, like the early death of his parents, or
his marriage to Barbara, but he did think to himself occasionally that it was perhaps as well that most prospective
parents had no real conception of what having children
would mean, otherwise hardly anyone—and certainly no
one with any imagination—would even attempt it.

At fifteen months, everything changed. The twins transformed themselves from undersized, sallow grizzlers into
admirable, healthy toddlers, peach-bloomed and enterprising. They walked early, talked early, and showed a pleasing
enthusiasm for books. Barbara, who had looked after them
with the grim conscientiousness she applied to the kitchen
paintwork and the household accounts, began to display
something approaching pride in them. She also tried to
detach William from his intimate participation in their
lives, a participation she had demanded during the first
terrible year. William, as with the twins' names, had refused.

"I've bathed them since they were born, and I'm going
on bathing them. I shall also go on feeding them and taking
them for walks and reading to them and discouraging them

from poking sticks in dogs' eyes and being impertinent to your mother."

"You should be interested in your career," Barbara said.

"You mean you think it's time I was a housemaster?"

"You're twenty-eight, you know. Even headmasters are beginning to get younger—"

"I don't want to be a headmaster," William said. "I don't want to administer, I want to teach. And I want to be with my daughters."

When the twins were four Barbara and William had a serious quarrel. Barbara, reared exclusively in the world of private education, wanted them to go to a nursery school in Langworth, run by the wife of a master at her father's school. William defied her, and his parents-in-law. Impelled by an instinctive feeling that the rule of convention in lives like his and Barbara's amounted almost to a stranglehold, he announced that his daughters would go to the local village state school. There was a tremendous row. It went on for several days and evenings and Frances and Lizzie—whose opinion was never considered—listened uncomprehendingly from the landing outside their bedroom, sucking their thumbs and holding opposite ends of the same comfort blanket.

In the end, there was a bargain. The twins would go to Moira Cresswell's school in Langworth for two years, then they would go to the village school until the time came for them to sit their eleven-plus examination. Then, said William, they would go to grammar school, in Bath. Over her dead body, Barbara shouted. It was to be Cheltenham Ladies' College or Wycombe Abbey School, or nothing. The twins sucked and listened. The only school they knew was the one where Daddy taught, full of cold corridors and raw boys and shrilling bells. There were no girls there.

When it came to it, William had his way almost entirely, because something extraordinary happened. When the twins were ten, and Frances, in particular, was beginning to be naughty, in a dreamy, elusive way that was very hard to pin down and punish, Barbara suddenly went away. One minute, it seemed, she was tweaking chair covers into place, saying organising things into the telephone, watching you like a hawk to make sure you didn't put your spinach into the vase of anemones on the kitchen table as once you had ingeniously done, and the next, she was gone. It was very weird. She went as neatly as she did everything else, leaving no sign of her going, and no apparent gaps in the house either. Lizzie and Frances were almost too stunned to cry.

William said she had gone to Morocco.

"Where's Morocco?"

He got out an atlas and put it on the floor and they all knelt round it.

"There. That's Morocco. And there's Marrakesh. Mummy's gone to Marrakesh. For a long kind of holiday, I suppose."

"Why did she go?"

"I'm breaking out," Barbara had said to William. "Living here is like living in a straitjacket. I'm forty. If I don't break out now I never will and I'll break down instead."

"But are you telling me in all seriousness," William said, "that you're joining the hippie trail?" He looked at Barbara. It was early autumn and she was wearing a corduroy skirt, a Viyella blouse and a profoundly middle-aged lovat-green cardigan. "The *hippie trail*? Seriously? Caftans and love beads?"

"Yes," said Barbara.

"I think," William said to his daughters, "that she has gone away because she has been too well-behaved for too long. Perhaps it's being a headmaster's daughter. She's gone away to behave badly for a bit, to get it out of her system."

"Do you mind?" Frances said.

William looked at her. "Not really. Do you?"

The twins exchanged glances. "I should have preferred her to have said goodbye," Lizzie said severely.

She was away for ten months. In those ten months, the twins took their eleven-plus examinations and gained places at the grammar school. William put the brochures for Cheltenham Ladies' College and Wycombe Abbey School in the dustbin. He also, supposing that Barbara was both smoking marijuana and being unfaithful to him, started having a single glass of whisky in the evenings, and taking to bed a local woman called Juliet Jones, who lived in an isolated cottage and was an excellent and successful potter. The twins completed the last year of their junior school, acquired gentle Somerset accents without Barbara there to correct them, grew used to having Juliet about (she was a better cook than Barbara) and wrote long joint letters to Marrakesh describing their daily rounds, and asking Barbara to bring them back gold-thonged sandals, worry beads and some desert, in a jam jar.

Barbara came home and no one recognised her. She was very thin, with kohl-smudged eyes and hennaed hair and the backs of her hands and tops of her feet were painted with indigo-blue patterns. She gave each of the twins a little silver hand of Fatima, to ward off the evil eye, and told William, in front of the children, that she loved him and was thankful to be back.

"But I'm also," she said firmly, "thankful that I went."

William didn't know what he felt about her, but then, he never had. While she was away, he had considered leaving her for Juliet, but now he reconsidered this. Barbara went upstairs to the bathroom and was locked inside for a time. When she came down, her hands were still painted, and her hair was still burnished, but she was wearing conventional clothes and her eyes had reverted—rather boringly, the twins thought—to normal.

"I think I shall make a shepherd's pie," Barbara said.

"Please don't," Frances said. She held her hand of Fatima very tightly for courage. "We'd so much rather have Juliet's."

"Who's Juliet?" Barbara said. She looked at William.

He looked back at her. Even Frances, at eleven, noticed how elated he looked, quite unafraid.

"I was just coming to that," William said.

·   ·   ·

Life was quite different, after that. The twins were suddenly given their independence, great dollops of it, going in and out of Bath for school on the bus, on their own, allowed to go to the cinema, or for bicycle rides, permitted to help themselves to food from the refrigerator. Barbara continued to live with William, and William continued, with unaffected discretion, to see Juliet. Books began to appear, books of a kind that William had never even conceived, let alone heard of, books by Betty Friedan and Simone de Beauvoir. Barbara, at forty-two, her adventure behind her and her marriage determinedly still ahead, had taken to feminism.

Barbara's version of feminism coloured the whole of the twins' adolescence. Lizzie was discouraged from domesticity, for which she showed such aptitude, and Frances from the wayward introspection which was her natural inclination and which wasn't, in Barbara's view, positive enough. Barbara went up to London for meetings of a women's group, and brought members of it home to a house which no longer gleamed and smelled of polish and Dettol. Lizzie took to going up to Juliet's cottage, where she was introduced to clay, and the first principles of sculpture. Frances, brandishing a copy of Doris Lessing's *The Golden Notebook* as cover, vanished for fumbling and frustrating assignations with the head boy of William's school. William himself, performing a quiet juggling act with his four women, wondered, every so often, how things had come to pass as they had.

He was quite pleased when Lizzie got married, but only quite. He liked Robert, who he rightly believed would look after her and respect her, but he thought she was too young to be married. He had been delighted by her choice of going to art school and had looked forward to using some of the capital his parents had left him thirty years before and setting her up in a studio of her own—helping her get commissions for the portrait heads she seemed to have a gift for. But Lizzie chose to get married. Barbara was strongly opposed to it.

"I see you are simply conforming to stereotype," Barbara said.

"Look here," Frances had said indignantly, defending her sister. "Don't you go for Lizzie. How dare you, anyway? Deeply married for twenty-five years, it's sheer hypocrisy—"

"You are the first generation with real choices," Barbara said, interrupting. She frowned at Frances. Frances had been to Reading University and had read English Literature, which was completely useless, instead of something with a purposeful application, like sociology. She seemed to have no driving career ambition but merely said, vaguely and annoyingly, that she thought she'd get a job. Barbara sometimes despaired that Frances was much less of a personality than Lizzie, too dependent upon her sister, too content to see Lizzie take decisions for them both. After Lizzie's marriage, Barbara counted the number of weekends that Frances shot down to Langworth, like a rabbit bolting home. It seemed to her far too many, and she wrote Frances long, articulate, reproving letters, explaining how unfair this was on Lizzie and Robert, and how she, Frances, would never grow up if she continued.

"I told you," Barbara said to William, "I told you how it would be, with twins. Frances will never come to anything."

William, adept now at saying nothing, said nothing. When Frances started Shore to Shore, Barbara was elated. She forgot she had despaired of Frances. She even urged William to lend her money.

"You must! You must!"

"I was going to anyway," William said.

"Of course," Barbara said, in the course of the talks she now gave to provincial women's groups, "my daughters are prime examples of young women who are profiting from what we fought for in the sixties. There is no question for them of underestimating their own career potential."

· · ·

When the telephone rang on the Sunday before Christmas, Barbara was up in the roof loft, hunting for one of her old caftans, to take to Harriet. She rather hoped Harriet would see it as a talisman. She had found what she thought was the right suitcase—an old one of her father's covered with the remains of pre-war P&O labels—when the telephone began ringing, two flights down in the hall. Barbara went to the square hatch above the landing.

"William!"

William hated answering the telephone; always had. If he knew Barbara was within earshot, he'd let it ring ten or twenty times, lurking somewhere with his breath held, as if he were afraid of it.

"William!"

A door opened cautiously downstairs.

"William!" Barbara screamed. "Answer it, for heaven's sake! I'm in the attic!"

His reluctant footsteps crossed the hall—the parquet shining once again, after Barbara's initial anti-domestic defiance had abated—and then his reluctant hand rattled the receiver.

"Hello?" William said cautiously.

Snorting, Barbara crouched in the hatch.

"Lizzie!" William said delightedly. "Darling, how lovely. We shall see you tomorrow—What? What about Frances—" He stopped. Barbara held the ends of the galvanised extending ladder and put one foot, and then the other, on the topmost rung. "Good Lord," William said. "Is she all right? I mean has she—?" He stopped again, listening. Barbara slithered gracelessly down the ladder and landed heavily on the landing floor. "Yes, of course," William said. "Terribly upsetting for you. Quite incomprehensible. It doesn't really seem a reason—" He glanced up. Barbara was coming downstairs at great speed, one hand held out for the receiver. "Look, darling," William said rapidly. "Look, I'll tell Mum and then we'll ring you back. No, no, she's fine but I'll tell her myself, no need for you to—bye, darling," William said firmly, banging down the receiver just as Barbara's fingers closed about it.

"What?" Barbara demanded.

"Something odd," William said. "Something very odd—"

"*Tell* me—"

"Frances isn't spending Christmas with us. Frances is going away."

"What? Where—"

William looked at Barbara.

"She's going to Spain."

"Spain!" cried Barbara, as if William had said "Siberia." "But why?"

"To see some hotels, apparently."

"At Christmas? Is she mad? Spanish hotels will be closed at Christmas!"

"Not these ones, apparently. They are a tiny private group of hotels called, says Lizzie, the Posadas of Andalucía. The son of the owner is going to show Frances round."

Barbara seized William's arm.

"That's it! That's why she's going! It's a man, a Spaniard—"

"Lizzie says not. She says she asked Frances and Frances says she's never met him. She's just going. Poor Lizzie, she's so cut up—"

Barbara let William's arm go. She suddenly looked thoughtful.

"Yes. Of course."

"Do you think," William said slowly, "that Frances is running away?"

"Running away? From what?"

"From us. From being like me, just drifting and bobbing—"

"Nonsense," Barbara said. "She runs a highly successful little business. You can't drift and bob and run a *business*."

"I said you'd ring Lizzie back—"

"Yes, I heard you—"

"It will be so different, without Frances, won't it, I mean we have never, in thirty-seven years, had Christmas without Frances—"

"I had one," Barbara said, "in Morocco. But then, I didn't *have* Christmas that year."

"You ran away—"

"Don't jump to conclusions," Barbara said briskly. "We don't know that Frances is doing anything of the sort. I shall ring her before I ring Lizzie."

"She's gone," William said.

"Gone?"

"Yes. She flew an hour ago. She went straight from Lizzie to the airport. She's left us a letter."

"How melodramatic—"

"No more melodramatic," said William with some energy, "than running away to Marrakesh."

"Why do you keep bringing that up?"

"To remind you that people do do unexpected things, people who haven't taken final leave of their senses."

Barbara seized the telephone and began to dial Lizzie's number with fierce, jabbing movements. William went slowly back into the sitting room, where he had been snugly buried in a drift of Sunday newsprint. He thought he might go down to the pub, buy himself a Scotch and then take his drink over to the pub payphone, as he so often did, and ring Juliet. He thought he knew what Juliet would say, but he wanted to hear her actually saying it. He saw himself standing there, in the corner of the public bar, telephone receiver in one hand, whisky in the other, listening to Juliet.

"Ah," Juliet would say. "Ah, William. I've been waiting for this to happen . . ."

THREE

Frances lay back in her aeroplane seat, and closed her eyes. The woman next to her, who was going out to Spain to spend Christmas with her son who had married a girl from Seville, was very anxious to be conversational, so Frances had had to say, gently and untruthfully, "I'm so sorry, I've got a wicked headache. I'm just going to close my eyes."

"Shame," the woman said. "Poor thing."

She tried to give Frances two paracetamol tablets, and then a peppermint wrapped in green-and-white waxed paper. Smiling and shaking her head, Frances declined and leaned her head back, closing her eyes to shut the woman out. She heard her turn to the person on her other side, a spindly boy in a black leather jacket and a white T-shirt with a black and red and yellow sun emblazoned on it, over the word "España."

"I've never flown to Seville before, you see, because formerly my son and his wife lived near Málaga, they ran a bar, called the Robin Hood, a theme bar, you understand, my son used to dress up, you know, but now that my daughter-in-law is expecting the baby, in March, that is, she wanted to be nearer her mother, quite understandable, in my opinion, so you see—"

"Sorry," Frances heard the boy say in thickly accented English. "Sorry, madam, not spik English, not unnerstand—"

"Oh?" the woman said sharply. She twitched her flight magazine out of the hammock on the back of the seat in front of her. Frances could hear her ruffling indignantly through the shiny pages. "Oh indeed," the woman said, only half to herself. "Fine show of Christmas spirit, I must say."

Christmas. Frances thought about it. She thought of her room at the Grange, Harriet's room, with its blue-striped ticking curtains chosen by Lizzie, and its walls of posters of brooding, sulking, pop-star boys, chosen by Harriet. When Frances came to stay, Harriet moved out to share with Alistair, at least technically she moved out, but in fact stayed and lounged on the bed, watching Frances dress and undress, and asking her questions. On Christmas morning, Harriet waited for Frances to say, "Please, *please* don't eat all that chocolate before breakfast or I shall throw up," and Harriet would peel the foil off a chocolate Father Christmas and open her mouth as wide as she could and say, "Watch. *Watch!*" Frances was very fond of Harriet; it gave her a slight pang, sitting in this aeroplane, that by not being at Langworth for Christmas, she was letting Harriet down.

But then, she was letting everyone down, quite spectacularly, most of all Lizzie. Lizzie had been so hurt, and then so angry, that Frances had had to pretend that her flight was an hour earlier than it was, in order to have a pretext for leaving Langworth.

"I can't explain any better," Frances had said. "I had this invitation to go to Spain a week ago, from Mr. Gómez Moreno. I said wasn't Christmas a bit of an odd time, and he said no, it was an excellent time because his father's hotels are open, but not full, which meant that I could see everything properly, really meet the staff. He said he and his father usually work at Christmas because his father doesn't like Christmas."

"But you could have gone on Boxing Day," Lizzie insisted. She had taken the armful of presents Frances had brought and had dumped them, just anyhow, on the floor by the Christmas tree, as if she didn't care about them in the slightest.

"But I didn't want to," Frances said. "I wanted to go *now*."

"Want!" Lizzie shouted. "Want! When do I ever get to do what I want?"

"Lizzie," Frances said, trying to take her sister's hand and finding it snatched away, "I'm your sister, but I'm not *you*. I can't take your life into every consideration about my life, any more than you can about mine."

"*Please* don't go," Lizzie had begged then. "Please don't. I need you here, you know what it's like—"

"It's only a day," Frances said. "Christmas is only a day."

Lizzie burst into tears.

"But why won't you tell me the truth? Why won't you tell me why you want to go, why you don't want to be here?"

"Because I don't really know," Frances said.

Lying back in the plane, she knew that to say that had been an evasion. There were things in Lizzie, aspects of Lizzie, that Frances had always evaded, had learned, in fact, to evade. From their earliest times together, those times when they had done nothing separately, not even the most intimate things, Frances had kept something back. It wasn't a large something, but it was private, an area of herself that was her own and which therefore had to be kept secret. As a little girl, she had loved the physical closeness of Lizzie, but she hadn't wanted to talk all the time; she had liked lying or sitting cuddled up to Lizzie, but thinking her own, silent thoughts. They hadn't been very profound thoughts, Frances considered, being mostly dreamy stories set in mysterious and misty places, but they had been very satisfying and very necessary. It was also very necessary that they shouldn't be told. Lizzie had never asked her what she was thinking; perhaps it had never occurred to her to, perhaps she assumed that they were both thinking the same thing.

Frances loved Lizzie. She loved her strength and her competence and the energy that manifested itself in the

Gallery and the house and her brood of children and her love of colour. She had loved it too on the rare occasions when Lizzie's competence broke down, as it had on the death of Alistair's twin, and she turned to Frances with a kind of sweet, trusting dependence, all the sweeter for being so rare, and so honest. It was horrible to hurt Lizzie, horrible to see that Lizzie could not, would not, even begin to understand that they were, for the moment, divided by their own needs and preoccupations. Frances felt guilty that Lizzie should be so tired while she, Frances, flew away to Spain. But why should she feel guilty? She hadn't chosen Lizzie's life, Lizzie had chosen it herself. So why feel guilty? Because Lizzie had made her feel so, just as, in a smaller way, the woman next to her, who so wanted to tell her about her son dressing up as Robin Hood in order to pull pints for English tourists in a Spanish bar, made her feel guilty.

"Don't feel guilty," Frances told herself. "Just don't. You aren't responsible."

"Pardon?" the woman said.

"Why are women so prone to feeling guilty?" Frances said, giving up and opening her eyes. "Why do women always feel so *obliged* to everybody else?"

The woman looked hard at Frances for a few seconds, then she picked up her flight magazine again and looked intently at a page of ads for duty-free scent.

"I'm sure I don't know," she said, and then added, with something like relief, "Only another hour and ten minutes to Seville."

At Seville Airport—battered and abandoned-looking like all minor airports—a small man waited, in a blue suit. He carried a placard which read, "Miss F. Shore to Shore," and which he held over his face so that he resembled a drawing in a game of Heads, Bodies and Legs.

"Mr. Gómez Moreno?" Frances said. She said it without much conviction, not trusting her phrase-book Spanish not to disintegrate into her, by now, better Italian. The man lowered the placard, revealing a broad, beaming face.

"Señora Jore to Jore?"

"Just Shore," Frances said.

"Señor Moreno send me," the little man said. "I drive you. Hotel Toro. Señor Moreno meet you Hotel Toro." He stopped for Frances's luggage. "Coming with me, Señora Jore to Jore."

He set off at a rapid trot, Frances following with her flight bag and her mackintosh.

"Please holding bag!" the little man called behind him. "Hold all-a your time. Is *tirón* in Sevilla!"

"*Tirón?*"

"Boys taking bags, quick, quick from motoring bicycles—" He reversed deftly into the glass swing-doors of the airport entrance, pressing himself back so that Frances could pass through.

"Is it far? To Seville?"

"*¿Qué?*"

"Is—*¿está lejos Sevilla?*"

"No," said the man. "In car, is quickly."

It was dark, sharp, winter dark with a cold wind, but the sky overhead was brilliant with exaggerated foreign stars. The man stowed Frances away in the back of a car, banged her luggage into the boot behind her, and sprang into the driver's seat as if they had not a moment to lose, starting the engine and roaring along the airport exit roads like a getaway driver after a bank raid.

I wonder, Frances thought, without much agitation, if I'm being abducted. It was most unlikely, but it wasn't impossible. Nothing, at the moment, seemed entirely impossible, nor, having broken out in a small way, was there any reason to suppose that she mightn't find she had broken out in a much larger way than she had intended. She looked out of the window. Buildings, factories perhaps, and high, squared wire fences were racing past in the orange-yellow light of the street arc lamps, looking both industrial and dull.

"Where is the Hotel Toro?" Frances said. "I mean *¿dónde . . . ?*"

The little man was leaning forward now, urging the car to overtake a bus.

"Barrio de Santa Cruz! By Giralda! By Alcázar!"

Frances had idly supposed that she would be staying at the Gómez Morenos' own hotel in Seville, the original Posada of Andalucía, which was called La Posada de los Naranjos. Frances had seen a brochure. On the front was a photograph of everyone's dream of Seville, a tiled courtyard seen through a wrought-iron gate, with a fountain and flowers and lollipop-neat orange trees in tubs. The brochure said that all the bedrooms looked down into this courtyard, which had typical Spanish atmosphere. The bedrooms, it was promised, were gay and modern, and a stay in one of them would not be quickly forgot. There was central heating and telephone and everywhere private bath.

The car swung suddenly left and rushed over a bridge, a long, impressive stone bridge. Beneath it, water glittered and glimmered in the lights from the further shore, the water of the Guadalquivir. Frances said the name to herself, "The Guadalquivir." In the one serious guidebook she had had time to read, Frances had discovered that George Borrow considered Seville to be the most interesting town in all Spain.

"Plaza de Toros!" the driver cried, waving a hand at the high, blank, curved walls of the bullring.

"Horrible," Frances said firmly. "Cruel and horrible." None of her clients would countenance a holiday in Spain that even glanced at a bull fight. Perhaps she would have to make that very plain to Mr. Gómez Moreno, both junior and senior. "I'm afraid that the English consider such a spectacle barbaric," or, more tactfully, "I'm afraid that, as a nation of animal lovers, we really cannot bear to see—" What would they be like, the Gómez Morenos? Would they be small and square and energetic like their driver, similarly dressed in blue suits, with gold teeth and an unshakeable view that the only kind of English person who came to Spain was the kind in search of sun, *sangría* and golf courses? Would it be terribly difficult to explain to them that the clients of Shore to Shore knew about Lorca and Leopoldo Alas and the haunting death of Philip II, and had been to the great exhibition of paintings by Murillo at the Royal Academy in London? Had she been too impulsive? Was it, in truth, nothing but insanity to upset everyone in the family at Christmas for the sake of a pretty brochure, a pleasant-sounding chain of small hotels, and a friendly telephone call or two from a young man in Seville anxious to drum up business?

Heavens! thought Frances, and then, a second later: Pull yourself together. This is an adventure—

The car, having sped about a confusing maze of streets, stopped abruptly in front of a high white wall. It had, it appeared, simply run out of road.

"Stopping," the driver said. "End. Is Barrio. No motoring cars."

He sprang out and began to open doors and the boot. Frances got out on to the pavement. She was in a small, lopsided square, quite quiet except for her escort's slamming of car doors and gruntings over luggage. At the far end was a little restaurant, its façade hung with rustling greenery and yellow lamps in its windows.

"Coming with me, Señora," the driver said, and darted down an alley beside the high blank wall.

The alley was narrow, lit only by a pretty wrought-iron lamp on a bracket ten feet above Frances's head. At the end, the little man vanished to the right, and then to the left, and then led her, panting slightly in his wake, to a broader alley, one side formed by a tall, cream-painted building, its windows obscured behind formidable iron grilles.

"Is Hotel Toro," the man called. "Very luxey!"

To Frances, it looked like a penitentiary.

"Are you sure?"

He performed his reversing manoeuvre into the doors to the foyer.

"Come!"

"Why am I not staying at the Posada de los Naranjos?"

"Señor Moreno is coming," the driver said. "Coming more later. Is good hotel, Hotel Toro."

It was, at first glance, the most bizarre hotel Frances had encountered in five years of intensive hotel spotting. The long foyer, floored in green marble chips and with a deeply, richly coffered ceiling, was furnished as an unintentional parody of the antique Spanish style, all carved oak and tooled leather and brass studs as big as walnuts. Between every piece of furniture stood either a suit of armour or an old-fashioned shop-window dummy in full flamenco frills, and the walls, heavily stuccoed as if with a garden fork, were adorned with bull fighters' capes and swords and also, in lugubrious rows, with the horned heads of their victims mounted on varnished shields. The impression was of a macabre party, halted by the casting of a sudden spell.

"Ambiente tipicamente español," the driver said reverently. He put Frances's case down on the shining green floor. "Mos' beautiful."

Behind the reception desk stood a lean, grave young man in a dark suit. He gave Frances a long look and then a slow bow.

"Miss Shore."

"Yes, I believe—"

"Señor Gómez Moreno has booked you a room with us. He left you this letter."

Frances looked at the proffered letter. She wanted very much to say that she was here on business, that she did not wish to stay among the phoney Falstaffian splendours of the Hotel Toro and that she was by now quite certain that there had been considerable confusion over all the arrangements. However, as it seemed plain that she was a guest of the Gómez Morenos, she felt she could not object until she saw one of them, face to face, to object to. She took the letter and opened it:

Dear Miss Shore! Welcome to Sevilla. We hope you will find the Hotel Toro comfortable and the staff obliging. I will, if you will allow me, call for you at the hotel at 9 P.M. this evening. Yours sincerely, José Gómez Moreno.

Frances turned to her driver.

"Thank you so much for bringing me here."

He bowed.

"Is no problem." He gave her another smile flashed with gold. "I hope you will be having a good time in Sevilla."

She watched him trot briskly across the foyer, reverse into the doors and swing himself out into the darkness beyond. The young man behind the desk held out a room key on a huge bronze plaque with a bull's head in relief upon it.

"Your room is on the third floor, Miss Shore. Room 309."

Room 309 had yellow walls, a yellow-tiled floor, brown wooden furniture and brown-and-yellow folkweave bedspreads. A single tiny lamp between the beds gave off as much light as a sick glow-worm, and high above, from the ceiling, hung a second unenthusiastic bulb in a yellow glass globe. The walls were quite bare except for a mirror hung at the right height for a dwarf, and a small dark panel which turned out to be an anguished Deposition of Christ from the Cross, full of grimaces and gore. In one corner, a small, flimsy plastic cupboard passed for a bathroom, with a notice stuck up above the lavatory which read, "By order! Please Use Softly!" Besides the twin beds—each as narrow as a school bed—there was a veneered wardrobe, a table bearing an ashtray and two red plastic gardenias in a pottery vase, two upright chairs and a tiny television set on a wrought-iron trolley. As well as being ugly the room was also cold.

Frances dumped her suitcase down on one of the beds.

"If I was paying for you," she said to the room, "I wouldn't stay in you another second."

She marched across to the window and flung open the long casements, which opened inwards and were lined with grimy pleated net. Behind them brown shutters were firmly bolted against the winter night. Frances wrestled them open, and leaned out. She took a breath, a breath of Seville. It smelled of nothing but cold. Perhaps it was unfair, on a December night, to expect it to smell of orange blossom and charcoal and grilling and donkey dung but really,

Frances thought, it could do better than this. I could be anywhere, she reflected crossly, anywhere in Europe, in a shoddy hotel room that isn't charming enough or comfortable enough or warm enough to justify *anybody* staying in it, unless they were completely desperate.

She looked down into the alley, lit by gleams from the hotel windows. A couple was coming by, an oldish couple in dark formal clothes, with a miniature dog darting about beside them on a scarlet lead. They paced slowly by, under Frances's gaze, the dog's claws clicking on the cobbles, and then vanished round a corner where a blue neon sign said Bar El Nido, with a helpful indicating arrow. Then the alley was empty again.

"Seville's social life," Frances said, and banged the shutters shut. She was reminded of a night she had once spent in Cortona, in the rain, in a hotel that had promised so well, being a former monastery, and had turned out to be grim and comfortless with no bar, no extra blankets, and the dining room locked against all comers by eight-thirty in the evening. She had been too tired, that night, to trail out and find another hotel. This night, she wasn't tired, but she appeared to be under an obligation—which was worse.

She sat down on one of the unfriendly beds and pulled off her boots. It would have been a relief to ring Lizzie. Under ordinary circumstances, and particularly with the wretched Gómez Morenos paying, she would have rung Lizzie at once, to tell her how dreadful the hotel was, and make a joke of the egg-box bathroom and the poor, gloomy bulls' heads and the pretend Spanish ladies, frozen in vivacious mid-flamenco for evermore. But in the current circumstances, she couldn't ring unless—unless it was to say Look, I've made a really bad mistake, backed quite the wrong hunch, and I'm coming home for Christmas after all.

"And that," Frances said out loud, "I can't do. At least"—she looked at her watch; it said eight forty-five—"at least, not yet."

• • •

At nine o'clock, having brushed her hair and put on more lipstick, but having decided against the tepid trickle that came from the shower head, Frances went down to the foyer and stationed herself between a lady in royal-blue ruffles, with a fan and castanets painted with panniered donkeys, and a bull who had lost his nearest glass eye. She watched the doors. Ten minutes passed, and no one came in or out. A stout couple emerged from the lift and sat as far away from Frances as possible, speaking in some Scandinavian language and studying a guidebook. Frances got up and asked the grave young man behind the reception desk for some red wine. He said he was afraid the bar was closed. Frances said then she was afraid that someone from the hotel was going to have to go all the way to the Bar El Nido for her and bring some back. The young man looked at her for a long, long time and then said he would make enquiries.

"Please do," Frances said. "And quickly."

The young man picked up the nearest telephone and spoke a great deal of rapid, quiet, nimble Spanish into it. Then he replaced the receiver and said to Frances, as if he were a doctor speaking to the anxious relation of an extremely ill patient, "We will do all we can."

"Good," Frances said. She went back to her chair. "This is a dump," she said to the one-eyed bull. The Scandinavian couple stared at her.

"Good evening," she said. "Do you think this hotel is comfortable?"

"No," the man said in a clear English. "But it is cheap." Then went back to his guidebook and his Nordic mutterings.

Frances went on waiting. The telephone rang once or twice, a boy in motor-bike leathers came in with a parcel, a handful of depressed-looking guests crossed the foyer on their way out to dinner, but no wine came, nor did young Señor Gómez Moreno.

"Where is my wine, please?" Frances called.

"One moment, Miss Shore," the young man said.

An elderly telex machine behind the desk began to chat-

ter out a message, claiming his attention. Frances looked at
her nails—clean, unpolished—at the heels of her boots, at
the Spanish lady's bright, fixed, painted face, at the darkly
gilded depths of the ceiling, at her watch. At half-past nine,
she marched back to the reception desk. The young man
saw her coming, and melted, without hurrying, into an
inner cubicle, obscured by a curtain. There was a brass bell
on the reception desk, shaped—oh my God, I can't stand
it, Frances thought—like a flamenco dancer. She picked it
up and rang it ferociously.

"Where is my wine?"

A cold blast of air swirled into the foyer as the doors
were pushed open. A young man came in, a tall, attractive
young man in an English-looking camel-hair overcoat and
a long plaid scarf.

"Miss Shore?"

Frances turned, still holding the bell.

"I am José Gómez Moreno." He held out his hand and
smiled with enormous warmth. "Welcome to Sevilla."

Frances looked at him.

"You are late," she said.

"I am?" He seemed amazed.

"In your letter, you said you would be here at nine
o'clock. It is now almost twenty-five to ten."

He smiled again, making a balancing movement with
his hand. "One little half hour! In Spain—"

The foyer doors opened again. A youth in black trousers
and a black leather jacket appeared, bearing a tin tray with
a single glass of red wine on it. The receptionist emerged
from his retreat.

"Your wine, Miss Shore," he said with quiet triumph.

The youth put the tray down on the reception desk.
Frances and José Gómez Moreno both looked at it.

"Please," Frances said. "Take it to the couple sitting over
there. With my compliments. They can share it."

"*¿Qué?*" said the youth.

"You explain," Frances said to the receptionist and then,
turning to José Gómez Moreno, who was gazing at her

with an expression of profound puzzlement, "and then *you* can start."

He took her to a restaurant in the Pasaje de Andreu. It was underground, in a vaulted cellar that had once, he explained, held great oak barrels of wine.

"White wine," he said, smiling again, "Moriles and Montilla. The best vineyards for these wines are near Córdoba."

Frances wasn't interested in Córdoba. She held the menu—*"Entremeses,"* it said in flowing script, *"Sopas, Huevos, Aves y caza"*—well away from her in order to show José Gómez Moreno that she was not to be sidetracked and said, "I think there has been some confusion."

He smiled. He was really very beautiful, with a decisively boned face and clear dark eyes and the smooth, obedient dark hair that is so rare in England.

"Confusion? Surely not—"

Frances laid the menu down and folded her hands on it.

"When we spoke, Señor Gómez Moreno—"

"José, please—"

"José, you said that your hotels were open but not busy at Christmas and that, as you and your father would both be working, there would be ample time to show me—"

"There will be! There is! Please look at the menu. Here is most excellent *sopa de ajo*, a soup of garlic, paprika—"

"I don't want to look at the menu, Jóse. I want to know why I am staying at that most inferior hotel when you are supposed to be impressing on me the suitability of your *posadas* for my clients."

José Gómez Moreno gave a deep and sorrowful sigh. He poured wine into Frances's glass.

"There comes something surprising."

"I beg your pardon?"

He sighed again. He spread his elegant hands.

"My father goes to Madrid for two nights. All is here as usual. Your room is ready. Then comes the telephone, quite unexpected, quite unforeseen. It is a party from Oviedo, from the north, wishing to stay for four nights, an excellent booking, of much benefit at a quiet time."

"So someone from Oviedo, who may never come to your

hotel again, is given the room I was to have and I am—am fobbed off with the Hotel Toro?"

"I don't understand fobbed off—"

"José," Frances said. "Do you think this is any way to do business?"

She leaned forward and peered at him. She saw that he was not only beautiful but also very young, perhaps no more than twenty-four or -five.

"Does your father know about this? Does he know that I have been thrown out for the last-minute party from—from wherever it was?"

"Oviedo."

Frances said crossly, "It doesn't matter where it was. I think you are making me far too furious to be hungry."

"Please—" He put a hand out and laid it on hers. "I make mistake. Truly I am sorry. The Hotel Toro is—"

"Dreadful."

"You do not like the Spanish atmosphere?"

"I do not like the cold bath water nor the ugliness nor the lack of service *nor* the Spanish atmosphere."

He gazed at her.

"I have offended you."

She picked up the menu again and glared at it.

"You have made me feel that I have come a long way for nothing when I might have been spending Christmas in England with my family."

There was a silence. Frances read the menu. She was not going to look at her phrase book, with José Gómez Moreno regarding her like a kicked dog, so she stared uncomprehendingly at words like *chorizo* and *anguilas*, and tried not to think of family supper in the kitchen at the Grange, with Davy allowed to stay up for the first course, drowsy in his pyjamas.

"Tomorrow," José said soberly, "all will change."

Frances said nothing.

"Tomorrow, I move some of the party from Oviedo into the Hotel Toro, and you will have the room my father instructed."

She glanced at him. His eyes were cast down.

"When tomorrow?"

"By midday."

"Your midday or my midday?"

"Please?"

"Punctual English time or unpunctual Spanish time?"

He straightened his shoulders.

"I come to the Hotel Toro at midday, as it strikes from the cathedral, and take you to our *posada*."

She looked at him. He was trying a smile out on her, a hopeful, boyish, pleading smile.

"You promise?"

He nodded. His smile grew more confident. He even gave the merest wink.

"Otherwise my father will kill me."

FOUR

Frances slept badly. Her bed was hard as well as narrow and there seemed to be no way to get warm. Soon after she had gone to bed, the occupants of the next room spent a long time running taps and pulling plugs, causing the pipes in the communicating wall to bang and gurgle. At three in the morning, someone in metal-heeled shoes went down the tiled corridor outside singing an unsteady song in German, and shortly after five, a party of municipal workers in the alley below threw a few dustbins about and brushed at the cobbles with twig brooms that made a sound like hissing snakes. At six-forty, the people next door went back into their bathroom to begin on more water games, and Frances crawled groaning out of bed, and climbed into her makeshift plastic shower cubicle, to stand with her eyes shut under the lukewarm trickle.

A different receptionist—a busty girl with luxuriant dark hair and lipstick the colour of black-cherry jam—said that breakfast was not served until eight.

"Then I will just have some coffee, brought here, please."

"It is not possible until eight, madam."

Frances held on to the edge of the reception desk.

"Where," she said, spacing her words out in an effort not to smack the cherry-lipped girl, "can I get a cup of coffee in Seville before seven in the morning?"

The girl looked at her.

"At the bar in the next *pasaje*."

"The El Nido?"

"Yes," the girl said.

Frances went out into the alley. High above her shone the kind of blue sky familiar from skiing-holiday advertisements, clear, strong, delphinium-blue sky without a single cloud. There was a sharp wind, too, and a distinct bite to the air. Frances turned up her mackintosh collar and longed for the dark-blue overcoat she had rejected as too heavy for Spain, even in winter, and left hanging in London, an unoriginal coat, but a warm and faithful friend.

The Bar El Nido was only half awake. A skinny, haggard waiter was sweeping the floor of last night's cigarette butts, and another one yawned behind a coffee machine. Two men in workmen's clothes leaned against the bar with newspapers and glasses of brandy, and the walls were covered with posters for bull fights and for football matches. Frances seemed to be the only woman there.

She went up to the bar and asked in careful, Anglicised Spanish for coffee and bread and orange juice. She was given exactly that. She asked for butter. She was handed a single minute rectangle wrapped in gold paper.

"And jam? *¿Mermelada?*"

The waiter produced a tiny foil pot of apricot jam, made in Switzerland.

"*¿Mermelada de Sevilla?*" Frances said. "*¿De naranja?*"

"No," said the waiter, and went back to his coffee machine.

Frances carried her breakfast to a little glass-topped table in the window. She felt more weary than hungry, more in need of the comfort of food than its sustenance. She picked up her coffee cup and held it, for warmth, in her hands.

She took a mouthful. The coffee was bitter, flavoured with chicory. Her eyes were sore, and despite her shower, she felt travel-weary and much rumpled, as she used to feel

on the occasions in Italy when she had been stranded for
the night and had slept in her car. She wondered if she
had, in fact, any inclination at all to trouble to give Seville
a second chance, even with the prospect of being made
more comfortable by lunchtime. She stared out of the window. A stout young woman went by, in patent-leather
shoes and a thick black coat, holding the hands of two sober
small children, dressed like miniature adults. Were they
going to church? Or going to see Granny? Or even going
to the dentist? Once, and only once, Frances had taken Sam
to the dentist, and Sam had bitten him, hard enough to
draw blood.

"You little bugger," the dentist had said, startled out of
his polite professionalism.

Those good little Sevillians would never bite anybody,
Frances thought, those good little Catholic children. She
tried to put herself in the stout mother's place, holding
those neatly gloved little hands.

"Come along, María, come along, Carlos, don't dawdle—"

It didn't work, she couldn't convince herself. Those children were inescapably Spanish, utterly foreign. Frances
wondered what their father was like: a lawyer perhaps, or
a doctor, a smallish, solid man to match his wife, anxious
to keep his children safe from the alarming liberalism
sweeping Spain.

"Drugs, sex," José Gómez Moreno had said last night
over tough little roasted partridges. "They are everywhere
in Spain now. Sevilla is very bad for drugs. Parents are all
the time afraid for their children. The television sex
shows," he said, his eyes gleaming, "are *terrible*."

He had talked a good deal about his father. He assured
Frances that she would be quite amazed by the beautiful
English his father spoke. "English," said José, "just like an
English person, no difference." He said his father was a
businessman and that the hotels were only one of his in-
terests, and that he had lived apart from José's mother for
fifteen years, and that this fact had made both the grandmothers angry and disapproving.

"They are strict Catholics, you see. Me—I can take religion or leave it. My generation can't be bothered."

"And your father?"

"He never speaks of religion. He doesn't like to be serious. Have you a boyfriend?"

"No," said Frances, "*if* it's any of your business."

He had laughed. He had recovered his equilibrium once and wasn't going to lose it again in a hurry, so he refrained from paying Frances fulsome compliments like how a beautiful woman like you should never, etc., etc. Just as well, Frances thought now, spreading butter and jam on her papery Spanish roll, or I might really have flipped. People never seem to use their imaginations, when dealing with those of us who aren't part of a couple, they never seem to display a quarter of the sensitivity when dealing with you that they simply *demand* when you are dealing with them. You get used to this in a way, just as you get used to singleness and to not being essential to someone and to both the pleasures and pains of not having someone else to take into account—you get used to it, but you still hate being asked about it. It makes you think about it, all over again, it makes you start to wonder . . . She bit her roll. Barbara's theory was, of course, that Frances couldn't sustain a wholehearted relationship because she was the weaker half of a pair of twins, but Frances was long used to her mother's theories and told herself she wasn't much inclined to believe them. And yet, she hadn't ever had a wholehearted relationship with a man, had she? She had fallen heavily for several men, in a desperate, almost headlong way, but she had never felt satisfied, in bed or out of it, by any of them once the fervour of the first stage was over. Always, it seemed, she would begin to withdraw, disappointed and empty-handed, just as the man was beginning to think that there might indeed be something more than met the eye to this tall girl in her conventional clothes with her funny little travel business and her oddly impersonal flat. But it would be too late then, he would have mistimed his interest, missed the emotional boat, and Frances would have gone, drifting back into her singleness, sadly but unavoidably. So

weird, Frances told herself, when I know that I'm a loving
person, that I like loving and being loved. Don't I? Or am
I just very short on self-knowledge and very long on self-
delusion? Could Mum be even partly right? Could it be,
really and in physiological fact, that Lizzie has all the emotional, sensual and reproductive instincts that should by
rights have been shared out between us?

Frances finished her roll and her coffee, and wiped her
mouth on a tiny, slippery paper napkin. She stood up. She
would do, she thought, what she always did on trips
abroad, which was to start with the church or cathedral of
any town or city, and work outwards. She went over to the
bar to pay for her breakfast. The waiter, eyes half closed
against the smoke rising from the cigarette in his mouth,
was drying glasses. He didn't look at her. She laid exactly
the right number of pesetas down on the bar with emphasis—"No tip," she said to him in English, "because there
was no service"—and walked out of last night's atmosphere
into the new morning's sharp, cold air.

It was, she remembered, Christmas Eve. It was impossible, somehow, to feel this emotionally, despite the cold.
Stuck as she was in the middle of an elaborate and undig-
nified mistake, the day didn't feel like anything; it simply
felt like an odd foreign day, similar, in its oddness, to many
foreign days in Frances's past. She thought of Langworth.
The house would shortly be in uproar, the kitchen strewn
with bowls of turkey stuffing and piles of vegetable peel-
ings, the house with the litter left by the children's robust
and chaotic approach to Christmas decoration. In the midst
of it, pipe in mouth, serenely absorbed in a crossword or
in one of Alistair's endless models, William would be the
still centre in the eye of the storm. Frances thought suddenly how nice it would be to have William with her now,
impenetrably English in these Spanish streets, gently
amazed by the otherness of it all.

"Extraordinary building," she could hear him say of the
cathedral. "Perfectly extraordinary. Now who do you suppose admires it?"

Frances couldn't think if she did or not; it was too pe-

culiar at first glance. She paused at a newspaper kiosk—
its upper shelves stuffed with pornographic magazines—
and bought a guidebook to the cathedral, a small, thick
guide book printed on shiny paper. "All you need to
know," said the title page, "about the Cathedral of Seville
and the Monastery of St. Isidoro del Campo."

Frances twitched her bag on to her shoulder and risked
another glance at her goal. She stood across the street from
its western façade, and gazed at it across Seville's swirling
traffic. It was simply enormous, and very complicated,
Gothic and flamboyant. Behind it, there appeared to be—
could there be?—a minaret. Frances opened her guide
book.

"In this cathedral are many beautiful doors, the Market
Door, the St. Christopher Door, the Door of the Bells, the
Door of the Sticks, the Door of Forgiveness, the Door—"

Frances shut the guidebook, and put it in her mackintosh
pocket. Perhaps, like some Italian cathedrals, a forbidding,
or even hideous, exterior would give way to treasures
within. This was not hideous, but it was startling, so vast,
so complex, so grand, so—so bragging, Frances thought,
that it made one feel apprehensive. Still, there wasn't much
point in standing shivering on the opposite pavement, feeling daunted before one had even begun. She remembered
doing that once in front of Parma Cathedral, thinking:
What a horror, just like a factory, and nearly, very nearly,
bypassing it for a Campari and soda in the nearest bar, and
then, driven by her decently cultural conscience, going in
reluctantly and being enchanted. There was a painting of
the Assumption by Correggio in Parma, full of cherubs
tossing flowers about. It didn't look, from the outside at
least, as if Seville Cathedral was the sort of place where
anyone, even a defiant cherub, would dare to chuck flowers
around.

The thing about southern European traffic, Frances had
learned long ago, was to confront it. Northern principles
of orderly obedience to red and green lights were pointless,
because nobody south of Paris took any notice of them at
all. The answer was to turn yourself into a confident pe-

destrian presence, striding out, as tall as possible, even, if necessary, holding out a commanding hand in a STOP attitude as traffic rushed at you like a pack of mad dogs. It upset Italian traffic policemen, behaving like this, but, in Frances's view, they were too easily upset anyhow. No doubt being isolated in foolish little comic-opera castles from which they flapped their white-gloved hands and impotently blew whistles at racing tides of impervious Fiats accounted for it. She would discover if Spanish policemen were the same. She turned up her mackintosh collar more resolutely, put her chin up and marched across the Avenida de la Constitución.

On the far side, an old man seized her. Jabber, he said to her in lightning, incomprehensible Spanish. Jabber, jabber, jabber. He pointed at the traffic, at Frances, at the well-behaved clump of people waiting on the pavement corner of the Plaza del Triunfo, he rolled his eyes to heaven, he crossed himself.

"Thank you," Frances said, smiling and disengaging her arm. "Thank you for your concern, but I am perfectly all right."

He shook his finger at her. No, he seemed to be saying. No, it is not perfectly all right to behave like that in Seville.

"Next time," Frances promised, "I'll trot tamely across with the others. Happy Christmas." She moved away. He called something after her. She turned to smile at him, but he was scowling. What a place, she thought, what a city, what people! No wonder the English headed off in droves for Italy, as if the rest of Europe hardly existed. An Italian might swear at you or grin at you, but he wouldn't *lecture* you. Huh, Frances thought, pushing open a tiny door within an immense door on her way into the cathedral, huh, but at least feeling indignant has got me warm.

Inside, Seville Cathedral was even larger than outside. The spaces were awe-inspiring, vast landscapes of gleaming floors and soaring pillars and vaulted arches, dark, hushed, menacing, and holy. Frances walked a little way inside and then stopped. She had come abreast of an enormous and sombre queen, made, it appeared, of darkly gilded wood.

She peered more closely in the gloom. There were three more queens arranged in formation, two by two, moving with stately tread across a carved stone platform, carrying what looked like a tabernacle on poles across their shoulders. Frances walked round them. Their expressions were at once majestic and far away; their tunics emblazoned with castles and heraldic beasts. Frances took her pocket torch out of her handbag, and shone its beam on the stone carving. She was looking, she found, at the tomb of Christopher Columbus. Poor Christopher Columbus, demoted from the podium of the heroes of history by the obsessive modern need to find feet of clay attached to anyone of stature whom the past had admired. Poor Christopher Columbus, no longer a great adventurer, now merely a greedy pirate. Frances put her hand appreciatively on the nearest wooden foot of the nearest, mighty, impassive queen. Banished to the ranks of the merely self-serving Columbus might be, but at least he had his tomb.

She wandered away from him into the dim and vast spaces of the cathedral. A thousand tapers glimmered from a hundred chapels across the distance of the floor, great screens of wood and forged iron vanished upwards into the shadowy heights of the roof, holy faces, carved and painted, eyes downcast in piety or upcast in agony wheeled slowly past in endless procession. She came to a kind of central room, black carved screens enclosing choir stalls, with huge, gilded metal gates at one end, like the gates of a fortified castle.

Heavens, Frances thought. How fierce this is, how angry the Spanish seem to be—

She turned. There was something extraordinary behind her, a gleaming something, apparently a wall of gold, a sheer, fantastic cliff of gold rising up and up like a broad and shining fountain between dark walls of stone. It too was confined behind a grille. Frances grasped the bars, and stared. The wall was sculptured, sculptured all over with figures and scenes, panels and pillars and little canopies, and at the top, miles above Frances and the dwarfed altar

below, Christ hung drooping on his cross, gilded too like
a great, broken, golden bird.

Frances gazed and gazed. She had never seen anything
like it, she had never, in all her travels, seen anything that
was so Christian and so unfamiliar all at once. She let go
of the bars in her grasp, and subsided on to a wooden chair
nearby, taking her gauche little guide book out of her
pocket.

"The great retablo of the main sanctuary," said her
guidebook, "was designed by the Flemish master Dancart
and fashioned between 1482 and 1526."

So it was there when the Armada sailed. When those
little ships came in their straggling groups up the English
Channel, and the watchers on the cliffs built their defiant
bonfires, this huge golden wall, redolent of all Spain's ambition and power, was standing here in Seville. It wasn't
often, Frances thought, raising her eyes again, that you really felt, along your arteries and veins, the thud of history,
the sensation that the passing of time was at once both
everything and nothing. She had felt it sometimes in England, only occasionally in Italy for all her love of the country, but it was really most peculiar to feel it with such
intensity in this almost hostile building, full of darkness and
swaggering, threatening strength; in a city she had so far
considered utterly alien.

She got up and walked slowly away towards the south
aisle. Perhaps because it was Christmas Eve there weren't
many people about, and the winter sunshine fell through
the high windows of the upper nave in long, dusty shafts
on to the empty and shining squares and triangles of the
floor. The place seemed ever more timeless, drifting ever
further from the newspaper kiosk outside, the scolding old
man, the waiters in the bar, the cars on the avenue, whose
noise came through the walls and distances like no more
than the sound of the sea. Frances leaned against a pillar,
putting her head back against its ancient, impersonal, cold
bulk. If she closed her eyes—if she half-closed her eyes and
gazed up that extravagant aisle through her lashes, at the
stupendous stretches of light and shadow, of gleaming mar-

ble and soaring stone, of shimmering surfaces and fathomless pools of darkness—she might just see, just glimpse
for a second or two, a procession, a fifteenth-century procession, clothed in velvet and damask, heralded by priests
and gilded crosses, with at its heart the Catholic Kings,
Fernando and Isabel, swaying across the marble spaces to
give to Christopher Columbus the mandate to explore the
Western world and bring its treasures home to Spain.

She opened her eyes. Someone was blowing a whistle, a
hideous, mood-destructive whistle, and vergers and sacris-
tans were hurrying about the cathedral, shooing visitors before them like flocks of bewildered hens. It was time for
the first Mass of the day. The cathedral, survivor of Moor
and Christian, was preparing itself for its central spiritual
function. Frances stood upright, gave her pillar a fond and
regretful stroke in parting, and followed the crowd out of
the past into the present.

The rest of the morning was unsatisfactory. The mood in-
duced by the cathedral hung about Frances like a dream
and made her feel irritable about the need to look at maps,
buy coffee, absorb the fact that Seville is the fourth city of
Spain, that it started the Spanish Civil War on the Republican side but was seized by the Nationalists, that it was the
favourite city of Pedro the Cruel (succeeded to the throne,
1350) and that it suffers now from a sad increase in petty
crime. The spirit of the thing, of the place, seemed absent
from these facts; something about both Spain and Seville
that had seemed, inarticulately, powerfully, comprehensible
to Frances inside the cathedral now escaped her. She simply
seemed to be back, rather crossly, in a modern foreign city
at the one time of year when every instinct told her to be
where everything was familiar and of her own kind.

Frances walked and walked. She saw the river and the
bridge she had crossed the night before; she saw long, tree-
planted formal gardens and buildings with exuberant baroque façades; she saw streets lined with houses and blocks
of flats, and streets lined with shops, some selling electrical

goods and groceries and plastic buckets, some selling leather clothes and souvenir castanets and ceramic holy figures, sentimental or macabre. She passed churches and garages and high blank walls hiding goodness knew what; she passed dingy newsagents and endless underwear shops and one beautiful building on whose first-floor balcony five skeletons stood dressed in the frocks and hats of high fashion, frozen in a grisly parade. She also passed people, crowds and crowds of hurrying people, absorbed in the admirable European habit of leaving the preparation of Christmas until Christmas Eve instead of exhausting themselves in a heartless, relentless, three-month Protestant hype. Everyone was carrying something, food and flowers, boxes of cakes and chocolates, bottles of wine, Christmas trees, baskets of clementines with their dark glossy leaves still attached, nets of nuts, armfuls of things done up in coloured paper and ringlets of ribbons. Only Frances, it seemed, was carrying nothing but an everyday handbag and a guidebook.

At half past eleven, Frances skirted the northern precincts of the cathedral—she gave it a respectful and grateful glance this time—and threaded her way back to the Hotel Toro, through the Barrio de Santa Cruz. It had been the old Jewish quarter, mazelike and secret between white walls, the houses turned in on themselves round their gardens and courtyards. It too was now full of busy people and chatter. A man went past her carrying a huge wooden angel with a pinkly painted face, and another with a lavatory seat slung jauntily over his shoulder. It didn't feel like Christmas—did Christmas ever feel like Christmas to a northerner in the south, or vice versa?—but it did suddenly begin to feel festive. Frances pushed open the glass doors to the foyer of the Hotel Toro with something almost like high spirits. It was five past midday.

José Gómez Moreno wasn't there. He wasn't there, and he hadn't been there. There was no message from him by telephone either. Frances went over to the telephone booth that was disguised as a medieval sentry box, guarded by two huge suits of armour, in a corner of the hotel lobby. She rang the Posada de los Naranjos, and asked for José.

An uncertain voice in hesitant English said that he was not available.

"What do you mean, not available? Is he in the hotel?"

"Yes, he is in hotel but—in meeting."

"With whom?" Frances shouted.

"Is private meeting," the voice said. "Of hotel business."

"Will you give Señor Gómez Moreno a message?"

"If you wish—"

"I do wish. Tell him that Miss Shore no longer wishes to have any further communication with him of any kind."

"*¿Qué?*"

"Tell him—" Frances began and then stopped. She took a breath. "Tell him to get knotted," she said, and banged the telephone down before the voice could say "*¿Qué?*" again.

She returned to the reception desk. The cherry-lipped girl was tearing a telex form into long, inexplicable strips.

"Are there any direct flights from Seville to London today?"

The girl picked up the nearest telephone.

"I enquire."

"Don't you *know*?"

"I enquire," the girl said repressively.

Frances turned away and began to pace the green floor. The need to be gone was abruptly so urgent that she couldn't have sat still if she'd been paid to. She knew exactly what was happening at the Posada de los Naranjos. José Gómez Moreno had asked a member of the party from Oviedo to move into the Hotel Toro and he or she had refused point blank. Of course they had, Frances thought, she'd have done just the same in their place. So José was hopping about, pleading and wringing his hands and not daring to come to the Hotel Toro and confront her.

"Madam," the girl called.

Frances went back to the desk.

"There are no direct flights today. You must fly to Madrid this afternoon, and take a flight to London after. All the flights are full, so you must be standby."

Frances glared at her. In her present mood, she could

see no charm in her cream-skinned, black-eyed Spanish face.

"Please get me a taxi. For ten minutes' time."

"Is very busy," the girl said remorselessly. "Will be fifteen, twenty minutes."

"Just *get* one."

The lift-indicator light revealed that the lift was presently on the top floor. Frances jabbed at the summoning button. The lift took no notice. She turned away, and rushed up the staircase instead, three flights of green marble stairs and black-carved wooden balustrades with, on every landing, a glittering shrine containing a highly made-up madonna and surmounted by a pair of bull's horns. Frances arrived breathlessly at her door and flung it open. The chambermaid had left the room immaculate, ugly and as dark as pitch, having shut all the windows and shutters tightly as reproof against sunlight and air.

The telephone shrilled.

"Yes?" Frances shouted into it.

"Miss Shore?"

"Yes—"

"Miss Shore, my name is Gómez Moreno—"

"Go away!" Frances shrieked.

She put down the receiver and dived into the bathroom to retrieve her sponge bag. The telephone rang again. She sped across the room and seized it and cried, "Listen, I want nothing more to do with you, *ever*. Do you understand?"

"Madam, taxi is here," the girl from reception said. "Is urgent taxi."

Frances swallowed.

"Thank you."

"He is waiting."

"I'll be right down."

She flung her possessions into her case, her nightie, her extra jerseys, her tidy dress and shoes, her hairbrush, underclothes, paperbacks, hairdryer, sponge bag. It now seemed to her not just imperative to get out of Seville before she exploded, but to do this before the Gómez Morenos could catch up with her. That one had been the father—deeper-voiced, with more confident English. José said his father had learned English at the London School of Economics in the sixties, and had insisted his children learn to speak it too.

"For Europe, you see. It is necessary for us all to be brothers and sisters in Europe."

Frances shut her case and locked it, slung her bag on her shoulder and picked up the case. What a performance, what a waste of time, what a stupid, amateurish, exhausting muddle the whole thing had been, and almost all her own fault for backing a hunch, indulging a whim.

"I'll tell you something," she said to Room 309. "And that is that I'll make sure I never see you again, or Seville, or Spain, for that matter."

Then she stamped out into the corridor and slammed the door behind her.

Downstairs, the taxi driver was flirting idly with the receptionist. She wasn't taking much notice, being engaged in adding up Frances's bill very slowly on a calculator with a dark, red-nailed forefinger.

"My bill is being settled by Señor Gómez Moreno."

"I have no instruction—"

The taxi driver looked at Frances without admiration—too little make-up, no visible curves, small jewellery—and leaned across the reception desk to whisper something to the girl. She gave the calculator a tiny smile by way of response.

"I shan't sign that bill," Frances said. "I am not paying it."

The girl took no notice.

"When is the next flight to Madrid?"

The taxi driver turned his head. "Two hour," he said. "No hurry."

"I want to get out of here."

The glass doors opened and a man came in at a run, a solid, middle-aged man. The girl stopped tapping at her calculator and smiled at him, a wide, charming smile full of white teeth.

"Miss Shore?"

Frances moved back.

"Miss Shore, I am Luis Gómez Moreno. I don't know how to apologise enough. I am mortified."

He had a square, open face, not the kind of long, grave Spanish face that had stared at Frances from the churches and streets of Seville that morning, but a more genial one, more extrovert.

"I'm afraid it's too late," Frances said. "I've been dragged here for nothing. I've been cold, uncomfortable and neglected and all I want to do is go home."

"Of course you do," Luis Gómez Moreno said. He turned to the girl at the desk and uttered a rapid instruction. She picked up the bill she had been preparing and began, as she had with the telex form, to tear it into careful strips. Then he said something to the taxi driver.

"Don't dismiss him," Frances said sharply. "He is taking me to the airport."

"May I not do that?"

"No," Frances said. "I haven't any patience left for the Gómez Morenos."

Infuriatingly, he smiled at her. He smiled as if she had made a really good joke.

"I like your spirit."

She said nothing. She turned to the taxi driver and indicated her suitcase.

"Please put that in your taxi."

"Is there nothing," Luis Gómez Moreno said, "that I can say or do to make you stay? I had no idea of this dreadful confusion until one half hour ago. Now I want you to try and forget the last twenty-four hours, and allow me to assist you in every way to do the business you came for."

Frances snorted.

"You've got a nerve—"

"I also have a heart and a conscience. I am truly sorry. You shall have a suite at the Hotel Alfonso XIII—"

"I don't want a suite at the Alfonso XIII. I don't want

any more dealings with you or your son or your hotels. I don't want to see Spain ever again."

"Not even—"

"Never," said Frances.

"How sad," he said, "when there is so much to see, so much that no one European knows about except the Spanish."

She looked at him. His face, framed by the upturned collar of his overcoat, was full of warmth, and hope and humour. He held out his hands to her, palms upward.

"Please, Miss Shore," said Luis Gómez Moreno. "Please give Spain, including me, just one more chance."

FIVE

On Christmas morning, Lizzie woke quite unnecessarily at
five and waited for Davy to come in, urgently requiring an
audience for opening his stocking. He didn't come. She
strained her ears into the chill darkness; the house was quite
quiet. Beside her, Robert breathed with what seemed a
most selfish regularity, deeply, evenly, comfortably. Nobody, Lizzie realised with indignation, was awake except
her.

She wondered whether to lie there and attempt to go
back to sleep. She humped over on to her other side, away
from Robert, and closed her eyes. Immediately, on the inside of her eyelids, was printed a list which began, "Empty
dishwasher from last night, lay breakfast, check time turkey
ought to go in oven, lay sitting-room fire." She tried to
replace the list with images of colour and shape that were
her usual sleep-inducers, and saw instead a clear picture of
Frances at a restaurant table lit by candles, with a glass of
wine in her hand and being offered a dish of glistening
paella to the sound of guitars. Lizzie groaned. She waited
to see if Robert had heard her. He hadn't. She groaned
again. He slept on. Lizzie sat up, swung her feet out from

under the muffling warmth of the duvet, and stood up.

She padded out to the bathroom and looked sourly at her Christmas face in the mirror above the basin.

"You are being very childish," she told herself out loud. She brushed her teeth and hair, pulled on her dressing-gown—a handsome, full-length, hooded one, stocked by the Gallery and much admired by Frances, who still wore the old kimono Lizzie had given her for Christmas at least ten years ago—and went firmly downstairs. All the bedroom doors, even Davy's, were shut. Nobody, it seemed, was in the least interested in Christmas.

The kitchen, fragrant still with the clove-breathed memory of last night's supper, was at least quite warm. Everybody had been too tired—or unhelpful—last night to clear up properly, and there were still pans, unwashed up, in the sink and newspapers on chairs, and trails of black pepper and breadcrumbs across the table. Rob had been terribly tired; the Gallery had been humming until after seven with last-minute customers, mostly men, and he hadn't got home until nearly nine, by which time Davy was asleep and Sam, having sneaked two glasses of wine, was being both obstreperous and silly. Harriet had wondered, out loud and far too often, whether Frances would ring from Seville, William had looked too much as if he was just longing to go away quietly and telephone Juliet, and Alistair had provoked his grandmother into an instant rage by saying, quite casually, that he didn't see the point of girls going to university if they were just going to shop and cook and have babies afterwards. In the midst of this, Lizzie had produced baked gammon, potatoes, cauliflower cheese and red cabbage, followed by mince pies and tangerines, and refrained—just—from thumping Harriet every time she said, "Honestly, it doesn't feel a bit like Christmas does it, it just feels like a weekend, doesn't it, any boring old weekend. I wish Frances was here."

Lizzie filled the huge Aga kettle and set it on the hotplate. The cat, named Cornflakes by Davy, emerged from the dresser drawer where he slept and which had to be left half open at night for this reason, and began his steady whining for attention and milk around Lizzie's ankles. He was, Lizzie thought, like a spider; he had nothing to do all day but besiege her, just as spiders had nothing to do but spin webs, endlessly, patiently, in every corner of the Grange. Outside the house, nature wasn't any better, either; it had all the time in the world to knit bindweed painstakingly round the rose trees and stifle the lawn with creeping moss. Lizzie yawned and put a teabag in the pot.

The door to the hall opened with a bang and Davy trailed in, sobbing, towing his stocking like a dead and lumpy snake. Lizzie stopped pouring water into the teapot.

"Darling! What is it, Davy? Why are you crying?"

"Sam!" wailed Davy. He dropped his stocking and began to tear at the jacket buttons of his primrose-yellow pyjamas.

"Sam?"

"Yes! Yes! I hate my pyjamas!"

Lizzie knelt down by Davy and tried to take him in her arms.

"Why? Why do you when they are brand-new and you look so sweet in them?"

"I don't, I don't. I hate them!" Davy wept, still wrestling inside Lizzie's embrace. "Sam said I looked *sexy*."

"Sam is very silly," Lizzie said. "He doesn't know what sexy means."

Davy glared at her.

"He does! He does! It means showing your bottom and your—"

"Davy," Lizzie said, "it's Christmas. Have you forgotten?"

"Sam said—"

Lizzie stood up, lifted Davy and set him on the edge of the table.

"I don't want to know what Sam said."

"He was going to open my stocking, he said he was perfectly allowed to."

Lizzie retrieved Davy's stocking from the floor.

"How's about you opening it now, with me?"

Davy looked doubtful.

"You ought to open stockings in a *bed*, you know."

"Not necessarily. You've got me and Cornflakes for company. Won't we do?"

Davy twisted round and wriggled off the table on to the floor. He bumped his stocking down beside him.

"No," he said, and trailed out of the kitchen again. Lizzie heard him going up the stairs, one step at a time, on his way back to certain persecution. Sam was a horror, but at least you didn't lie awake worrying about his fragile self-esteem and his chances of emotional happiness. He was like a terrier, cheerful, inquisitive, pugnacious and un-squashable. Lizzie adored Sam. In no time at all the girls were going to start adoring Sam too, and the kitchen would then be full of his sobbing discards being comforted by Alistair, who had always liked mending things and would find the transition from mending model aeroplanes to broken hearts perfectly comfortable. Lizzie smiled ruefully. How shocking it was to take a small but certain pleasure in thinking of Sam as a future heartbreaker, while knowing that, if anyone tried to break his heart in return, she, Lizzie, would probably murder them. Oh God, the mothers of sons . . .

"Good morning," Barbara said, coming in, in a blue chenille dressing-gown. "Happy Christmas."

"Oh Mum," Lizzie said, going forward for a kiss. "Did they wake you, the boys? I'm so sorry."

"Davy came in to ask if his pyjamas were sexy. I told him that in my view and in the view of ninety-nine per cent of sane women, pyjamas were the least sexy garments in the world, after galoshes and string vests."

"It was Sam," Lizzie said. She poured tea into mugs. "So typical of Sam, to try and wreck Christmas morning before it even has time to draw breath." She held a mug out to Barbara. "Tea?"

"I was awake anyway," Barbara said, taking the mug.

"Oh dear—"

"William was snoring."

"Why don't you wear ear plugs?"

"I thought of that," Barbara said. "But then I thought I

wouldn't hear a fire, if one started, so I've gone back to kicking him."

"Separate rooms, then."

"Oh no," Barbara said firmly.

Lizzie swallowed some tea. Nothing all day, not the champagne Robert had finally bought after saying they couldn't afford it, not the prune-and-chestnut turkey stuffing she had taken such trouble over, not the brandy butter nor the smoked salmon planned for supper nor the cashew nuts nor the Belgian truffles, would taste one tenth as good as this first, strong, hot swallow of tea.

"Why not? I mean, surely, after being married so long there's hardly much left to prove—"

"There's Juliet," Barbara said shortly.

Lizzie groaned inwardly. Davy's anxiety about the sex appeal of his pyjamas, followed by Barbara wishing to discuss Juliet, seemed more than she could bear before six o'clock on Christmas morning.

"He telephoned her last night," Barbara said. She went over to the Aga and leaned against its warm bulk, gripping her mug.

"Mum," Lizzie said, "you have known about Dad and Juliet for twenty-seven years. You could, if you had found the situation intolerable, have left him at any point during those twenty-seven years. But you haven't. You've chosen to stay. It doesn't seem to me to fit in with any of the things you say you believe about women, but never mind, that's what you've chosen. Dad always rings Juliet at Christmas, sometimes you even talk to her yourself. Juliet is a nice woman, Mum. Remember?"

"I did not like it last night," Barbara said. "I don't really know why, but I didn't. He looked—"

"Stop it, Mum," Lizzie said, putting her mug down and beginning to open cupboards in search of plates and jars and packets for breakfast. "It's Christmas morning."

There was a series of thumps upstairs, then a crash, then a squeal and then silence.

"I'll go and see," Barbara said.

"Don't bother. I've stopped going every time it sounds like disaster, or it's all I ever do."

Doors began to open and shut above them. Robert's voice, thick with sleep, shouted, "Shut up, will you?" and then Alistair's shouted back, "Happy Christmas, actually."

"Think of Frances," Barbara said, "waking alone in a hotel room in Seville and spending the day with a strange foreign businessman who doesn't believe in Christmas."

"I'm trying," Lizzie said, peeling the paper off a new block of butter, "not to think about Frances. At all."

"I wonder if that's what's the matter with William, I wonder if that's why he was so peculiarly pathetic about ringing Juliet—"

The door opened. Robert, his hair tousled, tying himself into a towelling bathrobe, came in yawning and said there was a notice on Harriet's door saying she was not to be woken under any circumstances whatsoever. He stooped to sketch a kiss on Barbara's cheek and plant one on Lizzie's.

"Why is everyone being so frightfully un-Christmassy?" Lizzie demanded.

"The boys are all in bed together," Robert said, pouring tea. "I dread to think what's going on. They are under Alistair's duvet."

"Davy was preoccupied earlier with looking sexy."

"Alistair is far too prissy for sex. God, is it really only five past six? I'll go and get some wood in."

"Was William awake?"

Robert thought about this.

"Someone was singing in the loo—"

"He always sings in the loo," Barbara said. "It's the mark of a public-school boy of his generation because they weren't allowed locks on the lavatories and sometimes not even doors."

Lizzie began to rub vigorously at a sticky jar with a damp cloth.

"Why not?"

"Because of buggery."

"Honestly," Lizzie said. "*Honestly*. What a disgusting

conversation. Don't you realise," she went on, raising her voice, "don't you realise that it's *Christmas*?"

"Is this Christmas?" Davy said to his grandfather.

"Yes."

"It feels quite cross for Christmas—"

"Yes," William said. "It does."

Breakfast had happened, in an atmosphere of acrimony, and without Harriet, soon after seven because everyone was up. Alistair pointed out that this was far, far earlier than a school day. Robert was the only one who had dressed, having gone out to get logs for the sitting-room fire in his dressing-gown, and having then got locked out by mistake, and been temporarily forgotten by Lizzie and Barbara, so that he was forced to roam about in the sleety dark outside alternately bellowing furiously and pleading piteously for readmittance. It was William who finally heard him and came down to let him in.

"My dear boy, I do hope you haven't been there all night."

Robert resisted the temptation to say, Don't be perfectly fatuous, and went upstairs for a bath. He was fond of William, and grateful to him, but easily irritated by him too. Either William's bumbling benevolence hid a mind like a steel trap, or else his father-in-law had the luck of the very devil. Robert found the relationship with Juliet both incomprehensible and old-fashioned, a sort of babyish, comforting, retarded habit, never grown out of. Robert had never been unfaithful to Lizzie in seventeen years. He didn't want to be. How somebody like Lizzie could emerge from that family of near half-wits, Robert couldn't imagine. There was William; there was Barbara with her bossiness and her phoney, half-baked feminism; there was Frances, drifting about through life like a ship without a pilot—and then there was Lizzie. Running a bath, and draping his sodden robe over the bathroom radiator to dry, Robert decided he would not tell Lizzie how badly the Gallery had done in the run-up to Christmas this year, until she had less on her plate. He longed to tell her, to share the anxiety and the burden, but not telling her for now was kinder.

After his bath, he felt, briefly, more alert and cheerful. Breakfast soon put paid to both. Davy, full of stocking chocolate, wouldn't eat, but cowered shivering on his chair in his despised pyjamas, refusing to put his dressing-gown on because Sam said it was a girl's one since it didn't have a cord girdle. Sam ate robustly and sniggered, as if amusing himself with an endless series of private lavatory jokes, and Alistair, peering through smeary spectacles and breathing heavily and theatrically, read the competition rules on the back of the nearest cereal packet as if they were the most absorbing literature in the world. Lizzie looked worn out, Barbara looked indignant and William abstracted. Harriet's empty chair was eloquent of an impending storm—she had fired the first shot in a war of nerves that wouldn't satisfy her until it was fully engaged.

I wish Lizzie and I were in Seville, Robert thought. Just the two of us, no children, no parents-in-law, no Christmas, no responsibility to make things fun for everybody else.

He tried to catch her eye. She was pouring coffee for William, her heavy hair swinging forward across her cheeks. She took a deep breath, as if gearing herself up for something and said, "Now we are *all* going to church. Ten-thirty and carols."

Sam gave a yowl and slid under the table.

"Don't be silly," Barbara said. "I never go to church."

"Mum—"

Alistair looked at his grandmother in admiration. "Don't you?"

"You know perfectly well I don't. It's a lot of mumbo jumbo."

"Mum," Lizzie said, "this is Christmas. You usually—"

"I shall come with you," William said, interrupting. "And so will Davy. Davy and I need to do a bit of singing."

"I don't," Alistair said.

Lizzie put her hands down flat on the table.

"On Christmas morning, for the last umpteen years, we have all, as a family, gone to Langworth Parish Church and sung carols. We are doing it again today."

"Sorry," Barbara said.

Robert leaned forward. "I'll come."

"I won't!" Sam shouted from under the table.

William got up and came round the table to where Davy sat. He lifted him into his arms.

"Davy and I are going to dress for church."

Davy looked deeply uncertain. If only Sam . . .

"I suggest," Alistair said, "that those who want to go and do a bit of mumbo jumbo, just do it, and send one up for me."

"Don't show off," Robert said.

"My dear father—"

"The thing about carols," William said, bearing Davy from the room, "is that you know all the words anyway so it doesn't matter if you can't read them all."

They went upstairs. Harriet's door was open, but the bathroom one was shut and rock music thudded away behind it. William put Davy into his bed and pulled up the bedclothes round him, to get him warm. He used to do this to the twins, long ago, on Sunday mornings, when he was left in charge of them while Barbara, who had then been as strongly pro-church as she was now anti it, went to early communion. William had always preferred evensong; it had always coincided better with the quiet reflective tempo of his own appreciation of the ancient Christian virtues of tolerance and compassion combined with an antipathy to anything strident or proselytising. There was, inevitably, a stridency about large family life, where all the separate personalities fought for the same space, not because that was the only space there was, but because they all determinedly perceived it to be so. Was that what Frances had run away from? Was her life, inevitably much more private than Lizzie's because of its circumstances, making it difficult, almost unbearable, for her to join in? Or was it that she—most understandably, William thought—was pointing out, by absenting herself, that it was both unimaginative and patronising to assume she would be grateful and relieved to be swallowed up automatically in the circus of family Christmas at the Grange? Her letter, left for them in the spare bedroom, had said so little, merely that she was sorry if she'd upset anyone but she was taking a promising chance for the business. It was a foolish letter really, evasive, even untruthful. But perhaps she not only couldn't tell the truth, but also didn't *want* to?

"Half the world," Juliet had once said to him, "lives envying the other half, and the other half can't think why the first half doesn't pull itself together and live the way the other half does. Do I make myself clear?"

"No," William said.

"I suppose I mean, then, that half the world are the bossers, and the other half are the bossed."

William sat down on the edge of his bed and looked down at Davy, drowsy now in the reassurance of an adult bed. Was he one of the bossed, as William was? And was Frances? Was Frances the bossed and Lizzie the bosser? And if so, had Frances at last recognised this and started to get the hell out of it all, just in time?

Davy opened his eyes. He regarded his grandfather.

"Are you sure this is Christmas?" he said.

In the end, Lizzie, Robert, William, Sam and Davy went to church, and a number of the rest of the congregation, who knew the Gallery family well, did a bit of counting and wondered where Barbara, Harriet and Alistair were. Lizzie didn't like to admit, when questioned, that Barbara had started a revolutionary movement against church at breakfast, so she simply mumbled untruthfully that they all knew how Christmas morning was and that they somehow simply hadn't got their acts together. Strangely, church cheered them all up a little, Robert because it ate up an hour of this endless day, Lizzie because it got her out of the house, William because he enjoyed the familiar ritual, Sam because he liked being in a crowd of any kind and Davy because he was wearing cast-off clothes of Sam's which could not, therefore, by simple definition, be called either girly or sexy.

When they returned, humming snatches of carols and feeling a mild anticipatory enthusiasm for the food and drink ahead, they found Barbara in the kitchen ostentatiously instructing Alistair in the art of basting a turkey—"I cannot imagine how you suppose he will make a fit husband for anyone if you indulge his rampant chauvinism so pathetically"—and Harriet, dressed in leggings, gold lurex ankle boots, one of Robert's jerseys and far too much make-up, yawning over drawing elaborate place-cards for the lunch table.

"Where did those boots come from?"

"They're Sarah's."

"They are truly tarty—"

Harriet eyed her father. "And how would you know?"

"Can I," Davy said, writhing out of his half-unzipped anorak and dropping it on the kitchen floor, "open my presents now?"

"Not till I've found something to write on, to make a list—"

"And now," Barbara said loudly, "we shall turn the potatoes."

Alistair slumped against the Aga.

"I really am exhausted. Prostrated, you know. And I have to say that women do these things so much better—"

"Pack that in," his grandmother said crisply.

Sam, still anoraked, appeared in the kitchen door armed with a silver plastic raygun.

"Look!" he yelled. "Look! Look what I've got!"

He pressed the trigger and a deafening explosion of chattering sound hit them all like smacks in the face.

"Stop that!"

"Where did he get it? I *said*, Sam, I *said* to wait till I'd found a piece of paper—"

"Can I have it? Can I have a go, can I, can I, can I—"

"It makes me furious, simply furious to see boys fed these ridiculous stereotypes—"

"Turn it *off*, Sam!"

But he was wild with excitement. Clutching the gun,

which glittered with intermittent lights like little deranged eyes, he spun round the kitchen, blazing away at everyone, hysterical with power and pleasure. As he reeled past the door to the outside, to the back drive and the garden, it opened, almost knocking him flat and sending the gun flying out of his hands. Before his screams began, there was a tiny silence, and during it, Frances appeared, wearing her mackintosh with a sprig of holly in the lapel.

"Hello," Frances said, almost uncertainly. "Happy Christmas."

SIX

Juliet Jones relished the particular solitariness of Christmas Day. Because the rest of the world was so deeply preoccupied with Christmas, the day, for her, hung suspended, without time or place, a day that hardly existed, and which therefore did not have to be treated with all the wearying domestic obligations that other days required. It was a day to be relished, or squandered, on a whim, a day to be celebrated or totally ignored, to be spent in bed or tramping the hills, guzzling or fasting. The only rule about Christmas that Juliet had evolved over the years was that she would never spend it with anybody else.

She did not consider herself by nature misanthropic. If asked—and people did, constantly, ask her, being convinced, as people are, that there is something freakish and unnatural about choosing to be alone—she would say that she had made a virtue out of necessity and had come to like her own company since that was the most of anyone's company she got. She knew herself to be also slightly perverse, always, even from childhood, wanting things she couldn't have, largely because she couldn't have them. Surely that accounted, certainly at the beginning, for Wil-

liam? After all, William Shore was the last kind of man
that a woman like Juliet Jones would choose. At least,
twenty-seven years ago, he was. Now, he was so familiar
he was an extension of herself, an extension which, to her
mild relief, took itself away after every meeting, to be ad-
ministered to by Barbara. Long ago, Juliet had wanted William's baby. To be strictly honest, she had wanted a baby,
and William, such a tender-hearted father to his twins,
seemed to be the perfect choice to assist her. She never told
him this; she just took no precautions, and hoped. The hope
came to nothing, and William stayed.

Juliet had always been regarded as very bohemian by her
own generation. Tall and strong-featured with long,
vigorous hair, she had, as a young woman, provided a remarkable contrast to her gloved and waisted contemporaries in the early fifties. She had been to art school, and then
to Paris, and to Florence, where she led, it was assumed by
her old schoolfriends in Bath, a life only to be hinted at for
physical extravagance. Then she returned to England, said
she wasn't going to be a painter but a potter, and set up
home and workshop in an isolated cottage up a track two
miles out of Langworth.

The cottage was no beauty. It was Victorian, sturdily
built, but of uncompromising brick in an area of golden
stone. All around it, the uplands rolled and swept away, so
that Lizzie, toiling up the track on her bicycle as a teenager,
felt she was somehow ascending on to the roof of the world.
Juliet's cottage was a treasure trove to Lizzie, an Aladdin's
cave of colour and texture and muddle after her own house,
which was painted either green or cream with not quite
enough furniture or pictures. The bones of Juliet's rooms,
the walls and windows and tables and chairs, had vanished
under a riot of fabrics: rugs and shawls and cushions,
lengths of Paisley cottons and gleaming brocades, pieces of
crushed velvet and embroidered linen lay layered on everything like exotic leaves. And out of this rich confusion came
Juliet herself and her pots; Juliet so self-possessed and decided, her pots, creamy, smoky and cloudy from the wood-
ash glazes that were her speciality, as cool as classical

columns. Lizzie had been head over heels in love with it all, with Juliet, with her skill with her cottage and her clothes and her pungent cooking full of cumin and nettles and the olive oil which Barbara would only buy suspiciously from a chemist, in little bottles, like a medicine. Lizzie longed for Frances to come with her to Juliet's. She told her all about it, she described and raved and promised Frances paradise. But Frances wouldn't come.

"Is she exploring sex?" Juliet had once asked Lizzie.

Lizzie thought of the head boy at William's school.

"I think she's *trying* to—"

Juliet had never got to know Frances as she had known Lizzie. Lizzie made it so easy; she was longing to be known, as William was. Even Barbara, between whom and Juliet there should by rights have existed a great awkwardness, was in some ways easier to grasp than Frances. Barbara and Juliet had had one mighty quarrel, in which Juliet said she was not leaving the area, and if Barbara wanted to move William away she'd better get on and do it, and then, except for minor eruptions, no further ones. A kind of strange friendship even grew up, founded on Barbara's tacit acknowledgement, for which Juliet was both grateful and respectful, that Juliet wasn't in fact taking anything that Barbara desperately wanted herself. Even Barbara didn't seem quite sure why she still wanted, as it were, the outer husk of William, his body in her life, but she did. Juliet recognised this, just as she recognised that she didn't want William always and all the time, and also that Frances, Lizzie's double to all appearances, was as elusive as Lizzie was accessible.

From her vantage point outside the family, Juliet could see them clearly. She could see that William, although he couldn't bring himself to like much in Barbara's temperament, loved her for being the mother of his children and for taking decisions for him. She could see that Barbara was torn, all the time, between the strength of her natural desires for self-fulfilment and the grim and abiding corset of her upbringing in a generation of middle-class women who, by and large, did no work after wedlock but social work. She could see that Lizzie, probably unconsciously, wished to show her mother that a woman could indeed run the whole gamut of womanly possibilities, wife, mother, worker, and be a living proof of the practicality of feminism, not just a noisy inconsistent theorist. But Frances... Juliet could not see so clearly when it came to Frances. There was something both bright and shadowy about Frances, open and yet half-hidden, something playful, a little erratic, vulnerable, something that didn't want to be known. There was a time when Juliet had thought Frances disapproved of her relationship with William, but Lizzie had assured her that wasn't it.

"Frances never disapproves of anything much, you know, and she thinks if Dad didn't have you, Mum'd leave him."

"Really?"

"Yes," said Lizzie, who had, the night before, expounded this theory to Frances and not been disagreed with. "Yes, really."

When William had told Juliet that Frances had suddenly decided to go away for Christmas, Juliet had felt a small elation. It was always thrilling to see someone turn protagonist, particularly someone whose life had always appeared a little hazy and evasive. "Good for Frances," Juliet had said to William on the telephone, listening to the pubby chink of glasses and rumble of talk behind him, "not before time, I was waiting for this, I love seeing people start steering their own lives."

"I don't think I ever have," William said sadly.

"More than you think," Juliet said, almost sharply. "You're sometimes a shameful old poser."

Nobody seemed at all sure why Frances had gone, and nobody seemed to wish to believe the reason she had given. Lizzie had been deeply hurt. She had come up to Juliet's cottage late on the Sunday evening and sat by Juliet's fire.

"It isn't that I resent her doing her own thing, it really isn't, but it's the not telling, it's the bouncing of the news on me when the whole plan is already made, as if, somehow, I'd have tried to stop her, as if—oh Juliet, it's as if she didn't *trust* me."

People went on so about trust, Juliet thought. They spoke of it as if it were a sacred vessel, and once you'd even cracked it, with only a hairline crack, the whole thing was then useless afterwards, thus invalidating relationships.

"Nobody's to be ultimately trusted," she said briskly to Lizzie, "not me, not you, not Frances, not anyone. It isn't in human nature to be utterly trustworthy; we just can't do it."

Lizzie had gone home shocked as well as uncomforted, leaving Juliet unable to sleep. As she got older, she had found she had to woo sleep, beckon it seductively with no disturbing shocks of late-night news or quarrels. That night, something about Lizzie, about her real misery and sense of rejection, had set all kinds of wheels of memory in motion that Juliet had hoped would never turn again, reminding her of past pains and rebuffs and unwanted solitariness, from which the road to her present reasonable contentment had been so long and hard and stony.

Having slept poorly, she spent Christmas Eve with a headache. She had asked, as she always did, the other waifs and strays from the nearest village—a retired nurse, a senior county librarian, a silent man who made weather vanes, a widower doctor, a journalist on the local paper— up to the cottage for mince pies and mulled wine and saw, as she always saw, the gallantry on their faces as another lonely Christmas challenged them to make the best of it. When they had gone, an uneven procession of red tail-lights jerking down her track like a line of bouncing scarlet stars, she quelled the fire, put the glasses and plates on the slate slab beside her kitchen sink, and went upstairs to fall into the kind of absolute sleep usually granted only to babies and adolescents.

She woke at three. A disagreeable night was in progress outside her window, a whining wind and the lashing slap of either heavy rain or sleet. She got up and went downstairs to make some tea. She felt, when she got down there, alert enough to wash up, rake out the fire and plump the cushions. Then she carried the tea upstairs, remade her bed and prepared to start the night again, remembering to say, "Happy Christmas," to herself, with a satisfaction that was, she told herself, almost smug.

She woke the second time to shouts. She thought at first that it was just the wind, whose many insistent voices she knew extremely well from her upland years, but then she realised that the wind, however ingenious, did not know her name. She climbed out of bed, pulled on the patchwork robe she had made years ago out of scraps of velvet and brocade, and went to the window. It faced the valley, the track and the best view. Juliet pulled back the curtains, opened the window and leaned out. There below her in the dim grey light, stood Frances Shore, with a suitcase.

"I've come to calm down," Frances said. "I've come to use you as a halfway house. I hope you don't mind. I couldn't face the thought of going back to my flat and waking it up, so I just drove straight here. I came on some Latin American plane which left Madrid in the middle of the night and was going on to Rio, or something. I spent hours on a bench in Madrid Airport wondering what I was doing and what I thought I'd been going to do in the first place. I still don't really know. I'll go to the Grange later, of course, but I hope it's all right if I just simmer down a bit here first."

Juliet smiled but said nothing. She went on spreading things on the table round Frances: a loaf, butter, a coffee pot, a dish of tangerines, a jar of honey.

"I had to sit in Seville Airport too," Frances said. "And Mr. Gómez Moreno came and sat too, to try and persuade me to stay. He was awfully nice, really, not a smoothy at all."

"Why didn't you stay?"

"Because of the mess they'd made. When something goes sour, it not only wrecks the future, but it destroys the past. I went to Seville for a little adventure and I landed in one of those long-drawn-out, tedious, depressing failures and disappointments that you can only have abroad. Instead of being foreign and fascinating, it was foreign and miserable. I've almost never felt like that abroad, but I did in Seville."

Juliet cut bread and pronged a slice on an old-fashioned toasting fork.

"So you've come home."

"Juliet," Frances said, "I could hardly go back to my flat and lurk there pretending to be in Spain, could I?"

"I suppose not," Juliet said. She stooped over the fire, holding out the fork. The thick, greying pigtail in which she confined her hair at night swung over her shoulder. "They are all, in varying degrees, very upset about you."

"Oh," Frances said.

"What else did you expect? You know your family, you know Christmas—"

"Yes," Frances said. She poured coffee.

Juliet turned the toast.

"William thinks that's why you went. To get away from them all."

"Only partly," Frances said. She leaned forward. "Juliet—"

"Yes?"

"I wanted—I want some richness to things, I want to go to places—" She stopped.

Juliet came away from the fire and dropped the slice of toast on a plate in front of Frances.

"What places? Foreign places?"

"Oh no," Frances said. "Not abroad. Inside me, places inside me."

Juliet looked at her. She poured coffee for herself.

"Then why run away from Seville?"

"I told you, it had all gone wrong."

"But it sounds as if you finally ran away just as it was all beginning to go *right*. You said Mr. Gómez Moreno was a nice man."

"He was," Frances said. She began to butter her toast. "He said something to me—"

"What thing?"

"I can't remember quite how it came about, but I was

telling him about the way, as a child, I used to make up
stories and how I sometimes caught myself doing it now,
and that I'd almost done it in Seville Cathedral that morning, thinking I could see the ghosts of Fernando and Isabel,
and he said"—she reached for the honey—"he said, 'But,
Miss Shore, that's what we humans all do when we have
an inner vacuum, we fill the space with stories.' I'd never
thought of that before."

There was a silence. Juliet drank her coffee; Frances
drew the knife blade across the honey on her toast.

"He's perfectly right," Juliet said.

"I know. It made me think—"

"About what?"

"About the inner vacuum. Have you got one?"

"Everybody has, of some kind. Mine has got smaller with
age. What did Mr. Gómez Moreno say to you when you
got on your plane and said goodbye?"

"He said, 'I am glad at least that you saw the Catholic
Kings.' I think it was a joke."

"And what did he propose you should do if you had
stayed?"

"He was going to show me his hotels, the one in Seville,
the one near Córdoba and the one he likes best, in the
mountains south of Granada."

"And instead of that," said Juliet, putting down her coffee mug, "you are going back to the Grange?"

Frances looked up at her, her wing of hair partly hiding
one eye.

"I want to go to the Grange," Frances said.

"I must say," Robert said, "I've almost never been so thankful to see anybody."

He reached forward and poured more wine into Frances's glass. They were, temporarily, the only ones left conscious around the wreck of the orgy of the Christmas lunch
table. The three older children had disappeared with the
skill of those long practised at scenting the approach of
clearing up; Barbara was upstairs trying to sleep, Lizzie was

attempting to persuade Davy to imitate her, and William, at the far end of the table, blissful in a purple paper hat, was snoring.

"I love this mess," Frances said. She looked down the table, at the confusion of plates and glasses, the scrumples of cracker paper, the depleted bowls of nuts and fruit, the bottles, and the candlesticks with the candles in them melting fatly into themselves, dripping and spilling scarlet waxy trails. "There's something so abandoned about it."

"I'm afraid I detest Christmas," Robert said. "I'm just too tired to see it as anything more than a nuisance. And everybody quarrels. If you hadn't arrived in the nick of time, there'd have been bloodshed."

Frances drank some wine. She'd had quite a lot already and felt, after two nights of broken sleep, heavy and dreamy.

"I went to Juliet's first."

"Did you? Why?"

"I—I thought I probably couldn't arrive at breakfast—"

"I wish you had. Breakfast was hell. Poor Lizzie."

"She does look tired."

"She is tired. Of course she's tired."

Frances looked at her brother-in-law. His strong-featured, high-cheekboned face was wearing well, but the queer, thick, reddish hair that had always given him a romantic, almost Irish air was beginning to recede a little at the temples, sharpening his hairline into a prow.

"Couldn't you and Lizzie have a bit of a holiday? You know I could fix you up, whatever—"

"Thing is," Robert said, leaning forward on his elbows, "thing is, we're going to be badly strapped for cash next year. The last six months have been terrible, worst ever. Lizzie knows it's been bad, but I haven't told her how bad and I won't until Christmas is over." He looked at Frances. "You must be feeling it too."

"A bit, but you see, so many retired people travel with me, all those flower and bird people, and people who want to paint and take photographs, and they don't feel the pinch in bad times as much as the employed do—"

"What bad times?" Lizzie said, coming in. She was loyally wearing the earrings Sam had given her, huge irregular holly leaves he had made out of modelling plastic, emerald-green studded with brilliant berries the size of big peas. "Davy has finally gone to sleep on condition I give his yellow pyjamas to the secondhand shop and never say he looks sweet again. That's going to be hard."

She sat down next to Frances and borrowed her glass of wine for a gulp.

"Look at you," she said affectionately to Frances. "Just look at you. I'm really sorry it went wrong, but I'm not really, too."

"I think we won't talk about it," Frances said, looking at William, unconscious and smiling under his tissue crown.

Robert and Lizzie exchanged a lightning look.

"No, of course not."

"I told Robert," Frances said, "that I went to Juliet's first, this morning."

"Why didn't you come straight here?"

"It was only seven—"

"Honestly," Lizzie said. "By seven we'd been up two hours and were well into a screaming match about church."

Frances said, as if she hadn't heard her, "I don't know why I never got to know Juliet when I was growing up—"

"You wouldn't come."

"I know. I remember."

"Mum started going on about her at six o'clock this morning—"

"It's Christmas," Robert said. "It has that effect on everyone. If there isn't something that naturally arises to take issue with, you find yourself hunting for an excuse for a row." He looked down the table at his father-in-law. "Sometimes I can't believe that he's actually managed a wife and a mistress for a quarter of a century. *William, of all people.*"

"He only has because the women did the deciding," Lizzie said.

Frances looked at her. "Are you sure?"

"Oh yes."

Robert stood up slowly, as if testing every limb and joint before he trusted it with any weight.

"I'm afraid I simply have to go to sleep."

Lizzie glanced at Frances.

"Do you want to?"

Frances wondered. Weighed down by food, wine and homecoming, she would, like Rip Van Winkle, sleep until this age had given way to quite another.

"No. I don't think so. We'll clear up."

Lizzie regarded the table.

"You're a heroine. Then we'll drag the team out for a walk."

Frances got up.

"I'll get a tray."

In the kitchen, Cornflakes had settled down, paws folded, to take his time over the turkey carcass.

"Bloody cat!" Frances shouted.

He streaked from the table and out through the cat flap in a single, arrowlike movement, born of long years of burgling butter dishes and milk jugs. Frances peered at the turkey.

"Can we tell where he's been?"

"Well, I'm not throwing it out, cat germs or no cat germs, I'll promise you that. It's a free-range turkey and it cost a fortune. Frances—"

"Yes?" Frances said, straightening.

"I really am so sorry, you know. About Spain."

Frances made a small, dismissive gesture.

"I know. I know you are."

"You mustn't let it weigh on you. Things do go wrong, sometimes, things that could just as easily go right, and for no apparent reason. You mustn't feel a fool."

Frances gave her a sharp look. She unhooked a plastic apron from behind the door and tied it round her waist.

"How do you know I do?"

Lizzie gave a little smile and said nothing.

"I don't think you should assume anything," Frances said.

"What were the Gómez Morenos like?"

"Junior was very attractive and rather hopeless and Senior was solid and dark and European."

"Nice?"

"Yes."

"Charming?"

"Not really. Just nice."

"I do so want you to be happy," Lizzie said, with sudden vehemence.

"But what *is* happy?"

"Being fulfilled," Lizzie said. "Using all the capacities you have, emotional, physical, mental. Filling yourself up."

"Are you trying to say husband and children and home and an art-and-craft gallery? Because—"

"Because what?"

"Because I think we all have different interior landscapes. Even twins."

"But you see," Lizzie said earnestly, putting down the carving knife and fork with which she had been dismembering the rest of the turkey, "even if we do have that landscape, it has got to have people in it. I mean, I know you've got us and we all adore you—"

"Don't patronise me," Frances said.

"I'm not—"

"Yes," Frances said, "you are. You think that I'm a half-empty vessel and therefore I'm inadequate."

"Oh no," Lizzie said, leaning towards her sister, her face full of affection. "No, I don't. I just think you are full of potential, and the potential is simply lying there."

"Stop sounding so sorry for me—"

Lizzie picked up the knife and fork again.

"I'm not sorry for you. You know what I think. I think you have taken the career and freedom chances for both of us, and that I've taken—well, other chances. I just don't want your life to become impersonal. That's all. That's one of the things that really got to me about your going to Spain, because by choosing to go now, at Christmas, you were deliberately turning your back on us, on some of your

best relationships. It was an impersonal thing to do. Don't
you see?"

"But I've come back."

"I know. I'm thrilled. It's made Christmas for me and
lunch was lovely, everybody being so nice when they had
previously been so horrible."

"I'll just go and get a trayload," Frances said.

She went back to the dining room, a room that spent
three hundred and sixty-four days of the year being a playroom. William had gone, no doubt in drowsy instinctive
search of an armchair. She began to pile plates, scraping
off black lumps of Christmas pudding and creamy lumps
of brandy butter, gathering up clattering handfuls of sticky
spoons and forks. Did Lizzie, she wondered, ever fill her
inner spaces with stories? Or only with arrangements and
lists and order books and responsibilities? Did Lizzie in
fact *have* any part of her particular interior landscape that
wasn't, by now, highly cultivated, productive and fruitful;
were there no corners for possibility left, or, if there were,
did she simply never consider them?

Frances marshalled glasses into a little regiment. Could
it be that Lizzie was trying to tell her that if she didn't
attend to the relationships in her life like some enthusiastic
gardener in a greenhouse of infant seedlings, they'd simply
wither away? But I have plenty of relationships, Frances
thought, I have the family and Nicky, who is my second-
in-command at Shore to Shore, and I have the London
friends that Lizzie knows little about. Why is it that she
says she wants us to be different yet the same, to comple-
ment each other, but she can't see, or won't see, that there
are other kinds of lives than hers?

She took a burdened tray back into the kitchen. The
newly sliced turkey lay on a big dish under plastic film,
and Lizzie was cramming the bones into a stock pot.

"Did I make you cross?" Lizzie said, turning.

"No," Frances said. "You almost never make me cross."

"I got such a fright, you see," Lizzie said, and stopped.
She put her arm up across her face, holding her turkey-
smeared hand well free.

"A fright?"

"I felt," Lizzie said, her voice not quite steady, "I felt that you were sort of *leaving* me."

"Lizzie!" Frances cried. She left the tray on the table and ran across the room. "Lizzie! How could you be so silly?" She put her arms around her sister.

Lizzie whispered, "Because we're a deal, aren't we? A sort of double-act deal, about life?"

"Yes."

"I'll always be here, you see, always here for you to come home to—"

"I know that."

"In a way, I'm sort of *for* you, and you for me."

"Yes. It's in our blood." Gently, Frances took her arms away.

Lizzie reached for a roll of paper towel, wrenched off several sheets and blew her nose hard.

"Sorry. Really sorry. What a display."

"It wasn't."

"Perhaps it needed to be said."

Frances nodded, slowly. The kitchen door opened and Harriet stood there in a long violent robe of orange and purple and scarlet and black and yellow and rust. She was in fits of giggles.

"What *is* it?"

"It's Granny's," Harriet said. She doubled up, heaving. "She said it was psychedelic—"

"It's one of her caftans!" Lizzie said, going forward. "One of the Marrakesh caftans. What a hoot!"

"Isn't it gross?" Harriet said.

Frances said, "She meant it as a compliment, giving it to you. She wants you to take yourself seriously."

The mirth was wiped off Harriet's face as if with a cloth. She plucked at the caftan.

"I don't see—" she said sulkily.

"Frances," Lizzie said, "aren't you being just a mite priggish?"

Frances shrugged. "Mum was three years older than us when she went to Marrakesh."

"What's Marrakesh?"

"It's a place in North Africa. It was one of the pilgrim places for hippies."

Harriet stared theatrically, widening her eyes like head-lamps.

"Granny was a *hippie*?"

"Yes, for a bit."

"Jesus!" Harriet said, and fell sideways against the door-frame.

"Harriet!"

"I know it's hideous," Frances said, "but it's important. Or significant, anyway."

Lizzie looked up at Frances, from her kneeling position. Frances's eyes were fixed on the caftan, not as if they were taking in the cheap and gaudy cotton, but as if they were seeing something other than the thing they rested on. Her expression was both thoughtful and sympathetic. But why should Frances defend Barbara? Barbara had left them, as ten-year-olds, for almost a year. Lizzie would rather have her hands cut off than contemplate doing anything so self-ish and unmaternal. And then today, Barbara had been frankly caustic when Frances appeared in the kitchen. "Heavens," she'd said, still holding the basting spoon, "they *do* seem to get Christmas over quickly in Spain."

"Frances?" Lizzie said.

Frances stirred, as if from a brief dream. Harriet and Lizzie watched her.

"Don't you think that sometimes, in every life, people do things that they mightn't do ten years earlier or later but which seem absolutely natural and imperative to do at the time they do them? Does it make you wicked?"

"If it affects other people in your life—" Lizzie began.

"No," said Harriet loudly, interrupting.

"What does it make you, then?"

Harriet smoothed the caftan over her narrow hips. Her sharp little face looked, for once, quite artless.

"It just makes you real."

• • •

On Boxing Day evening, Frances drove back to London. She had slept for twelve hours the night before and felt considerably worse for it. Her sole aim now was to get back to the most reliable source of satisfaction and comfort in her life, the office that held her little company.

The roads were almost empty; most people were stretching Christmas into at least the next weekend. In the back of the car was, besides her suitcase, a cardboard box of Christmas presents, and another one of food. Lizzie had terribly wanted Frances to take this, like a mother sending a child off to boarding school with a bursting tuck box. They had had another conversation before Frances left in which Lizzie had pointed out—quite fairly, Frances thought—that they were something of a Martha and a Mary, and that she, Lizzie, being inevitably the Martha one, would like it to be acknowledged that domesticity took a heavy toll of her, and that this should, in their future relationship after this hiccup, be remembered. Recalling her reflection in the aeroplane going to Seville that Lizzie had, after all, chosen the life she led, Frances was about to point this out, quite gently, when she saw a sudden gleam in Lizzie's eye, a gleam almost of desperation born of the complicated kind of fatigue—emotional, physical, administrative—which is all but exclusive to the mothers of large families, and said nothing after all. They had embraced with great affection when Frances left, as had Frances and William, Frances and Robert, Frances and all the children except Sam who affected to loathe being kissed while being, in fact, the most physically affectionate of the four children. Barbara had kissed Frances quite warmly, but wearing the expression of one who wished to say a good deal more than she was at present going to. When Frances drove off, they were all grouped on the front steps of the Grange, above the weedy drive and below the graceful pediment, backlit by the light from the hall behind them, waving in irregular silhouette.

·   ·   ·

Frances let herself into the side entrance of her narrow building, which gave directly on to the steep staircase up to her flat. She had been away three nights, and already, on the doormat, was a drift of mail, mostly junk, and half a chewed baked potato. Frances was used to these. There was a baked potato take-away shop two doors down her street and people never seemed to remember that the mixed pepper filling was spectacularly disgusting.

She switched on the light. One weekend, she and Nicky had painted this tunnel-like staircase terracotta, hoping to give it warmth and interest, and succeeding only in giving it the feeling, as Frances remarked, that you were climbing up some long internal organ. It was extremely ugly and she had never got round to doing anything further about it, beyond tacking up posters of Sienna and Florence and the towery skyline of San Gimignano.

At the top, a narrow door opened directly into a surprisingly large, light room looking over the street. Nicky was intermittently full of ideas for this room—for which she would have given her eye teeth—but Frances didn't seem to see it, or the room behind it, which was her bedroom and had a view of the cherry tree two backyards and one tiny garden away. She had painted both rooms magnolia when she moved in, furnished them with the things that were necessary, and left them. If people gave her objects—pottery plates from their travels, cushions, lacquered boxes, plants in pots—she hung them up or put them down somewhere, but not as if anything was part of a whole. It was all perfectly comfortable and decidedly dull. "Like my clothes, really," Frances said, when Nicky pointed this out. "The thing is, I don't really mind. How do you make yourself mind more?"

She carried up the suitcase and the mail, dropped the one on her bed, and the other on the sitting-room coffee table. Then she went back for the boxes, kicking the half-potato out into the street, and then shoving the door shut with her shoulder. She took the food box into her tiny kitchen, and unpacked everything conscientiously out of gratitude to Lizzie, and then, thankfully, collected up her briefcase and the handful of mail, opened a second door in the sitting room and descended an internal staircase to the office.

Even putting the lights on gave her pleasure. It was like being back on dry land after several uncomfortable days at sea in a very small boat. Nicky, the invaluable, conscientious Nicky with her long smooth hair tied tidily back and her air of being the perfect prefect, had left everything immaculate, machines shrouded in their covers, answering service switched on, blinds drawn shut, chairs parallel to desks, plants watered, waste bins emptied. Frances put her briefcase down on her own desk, read Nicky's brief typed note ("No problems left by 6 P.M. Christmas Eve except query Mr. and Mrs. Newby—is hotel in Ravenna in pedestrian zone because they can't tolerate noise? Also, Mr. Pritchard—why is his single supplement for Lucca £20 more in September than in May? Hope Seville a rave! See you Monday? I'll be in anyway—probably before you see this! Love, Nicky"), and went round the room, touching things lightly. This was one of the glories of her single life, this chance to revel in what satisfied her, in what she had made. Four years of it now, four steadily, quietly expanding years. Surely in four years, a mistake like Seville was not so very terrible?

She opened her briefcase and emptied the papers and tickets inside on to her desk. She began to make piles— one for the accountant, one for the wastepaper basket, one for the file Nicky kept called "Possibilities?" Into this would go the guidebooks to Seville, into the accountant's pile would go the air tickets and all invoices, even those tiny scraps, no bigger than big stamps, received for cups of coffee and so tempting to discard, and into the bin would go everything to do with the Gómez Morenos, including Luis's card, which gave addresses and telephone numbers in both Seville and Madrid.

Frances looked at the card. It was nothing special, just a business card.

"I have to give it to you," Luis had said. "Because to give out cards is the reflex action of a businessman. You may then put it in the nearest bin if you want to."

Frances flicked it with her thumbnail, added it to a few other papers, and dropped it in the wastepaper bin. Then, quick as a flash and driven by no impulse she could give a name to, she bent down and fished it out again.

PART
TWO

MAY

SEVEN

Luis Gómez Moreno waited at Málaga Airport. Dressed in the male-European casual summer uniform of cotton trousers, linen jacket, and polished loafers, he stood in the arrivals hall, his briefcase between his feet, and read a newspaper article about the growing dissatisfaction of the enormous number of Spaniards living in the Basque country. A Spanish town councillor in a Basque town said that Basque behaviour in council meetings was a lesson in racism. "They only allow their own language in council meetings. They won't even allow simultaneous translation!" Basque, said the writer of the article, is a language older than Latin with nothing in common with Spanish. The Basque country is a rural paradise and its invasion by the Spanish is bitterly resented. "These," said the reporter with relish, "are a most tenacious people."

As a small boy, Luis had been told, furtively, about the bombing of Guernica, the Basques' sacred city, by Hitler's Condor Legion. He had been told this by a young uncle, his mother's brother, and furtively, because in Luis's childhood, General Franco was an object of undiluted veneration. "Your mother," the young uncle had said disapprovingly, "your mother, my sister, was taught to obey Franco, God and your father, in that order!" That uncle was the first taste of rebelliousness in Luis's life, the first glimpse of his dominating mother as other than irreproachable. When Luis was twelve, the uncle took his radical political ideas to America; the family story was that he chose to go, but Luis rather thought otherwise, and his mother once, in a temper, confirmed his suspicion.

"Your uncle Francisco," she had shouted, "was a traitor to Spain!"

There had been a good deal of shouting in Luis's childhood. As in most post-war Spanish households, Luis's father's authority over them all was absolute, but this authority had to take into account the size of Luis's mother's personality and the strength of her will. She knew her duty and she rebelled against it all the time, buoyed up by the deeply Spanish belief that strength was to be gained through suffering. Her very frustration would, she knew, in the end be rewarded. Luis and his sister, Ana, instead of enjoying the home life propounded by Franco, a life of rhythm, discipline and order, lived in fact in a quarrelsome bear-garden. By the time he was fourteen, Luis dared to admit to himself that he disliked his mother and by the time he was a father himself, watching his relationship with baby José's mother disintegrate, he was beginning to wonder if he disliked all mothers; that motherhood was a state likely to turn any woman into a possessive, unbalanced monster. His own mother had screamed at him; now his wife, the minute she was a mother, was doing the same thing. His mother had wanted him to obey her implicitly, especially in matters of religious devotion; his wife wanted something else, something to do with freedom and esteem.

"It is not easy," she had once said to him with deadly emphasis, "to try and be a feminist in this land of machismo."

The effect of it all was to make Luis wary of profound relationships with women. He could see that some of his mother's generation felt cheated after lifetimes spent as virtual slaves in the house; he could see equally well that sub-

sequent generations of Spanish women wished to have the
freedom to work and to mix, but it was the handling of
women with either of those grievances that seemed so difficult; the barrage of their resentment and mockery seemed
to make any kind of mutual understanding almost impossible. He strongly disapproved of hearing his father say—
as his father often did—"Give a woman freedom, and you
get anarchy," but he equally disapproved of the violence
with which the opposite view was expressed.

Despite those early seductive whisperings from his political uncle, Luis knew he was not a radical. Indeed, there
were times when the notion of a life of rhythm, discipline
and order seemed not only attractive but civilised and better
able to ensure a general level of happiness than the seem-
ingly progressive pursuit of self-fulfilment. As a citizen of
one of the more socialist cities of Spain, he sometimes felt
out of step with the way things seemed determined to
move, while at the same time being unable to share completely a feeling common to many of his countrymen, that
General Franco had, in many ways, been no bad thing for
Spain. A foreigner, an American businessman with whom
he was having dealings, had once said, after an exhausting
meeting they had both attended, "Luis, what *excessive* people the Spanish are!" Perhaps, Luis thought afterwards, it's
the excessiveness of Spanish women that makes them such
a big deal to live with. Too big a deal. For fifteen years
Luis had lived, apart from visitors, alone.

Above his head, a clear female voice announced over the
loudspeaker system that the flight from London Gatwick
had just landed. Luis looked at his watch. The airport was
quite full so the baggage wouldn't be through for at least
twenty minutes. He considered going to buy a cup of coffee,
and then reconsidered it. Even if it took thirty minutes for
her to emerge, Luis decided he would not chance not being
there when Frances Shore came through customs.

When he had said goodbye to her at Seville Airport on
Christmas Eve, Luis had not thought he would hear from

her again. Briefly, he was mildly sorry about this, partly because he was furious with José for being so incompetent—José's continued incompetence was the source of many new quarrels between Luis and José's mother—and partly because Frances Shore was quite unlike anybody he had ever done business with in twenty-five years. He had known many Englishwomen during his time at the London School of Economics, but they had, on the whole, been a politically determined breed and not much interested in a young man from what they saw as the land of bull fights, religious bigotry and fascism. In the years since the sixties, he had never done business with an Englishwoman and met very few. His sense of adventure and taste for novelty had been aroused by the thought of defying Christmas and taking this Miss Shore to his three *posadas*. Then José had effectively scuppered the whole plan and when Frances had said goodbye at the airport—politely but not with any particular warmth—he had thought that was that. Miss Shore, in her unmistakably English mackintosh, would have other travel fish to fry.

But she had telephoned him. He had been in Brussels, discussing the EEC regulations for the setting up of organic farms—he was planning one, with an Andalusian consortium—and arrived back in Seville, to find a message from Frances. It was February. He rang her back immediately, and she said she would like to re-open negotiations with the Posadas of Andalucía. He said he would be charmed.

She said sharply, "I don't want you to be charmed, I just want you to be there, when you say you will be."

"I will be here in May."

"May is hopeless, I've got far too much business in May."

"Five days only. Andalucía is at its best in May. Or September. You fly to Málaga and I will meet you."

"Not in May."

"Then September."

"September is worse."

"Then—"

"All right," Frances said. "I'll juggle things. I'll come in May."

And here she was, in the baggage hall of Málaga Airport. He felt pleased. In fact, he felt more than pleased, he felt a kind of quickened interest, as at the prospect of something unknown, but attractively unknown.

He folded up his newspaper—if the Spanish were excessive, what adjective was left for the Basques?—put it in his briefcase, and moved across to the space of dusty floor in front of the doors that led to the customs hall. They were opening constantly, disgorging passengers with baggage trolleys and the mildly disorientated expressions that are the inevitable effect of air travel. Luis watched them closely; a few Spaniards came through but mostly they were English, and a lot of them the loudly confident, commercial English whose requirements had filled southern Spain with high-rise blocks of flats and mock Moorish villages, to the increase of its prosperity and to the detriment of its spirit. Then, suddenly, there was Frances. She wore a blue linen skirt and a white T-shirt with a cardigan tied over her shoulders, and she carried her own suitcase. She came straight over to him and held out her hand to him, smiling.

"Mr. Gómez Moreno," she said. "I hope you realise that I intended never to come back to Spain."

Having stowed her in his car, and climbed into the driver's seat, he asked if she would mind if he took off his tie.

"I cannot drive in a tie, somehow. I think I will strangle."

"Of course," Frances said, startled at the courtesy of being asked. She folded the lengths of her blue skirt around her legs. "It's so lovely to be warm."

"Twenty-two degrees," Luis said with satisfaction, as if he had arranged it especially for her. He started the car, and turned to look at her briefly, with a broad smile. "Well, here you are, Miss Shore, back in Spain."

"Frances."

"Thank you," he said. "Frances. Then Luis also."

He pulled the car out of the wired-off compound of the airport carpark. Above Frances hung the same strong blue sky she had seen on Christmas Eve in Seville, but this sky was full of warmth, not just light.

"I don't want us to have any more confusions," Luis said, "but I am curious to know why you changed your mind, why you decided to telephone me. Of course, I am pleased—"

"It rankled," Frances said, looking out of the window. "It wouldn't stop."

"Rankled?" he said, not understanding.

"Yes. It irritated me that it hadn't worked, that it was a good idea that went wrong. And a lot of my clients, the ones who have been with me since the beginning, were beginning to hint that they would like new horizons. Where are we going?"

"Mojas," he said. "I am taking no chances this time." He was laughing.

"Mojas? I've never heard—"

"You wouldn't have. It's a village. It's a tiny village in the mountains between Granada and the sea. It has my best *posada*, my favourite. We are too late, though, for the almond blossom."

"Almonds—"

"The village used to live by its almonds. Even now, the almond season is the busy season, the village streets full of donkeys with baskets, every house sounding with the tapping of the women and children shelling. We can hardly take the car into the village, the streets are so small. Donkeys are fine, cars are not."

"My clients," Frances said carefully, "would like that." She thought of them, cultivated, capable, respectful of the places they visited, repelled by the violation caused by mass tourism. "They are quite quiet people," she said to Luis. "They are the sort of people who will read seriously about Spain before they come, and who would never buy dolls dressed as flamenco dancers."

He laughed again. He was driving very fast through the shade-dappled suburbs of Málaga, slipping in and out of lanes of traffic as if he didn't need to think about it. Every so often, in bright glimpses between buildings to the right of the road, came a flash of the sea. Frances thought, with a sudden little inward clutch of pleasure: I'm liking this!

It had been truthful to say she had been irked by the Seville episode. Once it was over, she hadn't meant to think about it any more, but it kept popping up in her mind as something not only bungled, but unfinished. The newspapers seemed to be unnaturally full of pieces about Spain—surely they never were before?—and the telly seemed absolutely obsessed with the place all of a sudden, with programmes about Spanish women and crime and Catholicism, about Spanish gambling and food and drink and about the Spanish army. Frances had turned the television on one day soon after Christmas, quite idly, while wandering about with a mug of coffee and a slice of toast, and there, instead of a chat show or a police drama or a politician, was a very young Spanish army recruit, stooping in reverence to kiss the Spanish flag. Frances was amazed. It was such a theatrical, passionate, serious thing to do. Imagine telling an English squaddie he had to kiss the Union Jack!

In the end, Frances had given in. Spain was clearly campaigning for her, and so, in a quieter way, was Mr. Gómez Moreno Senior, whose business card, wherever she tucked it away, wormed itself to the surface of drawers and piles of paper like a fragment of broken china in a flowerbed.

"I'm jinxed," Frances said to Nicky. "Bloody Spain."

"Ring him, then," Nicky said. "Go and see his hotels. If they're great, hurray, and if they're grotty you'll defeat the jinx."

"They're in wonderful places—"

"I know. I read that piece about the cathedral in Córdoba that's inside a mosque."

"And it's a much better spring and autumn climate than Italy—"

"Ring him," Nicky said.

"And flights to Málaga are frequent and reasonable—"

"Then ring him."

"And the hotel that's in the mountains sounds as if it would be good for the flora and fauna lot—"

"Frances," Nicky said, raising her voice almost to a shriek, "ring him!"

So she did, and he said he would be charmed to see her. Then he wrote and said he would escort her personally to all three *posadas*, that he would show her the countryside and the glories of Granada, Córdoba and Seville. He said, in his letter, that he would devote himself to her.

"Wow," said Nicky.

"Don't be silly—"

"You watch it. Mediterranean men—"

"He's a middle-aged, married Catholic and I hardly know him."

"Do you disapprove of associating with married men?"

"Yes," Frances said.

Nicky pecked a bit at her typewriter. "Trouble is, there aren't many others. If they aren't married, they're either gay or they're goofy."

Frances gave a quick glance sideways at Luis. He didn't look at all goofy. He didn't, if it came to it, look particularly married either, in the way that William looked married, arranged and ordered by somebody else. Luis Gómez Moreno looked very independent, almost detached. Perhaps that was what happened to you when you had chosen your own shirts and socks for fifteen years; you stopped looking as if somebody else had a hand in you, you stopped looking *owned*. That excellent haircut—curlier hair than his son's—that well-laundered shirt, that collection of maps and objects in the glove pockets and on the dashboard of the car, the efficient-looking car telephone, were all his choices just as her blue skirt and the things in her suitcase and the fact that her toenails weren't varnished were hers. That's the single life, Frances thought, married or not; you decide everything for yourself, all the time, and sometimes that's exciting, and sometimes it makes you very tired.

"What are you thinking of?" Luis said.

They were bowling along a stretch of open road, with only a few garages and half-finished buildings between them and the shining sea. Frances turned to look at it.

"I'm afraid," she said primly, "that I don't know you well enough to say."

He laughed again. Frances caught the glimmer of a gold tooth-filling.

"Do you think, by the end of the week, we shall tell each other everything?"

"I've never told anyone everything in my life, not even my twin sister."

"A twin? You have a twin sister? Are you very alike? Can I be sure I have the right one here?"

"Quite sure," Frances said. "My sister has a wedding ring and four children."

He gave her a quick look.

"Don't envy her the wedding ring."

"I don't. She has one kind of life and I have another."

"This is interesting. Differences are always interesting. The difference between the Spanish and the English is interesting. If I met you in the middle of the Sahara Desert, I should know you were English."

"And if I met you," Frances said, slightly nettled, "I should think you were any old Mediterranean or Latin American, just one of millions of olive-skinned, dark-haired men with brown eyes."

"Black," he said, grinning, hugely enjoying himself.

"Nobody has black eyes. Not really black."

"Mine are. And yours are blue."

"Blue-grey."

"Like English sky."

"Luis, I can't bear that kind of talk."

He smiled broadly, took one hand off the wheel, and lightly touched Frances's forearm.

"Nor me," he said. "Just testing."

They drove for two hours. The road went along stretches of flat coastal plain, through scruffy, concrete ribbon developments and the odd anonymous resort with signs to *"La Playa"* nailed to every tree and building, and then, in a vast, delta-like area filled with the torn and flapping remains of abandoned plastic greenhouses—"The melon madness," Luis said. "The courgette craziness. It was like a gold rush"—there appeared a great fork in the road, the coastal arm running on towards Almería, the other swinging left into some low, advancing hills.

"The mountains now," Luis said. "The lovely mountains."

Frances turned regretfully to look at the sea.

"Can we see the sea, from Mojas?"

"Far away. A small sparkle. I have put in a pool, a little blue pool, and around it there is a jasmine hedge."

"Do you know about gardening?"

"No," he said. "Certainly not." He waited a moment and then said teasingly, "In Spain, gardening is for women."

Frances ignored the implication of this remark. "Then how come the jasmine?"

"Because I am a very rare Spaniard."

"I see."

"You don't see," he said. "But you will. When you see the Mojas *posada*. Look at that, look at the view."

The road was running up rapidly into drama. Behind them lay the shore, the nondescript little towns, the failed market gardens, but ahead the hills were beginning to heave and fold themselves into mountains—brown, russet, rose-red and saffron—splashed with the new green growth of spring and backed by the steady blue sky.

"I love it here," Luis said. "The land is so big and so ancient, and tourism hasn't found it yet. The seashore towards Almería isn't so friendly for the sunbathers and these"—he waved an arm at the slopes beyond the road—"are not good for golf. You cannot make a playground from a country like this."

She murmured, "Your English is so good—"

"Twenty-five years I have it now. Are you tired?"

"Only a little."

"It is not much further, not so much as an hour. Shall I stop for you to walk a little?"

"No thank you," Frances said, "I want to get there."

"Come," he said. He twisted slightly in his seat, and with

his right hand turned something behind Frances. The back of her own seat sank backwards. "There now. Relax a little."

Through the raised glass of the sunshine roof, the sky shone like a blessing. Frances watched it idly, contentedly, reminding herself of Davy, as a baby, in his pram, watching the moving apple-tree leaves above him with the same lazy satisfaction.

"Europe thinks we Spanish are all Castilians, very formal and stately, always deep in thought," Luis said. "But we are all different, region to region, even village to village. There is the story of the mayor of a tiny place near Madrid who declared war on Napoleon personally, himself. You will find Mojas like that, with its own personality, very local. Everybody thinks of Andalusians as gypsies, as flamboyant, and these people are so, in their way, but they are also, most of all, just the people of Mojas, just—" He glanced sideways. Frances was asleep.

He slackened speed at once, to avoid having to brake abruptly and wake her. How extraordinary, how confident of her to go to sleep so suddenly and completely, her hands folded in her lap, her face turned up to the square of sky visible through the sunshine roof. He drove even more slowly so that he could have a good look at her, at her thick, heavy hair, at her peculiarly English skin with the suggestion, on its surface, of all the components underneath that went to make it up—never visible on a darker skin— at the pronounced lines of her eyebrows and eyelashes. It was not, he decided, a beautiful face but it was an arresting one. He liked looking at it. Asleep, it was calm and strong, awake, it was full of movement. He glanced at the rest of her. Why dress, he wondered, to say nothing? Why choose clothes that could be anybody's, any age? José had reported her as being good-looking but not at all sexy. Letting his eyes linger on the blurred lines of Frances under the white cotton and blue linen, Luis was inclined to agree with the former assessment but not with the second. Yet why should she be sexy? She was almost gawky; her hands and feet were far too big and she—

"Don't stare," Frances said calmly, waking up but not moving.

"I am so sorry."

"Are we almost there?"

"A few more kilometres. There." Luis pointed. "On that hillside. That is Mojas."

Frances sat up. Across the valley a village lay scattered across the ribs of the hillside like a handful of white sugar cubes.

"The green in the middle is the *posada*, the *posada* garden."

"Aren't you tired, driving so fast for so long?"

"This isn't long," he said.

The road zigzagged down into the valley, crossed a swampy bottom filled with whispering bamboo and a few dried-up, unharvested clumps of Indian corn, and began to climb again. The slopes either side were terraced in graceful curves along the contours of the hill, the terraces held up with low walls of grey-and-ochre stone. They passed a boy in a baseball cap with a herd of piebald goats, jingling softly with bells, and then a man with a tiny donkey almost obscured under a giant bundle of firewood.

Frances said, without meaning to, "It's hard to remember that I'm here on business, somehow—"

"We think too much of business. We think too much of purpose."

"Do you think so?"

"Miss Shore—"

"Frances."

"Thank you. Frances, we will have a philosophical conversation later, but now I am the guide and you are the tourist. There you see to the right an almond orchard."

Trees as gnarled and twisted as those in an illustration to a fairy-tale stood in rough russet earth, stony and harsh.

"And now we are here," Luis said, "close your eyes. We are going in."

"But you said no cars—"

"No cars but my car and a few others."

The road twisted sharply to the left to continue climbing

the hillside. To the right, there was a wall, a high white wall with an opening in it, a narrow, dark opening that looked hardly wide enough for a bicycle.

"We can't—"

"Shut your eyes," Luis said. "Usually with guests, we tell them to leave their cars out here by the orchard, and the hotel staff will guide them in."

The car slid through the opening with centimetres only to spare. Having shut her eyes obediently, Frances found that this was more nerve-racking than opening them, so opened them and stared about her. White lanes, white alleys, whitened steps, cobbles, cascades of something brilliant—could it be bougainvillaea?—pots of geraniums, shutters tightly fastened, gates closed, vines across terraces, flashes of view, of sky, of cats, of kitchen chairs outside doorways, all steep and slanting and crooked and impossible; then a tiny, angled square with acacia trees and two old men on a bench.

"Here," Luis said.

"Where?"

"There," he said, braking and sliding the car into a black square of shade. "In the corner."

In the corner was a miniature cul-de-sac, and at the end of it a saffron-washed building, windowless with a big wooden door in a white frame, and beside it, a brass plate.

"The *Posada* of Mojas," Luis said.

They led her to a room on the first floor. The way to the room was through a series of irregular interior courtyards, balconied and full of lemon trees in pots and blue trails of plumbago. The courtyards were painted white and the balconies were painted deep russet and on the floor were tiles the colour of the ribbed roofs of the village, apricot and terracotta, earthy and soft.

"You will be comfortable here," Luis said, in the same tone of pride with which he had announced the temperature. "From this room you can see the garden and all the valley."

It was a long room. In one wall there was both a conventional window and a casement window that reached to the floor and with a balustrade across it to waist height. Both halves of this window stood open and the sunshine fell in across the floor, and the breeze blew the curtains in soft billows, new cotton curtains striped in yellow and white and blue, their hems whispering on the tiles. There was a carved bed and high white pillows and a dark chest like a small altar. On the floor there were cotton rugs, and on the walls, washed so pale a blue they were almost white, hung two old wooden panel paintings, one of a lily and one of an angel's head, curly and haloed.

Frances took off her shoes, stepping from the cool shadowed spaces of the floor on to the warm sunlit ones.

"I will be in the garden," Luis said. "We will have tortillas in the garden when you are ready. There is no hurry, there is never a hurry here."

She crossed the room and held the sun-warmed wood of the balustrade. Below her lay the garden, fashioned, like the fields outside the village, from several tiny terraces, their edges and the several sets of steps punctuated with amphorae, jars and pots in earthenware, cascading flowers and variegated leaves. There were trees, too, another acacia, several eucalyptuses waving their greeny-grey branches in swooping arcs across the sky, and in their shade were garden chairs, made of white wrought iron. Below the garden, the tilting roofs of the village fell headlong down the slope towards the valley, the rush only halted here and there by the occasional level roof terrace across which strings of washing blew, bright and orderly.

It was almost silent. From faraway down the valley came the faintest sound of bells—those goats?—and from the hotel kitchen, sleepy in mid-afternoon peace, came the distant clatter of a tortilla pan. Frances closed her eyes. Sometimes in life, just sometimes, she thought, there comes a moment of happiness that is close to rapture because it is so innocent, so natural, so right, a moment when you feel that everything's in tune, when . . .

"Frances?"

She opened her eyes again and looked down. Luis was standing on the middle terrace below her.

"Everything is all right for you?"

"Yes, oh yes—"

"Then come and eat," he said. "I am waiting for you."

EIGHT

It was raining, not hard but with the soft, slightly sticky rain of early summer. Bath's tourists—now all year round—had put up umbrellas and were drifting along the greasy pavements in exasperating, aimless hordes, the dangerous ends of their umbrella ribs exactly, Robert thought crossly, at his eye level. Every year, the tourists in Bath, despite the comforting amount they spent, annoyed him more. Did it ever occur to them, he wondered, that other people used Bath too, to try and get their shoes mended, and their teeth seen to, and as a place to buy washing powder and rashers of bacon, and that these weary people were being tried to the limit by the sheer numbers of visitors in persistent pursuit of Jane Austen and Beau Nash and King Bladud and glasses of revolting spa water? You could hardly, even on a wet Wednesday in May, get up Gay Street in comfort, for the press of neat polyester rainwear coming down, Royal Crescent and the Assembly Rooms behind them, the Roman Baths and the Abbey ahead. They were decent people, these tourists, well-behaved and obedient, trotting in and out of their coaches like good schoolchildren, but even their decency seemed aggravating to Robert, a symptom of fundamentally incurious minds and passion-less hearts.

He gave up the pavement, and stepped into the street. To be truthful, anything and everything was likely to aggravate him that afternoon, and it was unfair to take his feelings out on inoffensive women protecting their holiday perms under plaid umbrellas. Lizzie had known Robert was coming in to Bath to see their accountant, indeed she had suggested that they go together, as they often did, but Robert had said no, don't bother, it's just a routine visit to tidy things up after the end of the financial year. Lizzie hadn't pressed the point, had seemed, in fact, rather grateful to be let off. She was busy thinking about autumn stock, she said; did he mind?

"No," said Robert. "Just don't order anything until I get back. Not finally, that is."

"I won't," she said, but she wasn't really listening. She was looking at some samples of silk-screen printing an art student had brought in, chalky pastels and black in abstract designs, faintly reminiscent of the work of Duncan Grant and Vanessa Bell. "Five years ago, I'd have snapped this up, but now I don't know, looks a bit *passé*—"

Robert kissed her. "I'll be back before five. Anything you want from Bath?"

She shook her head. He had paused for a fraction of a second, wondering whether to change his mind and insist she come—there was no reason to, only an instinct which might well have simply been his preference for having her with him—and then he had gone.

Now, two hours later, he was on his way up Gay Street back to the car, which he had left in a little street somewhere behind the Circus. The meeting with the accountant had begun by being what he had anticipated—a final review of the last year's accounts—and had then turned into something else, something more unpleasant. The accountant had pointed out that if the Gallery business did not pick up significantly and quickly, Robert and Lizzie would be in trouble over mortgage repayments on the Grange.

"You have borrowed," the accountant said, "a hundred

and fifty thousand pounds in the last five years."

"Secured against the Gallery."

"Indeed. But against a profitable Gallery. In the current conditions, it's a lot to ask of a business like the Gallery to support itself, all of you, *and* a borrowing of that size."

"Then you think that the last six months' dip in trade wasn't just a one-off, and that things will get worse?"

"Correct."

Why hadn't he said, I'm afraid so, Robert thought, flattening himself against a parked car to avoid a passing one. Why didn't he reply at least in a human way instead of snapping out "Correct" like some heartless robot? Of course, it was his professional duty to point out to Robert that for the first time in seventeen years of trading, things were not getting better, but worse, and that the steady, happy pace up the path of prosperity was unmistakably giving way to a slide down into something altogether more alarming and uncertain, but why couldn't he have tried to soften the blow, even a little?

I'm frightened, Robert thought.

The rain was getting heavier. He reached the top of Gay Street, turned his collar up, and ran across the circle of green in the middle of the Circus, through the clump of huge lime trees, which were the only living things about looking grateful for the rain, and made for Circus Place. A boy and a girl went past him huddled together and giggling under an old supermarket bag they were attempting to use as an umbrella and it struck Robert with a pang that they were as young and waywardly dressed as he and Lizzie had been seventeen years ago, with all the world before them and nothing to be responsible for.

When he reached the Gallery, it was ten minutes before closing time, and Jenny Hardacre, who had been their invaluable chief assistant for seven years, was beginning on the process of locking up. Jenny, who had a sweet face and prematurely grey hair held back off her face with combs, had been widowed soon after her only child, now a resolute little boy the same age as Davy, was born.

Usually, going into the Gallery soothed whatever sore feelings Robert might be afflicted with. The polished floor, the pools of carefully angled light, the racks and piles and shelves of seductive merchandise, the smell of seagrass and wood and potpourri were all not just lovely in themselves, but solid proof of achievement. This evening, however, their solidity seemed to have evaporated and instead an air of miserable vulnerability hung over everything, as if the bailiffs were poised to march in and seize the pictures and rugs and lamps and bear them away mercilessly, like helpless victims of rape and pillage. Robert gave himself a shake; he was getting horribly emotional. He needed to talk to Lizzie.

Jenny looked up from the till and smiled.

"OK?"

"Not very," he said.

Her face became instantly sympathetic. "Oh dear—"

"Is Lizzie in the office?"

"Yes. She's got the boys with her. They got dropped here after school."

The office at the Gallery was on the first floor, at the back, looking out on to the decayed tangle of a few of Langworth's very minor industries, now defunct. Knowing that he would have to spend a lot of time there, Robert had designed the office to be the kind of studio he had always wanted and now felt he would never have, with high desks for drawing at, and wonderful lighting and plenty of wall space for pinning up things. As he came in Lizzie, who was on the telephone, turned and gave him a wave, and Sam and Davy, who had been engaged in drawing spaceships all over Davy's bare knees with a felt-tipped pen, launched themselves at him and clamped him strenuously about the calves.

"Get off," Robert said.

"I tell you what," Lizzie said into the telephone, "make me half a dozen and we'll see how they go. No, sale or return, that's how I operate with individual craftsmen because this is a gallery as well as a shop. All right? Yes, different woods would be lovely but they must be English woods."

"Sam," Robert said. "Let go."

"Your shoes are sopping—"

"It was raining in Bath. Let *go*, Davy."

"I don't have to till Sam—"

"You do have to," Robert said furiously. "I've had a bloody awful afternoon and I'm in no mood for bloody awful children."

Lizzie put the telephone down.

"Was it awful?"

"Yes," Robert said. He had an ominous feeling that he was losing his sense of proportion entirely. Trying to free at least one leg, he lashed out with one imprisoned foot far harder than he meant to and caught Davy a blow on the chin. Davy, never far from tears at the jolliest of times, dissolved at once, clutching his chin with his hands.

"Now look," said Sam pleasedly. "I expect you've broken all his teeth and he'll only be able to eat yoghurt and yuk like that. For ever."

Rob stooped and picked up the sobbing Davy.

"I'm so sorry, darling, I never meant to hurt you—"

"I hate yoghurt," Davy wailed through his muffling hands.

"Let me look. Take your hands away and let me look at your mouth—"

Lizzie said, from where she still sat by the telephone, "What was so awful, Rob? Don't worry about Davy, he'll be fine, you know how he carries on."

Davy opened his mouth hugely wide and Robert peered inside.

"All there, thank goodness—"

"I expect, though," Sam said from where he still lay on the floor, "that you've cracked his jaw."

Davy gasped, eyes widening.

"Don't be daft."

"What was so awful?" Lizzie said again. "I mean, you

knew the figures before you went, you knew we'd had the worst half-year ever—"

"Things won't pick up," Robert said. He stooped again and set Davy on his feet. Davy was trying to arrange his hands like cups to support his cracked jaw.

"What d'you mean?"

"I expect your jaw will just dangle about like some dopey old ape—"

"Sullivan said that there is no sign as yet of a general economic recovery and that we, like all small businesses, will not find trade picking up in the foreseeable future. As he put it so charmingly, shopping in a shop like ours is the kind of luxury people will give up first."

"Don't let go!" Sam hissed at Davy. "Or it'll start dangling."

Lizzie got up and came across to Robert.

"I wish I'd come with you."

"So do I, but it wouldn't have made any difference to the facts. The thing is, the turnover's not at all bad considering the conditions, but the profit simply isn't enough to meet our outgoings."

Davy leaned against Lizzie and gave a subdued howl. Lizzie bent and firmly took his hands away from his chin. His eyes grew wide with terror, waiting for his lower jaw to flop downwards like a broken shutter. It didn't.

"See?" Lizzie said. "You are very silly and Sam's a bully."

"What's a bully?" Sam said hopefully.

"Somebody," Robert said, looking down at him, "who takes pleasure in being horrible to the weak. It's a form of weakness in fact, to bully. Bullies are always cowards inside."

Sam got up and went over to the nearest desk which he began to kick gently, with his back to them. Lizzie stepped forward and leaned her cheek on Robert's chest.

"I didn't order anything this afternoon, in the end. That was a nice young man who makes potpourri boxes, turned wooden ones with latticed lids—"

"I expect the Indians make them cheaper—"

She lifted her head.

"Shall we talk about all this later?"

"Yes."

"Mummy," Davy said. "Can I have for supper what Sam has?"

"You always have what Sam has!"

"I don't want yoghurt—"

Lizzie looked at Robert, smiling almost in despair. "We wanted this, didn't we, we wanted this rich, busy life full of work and children, with everything muddled up together, it's what we meant to have, isn't it?"

He moved away and began circling the room, straightening papers, turning off machines and lights. Lizzie watched him, waiting for his reply, and at last he said, from the far side of the office, bolting the window with its patent safety catch, "Of course it is. It's just life itself that deals you a nasty when you aren't looking, it's life that keeps moving the goalposts. We haven't changed, Lizzie, it's just the things around us that have."

"So we'll have to learn to?"

"I suppose so," he said, and she had seldom heard him sound so sad. "I suppose we'll have to."

The evening passed, as so many evenings seemed to, in a crowd of incidents which made up the necessary, repetitive process of getting everybody fed, homeworked, music practised, bathed, off the telephone, away from the television, and into bed. Lizzie had always intended that as each child reached twelve, they should have supper with her and Rob, instead of an earlier and more babyish children's supper, but two things had arisen to frustrate this intention. The first was that neither Harriet nor Alistair ever seemed to show the slightest inclination to eat with their parents, professing not to be hungry, or not hungry then, or not having finished their essay, or their French vocabulary, or being too tired or too deep in a book, which last Lizzie had learned to interpret as too deep in an episode on television of *LA Law* or *Inspector Morse*. The second reason was that

Lizzie discovered that by eight-thirty on an average evening, she and Robert had simply *had* the children. At first she had felt guilty about this—she had intended to have at least four, after all, she was proud and pleased to have a large family, just as she was proud and pleased at the children's intelligence and strength of character—but then it had occurred to her that she was as much Robert's wife as the children's mother and even, if there was time to consider it, her own self, Lizzie Middleton, and that if she didn't have a little adult time at the end of a busy day, she would go raving bonkers. So now she cooked pasta, or ground beef in some form, or sausages, at six-thirty, and two hours later, Robert repeated the exercise, more or less, for himself and Lizzie.

"Of course," Barbara said frequently, "it's perfectly ridiculous the way modern children are never sent to bed. You and Frances were in bed by seven until you were fourteen."

"Were we? I wish somebody would send me to bed at seven now."

This evening was no different to a hundred others except that Sam, mysteriously chastened in some obscure part of himself, tenderly tied Davy's head up with his own Manchester United football scarf to keep his jaw in place, and fed him little scraps of sausage, like a helpless fledgling. Davy glowed in this attention. Harriet too was unnaturally quiet, being, Lizzie suspected, in the grip of a blind and hopeless crush on a sixth-form boy at Langworth Comprehensive, the kind of careless, glamorous boy who would never notice her. Lizzie wished Harriet would talk to her about it, but Harriet had never considered Lizzie a fit recipient of confidences, and when Lizzie came into the room while Harriet was in the middle of one of her interminable telephone conversations to Heather, Harriet's voice would sink at once to a conspiratorial whisper. Alistair had vanished. He would be in his room as usual, his curious fusty lair, where he lived a powerful and private life among his models and his piles and piles of cherished cartoon books and magazines and comics, which he read with a manic intensity.

By nine o'clock, the house was almost quiet. Harriet had taken Radio One and her aching heart to the bathroom, Sam and Davy were asleep—Davy still carefully bandaged up in his scarf—Alistair, lying on the floor in his bedroom, was writing fervently about the evil effects of acid rain. Lizzie had loaded the washing machine to turn on before they went to bed, when electricity would be cheaper, had made a few more of her famous lists for the morning and fed Cornflakes. Robert had grilled two chump chops and some mushrooms, made a salad and put a loaf of brown bread in the bottom oven to warm.

"I sometimes wonder," Lizzie said, sitting down heavily in one of the kitchen chairs, "if what we do every evening is repeated all over England in thousands and thousands of households with several children and both parents working, and all parents have this alarming feeling that however hard you run, you are actually slipping further and further behind. I'm so tired I feel I've been hit with a sandbag. Are we tireder than people used to be?"

"No," Robert said. "It just feels like it, which comes to the same thing." He put a plate of chops and mushrooms down in front of her.

"Why does it? Do we do more?"

"No, but we want to achieve all the time. We aren't content with just staying alive, warm and clothed and fed, we take all that for granted. It's the achieving that's so exhausting."

Lizzie ate a mushroom.

"I told Frances, at Christmas, that fulfilment was the way to happiness."

"Did you?"

"Yes. I said you had to go into every room in yourself, as it were, and explore it and use it."

Robert sat down opposite her and ground black pepper vigorously over his plate.

"What's wrong with that?"

"You end up sandbagged, like I said. Frances doesn't

know what it's like to be this tired. Did I tell you, she's gone to Spain again?"

Robert stopped slicing bread.

"Has she? Why?"

"She said she felt she'd made an unprofessional move in walking out on those hotel people at Christmas, and that some of her clients were beginning to say they knew Italy like the backs of their hands and what could she think of next."

"Sounds fair enough."

"Yes," Lizzie said, helping herself to salad, "of course it does. It'll do her good, she's been so odd and dreamy lately—"

"She's always dreamy."

"Part of me," Lizzie said, "won't settle until she's happy."

"Till *she's* settled, you mean, till she's married."

"It isn't natural to live like she lives. She's so loving as a person, it's a waste."

"Lots of people choose to be single, you know. Men and women. It isn't because they're inadequate emotionally, is it? Isn't it because most of them don't find the right person to share with, and it's better to be alone than to share with the wrong person?"

Lizzie spread butter on her bread. "Frances is lonely. She's too dependent on too few people."

"Are you sure?"

"She's my twin," Lizzie said simply.

Later, when they had eaten some cheese, and an apple each, and were considering whether or not they wanted any coffee, Robert said he was sorry, but he couldn't go to bed before they had talked about the problems with the business.

"Tell me, then," Lizzie said, yawning.

"The bottom line is this. We are currently paying fifteen thousand pounds a year in interest, and that is, as you know, on top of the mortgage repayments on this house as well as keeping us all fed, clothed, insured and all the other stuff. It cost fifteen hundred quid to heat and light this

house last year and the last telephone bill was nearer three
hundred than two and that was for only a *quarter*. Then
there's the running costs of the business, which you know."

He stopped. Lizzie, who had been leaning against a cupboard, came and sat on the corner of the table.

"Oh Rob. It isn't as if we live at all grandly——"

"I know. I'm just scared that if things don't pick up we
won't be able to live at all."

Lizzie looked across at him with a face so tired, his heart
smote him.

"What is the difference between what we're making and
what we need to make?"

"About the amount of the interest on the loan. About
fifteen thousand."

She got off the table and came round to lean against
him, holding his head against her bosom. It struck her suddenly, and miserably, that even though they might be together in their trouble, it didn't somehow seem to make
the trouble any less terrifying. She had an image of herself
and Rob and the children in a tiny, fragile, leaking boat on
a very rough sea, and the children were crying piteously
and she was full of a terrible guilt as well as a terrible fear.
She was drowning, and all these little reproachful hands
were about her neck.

"I never realised," she said, holding Robert's head, "how
bad it was. I feel awful, that I didn't realise, that you've
had to know by yourself——"

His voice was muffled against her.

"I hoped you wouldn't have to know. I hoped it was just
a bad patch and all we'd have to do would be to tighten
our belts for a bit."

"So," her voice faltered a little. "The gap of fifteen thousand might get wider."

He attempted to nod, inside her embrace.

She whispered, "I must be very naive, but I never
thought money would be a real problem for us, I mean I
never thought we'd be millionaires, I don't want that, but
I didn't think either that we'd be in debt and not—not
able——"

"Shh," Rob said. He moved his head back so that he could look at her. "It's only money," he said, trying to make a joke of it.

"You can't say that," Lizzie said. "You can only say that when you've got enough of it."

They neither of them slept well, partly on account of worrying and partly on account of Davy's fixed belief in his injury, which brought him in to their bedroom four times between midnight and six-thirty. In the end, desperate for a last half-hour of attempted oblivion, Lizzie pulled him into bed beside her, where he lay, stiff with anxiety, his head still absurdly swaddled in red-and-white wool.

"I am a sad boy," he told Lizzie.

"I'm pretty sad, too," she said. She held him and thought of lying there holding him when he was only a tiny baby and they all took their security for granted. She couldn't believe how much money they had borrowed, and at the same time, she couldn't believe how easy it had been to borrow, how the bank had constantly and pressingly asked them if they were sure they had enough, and so they had thought: Well, with another few thousand we could paint another room, take the children to Austria (they had walked and cycled through the lovely valleys, carrying Davy on their backs or in a special little pannier), change the car, and they had taken the money and the debt had quietly grown until it now loomed over them, transformed from something manageable into something menacing. And however hard they worked at the Gallery, they couldn't, it seemed, make any more money out of it by their own efforts, because the only thing that made money was people coming in and buying lavishly, and nobody was feeling lavish just now. There are probably, thought Lizzie, reaching down to hold Davy's cold feet in her warm hands, people lying awake all over the place worrying like this, people with mortgages and children and this dreadful, impotent feeling that you are dependent upon forces outside your control for anything to improve.

Beside her Robert stirred, sighed and opened his eyes. He peered across her at Davy.

"How many teeth fell out in the night, Dave?"

Davy shut his eyes in disgust.

"I was wondering," Lizzie said, "whether I shouldn't ask Dad for some help?"

"I'd rather you didn't—"

"I know, but he's awfully easy to ask, bless him, and I'm sure he'd understand—"

Robert turned on his side so that his profile rested against Lizzie's nearest shoulder.

"Lizzie, I'm afraid I couldn't bear it. It's one thing to ask for money to build with, on the way up, but quite another to ask for it as a lifeline, because you fear you may be on the way down."

"Don't talk like that!"

"I can't help it, it's what I'm thinking."

Davy put a tentative hand inside the football scarf and felt his face.

"Are you going to school in that scarf?"

"No," Davy said.

"Then why have you worn it all night?"

"Sam said it would mend me."

"Sam has a guilty conscience."

Davy regarded her.

"Sam said Pimlott might let me play with them."

"Do you like Pimlott, Davy?"

"Oh yes," Davy said reverently.

Lizzie kissed him.

"You're too like your Aunt Frances," Lizzie said. "Too grateful for too little." She gave a small, ironic smile. "Think of Frances! Think of Frances and think of us!"

"You're always being so sorry for her—"

"I know, it's just that now, being able to roam about in southern Spain in May seems—"

"Shh," Robert said.

"There are footballers in Spain," Davy said, feeling for the huge, soft, woolly knot on top of his head. "Pimlott said."

"Would you mind," Lizzie asked Robert, "if I went and talked to Juliet?"

" 'Course not. But what on earth could Juliet do?"

"I don't know. Nothing, probably. But I'd like to see her."

Robert began to get out of bed. "Suit yourself—"

"Rob, don't be huffy—"

"I'm not huffy," he said huffily. "I just can't see the point of telling Juliet our troubles. But you tell her if you want to."

"I do want to," Lizzie said. "I do want to. Because I can't, at the moment, tell Frances."

Juliet was pegging out washing. She wasn't naturally domesticated in the brisk, domestic science-school way that Barbara was, but there were some soothing domestic tasks she really relished, and hanging out the washing was one. It was partly that the high, windy situation of the cottage was so tailormade for the job, and it was glorious to see sheets and towels cracking and bellying in the wind like the sails of tall ships. Sometimes they cracked and bellied so tremendously that they blew away across the downs and Juliet would have to retrieve her laundry from bramble bushes and five-barred gates. She was just hoisting her clothes prop—she scoured the woods for these; ash and hazel were usually the most promising—into place, when she saw the glint of a car roof catching the sun at the foot of her track. A few seconds later, she saw that it was Lizzie.

"You look like an illustration out of *Mother Goose*," Lizzie said, getting out of the car.

"It's my grey feather hair. You, on the other hand, look exhausted."

"I didn't sleep. I hate not sleeping, I simply can't function the next day at all."

Juliet took her into the cottage. There was a sewing machine on the table, and a great chaos of pieces of fabric, and a jar of cow parsley on the hearth. One of the windows was open to the windy morning and the curtains were rippling back and forth in the draught and for no reason she could immediately think of, except sleeplessness, the sight of Juliet's sitting room made Lizzie feel slightly tearful, because of its timelessness, its air of suspended but constructive activity, its security.

"Have you ever been short of money?" Lizzie said.

"Always."

"In debt?"

"Never. Can't bear it. It's the one orthodox element in my moral code. I bought this cottage outright thirty years ago for three thousand pounds that my mother left me. I couldn't have borrowed the money for dear life."

"We've borrowed," Lizzie said, crouching down and putting her face against the pepper-smelling heads of the cow parsley.

"I'm sure you have. Everybody does, but me."

"And now it's become—very difficult to pay it back."

Juliet ran water into her kettle. She thought of the Grange, and Lizzie's children, and the industrialist she had heard on the radio that morning who had said that for the first time in twenty-five years, his order books were empty.

"I don't expect you to have a solution," Lizzie said, straightening up. "I don't expect you even to react. I just had to say it to someone who wasn't Rob, and I don't want to say it to Mum."

Juliet put the kettle on to boil and came back towards Lizzie.

"I'm so sorry."

"I feel we've been awful fools, so gullible—"

"You aren't business people after all, you're artists—"

"We've learned business," Lizzie said. "At least, we thought we had." She looked at Juliet. "What I can't bear is not being able to think of what to do. If I could think what to do, I'd do it."

"In that case," Juliet said casually, "why doesn't one of you go out to work?"

NINE

Luis took Frances to Granada along a tortuous and beautiful road through the mountains. He told her that although he was born in Seville, Granada was his favourite city in Spain because it was at once so full of vitality and so full of melancholy as well as being full of wonderful buildings. The last Moorish king of Granada, Luis said, had been unromantically called Boabdil, and when he had to flee from the city in 1492 he wept and wept at leaving its courtyards and its fountains and its minarets.

"He had a terrible mother," Luis said. "His mother said to him, 'You weep like a woman for what you could not defend like a man.'"

"That's the sort of thing my mother might say," Frances said.

"And mine—"

They glanced at each other, laughing.

"I wanted to go to university here," Luis said, "but my father sent me to London, believing that the London School of Economics was a business school. He had no idea of its politics, and I never told him."

"Do Spanish children confide in their parents?"

"Not my generation, certainly."

"And José? Does José talk to you?"

"José," Luis said, frowning a little, "talks to his mother."

Frances looked out of the window and then, because the drop her side of the road was so sheer and so deep, looked hastily back again. She wanted very much to ask Luis about his marriage, to which he had never referred. Yet he wore a wedding ring, the standard third-finger, left-hand, married gold band of a standard Catholic husband.

"I've forgiven José," Frances said. "I think you ought to."

Luis shrugged. "He can be just a charming boy to you, but to me he is a disappointment. He wants only to play."

"Perhaps you shouldn't give him so much money."

He glanced at her. "Do you have much money, Frances?"

"No," she said, "just enough."

"Do you approve of that?"

"Yes, I do."

"But then you are a puritan."

She glared at him.

"I'm not!"

He was grinning, teasing.

"Are you sure?" He began to imitate her. " 'No, Luis, I won't have another glass of sherry, even though it was delicious and I would love to . . . No, Luis, I won't stay up any later and argue about philosophy with you because I am here on business so I must sleep enough and keep a clear head . . . No, Luis, I will not ask you personal questions because it would not be proper.' "

She stared ahead soberly for a moment.

"Am I really like that?"

"No," he said, "not really. That's why I tease you. You say these things to me but I don't think they are true."

"I hate being flattered," Frances said. "I distrust it."

"I don't flatter you. I tell you often that you are wrong, your views are often too soft—"

"And yours are too hard."

"I am a Spaniard," he said. "We are conservative people,

and a little tragic. Everything happens on a grand scale here, including the disasters. Look ahead."

Frances looked. Across the great agricultural plain they were approaching, she could see a wall of mountain, and snow.

"The Sierra Nevada. Soon you will see the city. I will drive round to the north of it, and take you in through the old Arab gate, the Puerta de Elvira, and we will walk in the Albaicín, where the falcon keepers used to live, which is the poor quarter now, but interesting, and then we shall look at the Alhambra, which is the glory of Granada, and then I will give you lunch at the *parador*."

Frances, filled with joy, said, "It's so kind of you, Luis, to go to all this trouble but really, you know, I've decided in favour of the *posada* anyway, so—"

"It's not trouble. I like it."

She said nothing. She looked for a moment at his hands on the steering wheel, and then quickly away at the advancing mountain wall under its crest of snow.

"I am happy to do this," Luis said. "I am happy to be with you. You see, I am doing what I like."

In the gardens of the Generalife, Frances sat down to make notes. "Generalife," she wrote in her large, firm handwriting, "Arabic for 'the Garden of the Architect.'" She closed her eyes for a moment and briefly turned her face up to the clear, decided, early summer sun. When she elected to open them again—at her leisure and pleasure as everything was being on that day—she would see the long green length of the Patio de la Acequia, and the roses and the myrtles and the orange trees and, arching over them, the ceaseless shimmer of the fountains, rising and falling in a soothing, seductive, hypnotic rhythm. If she looked a little to her left, she would see an ancient arched wall over which bougainvillaea fell, and if she lowered her gaze a little, she would see Luis. He had stretched himself out in the shade of a kind of lookout balcony and had his eyes shut. She did open her eyes; she did look at him. He had arranged

himself on the stones, she thought, in a way that was very
graceful for such a solid man.

Frances went on with her notes. "These gardens and the
palace here were the summer residence of the rulers of
Granada. Moorish influence paramount, wonderful plant-
ing and views, and *water*, water everywhere. Excellent for
painters, photographers. Food in city also interesting, being
Moorish still in large measure"—Luis had made her eat a
particular kind of dried ham at lunch, with beans, broad
beans called *habas* which he said the Moors had loved—
"in fact, I have a feeling that Moors here knew about real
quality of life, air, water, flowers, music, prospects, how to
delight the senses."

She wondered, briefly, with a kind of professional reflex,
about the senses of the clients of Shore to Shore. Would
they find that the exotic and sophisticated charms of the
Alhambra with its screens and fretted arches and reflecting
tanks of water were quite obliterated by the nightmare of
trying to park their hired holiday cars? The trouble was,
today, did she care about that? Had she, if she was honest,
cared at all, since she stepped out of her shoes on to the
sun-warmed tiles of her bedroom in the *posada* at Mojas
and felt the unmistakable siren call of something that had
nothing to do with that neat office in Fulham, with telephoning punctilious Nicky, with worrying whether the new
holiday she had dreamed up that year of Etruscan sites and
Renaissance gardens was, in fact, going to involve far too
much walking for many of her loyal but elderly clients?
Had she not, for these few days at least, simply climbed
into the infinitely alluring hammock of quite another kind
of life to any she had previously known, and just let herself
sway to its rhythm in the sunshine? She put her notebook
down and spread her hands on the warm old stones either
side of her, the stones laid at the commands of the Sultan
Abul-Wallid Ismail I over which his wife Zoraya then
softly trod on her way to secret meetings with her lover in
the Court of the Cypresses. Bewitching stuff, Frances
thought, quite bewitching, but am I really just being rather
silly? I do hope not, because that would be such a disap-

pointment, and I am so very, very tired of being disappointed. At least today is not disappointing, and nor was yesterday, nor the day I arrived. Since I arrived I haven't once felt I was being balked of something I wanted; in fact, it's been rather the opposite, I've been given things I hardly dared to hope for. When Luis wakes up, I will ask if we can go and see the tomb of the Catholic Kings. After Christopher Columbus, I feel drawn towards significant Spanish tombs.

Luis was not asleep. His eyes were closed, certainly, but not completely, and every so often he took a long, covert look at Frances, sitting out there in the sunshine in a straw hat which he would, if she were his, have made a bonfire of, for its quelling and spinsterish qualities. If she were his, indeed, he thought, he would not dress her in the bold and elaborate clothes that Spanish women carried off with such flair, but he would certainly like her to stop shrouding herself in all these anonymous folds of fabric, as if she wished nobody to be able to guess a thing about her, just by looking. But people did look at her; Luis had noticed that. It wasn't very surprising. After all, he wanted to do it a good deal himself; he wanted to know more about her.

He had, rather to his surprise, told her quite a lot about himself at lunch. He made a point, on the whole, of not talking about his marriage, whose failure, yet continued technical existence, seemed to symbolise so much in himself that he had never quite resolved, the lifelong girders of Catholicism that seemed to remain whether he took any notice of them or not, the struggle between the order of traditional values and the inevitable confusion but freshness of progressive ones. As a businessman, he applauded the chances offered by European economic unity; as a Spaniard, he deplored the smallest influence that might diminish Spain's proud, difficult, capricious Spanishness. "Every day in Spain is some kind of adventure," he said, laughing, to Frances. "Even catching a train—" And then, for some reason, he had told her about his marriage.

She had listened with that kind of stillness people have

when everything you say is saturated with importance for them.

"I was in love, certainly, she was very charming, but you must also understand the strictness of a good middle-class family like ours, in the sixties. We could not get to know each other very well in many ways, we could not relax, we could not be"—he paused and then said circumspectly— "be intimate. There could be no easy friendship between boys and girls then, no fooling around, no experiments. Our parents were much involved, as their parents had been with them. I don't complain. Often it's as good a way to make a marriage as completely free choice. It's hard to choose when there is all the choice in the world. José will never choose. Why should he? His mother looks after him like a baby and he has as many girls to play with as he likes. I disapprove but his mother takes no notice. She thinks I disapprove of everything that gives freedom to anyone in Spain but myself."

"And do you?" Frances said.

He looked at her with a flash of something like contempt.

"What a question! I don't believe anyone on this earth should behave as if they had nothing to prove, neither man nor woman. But my wife thinks she has nothing to prove. It is not possible to live with someone who thinks that, it makes every conversation a farce because the assumption is always that she is right because she is a woman and a mother and I am wrong because I am a Spanish man. I tell you," he said, grinning again, "there is an armed woman in the Seville police. She is wonderful. I told José's mother she should imitate her and she threw a big dish at me."

"I expect she did," Frances said. She was eating, with a teaspoon, a thick, dark quince paste that Luis had told her was as much an ancient speciality as the broad beans had been.

"You are so cool," he said. "Why don't you shout at me?"

"That would be pretty stupid."

"I am afraid that perhaps José's mother is a little stupid. She is my son's mother and when I married her, I loved her. You can only be sad when love dies because it was living once and everything living is important. Why did you not marry?"

Frances put her teaspoon down on her now empty plate. She looked at her wine glass. It too seemed to be empty. How many glasses had she drunk?

"I never wanted to."

"You don't believe in marriage?" His voice had a tiny edge of hope to it.

"I do believe in marriage. I don't think it would have lasted so long, as an institution, if it wasn't basically the best that men and women could devise for arranging society."

"Then?" Luis said, filling her glass.

Frances bent her head. Her wing of hair fell forward, obscuring her face from him.

"I would like," Frances said carefully, turning her wine glass by its stem, "to have a relationship with someone, with a man, that was enhancing. Suppose we were in a room together, this man and I, I would like him to feel that the room was better for him than any other room because I was in it too. And I would like to feel the same, about him."

He let a tiny pause fall, and then he said, "Well. And why should this not happen?"

"It isn't that it shouldn't," Frances said. "It's just that it never has." She picked up her glass and took another swallow.

Luis said nothing. She looked, from behind the cover of her hair, at his hand—brownish-skinned, below the pale-blue cuff of his shirt—lying on the tablecloth about six inches from her own hand, whitish-skinned with a plain silver bangle round the wrist, holding her wine glass. Neither hand moved. Then Luis said, "I am going to take you now to see some most beautiful gardens."

Lying now in the beautiful gardens, watching Frances, Luis felt a rush of something much stronger than curiosity, a mixture of protectiveness and possessiveness, of admiration and even, he thought with some amazement, a kind of awe. What *was* she? Why did she give him, so often, the feeling that she was walking away from him down some mental corridors, and that he longed to follow her and seize her and ask her to explain? And why, as now, when she did some perfectly ordinary thing like taking off her sandals, revealing pale, unexceptional, slightly-too-big-for-beauty feet, did she fill him with desire? He swallowed, making a sound so small, he thought, that nobody could hear him above the sound of the falling fountain.

"Luis?" Frances said. "Are you awake?"

He sat up, stretching. "Yes."

"Will you take me to the tombs? The tombs of Fernando and Isabel, that you told me about, with the marble lions?"

Knowing that she wouldn't like it, he resisted the urge to say, I will take you anywhere you like, and said instead, "Of course. I always like to see them. Charles V put up the tombs because he was so proud of his grandparents. Wouldn't it be something to think you would ever have a grandchild who thought so much of you?"

Frances was impressed by the tombs. They had been made in Italy, of white marble, and in glass cases nearby she could see Isabel's crown and Fernando's sword and, rather stirringly, the banners used when Granada was conquered for the Catholic Church and poor Boabdil was turned out sobbing into the harsh world outside his paradise. A tiny, low-wattage bulb burned by Isabel's tomb, which she had, Luis said, specified in her will.

"An electric lightbulb?"

"Of course not," Luis said, smiling. "When I was a boy, even a young man, it was always a candle."

Frances did not like the rest of the cathedral.

"It's all out of proportion, and it's far too heavy."

"The Spanish like heaviness."

"And all this bronzey-gold stuff. It's so ugly. Why couldn't they leave the stone?"

"They wanted it to glow, richly, to look as if it were full of splendid light. This cathedral is regarded as one of the most important works of the Spanish Renaissance."

Frances leaned against a pillar, a pillar even more massive than the one she had propped herself against all those months ago in the cathedral in Seville.

"Luis, I can't look at another thing—"

He said, "I should have stopped you long ago; you are exhausted."

"Only with looking. With thinking about the Moors. I've loved it but I—"

He took her hand.

"Can you walk? Can you walk back up to the *parador*, where we have left the car, or will you wait here and I will bring it to you?"

"I will walk," Frances said. "I'm all right, truly. Perhaps it's something about churches, particularly Catholic churches."

He drew her hand through his arm. She leaned on him, then, feeling that she was leaning too heavily for subtlety, but not as heavily as she would have liked, drew away a little. In response, his arm tightened.

"Come," he said. "No more the English miss."

He led her out into the sunshine.

"Don't look back at the façade. Even I, as a loyal Spaniard, think it's terrible. I am going to find you first a drink. The water here is famous and you shall have it with lemon juice and sugar."

"There," he said, a few minutes later, settling her into a green-painted metal chair under a canopy. "Take your hat off and relax."

"I don't think you like my hat."

"Shall we say, I think there are more pretty hats—"

"It keeps the sun off, otherwise I go pink and get freckles."

"Freckles?"

"Here," she said, tapping her nose. "Charming on children but not on adults."

Luis turned his own chair and shouted at a waiter.

"I must learn Spanish," Frances said. "For somebody in the travel business, I'm a shamefully bad linguist."

"Are you musical?"

"Not very."

"Come," he said, laughing at her. "What are your advantages then?"

She smiled, and said without coquettishness, "You tell me."

"Seriously?"

"No," she said.

"Oh," he cried, flinging his arms out. "Again you pull away!"

"Luis—"

"Listen," he said, leaning forward, his dark eyes shining, "listen, Frances, I want to know you. I have never talked to a woman in this way, I have never felt I was so much—in a mystery, and then I come a little close and you hide from me. Why always? What are you afraid of?"

She looked right back at him.

"I don't know."

The waiter came with two tall glasses of lemon juice, a jug of water and a little metal dish of white packets of sugar. He put it all down on the table. Luis took no notice of him.

"Frances, we are friends now. We tease, we laugh, we tell each other things. It's not long, I know, two or three days, but we have been together most of the time. I am not a dangerous man. Look at me. Forty-eight, three kilos too heavy, a middle-class—my mother-in-law would say bourgeois—businessman. I am not a wolf. We do business together and it turns into a friendship. Do you prefer to go on to Córdoba on your own?"

"Certainly not," Frances said, clutched by a fear that had nothing to do with going to Córdoba alone.

"Then do not," he said, almost fiercely, competently pouring and mixing their drinks, "behave as if I were a savage person and you were a whipped dog."

She waited. He finished stirring and handed her a glass.

"See if that is sweet enough—"

She took a sip.

"It is. It's delicious. Luis—"

"Yes?"

"I think," Frances said carefully, "that living alone has some good things about it and some bad. It also has some elements that just happen, that aren't either good or bad, but are just there. One of those, in my case, is that I tend to react to things now with a certain set of responses, and one of the chief of those responses is that when anything disconcerts me—even because it's simply new to me—I pull away. It's my defence, I suppose, to withdraw. It's not meant as a criticism of other people, it's just how I have come to react."

He nodded. He looked across the little square where they were sitting, with its small, unenthusiastically trickling Baroque fountain in the middle and cars parked densely round the edge.

He said, "But why do you assume that anything new will harm you? Why do you not think that something new could make you more rich, more happy?"

"I *do* think it could. I *do* think I would benefit."

"Then why—?"

"Because I don't know how," Frances said. "I want to— open up, but I don't know how. And *don't*—" she added fiercely, "tease me about it."

His face was perfectly serious.

"I never even thought of it," he said.

He reached for her hat on the empty chair between them.

"Now, put on this sad thing and we will walk slowly back up to the *parador*."

She nodded, obediently putting her hat on, slightly too much on the back of her head, so that it gave her an old-fashioned, innocent air. She looked at him for his approval.

"I am sorry," he said, "but I'm afraid I cannot bear it." He stretched his arms out and lifted the hat gently from her head. "It will be my pleasure to buy you another, but this hat must stay here. It will amuse the children of the café owner to find it."

Frances looked at her hat, lying on the table with an air
of mild reproach about it. She had bought it, on impulse,
one hot day, from a market stall in the North End Road.

"Poor hat," she said, not meaning it, faintly excited to
have it taken from her. "What kind of hat will you buy
me instead?"

He was counting change and small crumpled notes on
to the tray that had held their drinks.

"One like our donkeys wear," he said, without a glimmer of a smile. "One with holes for your ears."

On the journey home, he asked if she would think him
very rude if he made some business calls. She said she
wouldn't think it rude at all. He adjusted her seat so that
she could, as she had on the day of her arrival, lie back
and watch the blue sky soften and fade above her as the
sun sank slowly in the west and threw the mountains of
the Sierra Nevada into high, dark, dramatic relief. He said,
"Are you sure you are comfortable?"

"Very," she said. "Blissfully. Never been more comfortable."

On the back seat, behind her, lay her new straw hat. It
was more shallowly crowned than her old one, and the
brim was three times the size and very supple. Luis had
made her try on eleven hats. She wasn't sure that she had
tried on eleven hats in her whole life before, certainly never
in the space of fifteen minutes. She owned only one other
hat and it was dark-blue felt, a standard English middle-
class hat, the kind worn by mothers at school speech days
and friends of the bride at winter weddings, and Luis
would certainly hate it too. He would say it had no life in
it and he would be right. She thought of her old straw hat
lying on the café table waiting for several incredulous Spanish children to find it with cries of comic amazement that
any human being could actually have bought, let alone
worn, such a thing, and she felt a little surge of triumph.
It was as if something tiny but significant, which was ham-
pering her, had been conquered in the abandonment of that

hat. When she had finally chosen the new one, and Luis had approved of it, she had said, to her own mild surprise, "I think I'd like to buy a scarf, to tie round it, now," and he had said, delighted, "You are quite right but I shall do the buying." So he had bought her a long, fine silk scarf patterned in purple and blue and green, and the woman in the shop had tied it deftly round the crown of the new hat, so that the ends fell in soft streamers over the edge of the big, wavy brim.

"Better," Luis said, looking at her. "Much, much better."

"Even worn with a Marks and Spencer T-shirt?"

"Even with that."

Now the hat lay behind her, its streamers spread carefully over Luis's folded linen jacket. Absurd, Frances thought, to be so pleased and excited about a hat. It was a very classy hat, to be sure, and Frances would never have contemplated paying a quarter as much for anything that was merely something functional to keep the sun off, but then it wasn't just functional really, was it, it was elegant and becoming and mildly romantic—and Luis had bought it for her.

Beside her, Luis was talking steadily into the telephone, streams and streams of quick, rasping Spanish, its rhythms so different from Italian rhythms, and so utterly different from English. He was on the board of a shoe-making company in Seville, he had told her, and another that made specialised scaffolding for the construction industry, and he owned a small vineyard and these few hotels and of course there was this new project, the organic farm. He wanted to employ women on his farm because, he told Frances, he thought they worked better. "Work is important for them because it is for a purpose, it is to provide for their children." He was intending to invest most of the money he had made over the last twenty-five years in this farm. He wanted it to be the biggest in Europe. He asked Frances what the turnover of Shore to Shore was. She told him.

"With two employees?"

"One full-time, one part-time, and me."

He sucked his teeth.

"Not bad," he had said.

Frances had said, without heat, "Oh shut up," and he had smiled.

"In ten years," he said, "when you are my age, you will be talking millions."

"I like it small."

She did, she reflected now, but the trouble was, small things would grow, try as one might to prevent them. After all, here she was in Spain, having vowed that Italy would satisfy her and her clients for ever, and there, on the back seat of the car, lay the hat bought for her by a man with whom she was supposed to be doing business. What business had they talked? Almost none.

"Speak to Juan," Luis said, referring to the hotel manager. "Talk prices to Juan. You like my hotel, I like your kind of company. We are agreed on that. All that is left is the money, so talk money to Juan."

Juan was small and quick and very eager for Luis's good opinion. This made him slightly deferential to Frances, who, after all, Luis had brought in person to Mojas, and smile too much. It did not look as if it would be a very complicated matter between them. Frances would reserve six of the hotel's ten double rooms for a week in May and a week in October the following year, at a special rate to include breakfast and dinner, and they would, on both sides, regard this as an experiment to see what kind of response they got from the clients of Shore to Shore. Personally, Frances was not very anxious about the response. The hotel itself, with its cool, hidden, crooked courtyards, its bedrooms furnished with a charming mixture of chapel and farmhouse, its pretty shaded garden, its excellent kitchen, couldn't fail to please. Nor indeed, could the surrounding countryside, where the opportunities for sturdy English walking were so enormous ("What a race you are for walking for pleasure!" Luis had said. "Here, we only walk to get somewhere"), with spectacular views and interesting birds and plants, and nor, now that she had glimpsed it, could Granada, steep, exotic and extraordinary, where the present Catholics could never even begin to forget those powerful centuries of their Moorish past. So strange, she thought now, gazing dreamily at the sky, that I hardly had to do business here, it has just come. It's like standing on the edge of the sea and letting each incoming wave bring you something that you want, even if it turns out to be something you didn't know you wanted until you have it, when you know you couldn't bear to let it go.

Luis put down the telephone.

"Modern economics!" he said. "So stupid. By next year, it will probably be cheaper to import the hides for our shoes from the Argentine than to use Spanish leather. Did I wake you? Were you asleep?"

"No."

"Are you hungry?"

"Not yet."

"Frances," he said. "There is one more thing I want to show you before we leave Mojas, and then we go on to Córdoba."

"Tomorrow?"

"Or the next day."

"But I must go home on Friday."

"Why?"

"Don't ask me why. You know why. I have a business to run, just as you have."

"Sometimes we must break the rules, or bend them. Are you not enjoying yourself?"

"You know I am."

"Then that is, for now, more important than your business, or my business. There is a terrible English word, 'sensible.' I cannot bear this 'sensible.' It has nothing to do with the senses."

"It used to have. It used to mean being very emotionally conscious."

"Really?"

"Yes."

"Then I forgive it. I will use it in the old way. For now, Frances, I want you to be sensible. I want you to be full of feeling. Will you be?"

But she couldn't answer, she could only turn away to hide a face full of rapture, so that, after a little silence, he merely grunted, picked up his car telephone again, and began to dial Madrid.

TEN

That night she dreamed of Lizzie. She was trudging up the track towards Juliet's cottage, and she could hear the sound of someone crying, and the crying got louder and louder and then she saw that the person who was crying was running down the track towards her. As the running person got nearer, Frances could see that it was Lizzie, looking very young, only about twenty, with very long hair, wearing one of Barbara's caftans, and so Frances held out her arms to catch her sister as they met, but Lizzie took no notice of her, but just rushed on, crying, past her, and went down the track like the wind and then vanished. After that, Frances had several other rapid dreams, one of them set in Granada, among the fretted arches of the Court of the Lions, in the Alhambra, but when she woke, in the morning, it was the Lizzie dream that she remembered.

Her room was wonderful in the morning, cool and blue and light, like a seaside room, with the curtains swishing softly on the tiled floor, and a woman who lived in the first little street directly below the hotel garden calling, as she called every morning, for her little boy. "¡Pepe!" she would call. "¡Pepe! ¡Pepe!" Frances never heard him reply. She supposed he had to go to school, to the little whitewashed school by the church, and that he didn't want to go, so he hid, a naughty, spirited little Spanish Sam.

She sat up in bed, pushing back the white sheets with their embroidered hems, embroidered, Juan had said, by two old women in the village who had been lacemakers as girls but who couldn't see well enough to make lace any more. Why should she think of Lizzie? Why, even more, should she dream in that worrying way, of Lizzie? She put her feet down pleasurably on the smooth floor. Perhaps it was raining in England, perhaps it was raining on Lizzie, perhaps, even, the age-old habit of guilt about Lizzie—not telling her everything, wanting some little freedom from her, loving her and her family but not needing them as once she had done—had stirred in Frances's subconscious as she slept, like a prehistoric monster shifting in the mud of a fathomless lake, and manifested itself as a dream. Frances gave herself a shake, and stretched her arms until they felt ten feet long, and then padded over to the window, and opened the curtains.

The windows were already open, as they had been all night. Down in the green and flowery garden, Juan was watering the pots and the fat waiter—there was a fat one and a thin one—was putting yellow cushions on the white iron chairs and brushing fallen leaves and petals off the white iron tables. On one of the tiny patches of grass, Juan's dog, a cheerful small mongrel with an absurdly curly tail, sat and scratched. Her clients would like that dog, Frances thought, just as they would like the spilling stone jars of pelargoniums and the plumbago that wound gracefully round the wrought-iron balustrades. All that would be missing, for them, would be deckchairs, in which to read fat novels and fatter biographies and three-day-old copies of the *Daily Telegraph*, bought in Málaga. She must tell Juan about the deckchairs; she would tell him that they were an English eccentricity, as necessary to a certain type of English person as marmalade for breakfast.

Below the garden, the falling roofs of the village were pale apricot in the early sun. The washing was, of course, already out, and so were a few cats, and there was that particular sound of Spanish sweeping, bristles on stones, and the echoing sound, too, of hoofs in narrow alleys, mules and men going out into the fields for the day. The mules lived, Frances had noticed, in stables that were such integral parts of the houses of Mojas that they were simply like downstairs rooms, and sometimes the family bicycles and motor bikes lived there too in a companionable way. It seemed such a natural life, so uncontrived, so properly concerned with the business of actual living, so rooted in these rolling, reddish hills and mountains with their olive groves and almond orchards and sudden, neat green vegetable plots, as brilliant as billiard tables. But it was poor, too, Luis had said, poor and harsh still, and, when Juan had advertised for waiters, thirty-seven boys from local villages had come to Mojas, seeking one of the only two positions on offer.

"The sun is a deceiver," Luis said. "It makes people from the north think that life must be easy. You would be amazed how monotonous is the diet of the people of this village."

It was a sobering thought. So, too, was the memory of the dream with Lizzie in it, running and crying. Frances went back to her rumpled bed, sat on the edge of it, picked up the bedside telephone and asked for an outside line.

"Frances! Oh Frances, how lovely!"

"I dreamed about you," Frances said. "And it was a worrying dream and so I'm ringing. Are you all right?"

"Fine," Lizzie said.

"Lizzie? Really?"

"Yes," Lizzie said. "We had to do the end-of-year accounts and you know how they are—"

"Rob said at Christmas that they mightn't be very good."

"They aren't."

"Seriously not good?"

There was a small, crackling pause.

"Lizzie?"

"I think I'll have to get a job," Lizzie said. "To help pay the mortgage. It isn't a big deal. I don't want to waste expensive telephone time—"

"A *job*? But you've got a job, in the Gallery—"

"An outside job. Rob and Jenny can manage the Gallery between them. Rob asked me if I'd like to get a job or I'd like him to, and I chose me and now I feel rather awful, as if I'm taking the easy option."

"When did this happen?"

"Yesterday, I suppose. I went to see Juliet. We could ask Dad for a loan but Rob doesn't want to, and I don't really."

"Can I help?"

"Frances, you haven't got any money—"

"I've got some, enough to help a little—"

"No. You're sweet, but no. We mustn't get this out of proportion, heaps of people are in the same boat. We just have to change our lives a bit and that's the hard part because we didn't think we'd ever have to. Don't let's talk about it any more, it's so depressing and it's pouring with rain here. Are you having a lovely time?"

"I'm afraid I am—"

"Why are you afraid?"

"Because I feel a pig, when you aren't having a lovely time at all."

"Frances," Lizzie said sternly, "I really am not as small-minded as that. What's it like?"

"Sunny," Frances said. "Simple, charming and quite fierce too. Spain seems to be fierce."

"Even your Mr. Whatsit Moreno?"

"No," Frances said. "He isn't fierce. He's—"

"What?"

"Wonderful," Frances said.

"Frances—"

"I'm very happy, you know."

"Frances, what's *happening*?"

"Nothing's happening," Frances said. "Except he takes me to look at things and we talk a lot, and I make arrangements with the manager here, business arrangements."

"Frances!" Lizzie called from wet England. "Frances, are you falling for him?"

"Yes," Frances said. "And for Spain and this village and—"

"And what?"

"For myself. I really like myself here."

"You sound quite unhinged!" Lizzie cried.

"Well, I'm not. I'm just relaxed and happy."

"*Please* be careful!"

"Lizzie, I'm thirty-eight, you know."

"I do know. I'm sorry. Is it—*very* sunny?"

"Yes."

"I'm so pleased for you, really I am—"

"I'll be home at the weekend, or soon after. Then we'll talk properly. I know thinking about you isn't much help—"

"It is. I went to see Juliet because I couldn't see you."

"But you've got Rob to talk to—"

There was another tiny pause.

"Yes," Lizzie said. "Ring me when you get back. Don't worry about us, we're fine really. Bless you for ringing, it's a big help, truly. Bye, Frances."

Frances heard the tiny click as the telephone receiver went down in Langworth. She should have asked Lizzie what kind of job she was thinking of, she should have asked after Rob, who was so prone to anxiety and would be, at the moment, so much in need of Lizzie to reassure him. She should— Stop this, Frances said sternly to herself, stop this at once. Lizzie's misfortunes are not your fault, you stupid, overemotional, guilt-ridden . . .

There was a knock at the door. Frances pulled up a slipped nightgown strap.

"Yes?"

"Good morning," Luis said from the other side of the door. "I saw your curtains were open. Are you going to eat breakfast?"

"You bet."

"May we eat it together?"

"Of course."

"Then I will go down," he said, "and wait for you."

"I'll be ten minutes."

"This is Spain," Luis said. "Do I have to remind you all the time? Ten minutes, one hour—"

She was laughing. She tipped herself sideways into the heap of sheets and laughed and laughed.

"Don't laugh with yourself," Luis said. "It is so selfish." But his voice sounded as if he were laughing too. Then she heard him going down the staircase outside into the little courtyard below and she thought she heard him singing.

"I want to take you to Mirasol," Luis said. "The road will be very rough, over the hills—"

"Why don't we walk?"

"Walk? Frances, it is perhaps ten kilometres!"

"So? Can't you walk that far? Think how good it would be for those three extra kilos."

He patted his stomach.

"I am fond of them now—"

"Let's compromise. We'll take the car part of the way, and walk the rest."

"This is a terrible prospect," Luis said.

"You are just lazy."

"In my youth, I play beautiful tennis, really beautiful—"

"That doesn't interest me at all. I want to walk in these hills and I want you to come with me. After all, I must be able to tell my clients that the walking is good, from first-hand experience. Why are we going to Mirasol, anyway?"

"There is something to show you."

"A church? A castle?"

"No," Luis said. "Something simple and sad. Go and get your hat."

When she came downstairs again with her hat in her hand, Luis and Juan were standing in the tiny white courtyard off the bar, where weeping figs grew and where hotel guests drank glasses of iced sherry before dinner.

"We have water problems, Juan says. They are the curse of this region. Two of the roof tanks didn't fill in the night." He turned and spoke rapidly to Juan. "Frances, we may have to go to Motril later, to shout at the authorities, but we will do that after Mirasol."

"Do you want to do that first, the water, I mean?"

"No," Luis said. He smiled at Juan. "Juan is the manager here, the water is his problem. It is merely mine to pay for it. Come."

Out in the little square, Luis's car, blond with dust, waited under an acacia tree. It was too early for the old men, so the square was empty apart from a hen in one corner, investigating the contents of a litter bin through the wire mesh, and a spindly cat in another, watching the hen with a show of elaborate indifference. The bar was shuttered, so was the post office, a decayed Baroque building with great lumps of plaster moulding missing from its façade, and only the single shop gave faint signs of life, the plastic strips that screened its open doorway half-heartedly against flies twitching in the slight breeze.

Luis drove out of the village to the north-east, first through the maze-like lanes, no wider than passages in a house, with their glimpses of courtyards and flowers and dark workshops and darker interiors, and then through a few more-open streets, where businessmen from Motril had built themselves raw and ugly modern villas behind fearsome fortified walls and grilles. In front of some lay great holes which might one day become swimming pools, and beside all of them were double garages. It was, Frances thought, almost a Spanish Langworth, with a dangerous philistine fringe of new building threatening the timeless old heart. Beyond the new villas, the village cemetery lay like a little township of its own, secure behind white walls topped with apricot-coloured tiles, and guarded by an imposing chapel and a sentinel host of cypress trees.

"When the last mayor of Mojas was buried here," Luis said, "every single person in the village came out to his funeral. He lived in the house that is now the *posada* and he ruled the village like a tyrant. The house had no sanitation and every morning, four men would carry him out, in his wooden chair, to the fields, and when he had finished, they carried him back again. They feared him and they hated him, and when he died, the village mourned for him, every man and woman and child. They raised a subscription for a statue of him to be put in the village plaza, but the priest would not allow it because he said that the man had been a communist."

"What happened to the money?"

"It vanished," Luis said.

"Do you think the priest took it?"

"Frances," Luis said, smiling. "That is a most improper suggestion."

A track branched off from the road beyond the cemetery, a track of soft, brick-coloured dust, winding among the darker, still-brickish stretches of an almond orchard. It ran along the side of a shallow hill, dipped into a small, domesticated valley where an old man and a young man were weeding a meticulous potato patch beside a ruined house, and then rose again through a miniature gorge, walled in red-and-ochre cliffs, to a kind of summit, a knoll tufted with wiry herbs. Beyond the summit lay a spectacular view, a series of sweeping slopes and valleys, threaded with the pale lines of tracks that linked the scattered buildings across the landscape like beads on a necklace. There were no visible roads, no pylons, no plastic-roofed greenhouse developments, no signs that this vast old tract of territory was inhabited by anything other than simple man and beast. In the distance, perhaps three miles away, hanging on a hillside above a wooded gorge, was a significant white village, the bell tower of its church sharp against the rising slope behind it. Luis stopped the car.

"Mirasol," he said.

"Can we walk now?"

"Yes," he said. "We can walk."

The air outside the car smelled of thyme. It was very quiet, except for the soft little wind and for the sound that Frances had come to love, of a distant herd of goats, all bells and bleating. She put on her hat, the streamers of the scarf fluttering in the wind behind her. Luis watched her.

"Now," he said, "for some of your English walking."

They walked mostly in silence. The track was soft underfoot, taking them gently down into the valley among bright clumps of broom and thorn bushes tangled up with wild sweet peas, sharp mauve-pink among the prickles. Every so often, they passed a little vegetable patch drinking greedily from a sudden spring, lines of tomatoes and beans neatly braced against criss-cross lattices of bamboo, fronds of carrot tops in orderly rows, clumps of potato and courgette. Some of them had a solitary man working in them, his mule tethered beneath a tree, but most of them were empty, as bright and symmetrical as samplers. Once, Frances's hat was blown off by a capricious gust, and Luis rescued it from a disagreeable tree laden with small leathery leaves and bunches of long leathery pods, and once Luis decreed a rest on a nearby rock, and Frances sat on the turf beside him and told him about Barbara running away to North Africa to be a hippie, which had seemed—and still did seem, in retrospect—like a bid for freedom, but, if so, it was a bid that had come to nothing.

"It was as if she took the cork out of a bottle when she went away, and then she just put the cork back in when she came home."

Luis wanted to know if Frances looked like her mother.

"Not very. She is dark and quite severe-looking. My father is fair. At least, he was; now he is just grey."

"I am going grey," Luis said.

"Are you? Do you mind?"

"Yes," he said, smiling. "Of course I do."

The climb up to Mirasol was steeper than it looked. The track became stonier, and darkened by woodland, climbing sharply up the rocky slope in twists and turns. Luis began to complain, but Frances simply climbed ahead of him, in and out of the sun and shadow, and when she reached the top and the junction with the roughly surfaced road, sat on a boulder and waited for him.

"That was terrible," he said, emerging, panting.

"It would have been terrible for the car too," Frances

said. "Think of the suspension." She waited for him to get his breath. "Tell me about this village."

She looked along the road. The first few houses of Mirasol clung to the steep slopes either side of it, half-buried or perilously balanced, whitewashed, shuttered, secret.

"It was Republican," Luis said, "in the Civil War."

"Poor place," Frances said. "It was a fearful war."

They began to walk along the road towards the village. It was a lovely road, dipping up and down along the hillside so that the old houses with their balconies and their shutters and their pierced wooden screens so redolent of their Moorish past were scattered up and down the slopes, only accessible by whitewashed steps and paths as narrow and vertical as drainpipes. The inhabitants of Mirasol were plainly green-fingered, because vines and tangles of climbing nasturtium and bougainvillaea swarmed over walls and roofs and every step and terrace had its pot of flowers.

"But there are no people," Frances said, amazed.

"No. You never see them."

Frances looked up. The sun hung there, a polished coin in the calm sky. She looked along the swerving street. Everything was picturesque and charming, and also, mysteriously, sinister.

"Why does it feel like this? Why does it feel so sombre?"

"Come," Luis said. He took her hand.

"Where are we going? Why have you brought me?"

He turned off the road and began to lead her up a steep flight of steps beside, and then behind, the church. The walls either side of the steps were white and blank and the space between them was so narrow that Luis had to go ahead, pulling Frances behind him like a child. They went up and up, past shut gates and shut doors, past openings to other alleys, past a tiny wired-in courtyard where a yellow-eyed German shepherd dog watched them go by in silent resignation, and then they came out onto a kind of platform at the top, a rough space above the village and below a cliff of brownish rock. They were both gasping for breath.

"Look," Luis said, panting and pointing. Frances turned.

Below them, the roofs and flowers of Mirasol cascaded down into the dark gorge below with dizzying steepness.

"Did you bring me up here for this? For another view?"

"No," Luis said.

"What then?"

"I have something to show you."

He came beside her and took her elbow in his warm hand.

"Over here."

They walked across the stony platform. It hugged the curve of the hill, turning eastwards as the cliff turned.

"There," Luis said, pointing again with his free hand.

Frances looked. Along the cliff wall, at heights varying from four feet to six feet from the ground, were painted crosses, crude, roughly painted crosses, dull-red against the rock, dozens of them, crowded and clustered together, all different sizes.

"What are they?"

"Memorials," Luis said. "This village was Republican. Franco's Nationalist troops raided the village, and brought every man and boy up here, and shot them, against this wall. The village has never recovered."

Frances took her arm out of his grasp and walked to the edge of the platform.

"Are you shocked?" he said.

"Of course I am," she cried furiously. "Shocked and angry. Who wouldn't be?"

Luis came close to her again.

"In the thirties, when my father was a young man, Spain was a symbol, for the whole world, of divided beliefs. You were right to call our Civil War fearful, of course it was, it was about hope and despair. You English now have no good word to say for Franco, to you he is a fascist monster. To me he was indeed a despot, and I believe that tyranny is a second-rate ideology, but he was not a monster. After the fall of France, Frances, in the last World War, when I was a child and you were not yet born, he refused to ally himself with Hitler. He saved Spain from the Nazis and he would not let them close the Mediterranean, so the rest of Europe owes something to him for that at least. Of course, this is a terrible place, but it is not evil in its terror, it is tragic."

Frances looked at him.

"Why are you telling me all this? Why did you bring me here and lecture me like this?"

He took both her hands. He leaned towards her and his eyes shone as they had shone at her across the café table in Granada.

"Because you must understand, Frances, about Spain, about the Spanish. I have shown you charming things, pretty things, ancient things, curious things. You have seen my hotel, and its garden, you have seen a little of Granada, you have smiled at some of the people who work for me, but that is not enough. It isn't enough to see the sunshine, it isn't even enough to see the magnificence, you have to see too how melancholy Spain is, how stubborn, and proud and full of violent conflicts of opinion. You have to *understand*."

His vehemence vibrated through his hands to hers. She said, almost in a whisper, "Why do I have to understand?"

"Because," he said, "you must know what you are taking on if we are to become lovers."

"Luis—"

"It is not easy, you see, between races. I know something of yours. I want to be sure, for both our sakes, that you understand a little of mine."

For a second, everything about her seemed to fracture, the sky, the dreadful cliff, the swooping valley, Luis's face. Then he let go of her hands and pulled her into his arms, holding her hard against him. Her hat slipped from her head and went skittering away across the platform like a kite.

"Frances, *amor*—"

"Shh," she said. She put up her face to be kissed, tilting just a little because she was very nearly as tall as he was. He kissed her. She flung her arms around him, pushing herself against him, longing for him.

"I can't believe this, I can't believe—"

He kissed her again and then he flung his head back, laughing, his teeth shining in the sun.

"What is it?" she cried indignantly. "What's so funny?"

"Oh!" he said, kissing her again. "Oh, you English! Can't you even tell the difference between a joke and joy?"

In the night, most surprisingly, it rained. Frances lay in Luis's arms and listened to it falling on the oval-grey leaves of the eucalyptus trees and the fringed green ones of the acacias, and visualised the grateful grass and flowers and the shining wet stones of the terraces. She lay very still, conscious of his sleeping, conscious of her quite unspeakable happiness and sense of deliverance, conscious, with a kind of joyful physical understanding, of this warm damp night in southern Spain.

They had made love twice. Or, to be more accurate, Luis had made love to Frances and then she and he had made love together. The first time he had told her not to talk.

"I want you just to feel things, sense things. I don't want you to think, you think too much, Frances. It wasn't an intellectual decision that we fell in love, was it? Of course not. Nor will the making love, it will be a matter of the instincts, the imagination. So, in your own words, shut up."

Afterwards she had said, "Oh but Luis, you are married!"

"Frances, I am not divorced. I haven't made love with José's mother for fifteen years, since I was thirty-three."

But she couldn't really care. It wasn't just the glory of the moment that was so wonderful, it was the feeling—a feeling she could never remember having had before—that this was just the beginning, that Luis was going to show her things, help her to see things about herself that she had never seen.

"We are a stupid age," Luis had said at dinner (oh, such a dinner, when she knew, with almost unbearable excitement, what lay ahead), "we are so mechanistic, so scientific, that we don't pay attention to our instincts and we are so *wrong*. Look at you."

"Me?"

"Yes, you. Look at you. Full of lovely things you were never trained to see. Too much hidden in you."

"Do you mean inhibition?"

"Only partly. I mean more this word I love now, this 'sensible.' I mean knowing your feelings, enjoying them. You are not eating."

"I don't seem—"

"Are you afraid?"

"Only," she said, looking at him with her straight gaze, "that you will find me dull."

"Dull?"

"Yes," she said. "I haven't had a very exciting life, sexually speaking, so of course I naturally assume I may be rather dull."

"You are mad," he said, "quite mad. What do you think I make love with? My eyes only? Like some boy?"

She began to giggle.

"No, of course not, not just eyes—"

"This is very indecent talk, Señorita."

"I can't help it. I'm disgustingly happy. I'm not responsible for anything I do or say."

He regarded her. She was wearing a narrow black dress—not narrow enough but better than almost everything else she possessed—and a long string of amber and silver beads, and silver earrings.

"I will never tire of looking at you," he said. "Your face is—is full of your personality. You are—" He stopped, searching for exactly the right phrase and then he said urgently, "You are so honest, Frances. I never knew a woman so honest. Even when you hide things, you never hide them to deceive me."

She looked down. Heavens, if this was love, no wonder people did such daft things for it, wrecking their domestic lives, throwing up their career prospects, starting wars.

"Do the staff here all know?"

"Of course they do. I expect they have taken bets in the kitchen—"

"Luis, have you ever—?"

"Brought a woman here before? Never. It is my refuge. Always, I confine women to Sevilla, between the hours of eight in the evening and two in the morning. You are a great nuisance. You have broken all my rules."

"And you mine. No married men, no using business for pleasure—"

"No foreigners?"

"Certainly no foreigners."

"Frances."

His feet trapped one of hers under the table.

"Frances, I am afraid I cannot wait one minute longer."

Then this. This room, and this dark carved bed and the white sheets and the whispering curtains and the release and the love, and now the rain on the warm dark earth filling the air with scents. Frances turned a little, moved Luis's lower arm so that she shouldn't crush it, arranged his other one to hold her across her side and breast, and slept.

PART
THREE

SEPTEMBER

ELEVEN

On the first day of her new job, Lizzie felt quite sick with apprehension. It had taken so long to find the job at all, and the finding of it had been a discouraging experience, with the dawning realisation that she was, in professional terms, only fit for the kind of job that would pay her so poorly as to make little sense of the time and energy it would take. It was, in the end, and yet again, Juliet who had come to the rescue with a suggestion. Try schools, she said, try all the private schools in the area.

"To teach art?"

"You could try that. But art isn't the only thing you know about, is it? You can bookkeep after all, you can type, you can run things, you understand these disagreeable modern machines."

Lizzie had been horrified. The image of the school secretary at her grammar school rose up before her, a small, terminally repressed woman in spectacles and grey cardigan and fog-coloured stockings. She never smiled and she treated the headmistress like a deity. She had given the impression of hating girls, of hating all their energy and cleverness and rampant promise.

"Juliet, I couldn't—"

"Sir Thomas Beecham once said," Juliet remarked, "that one ought to try everything in life just once except incest and morris dancing. Being a school secretary seems to me rather an easier option than either."

Then Barbara had found the school.

"Of course, it's hopelessly old-fashioned, still bringing up girls to expect to live lives like their mothers, but what else can you expect from a provincial community? I shouldn't think their fathers read anything except newspapers. It isn't even very well run. Your grandfather would have been appalled."

Barbara had been oddly sympathetic to their dilemma, oddly because sympathy wasn't something that came naturally to her. William had wanted to lend them money, at once, but Barbara, better understanding the matter of Rob's pride, dissuaded him.

"Put it into an account for the children if you want to, but don't bail them out. Robert will only resent you for being able to, and I shouldn't blame him. After all, you've hardly worked for your capital, have you?"

And he has, William thought sadly, Robert has worked for nearly twenty years to build up something that he may now lose. I've just pottered along, and the nice little lump my parents left me has pottered along behind me, like a kind and reassuring nanny. I've never been really worried about money in my life, and although you could fairly say I haven't spent much either, it's all been quite easy, too easy. I should feel so much better to give some to Rob and Lizzie—after all, it'll be half theirs in the end anyway—but I do see that my feeling better isn't the point.

"Robert and Lizzie are very young," Juliet pointed out. "Not yet forty. There's plenty of time for a whole new life, even two."

Lizzie's whole new life was now going to encompass Westondale. Westondale was the kind of school she and Frances used to despise when they were at school themselves, for its decorous social gentility and a narrow, undemanding curriculum, whose devisers would never think of teaching Greek to girls, and that was heavily inclined towards the domestic sciences. It was amazing, Lizzie thought, that such a school should still be alive in this age of conscious equality of opportunity, but, shabby though it was, and abidingly unadventurous, it was still there and so were over two hundred girls dressed in navy-blue and white, from eleven to GCSE-level. If it had been more modern, Rob had rightly said, if it had moved with the times any better, it would never have considered employing Lizzie, whose experience, in a lot of employers' eyes, would never have compensated for her lack of proper qualifications.

Westondale was housed in a pair of large, early-Victorian dwellings on the southern slopes of the hills running down from Langworth to Bath. The houses stood in their two original gardens, linked together by a concrete-and-glass corridor erected in the fifties, and surrounded by a hotchpotch of car-parking spaces (staff, parents, deliveries), tennis courts, hockey pitches and shabby patches of shrubbery in which the younger ones loitered in break and the more rebellious smoked. The no-smoking rule, so easy to avoid for day-school girls, was only any fun to break in school hours and in uniform. At the back of the houses various additional prefabricated classrooms—an art room, a biology lab, rooms nominally dedicated to geography and music— stood about on breeze-block stilts, and against the windowless wall of each leaned long, leaking bicycle sheds for those pupils who cycled up laboriously to school from the city. The whole place gave the impression of having grown at random, rather than ever having had the discipline of a plan, and was badly in need of a coat of paint. The parents told each other staunchly that it was such a happy school; the girls themselves simply knew that it was something boring to be got through before things, with any luck, became more interesting.

Lizzie had been appointed assistant school secretary, working under the present secretary, Mrs. Mason, until the latter retired at half-term on the very dot of her sixtieth birthday. She was retiring, she said, to devote herself to her local branch of the Townswomen's Guild, of which she aspired to be chairman.

"Or should we say chairperson, these days!"

Lizzie nodded, speechless. It seemed to her that this part-term with Mrs. Mason in her purple jumper and flashing spectacles might seem a very long part-term indeed.

"As you will find out," Mrs. Mason said, darting plump hands over drawers and drawers of index cards, "I have my own little ways, my own little methods. My husband always says to me, 'Your mind may not work like anyone else's, Freda, but at least it works!'" She gave a peal of merry laughter.

"Yes," Lizzie said.

She looked round the office. It had, for all its lines of steel cabinets and files, the air of a church bazaar, a small space crammed to bursting with knick-knacks and pointless knitted things.

"I never throw anything away, you'll find," Mrs. Mason said. "And I like to bring a personal touch to the work-place. My grandson made that"—she indicated a red-and-yellow papier-mâché lump that might have been a dragon or perhaps a pineapple or maybe just a lump—"and the little ones from the first form made me that pop-up cal-endar for Christmas. So creative!"

"Yes," Lizzie said.

She told Robert about Mrs. Mason, hoping to make him laugh, but he was too full of anguish at her having to take such a job to feel anything other than anxiety.

"Oh Lizzie. Can you stand her?"

"Of course I can. It's only about seven weeks and then I can have a bonfire of all her macramé plant-holders."

She spoke the truth. It wasn't Mrs. Mason she was going to mind; Mrs. Mason was just a temporary joke, if not a very good one. What Lizzie minded was that the money she would be earning would not be able to be spent con-structively on putting food in their mouths, or clothes on their backs, but merely, and aridly, in paying interest to the bank. What was worse was that the amount she earned probably wouldn't even be enough to cover that interest. It felt, quite literally, like pouring water into sand and it filled her with a misery that she couldn't possibly confide to Rob, because he, for some obscure reason, seemed to feel that he was to blame for their indebtedness, as if he could—and should—have foreseen that the boom times would end, quite suddenly, and that all their hopes and plans would be plunged into frightening darkness.

"It's *our* business," Lizzie kept saying, "and *our* house. I've been as involved as you all along, we've never taken a unilateral financial decision in our lives. If anything, I wanted the Grange more than you did."

He was easier to comfort than she was herself. She found she couldn't comfort herself, and for reasons of temperament and this tendency to blame himself, she couldn't ask him for comfort. And all this bleakness of feeling, this dread at the prospect of a long struggle in which something important would inevitably be lost, was made infinitely worse by the fact that, for the first time in her life, Lizzie couldn't talk to Frances.

At least, Lizzie told herself, driving in to her first morning at Westondale in the second-hand car they had bought for this purpose for seven hundred pounds, and in which Lizzie had no confidence, I can talk to her, but there isn't any point because she isn't listening. She hadn't listened for four months, ever since that second trip to Spain, from which she had returned so glowing and so preoccupied. Lizzie had never seen Frances like this before, even when in the grip of what looked like previous infatuations. Lizzie was sure this latest episode was an infatuation.

"Frances, you've only been with him a week."

"I seem to remember that you and Rob—"

"But we were young, we were students and impetuous. It was quite different. I'm so worried you'll be hurt."

Then Frances had turned on her. She turned on her, not with anger, but with a kind of quiet power.

"I've had enough of this, Lizzie. I've had enough of your lifelong assumption that I am somehow an inadequate human being, that I'm not fit to manage a relationship of any seriousness, that I'm just standing about waiting for other people, notably you, to wind me up like some clockwork toy and send me trotting off in the direction of your choice. I am in love, Lizzie, I am in love, properly, for the first time in my whole life, and nobody will tell me how I should conduct this love, or what mistakes I am liable to make. I haven't just found a wonderful companion, you see, I haven't just found an interesting and sympathetic other mind, I have found a *lover*." Lizzie had been deeply shaken by this, not least because the evidence of Frances having found a thoroughgoing lover was plain for all to see. You only had to look at Frances, at her skin and hair and eyes, not to mention an indefinable but unmistakable new coherence in her clothes, to know she had a lover. You only had to listen to her, indeed, with your eyes shut, and hear the shining confidence in her voice, to know it.

Of course, Lizzie wanted to meet him, was avid to know every crumb of information about him, but Frances wouldn't allow it.

"Not yet. This is our private time. We are trying to see each other most weekends, but it isn't easy, and there's too little time. You'll have to wait."

"Of course, I told you so," Barbara informed William over breakfast. It was National Prune Week and she had flung herself into it; a huge bowl of them lay glistening in front of William like a threat. "Didn't I? I said, when she cancelled Christmas, that there was a man in it somewhere."

William took a single prune and hid it under his muesli.

"There wasn't, then."

"Nonsense! A Spaniard! Why choose a Spaniard?"

"We don't choose love," William said. "It chooses us. Not always conveniently, I grant you, but then convenience is not a prime quality of passion."

"Passion!" snorted Barbara. She looked at his cereal bowl. "Where are your prunes?"

None of them had seen Frances, to speak of, since May. Lizzie had had one snatched visit to London, during the course of which Frances had spoken so sternly, but Frances hadn't been to Langworth once and, instead of telephoning every other day, as she used to, only rang once a week, or even fortnight.

"I suppose she just rings Spain—"

"Of course she does!" Robert said. "What else do you expect? Why aren't you glad for her?"

"I am."

"You do nothing but point out the pitfalls."

"Rob, there are so many. He's ten years older, he's married, he's Catholic, he's a foreigner. There are such agonies ahead—"

"Perhaps she thinks they are all worth it for the present. Anyway, why shouldn't she be able to cope? Why are you the one with a monopoly on coping?"

"I'm not, I just always feel with Frances—"

"Lizzie," Robert shouted, interrupting. "Will you please stop going on about Frances and just focus on *us*? We're your priority, not her. I'm your husband, remember, your companion, *your* lover when we're not too bloody tired—"

The trouble is, Lizzie thought, gripping the wheel of this unfamiliar and clattering car that felt as if it might, at any moment, simply disintegrate into a series of nuts and bolts and cogs and wheels spinning over the road, the trouble is that I am jealous. I've been, I have to admit it, jealous of Frances on occasion in the past when she seemed so free and I felt so tied, but I'm not jealous of her now—I simply can't summon up the energy even to imagine having a love affair—but I'm jealous of *him*. I don't know him and I really resent him having all Frances's attention and confidence. Particularly now. After all, I've hardly asked for Frances's help before, I've never needed it, and I'm not exactly asking now, but I could do with her. In this horrible situation when I'm so scared we may just lose everything we've worked for, I really could do with her. It isn't much to ask, is it, for your twin's support in a dark hour? It isn't greedy, is it? Isn't it just natural to turn by instinct to your other self, your other half? Of course I want her to be happy, I always have, but what she's doing is so dangerous, far too dangerous for happiness. Oh dear, thought Lizzie,

swerving to avoid a sudden cyclist emerging from a turning, perhaps I am just an awful managing cow, perhaps I
am what Rob says I am and Frances—oh *damn*, I'm going
to cry, can't cry, mustn't, can't arrive *chez* Freda Mason on
my first morning with a nose like a red balloon.

The small staff car park at Westondale was already full
when Lizzie arrived. She drove round to the even smaller
one allotted to the collecting parents of juniors—ingeniously designed for the maximum need for quarrelsome
reversing—and parked there. A gardener emerged from a
bush and said staff couldn't park there.

"I'm not staff," Lizzie said, locking the driver's door.
"I'm administration."

"Mrs. Drysdale won't have it."

Lizzie ignored him. Mrs. Drysdale was the headmistress,
a big, handsome woman who dressed in scarlet and tur-
quoise and orange as if to indicate that, whatever she had,
she was going to flaunt it, tremendous bosom included. She
had interviewed Lizzie in a flash, with the fluent, patronising, know-all manner of a professional agony aunt, saying
that she relied utterly on Mrs. Mason's judgement and that
she so approved of Lizzie's being a mother and why didn't
she send her own daughter to Westondale? Because we
can't afford the fees and also because Langworth Comprehensive is pretty good, Lizzie had said, whereupon Mrs.
Drysdale's eye had hardened and she had flourished Lizzie
briskly out of her office with a clash of bracelets and a
wealth of false smiles. Lizzie had not been left with the
impression that Mrs. Drysdale was the sort of headmistress
to worry about car parks; the grand gesture, the broad
sweep, was more in her line.

"I shall have to report you!" the gardener shouted.

Lizzie hurried away from him across the stretch of tired,
late-summer grass between the car park and the front door.
She tried very hard not to remember, as she climbed the
steps to the door, that this was the first day she had ever
spent in someone else's employ. Needs must, she told herself sternly, I chose this, I have to do it.

Freda Mason had arranged a trembling card table for

her to use as a desk in the corner of the office, and ostentatiously placed upon it a welcoming bunch of dahlias.
Lizzie hated dahlias.

"How kind," she said.

"My husband's pride and joy. These are his speciality,
these pompoms. This one is Pride of Berlin, and the sweet
little orange one is New Baby. Personally—"

The door of the office opened and a girl came in. She
had frizzy dark hair and a hunted expression.

"Georgina, you know you should knock."

"I did," the girl said. "I came to ask if I could ring my
mother because I forgot my violin."

Mrs. Mason shook her head. She looked at Lizzie.

"The day Georgina doesn't forget something will be a
day to remember."

Georgina looked furious. She trudged across to the nearest telephone and wearily dialled a number. She was Harriet's age, Lizzie guessed, and plainly, from her resentful
stoop, hated the way she looked, from her untamed hair to
her polelike legs.

"We add these calls to the individual bills," Mrs. Mason
hissed at Lizzie. "Surname Fellows, address St. James's
Square. The bigger filing cabinet, top drawer."

Georgina thumped the telephone down.

"No one there."

"Oh dear," Lizzie said, anxious to help. "Couldn't I take
you home to get it?"

Mrs. Mason looked appalled.

"No," Georgina said.

"Georgina!"

"I mean, no thank you. I hadn't practised anyway."

"Then why—"

"I had to have tried," Georgina said desperately. "I've
got to tell Mr. Parsons I've tried."

She trudged back to the door again, and vanished. The
telephone rang. Mrs. Mason pounced on it.

"Westondale!"

She paused, flapping her free hand at Lizzie for something to write with.

"I'm afraid that, unless it's an emergency, Mrs. Drysdale only sees parents between three and four on Tuesdays and Thursdays. I will try and make an exception, Mr. Murray, but I'm afraid I can't promise anything. May I take your number?"

"Parents," she said, putting the telephone down. "You'll find they're the bane of your life. That father wanted to see Mrs. Drysdale, at nine in the morning, if you please!"

"Perhaps he's working, perhaps he has to take time off."

"If you ask me," Mrs. Mason said, "parents these days simply don't put their children first." She looked at Lizzie. "Now, before that menace takes it into its head to ring again, shall we just get started?"

It was a long and weary morning. Even Lizzie, who had been with Robert to evening classes to learn how to keep accounts and who had since developed her own eccentricities about doing them, was startled at the laborious confusion in which Mrs. Mason worked, with every item of information cross-referenced in longhand across a perfect wilderness of index cards. A small computer stood in one corner of the office, and when Lizzie enquired about it, she was told, with an air of distaste, that it had been a gift from the Parents' Association, which was very kind of them, Mrs. Mason was sure, but wholly unnecessary. Mrs. Mason had been trained as a librarian and there was nothing, therefore, about the organisation of information that she couldn't do in her sleep. Lizzie listened, answered the telephone to queries she couldn't answer, gazed uncomprehendingly at everything that she was shown, drank an unpleasant cup of instant coffee brought by a woman in a green overall, and tried not to think about the Gallery, or the leaking pipe in the bathroom at the Grange she had forgotten to telephone the plumber about, or the pain Alistair had suddenly said he had at breakfast.

"What sort of pain?"

"Here," he said, laying a hand briefly against his lower stomach, but not taking his eyes off the comic that had come with last Sunday's paper.

"How long have you had it?"

"Oh, weeks—"

"Weeks?"

"Well, a week anyway."

Robert had said, a little testily, that he would take him to evening surgery if the pain was still there after school.

"But I'll be back then. I can take him."

"You'll be tired," Robert said with a kind of finality.

"So will you."

"I know, but it's part of the deal that I do more for the kids. I said I would if you took this job."

"Perhaps Jenny might?" Lizzie suggested.

They looked at each other.

"We mustn't exploit her—"

"I know, but she said she'd be thankful to help. I think she's lonely."

"We have our lunch in the staff room," Mrs. Mason said now.

"Not with the girls?"

"Oh no."

"I'd like to have lunch with the girls."

"Just as you please. You'd better speak to Mrs. Drysdale."

"I can't possibly need to bother Mrs. Drysdale about anything so trivial—"

Mrs. Mason looked deeply offended.

"I wouldn't say that creating a precedent was trivial."

In the end, Lizzie ate her lunch—shepherd's pie and carrots followed by an apple pudding in which the apple seemed to be merely nominal, and custard—in the staff room. The talk was all of girls she didn't know, problems she had never heard of, past examination results she could feel no interest in. She was given water to drink out of a plastic tumbler and was otherwise largely ignored. At one point the person next to her, a middle-aged man dressed in brown corduroy who said he taught geography, gave her a brief lecture on the misguidedness of the new national curriculum and the iniquities of any educational system based on continual assessment, but apart from that, he behaved as if she wasn't there.

After lunch, she eluded Mrs. Mason, who seemed to wish

to have a confidential few minutes over another cup of
instant coffee, and went out into the grounds. Clumps of
girls stood about gossiping or lay ostentatiously in the de-
clining sun, their school shirts unbuttoned at the throat and
tucked into the tops of their bras for maximum exposure.
The ones with the best tans were being treated like stars.
Lizzie spoke to several of them and explained who she was,
but although they weren't at all rude in reply, they made
it plain that during break they never mixed with the enemy—alias adults—and that after a long summer holiday,
they had so much that was vital to report to one another.
Only a solitary girl with a clever face reading alone seemed
pleased to speak to Lizzie. She was reading *Anna Karenina*,
and she said it was absolutely transfixing her. After a few
minutes' desultory chatter, it was clearly kind to move away
and let her return hungrily to the torments of poor Anna.

Lizzie fought yawns all afternoon. The strangeness, the
mixture of boredom and frustration engendered by being
in a small room with Mrs. Mason from nine until three-
thirty—two days a week it would be until five-thirty—the
self-discipline required to remember what she was there
for, and simultaneously not to remember how little she was
being paid for it, were, when combined, more exhausting
than Lizzie would have believed possible. It was incredibly
difficult not to be in charge, to have to submit to Mrs.
Mason's pace of work and way of work. By three-thirty,
still burdened by her unaccustomed weight of lunch—how
eagerly everyone else had devoured theirs!—Lizzie tottered
out into the pale-gold afternoon and found the grounds
swarming with girls and an illiterate notice on her wind-
screen telling her that the place she had parked her car was
reserved strictly for parents.

She reached Langworth soon after four, and went straight
to the Gallery. It was quite quiet, with only a handful of
customers drifting about with the air of sightseers rather
than people bent upon purchase. In the café on the top
floor, a few women were eating flapjacks (made of organ-

ically grown oats) and drinking coffee, and at a corner table, Jenny Hardacre sat with Sam and Davy and her own
son, Toby, having, as prearranged, collected them all from
school.

"Oh Lizzie," Jenny said. "How was it?"

Davy and Toby went on drinking milk through straws,
but Sam, on sight of his mother, pretended to have been
shot, and sprawled backwards in his chair with crossed eyes
and lolling tongue.

"I'm afraid that it was absolutely awful. Where's Rob?"

"In the office. With the rep from the candle people."

Lizzie sat down. Sam immediately reared up in order to
flop down dead again across her.

"Don't," Lizzie said. He took no notice. "I won't tell
Rob how dreadful it was because the poor thing's worried
enough about me doing it as it is."

"I know. Perhaps it'll get better."

"It's the most frightful mixture of inefficiency and petty
bossiness. Get up, Sam. How's today been?"

Jenny pulled a little face.

"Sort of average. I thought I'd sold a quilt this morning,
but she turned out to be one of those I-must-go-away-and-
think-about-it types, who never come back."

"Pity. There's so much stock still—"

"Lizzie," Jenny said.

"Yes."

Jenny leaned forward, her face full of concern.

"I really do want to help, you know. I don't mind doing
extra things, I promise I don't. I mean, I don't need to be
paid for extra things and I'd so like to feel you would lean
on me a bit, about the children and so on, if you need to."

Lizzie said, "You are a dear and a salvation, but we are
terrified of exploiting you."

Toby took a full straw of milk out of his glass and blew
it out into a pool on the table. Delighted, Davy did the
same. Sam watched them enviously.

"Boys—"

In silence, Jenny took Toby's glass and straw away. Davy
watched Lizzie, waiting for her to do the same. She didn't.

"I shall not bring you to public places," Jenny said quietly to Toby, "if you behave like a baby."

He went pink. He made as if to slide from his chair.

"Sit still," Jenny said. He stopped sliding.

"How do you do it?" Lizzie said admiringly.

"By only having one. He's all I've got to think about. That's why I wish you'd lean on me more. It would be doing me a *kindness*, Lizzie. Thanks to what Mick left me, I'm not too badly off, I don't need to work for money, but I do need to work for myself."

Davy began to play in his milk pool with his finger, drawing the milk out into points and promontories. Without speaking, Jenny gently took his hand out of the milk, and then removed his glass and his straw. Sam rose from the dead across Lizzie's lap and gazed at her. Then he returned to his chair and gathered his own milk possessively to him, drinking it with diligence.

"Brilliant," Lizzie said.

"I don't want to interfere—"

"You couldn't. Do you know if Rob has done anything about Alistair?"

"No. Shall I—"

"Alistair had a pain at breakfast, and Rob said he would take him to evening surgery after school if it hadn't gone."

Jenny half-rose.

"Let me check. I'll get you a cup of tea, you look worn out, and then I'll check."

"I could kiss you."

"Yuk," Sam said.

"I can bite my big toe," Toby told Davy. Davy looked nonchalant.

"Here's Rob," Jenny said, standing up properly.

"Darling," Rob said, stooping to kiss Lizzie. "How was it?"

"Fine," she said. "I'm just a bit bushed because it was so new."

He picked Davy up and sat down in his chair instead, placing him on his knee.

"I bet it wasn't fine. I bet it was dreadful."

"She said it was awful," Sam said.

"Oh Lizzie—"

She put her hand on his.

"It wasn't. It wasn't that bad, I was just having a little whinge to Jenny."

Robert smiled up at her.

"She's been great. Actually, I didn't know you were back or I'd have come and got you to speak to Frances."

Lizzie stared.

"Frances?"

"Yes. She rang ten minutes ago, wanting you, not realising you'd started at Westondale."

"What did she say?"

"She asked if she could come down this Sunday. For lunch."

"Yes, of course—"

Robert bent his head and absent-mindedly kissed the top of Davy's.

"She wants to bring the famous Spanish lover. To meet us. I said fine, so I hope it is."

TWELVE

"I bet he'll be spoddy," Harriet said.

Alistair, who was reading a book of Davy's about an owl who was frightened of the dark, said, without raising his eyes from the page, "Why?"

"Well, he's foreign. Remember those French boys we had to have at school? They were utterly spoddy."

Alistair began to twiddle a piece of hair on top of his head.

"He's quite old, though. Mum said."

"Spoddiness isn't a matter of age," Harriet said scornfully, "it just happens. It's like all those awful poets maundering on about the first pathetic aconite of spring. They're as old as the hills and they're *all* spoddy."

Alistair chucked his book on the floor. The owl had been coaxed out into the night and found it could see better then than by day, so that the ending was both happy and feeble.

"Well, our aunt seems to be pretty gone on him—"

Harriet flushed. The notion of love stirred her up and created an unpleasant inward physical turmoil.

"It's going to be so *embarrassing*—"

"What is?"

"Watching them."

"Well, don't look then."

But Harriet was longing to look. Clearly Frances was having sex with this potentially spoddy Spaniard and this, because they were not married to each other (married sex was too disgusting and embarrassing even to contemplate), was both panic-making and completely fascinating. Harriet had several times, drifting elaborately in and out of her bedroom, seen Frances naked. She had looked a lot like Lizzie—whom Harriet did not, at present, ever wish to see naked—except that she was both thinner and smoother. Their bottoms were too big, Harriet considered, but their legs were all right and their b ... well, their bosoms were awful, *really* embarrassing, and as for their ... Harriet swallowed and twisted round on the window seat to gaze furiously out into the street. If she let herself think about a man touching Frances with no clothes on, she thought she might just blow up.

"Granny says that he is unquestionably well off," Alistair said, sprawling off his beanbag to pick up *A Child's Guide to Dinosaurs*, which lay just out of his reach.

"I wish we were," Harriet said gloomily.

Alistair opened the book. The first picture was of a diplodocus standing despondently in a lake, to which Sam had added spectacles and a bow for its tail in red crayon.

"It's the recession, I'm afraid. A business like ours was bound to suffer."

"Why do you have to talk like that?"

"Like what?"

"All la-di-da and pompous."

"I merely," Alistair said, settling back into the beanbag and preparing to read about the brain size of the diplodocus, "take trouble to use the English language with some care."

Harriet got off the window seat. She decided to change her black tights for her other black tights. She stepped over her brother.

"Even if," she said precisely, "this Spanish person turns out to be a spod, he can't possibly be as spoddy as you are."

Alistair sighed. The diplodocus had been an unenter-
prising herbivore and had, it seemed, richly deserved its
inevitable extinction. Harriet crossed the playroom, opened
the door and went out, slamming it behind her.

"I look forward to this," Luis said.

"You don't feel it's too official?"

"No," he said, "I think it's interesting. You know my
son and my sister, after all."

Frances glanced at him. He half-lay in the passenger seat
beside her, quite relaxed, looking peacefully out at the
green miles of Wiltshire and Avon flying past the car windows. She had offered to let him drive, but he had
shrugged and said no, he would like to be the passenger
this time.

"I don't think your sister was very enthusiastic about
me."

He made a little gesture.

"Give her time. She is used to my leading a bachelor life.
And I'm afraid there are a lot of Spanish people who still
believe that a man may have a different freedom to a
woman. She was also—" He paused and then said, "I think
she was surprised to find you were English, that I had
chosen a foreigner."

"I felt, I must say," Frances said, changing gear prepar-
atory to turning off the motorway, "that she disapproved."

"No," Luis said, "not that. She is a modern woman, a
professional, a doctor. You saw how she was. She is just a
little formal at the beginning."

More than a little formal, Frances thought. She remembered the dinner in the flat in Seville, the dark furniture,
the table laid with old-fashioned ceremony and precision,
Ana de Mena in her bold, dressed-up Spanish clothes, her
silent professorial husband with his long, gloomy face like
that of a saint approaching certain martyrdom. They had
no children, Luis said, they were a profoundly professional
couple. They had a little English and with that, and Frances's slowly budding Spanish, they struggled through the

evening. But there were no jokes. Even Luis didn't seem
inclined to crack jokes, and when they got down into the
street again, he actually took her in his arms and kissed
her, almost violently, and she was much startled because he
was never, ever, demonstrative to her in public places.

"Will she tell your mother about me? And José's
mother?"

"No," Luis said. "We have neither of us told my mother
anything we could avoid telling since we were children, and
Ana does not like José's mother."

Frances's heart gave a little lift.

"Why not?"

"Because she talks all the time of feminism but wishes
not to earn her own living."

"Ah," said Frances, thinking of Barbara. "Why haven't
they any children?"

"Ana believes she has given up the chance of having
children for her medical career. She believes she made the
choice."

Frances had wanted to say, And do you think she was
right? but refrained. What was the point, when she already
knew Luis's answer. "Ana was brought up by our mother,"
Luis would say. "She knows the dangers. She saw the dangers of motherhood at first hand."

The first time he had said this had caused their first
quarrel. Frances had been furious with the free, passionate
fury born of a rebellion of the instincts.

"You simply don't know what you are talking about!
You can't judge all the world's mothers just because you
didn't like your own, and you don't love José's mother any
more! You don't know anything about it."

"I know enough," he said.

"What do you mean?"

"I mean," he said, gripping her wrist, "I mean that
women change when they become mothers, they cease to
be themselves, to think with dispassion and freedom, and
they are taken over, possessed—"

"It's absolute nonsense! I never heard such utter and
complete rubbish! Take Lizzie—"

"Lizzie?"

"My sister, my twin. She has four children and she hasn't been perverted by them into something else!"

"I did not use the word 'perverted.'"

"You implied it—"

"I should like to meet Lizzie. I should like to see your twin."

Oh this love, Frances had thought then, wrestling with her anger, this love that made you adore someone with whom you could have such terrible differences as well as such agreements, such glorious unions. It wore you out sometimes, but mostly it exhilarated you, energised you, gave you the feeling that you were like a house, previously sad and shuttered, with all its windows and doors flung wide open to the sun.

"You may meet Lizzie," she said severely. "You may meet her as long as you remember how much I love her."

"I would not forget that."

It was easy to love everyone now, Frances thought, easy and natural. She felt full of love, as if she had suddenly come upon a limitless supply of it and could throw handfuls of it in the air over everybody, like confetti at a wedding. Four months now, and still an almost ecstatic incredulity swept over her. To have Luis here, by her side, in her car, here because she was here and that was his sole reason.

"Only three more miles," she said.

He turned his head and gave her profile a long, un-hingeing, intense stare. Then he put up his hand and touched her cheek.

"My Frances," he said.

Lizzie had expected Luis to be dark and on the heavy side, and not as tall as Robert, nor so romantic-looking, and definitely middle-aged, and all these expectations were comfortably fulfilled, but she had not expected him to be so attractive. As for Luis, he had known that Lizzie would look like Frances, which she did, very like Frances, but it had been very difficult to visualise beforehand the fact that she would look so like Frances but, at the same time, not *feel* like Frances at all. It would not be easy at all, Luis thought, smiling at her, to take this Lizzie to bed.

"I am afraid," Lizzie said, letting her hand lie in his, "that we have been shamefully curious to see you."

"And I you," Luis said. "I have never known twins before. Now then, who are all these children?"

Davy said clearly, "Sam says you've got a Rolex watch."

"Davy!"

"Sam is right," Luis said. "Which is Sam?"

"That one," Davy said, pointing at the sofa and a pile of cushions from which two legs protruded.

"Has this Sam no head?"

"I am afraid he has no idea how to behave," Alistair said. "I suppose my parents are to blame for that."

"And who are you?"

"Alistair."

"And so," Luis said, turning to Harriet who blushed to the roots of her hair, "you are Harriet."

Lizzie said, "You see, Frances is a very special aunt."

Luis laughed. "You don't need to tell me she's special—"

"I should have had a twin too," Alistair said. "But the other baby died. Very inconvenient, if you think about it, because if he'd lived I probably shouldn't have had to put up with Sam. I mean, Sam simply wouldn't exist. Rather a blissful thought, one way and another—"

"Enough," Robert said. He was trying not to look at Frances. She was wearing a red silk shirt—red! Frances, of all people, in red!—and black trousers and her hair was longer than usual and paler than usual and her bare feet, in fine black sandals, were brown. She had gold earrings on, like gypsy hoops, quite bold earrings. Robert had never seen her wear any earrings but pearl studs before, small, almost apologetic pearl studs. He glanced at Lizzie. Lizzie was watching Luis with a completely open interest and Luis, while holding out his wrist so that Davy could admire his watch, was watching Frances.

"Could you be a deep-sea diver with this watch?"

"Oh sure."

"And go in a spaceship?"

"No problem," Luis said. He held his free hand out to Frances. "*Amor*—"

The room suddenly filled with electricity. "*Amor*," he called her, Lizzie thought, "*amor*"! What a word, what a—what a display of intimacy, of passion, of . . . Lizzie swallowed. "*Amor*." If anyone had ever called her that, she thought, she would probably have fainted. Beside "*amor*," "darling" suddenly had about as much sex appeal as a brown paper bag. She cast a brief, enquiring glace at Frances. Frances was stooping over Davy, saying, "I shouldn't admire it too much if I were you, Davy. I think it's extremely vulgar." She both looked and sounded perfectly normal. Perhaps—perhaps Luis called her "*amor*" all the time? If he did, then what on earth was the atmosphere of their private life like; how could you possibly do ordinary things like brush your teeth or make toast with a man around looking at you like that, and calling you "*amor*"?

"Lizzie?"

"Yes," Lizzie said, blinking.

"I just said could I help with lunch. Rob is going to show Luis the Gallery."

"Yes," Lizzie said quickly. "Good idea. Do—"

"And I'll stay here," Frances said. She was looking directly at Lizzie.

"Harriet will help—"

Harriet, consumed with the need to be out of the room and away from whatever was the matter with the atmosphere in it, muttered something about her history project.

"I'd like to help you," Frances said. "I haven't seen you for months."

"My fault," Luis said. He didn't sound at all sorry. He bent to secure the heavy gold strap of his watch around Davy's wrist. "There you are. Now you look exactly like a European businessman."

Davy held his wrist lovingly with his free hand.

"Would you say," he said, "that Sam really shouldn't have a turn of this?"

• • •

Luis was impressed by the Gallery. He told Robert that it displayed a more international and varied taste than you would find in such a shop in provincial Spain. He particularly admired the design of the interior; he said design was very, very highly regarded in Spain, notably in Barcelona. He wanted to know about the qualifications necessary to run such a business in England.

"Qualifications?" Rob said. "There aren't any, not for this sort of shop. You just learn as you go along, experience comes with time."

Luis said that in Spain all the professions were profoundly localised in all the various regions and that you had to be colleged for everything, there was no professional path you could take if you hadn't been to its specific college. He then talked about labour problems in Spain, about the strength of the unions—either socialist or communist, he said—about the minimum wage, about the conservatism of rural Spain and the socialism of some of her cities.

"But I am boring you," Luis said. He stood in front of a display of tall iron candlesticks, imported from the Philippines, their tops spiked to hold huge, devout candles of ivory wax.

"Not at all. I know nothing at all about Spain, I'm appallingly ignorant—"

"No," Luis said. He was looking at the candles, but he was smiling. "No. You are very polite but really you are thinking about Frances—"

"Naturally—"

Luis put a hand on his arm.

"Just say yes to me. Of course you are thinking of Frances."

"We are a close family," Robert said. "We're all rather bound up together. Lizzie and Frances are very close, of course, being twins, and they've stayed close to their parents. I hardly see mine."

"Nor I," Luis said. "My mother is now very pious and

my father was a soldier, so he is very right-wing, perhaps too right-wing for modern Europe."

Robert moved away across the floor of the shop to where some lithographs hung, impressionistic lithographs he had commissioned from a local artist, of seasonal beasts and birds, which had, to his chagrin, failed to sell. Lizzie thought they were too strong and dark, too powerful.

"I mean, I know people *know* that foxes kill pheasants," she said. "I just think they don't want to see them doing it."

"Do you like these?" Robert asked Luis.

"Yes," he said. "These would sell well in Spain."

"They aren't selling here. Lizzie says they are too brooding." He glanced at Luis. "The thing that worries Lizzie is, you see, what will happen?"

"Always this worries women. I can't tell you what will happen because I don't know what the events of the future will be."

"But we don't want Frances to be left *without* a future."

Luis straightened up. He turned to Robert. He said, looking straight at him, "You should not underestimate Frances. She will never be without a future. I have never met anyone like her for strength."

"Frances?"

"Oh yes. She keeps it very quiet but it is there. My sister, Ana, is strong too but she wears her strength like her clothes, you can see it. Frances is the opposite."

"I have known Frances since she was twenty, only about a month or two less than I've known Lizzie. And I've never seen her so—so deep in any relationship."

"So," Luis said, putting his hands in his trouser pockets, "you are warning me not to hurt her? Or your wife has said to you to warn me?"

"Please don't be angry—"

"I am not in the least angry," Luis said, smiling. "I am just trying to understand you."

"It isn't interference," Rob said earnestly. "It's just a kind of protectiveness, about Frances—"

"Yes, yes. I too know about that, remember. I may be a

poor foreigner, but I am also a human being."

"The thing is," Rob said, feeling suddenly that he was in an absurd position, a sort of surrogate heavy-father position which he had never sought and which he was disliking very much, "that the northern and the southern forms of passion are so very different. Don't you think? Perhaps we can't, in the end, understand one another because our instincts are so different—" He stopped. He looked at Luis. He said, "God, I'm so sorry. I never meant to say all this, I'm not sure I even believe it. Will you forget the last few minutes entirely? Can I just say that I have never seen Frances look better or happier?"

Luis looked back. Their eyes met. What was he trying to say, this nice brother-in-law of Frances? Was he trying to wish them well while at the same time saying that he doubted that things could, in the end, possibly be well for them? Did he have, too, this curious English habit of reticence, the habit Frances had had when he had first known her, which made its possessor reluctant to articulate feelings, almost afraid to? It was like a terrible politeness, a kind of courtesy, so self-denying that in the end it was an affliction and imprisoned the sufferer. It wasn't so much, Luis thought, that the Spanish were better at explaining their feelings, it was rather that they were not afraid of those feelings in the first place. They were, as Frances had pointed out, proud of their qualities and their emotions. "It makes you a noble race," Frances had said. "You're high-minded. The English are often excellent but they'd be afraid to be high-minded now. They'd feel silly, they'd think they looked imperialist." Robert Middleton didn't look either silly or imperialist to Luis, he merely looked unhappy, as if he had no outlet for what he was feeling. Luis took his hands out of his pockets, stretched both of them out and grasped Robert's.

"If she looks it, I feel it."

"Yes, I know—"

"Sometimes," Luis said, "we need exactly what is not natural to us, we need to look at everything through different eyes."

Robert thought suddenly of their situation, of the vulnerable Gallery, of Lizzie's dreary little job, of the great, weighty burden of the Grange.

"Sometimes it isn't need that changes your vision," Robert said. "Sometimes circumstances mean you just have to."

Luis dropped his hands. Something else had happened in Rob's mind, something not to do with Frances.

"Perhaps," he said politely.

"Couldn't I just book you a holiday? You and Rob, in Mojas? You've no idea how lovely it is."

Lizzie drained fat off the ducks she had extravagantly bought—and now obscurely regretted—for Frances and Luis, and said she thought not.

"But why?"

Lizzie put the roasting tin on the draining board and speared the ducks with a fork.

"We can't afford it. We can't afford anything, Frances, not this house, not the cars, nothing. We certainly can't afford a holiday in Spain."

Frances said, "But it would be a present. From me. I'd like to give it to you. I want to. Just you and Rob."

Lizzie put the ducks on a plate, and the plate in the warming oven. A dull misery was settling on her.

"Lizzie?"

"I can't—take things from you. I—"

"What?"

"It's so sweet of you," Lizzie said desperately. "Really kind. But I couldn't bear it."

"Why not? From me of all people—"

"Yes. From you of all people."

"Frankly," Frances said, slicing fiercely into the pineapple she had had been given to cut up for a fruit salad, "I think that's pretty churlish."

"It isn't. Believe me, it isn't. It's just that I feel control is slipping from me."

"Look," Frances said, "what are we doing eating duck and pineapple if things are so bad? Did you buy them specially for us?"

Lizzie winced at the "us."

"Of course I did—"

Frances threw the knife down.

"Oh *Lizzie*. Why? Why go on as if nothing's changed when everything has?"

"Because I hate some of the changes, I hate them so much—"

"Is your job really terrible?"

"No," Lizzie said, pouring stock into the roasting tin for the gravy. "No, of course it isn't terrible, it's just dull and wearing and a bad anticlimax after what I'm used to. You think, don't you, that shock is a sudden thing, a horrible fright, but once it's over, it's over and you slowly recover. But the trouble about our kind of shock is that there is wave after wave of it, each blow seems to be followed by another because anything to do with money seems to have such an appalling capacity for building up, when you aren't looking. I'm sorry, I'm not being at all clear and I know I seem terribly ungrateful but I feel absolutely trapped, Frances, as if I can't *affect* anything in our lives any more, and I can't bear that because I always *have* affected things. I expect people who are made redundant feel like this, suddenly powerless, as if they'd become victims of some remorseless machine. It's just awfully hard, somehow, to accept kindness, even from you. I don't want kindness, you see, I just want to *punish* somebody."

Frances dug out the horny little eyes from the remains of the pineapple skin with the point of her knife.

"But mightn't a holiday restore your sense of proportion, of perspective?"

"Of course. I just feel—I just feel that if I went away I could hardly bear to come back. I feel so guilty, you see, guilty about the children, as well as being worried and angry. I couldn't go off to Spain and leave them, not at the moment."

"But *they* aren't worried, are they? I don't expect they've even noticed."

"I don't want them to notice. Mum says it's about time they knew a bit of hardship and I just can't stand her saying things like that. Actually, I don't think I can stand this topic any longer. Can we talk about something else?"

"I could talk to you about Luis," Frances said simply.

Lizzie turned round. Frances was sitting there at the table, slicing pineapple, her hands and face pale-golden against her gleaming shirt. Nobody, Lizzie thought, had ever considered the twins beautiful, for the very simple reason that they weren't, couldn't be, because they lacked that necessary classical purity of line and feature, but by God, at that moment Frances came close. Lizzie went across and put an arm around Frances's shoulder.

"I'm sorry to be such a killjoy and a prize crosspatch, because I really, *really* am pleased."

Frances regarded her.

"Do you like him?"

"So far, so very good."

Frances leaned a little and kissed Lizzie.

"That's all right then," she said contentedly. "He's changed everything for me."

"Everything?"

"Even the business," Frances said. "He's finding me guides for the Spanish holidays next year. You know what headaches I've had with the guides for Italy, how difficult it is to find somebody good and responsible enough, who doesn't then want so much money that the cost of the holidays goes rocketing? Well, it won't be like that in Spain. If you want to get anything done in Spain, you have to know someone, and Luis knows *everybody*."

"Oh Frances," Lizzie said, laughing. "You have got it badly."

"I know. Really badly. And I don't in the least care if I get it even worse. We're going to see Mum and Dad after this—"

"Heavens—"

"Why 'heavens'?"

"Well," Lizzie said, abruptly losing her nerve for what she really wanted to say, which was that anyone would think Luis was a prospective *son-in-law*, for goodness' sake, "it just seems a bit of an ordeal for him."

"He wants to meet them."

"Does he?"

"Yes," Frances said with decision.

The outer kitchen door opened from the garden and Robert and Luis came in.

Luis said at once, "You have a beautiful shop."

"I know," Lizzie said, smiling at him, "I just wish it was a more profitable one just now."

"I smell something wonderful—"

"Duck."

"Magnificent! I adore duck. *Querida*, what are you doing with that dangerous knife?"

"*Querida*" now. Heavens, what a language! Lizzie said quickly, "Rob, do find Davy, would you? I'm worried about Luis's watch—"

"Luis, however, is not at all worried about his watch," Luis said.

"All the same," Robert said, opening the door to the hall, "we'd feel awful if anything happened to it."

"Frances, on the other hand, would be pleased."

"Yes," Frances said, composedly, "she would. There now. Shall I add these grapes?"

From the hall, Robert could be heard shouting for Davy. There was a long silence, then a door opened, letting out a blast of television, then it banged shut and slow feet came across the hall.

"Sam was far too frightened to touch this watch," they heard Davy say.

"I'm pleased to hear it."

"Alistair told him that if he even touched it with his baby finger he'd be landed the big one by Frances's man—"

"Davy," Rob said, "our guest is called Mr. Moreno."

He reappeared in the doorway with Davy in his arms. Luis was laughing.

"Frances's man!"

Davy went pink. He turned a little in Rob's arms and hid his face against his father's neck. Lizzie went over to them, putting her hand up to Davy.

"It's all right, darling, you couldn't know, look, Mr. Moreno doesn't mind a bit—"

"No, he certainly doesn't," Luis said.

"Darling," Lizzie said coaxingly, her hand on Davy's ruffled hair. He turned his head and looked down at her gravely, and at that moment Frances glanced up and saw the three of them there, Rob holding his son, Lizzie reaching up to him, their three faces tender and united. A pang shot through her, a nameless, powerful pang. She opened her mouth to say, You look like a painting of the Holy Family, and shut it again. It suddenly seemed too absolutely true to be uttered.

Luis was by her side at once, pulling out another kitchen chair from the table and sitting down.

"Come," he said to Davy, "come and let me show you how the watch will tell you what time it is in Australia."

Robert set Davy gently on the floor. Davy hesitated, pressed against Robert's thigh.

"Come," Luis said. "We are friends, Davy?"

With infinite slowness, Davy sidled round the table and stopped three feet away.

"But I cannot see the watch from there. I am so old now, Davy, that I have to have things close to my face to see them at all. You must help."

Gradually, Davy inched forward.

"Which arm did we put the watch on?"

Stiffly, like a soldier, Davy thrust out his right arm. Luis took his hand.

"Come a bit closer."

Davy came.

"Closer still. This dial is so small. Look now. I press this and we look in this tiny window and we see the places in the world. Are you a good reader, Davy?"

"Quite," Davy muttered, torn between ambition and honesty.

"Can you see that A there?"

"Alistair has A—"

"So does Australia."

Davy bent close to the watch, and, as he did so, Luis put an arm around him.

"Now press this."

Davy pressed.

"Look what you have done, you have made numbers! Can you read numbers?"

Davy looked up at him. Their faces were inches apart.

"I can do up to five," Davy said confidently.

"You are a clever boy, then."

Davy watched him for a few seconds, then bent again over the watch.

"A clever, charming boy," Luis said, and over Davy's head, he looked across at Frances. She was looking back at him, he thought, as if she had seen a vision.

THIRTEEN

"It's preposterous," Barbara said.

"You said that," William reminded her, "when you were told you were pregnant with twins. You also said—"

"The whole thing is absurd," Barbara said. She was wiping the table with a damp cloth and William wasn't even halfway through breakfast. She often did this now, picking up bowls and jars and wiping pointlessly underneath them in the middle of meals. It was a maddening habit. William seized the marmalade and held it against his chest possessively.

"But you liked him."

"Oh," Barbara said crossly. "Of course I liked him, he was a perfectly nice, civil man. That isn't the point. Put the marmalade down or your jersey will get sticky."

"No it won't," William said. "The marmalade is *inside* the jar. You said you had never seen Frances look better and that Luis was a nice man."

"But he's *foreign*."

"Everybody," William said patiently, "is foreign to anybody else who isn't of the same nationality. Please leave the toast, I want some more."

"Mixed marriages—"

"Barbara!" William shouted.

"Don't shout."

"They aren't *getting* married!" William shouted, taking no notice. "Luis *is* married! They are having a love affair!"

"And you, of course, would know about such things," Barbara said, taking the butter away in revenge.

"Frances has had several love affairs," William said, ignoring her and spreading marmalade thickly on his toast to compensate for the lack of butter. "They've none of them been very serious and I think this is the most serious one so far. That's all."

Barbara put the butter in the fridge and slammed the door shut so hard that all the bottles inside clattered nervously together. Then she stood there, with her back to William.

"Barbara?"

She didn't say anything. She simply stood there, visibly tense, staring at the wall above the fridge where a regrettably soppy calendar hung, the well-intentioned Christmas calendar sent by their local garage. William waited for half a minute, politely, then he bit into his toast.

"It's not that," Barbara burst out.

"It's not what?" William said, crunching.

She turned round. She was fighting to look normal. All her life, she had striven to prevent any emotion—except temper, William often thought—appearing on her face.

"It's not that I disapprove of Frances having a love affair. And I don't really mind about his being foreign—"

"Oh good."

"But she's in love this time."

William stared.

"What?"

"She's really in love. Properly. Deeply."

"So?"

"He's married," Barbara said.

"Yes, I know—"

"So she'll be *hurt*," Barbara said.

William put his toast down.

"I don't see—"

"No, of course you don't see, you never see, you are the original Mr. Have-his-cake-and-eat-it, so I wouldn't even cherish the faintest hope that you *might* see. But Frances is in love with a married Catholic foreigner so it is bound, absolutely *bound*, to end in tears, most of which will be shed by Frances."

William picked up his toast again. His hand shook a little and a blob of marmalade fell on to the gentle front curve of his jersey.

"Why can't you let her be happy in peace? Even if there *may* be problems ahead, there aren't problems *now*. Why can't you just rejoice for her instead of cawing round her like some malevolent old rook of a Cassandra?"

"You have marmalade on your jersey," Barbara said. "I knew you would."

"Shut up!" William yelled. He hurled his toast across the kitchen and watched it land face down in a basket of ironing.

"Men," Barbara said, witheringly. "Hopeless romantics, useless realists. What is the point of rejoicing idiotically over something that is doomed to disaster? Luckily, I don't share your taste for romantic sentimentality."

William bent his head. He reflected, and not for the first time, that it was a great pity he suffered from a middle-class male reluctance to thump his wife.

"Don't think I don't love Frances," Barbara said. "And don't think I don't understand her either. It's because I love and understand her that I'm not going to join in this ridiculous game of pretending she's found a solid emotional future when that's the last thing she's done. Now I am going to make our bed and I shall leave you to sort out the childish mess you have made in the ironing."

She went out, closing the door in what William's mother would have called a marked manner, and William heard her feet going heavily and steadily up the stairs. They crossed the landing and entered the main bedroom and were then drowned by the incomprehensible quacking of the distant radio which Barbara switched on, as she always did, at antisocial volume.

William got up and went to the sink and scrubbed at his jersey with a damp cloth. He looked out of the window. It gave on to almost exactly the same view as it had given on to nearly forty years before when Barbara told him she was going to have twins, the same pleasant, unremarkable fields, the same hedgerows, even the same row of black poplars with their scarred sturdy trunks and their magnificent crimson catkins in spring. The only thing that had changed was that the farm beyond the fields had put up a hideous silage silo and even uglier Dutch barn, painted bright, hard, unnatural green and now blotched with huge brilliant patches of rust.

William held the edge of the sink. Perhaps he was romantic, perhaps he did feel that whatever happened in the future would be worth it because of how Frances felt now, looked now. Perhaps he did feel, with an instinct that had nothing to do with reason—and he had never, after all, had much respect for reason as a creed for living by—that nothing lovely was ever, somehow, wasted, even if it came to an end. Yet of course Barbara, however bloody, was in some ways right to feel chill apprehensions even in the midst of current joy. She was also, however strangely she often expressed it, the twins' mother and therefore bound to feel a kind of protectiveness, even if it did emerge in a weird and strangulated form. It was a wonder, really, that Barbara was taking Frances's present happiness at all seriously, and wasn't simply snorting with contempt that anyone, anywhere, in their right minds, could find the mere notion of romantic love anything other than utterly ridiculous.

William gave an enormous sigh and turned away from the window. Poor twins, poor little twins, both now in their various ways so beleaguered, Lizzie by present problems, Frances by the looming threat of future ones, even if she didn't yet perceive them. He remembered how he once used to think, during the twins' turbulent babyhood, that nobody would embark on parenthood if they knew the re-

lentless exhaustion it was going to involve. What a naive
view, he now thought, what inexperience! Looking back,
those early years were actually the golden years of parenthood, for the simple reason, William told himself, that it
had still then lain within his power to make his children
happy.

He crossed the kitchen and looked into the ironing basket. The toast lay on a pair of his chainstore pyjamas, pale-
blue cotton piped in darker blue, neatly ironed. He decided,
after staring at it for a few minutes, simply to leave it there.

The new bank manager in Langworth was youngish, with
a narrow face, short hair and the kind of ubiquitous sober
suit that everybody seemed to be wearing for work nowa-
days if they weren't looking after either cows or cars.

He said to Robert, "I am glad, Mr. Middleton, to have
this opportunity of meeting with you."

Why the "with," Robert wondered. Did it signify something different from just meeting someone? Anyway, it
wasn't a meeting, it was a summons.

"You asked me to call."

"Indeed I did. I believe my letter was addressed to both
you and Mrs. Middleton. I rather expected—"

"Mrs. Middleton, as I told your secretary, is working
during the weekdays of termtime at Westondale School in
Bath."

The bank manager raised his eyebrows and pursed his
lips.

"Was I informed of this?"

"Why should you have been?"

"In your present position," said the bank manager, in a
tone that implied that Robert's indebtedness was some kind
of criminal offence, "it is necessary to inform us of everything."

Robert opened his mouth to say, Do not speak to me
like that! and shut it again. What would be gained, after
all, but a brief, delicious surge of adrenaline followed by
the necessity of having to apologise, thereby giving the en-

emy the upper hand. Robert looked at the manager's reddish hair and pale, almost lashless eyes, and skin that still
bore the scars of adolescent acne. He not only looked like
the enemy; he looked as if he liked looking like the enemy.

"Please sit down, Mr. Middleton."

Robert obeyed, reluctantly, and chose a chair upholstered
in charcoal-grey tweed. The bank manager sat down behind his own desk and folded his hands on a fat file that
presumably contained the Middletons' records.

"I am afraid, Mr. Middleton, that I cannot tolerate this
situation any longer."

"How dare you use the word 'tolerate'?" Robert shouted,
forgetting his resolve. "How *dare* you? You banks are a
service, let me remind you, a bloody expensive *service*, not
some kind of moral committee sitting in judgement on er-
ring customers!"

The bank manager looked down at his clasped hands in
pained silence as if waiting for an unpleasant smell in the
air to evaporate.

"My loans committee, Mr. Middleton, my loans committee at the regional head office in Bath, have made it a
requirement that you put in hand immediate measures to
repay the bulk of the present outstanding loan. It was
granted, if you remember, on the understanding that a sub-
stantial reduction would be made within a period of nine
months. Those nine months are up, and the loan has not
been reduced by any significant degree. The bank is anxious, Mr. Middleton, that the loan may harden."

"Harden?"

"That you will, Mr. Middleton, become used to it and
therefore not look further than the paying of the interest."

Robert looked down for a moment. His head swam. It
was not only incredible that this sandy clerk was speaking
to him in this way, but also that he was actually saying
what he appeared to be saying. He took an enormous
breath.

"Does it not occur to you that we detest this loan a hundred times more than you do, for the simple reason that
the sum involved threatens all that my wife and I have

achieved over the last eighteen years? Do you imagine we
have had a quiet moment since we found ourselves in this
situation, and that we aren't straining every nerve and
sinew to think of and implement ways of improving it?
Why else do you suppose that my wife has taken an outside
job if it isn't to try and ease the burden on the business
and pay your appalling interest rates? My wife is a highly
talented and experienced woman, and she is forced to work
at a level I don't think you'd expect of your counter
clerks—"

"Excuse me," the bank manager interrupted, "but it
won't help to get personal."

"But what else can we do?" Robert almost shouted. "We
are working harder than we've ever worked for smaller
returns than we've ever had. What on earth else can you
possibly expect us to do?"

The bank manager shifted his hands so that his elbows
were on the desk and his fingertips came lightly together
in a gesture which seemed to Robert both authoritarian and
sanctimonious.

"My loans committee—"

For some reason, Robert's stomach sank like a stone.

"My loans committee," the bank manager continued,
looking straight at Robert, "now requires a positive indi-
cation that the bulk of the loan can be repaid in the near
future."

"And how the hell am I supposed to do that?"

"It's quite simple, Mr. Middleton. It merely means, I am
afraid, that you must put your house on the market."

Jenny stood on the landing outside the office in the Gallery.
She carried an individual-sized bottle of mineral water, and
a tuna sandwich, on a tray. Robert had been inside, with
the door shut now, for two hours, and it was almost three
o'clock and she knew he'd had nothing to eat at lunchtime.
She tapped.

He called, "Who is it?"

"Jenny," Jenny said.

"Oh Jenny," Robert said. "Come in."

She opened the door cautiously. He was sitting at his desk with the ring binders of their collected bank statements open all around him.

"I thought you might like something to eat, I didn't think you'd had any lunch—"

"I didn't. You're a dear."

"The sandwich is tuna. It was all they had left upstairs. I hope that's all right."

"It's fine," he said.

She put the tray down on the table by his desk.

"Mineral water seems so dreary. Would you like some coffee, too?"

He looked up at her. He was very pale.

"Jenny."

"Yes," she said.

"Sit down a moment."

She sat on a nearby swivel chair, folding her hands in her lap. There was a silence for a moment and then Robert said suddenly, with no preamble whatsoever, "We've got to sell the Grange."

She gasped. Her hands flew to her face.

"Don't—"

"We have to," he said. "I went to the bank this morning. We had nine months in which to start reducing the overdraft, and of course, we haven't been able to, we've hardly been able to pay the interest, so they are putting on the slammers."

Jenny had a fleeting glimpse in her mind's eye of her own cottage, which had represented to her, since Mick died, so much more than just somewhere to live. She saw its dear and familiar façade, with the Maigold rose climbing over the porch and the dormer windows set in the roof like surprised eyebrows, and felt, with a pang so violent that it frightened her, what unrelieved agony it would be to have it taken from her.

"Oh Rob—"

He picked up half the sandwich and took a dutiful bite. "How am I going to tell Lizzie?"

"I don't know—"

"She adores that house," Rob said, laying the rest of the sandwich down again. "She had her eye on it the moment we got to Langworth, we used to walk past it at weekends saying, 'One day, one day,' to each other and having fantasies of what we would do to it. Then we got it and you know how she flung herself into it. Now I've got to tell her it has to go."

"Perhaps—"

"Perhaps what?"

"Perhaps," Jenny said, twisting her neat, small hands together, "it'll satisfy the bank if you just put it quietly on the market, and then maybe business here will pick up and you won't actually have to sell it after all."

Robert said, "They want a hundred thousand pounds, minimum, before the end of six months."

They looked at one another. A hundred thousand pounds, Jenny reflected, was far more than her capital had been after the insurance company had finally paid up for Mick's dying in a car crash. Everything she owned, including the cottage, amounted to less than the sum of the Middletons' debt. It made her feel cold to think about it.

"Lizzie's so brave," Jenny said, "and strong, I'm sure she'll be able to take it. I'm sure she'll think of something."

"Are you?" Robert said. He looked at Jenny's sweet, ordinary little face, at the crisp, piecrust-frilled collar of her striped shirt, at the graduated pearls lying in a perfect loop against her green jersey. She suddenly wore, for him, an air of such absolute security and unchangeableness that it was all he could do not to fling himself at her and bury his face in her reassuring bosom and beg her to tell him soothingly that it would all be all right in the morning, she promised it would.

"The trouble is," Robert said, restraining himself, "that I don't think there *is* anything left to think of, or we would have thought of it, and done it."

·   ·   ·

Later, he left Jenny to lock up the Gallery and went home early, taking Sam and Davy, whom Jenny had, as usual, collected from school and given tea to. Sam disliked this collecting arrangement very much, being in awe of Jenny for some reason he simply couldn't fathom—she was after all only a mother and a small and quiet mother at that—and finding that he was inclined, in consequence, to behave soberly in her presence. This was against his own unarticulated code of conduct, so, in order to compensate himself for having let himself down, he was always perfectly awful on the brief walk from the Gallery to the Grange, using forbidden words at the top of his voice and darting insanely into the road like a kamikaze pilot, so that Robert usually reached home in a state of enraged nervous collapse. If Lizzie left Bath in time to take the boys home, she drove them in her clattering car, and this, in some measure, deprived Sam of the best opportunity to be awful because the journey only took three minutes.

When Robert got Sam and Davy back—Davy sniffing ominously because Sam had told him he had a face like a baboon's bottom—he found Alistair in the kitchen eating cereal by the handful straight out of the packet while reading a comic called *The Rules of Id*. Harriet was nowhere to be seen.

"Hello," Robert said.

Alistair, scattering cereal flakes as he crammed another handful approximately into his mouth, ignored him.

"Stop that," Robert said. "Speak to me when I speak to you and don't eat cornflakes at all if you aren't going to eat them in a civilised manner."

Sam slithered from the room in beady-eyed search of television and Davy, still grizzling faintly, trailed after him. Alistair raised his eyes slowly from the comic strip as if perfectly amazed at what he had been asked to do.

"I *beg* your pardon?"

"You heard me," Robert said. He reached forward and snatched both the cereal box and the comic.

"Excuse *me*—"

"Go and get a dustpan and brush and sweep up the mess

you've made. Then go and do your homework until I tell you supper's ready."

"I am most unlikely, at this rate," Alistair said, "to feel remotely inclined for supper."

"Then you can go hungry," Robert said. "And see if I care."

Alistair stepped back prudently, just out of reach.

"Temper, temper, I *must* say. I wonder what's brought this on?"

Robert went over to the fridge and opened it and began taking out packets and objects wrapped in plastic film and greaseproof paper.

"Do as you're told, Alistair. Where's Harriet?"

"Don't ask me. Last sighted in the Market Place with Heather, no doubt lying in wait for Jason Purdy, which does, if you ask me, show a *singular* lack of taste even in someone as utterly desperate as my dear sister."

"Alistair," Robert said, getting out a baking sheet and laying chipolata sausages on it in neat, pale ranks, "if you don't go and get the dustpan now, I shall clobber you."

Alistair went out, very slowly, remarking to Cornflakes, who had risen interestedly from his dresser drawer to watch the argument, that losing one's rag was commonly recognised to be the surest sign of conceding victory in battle to the other side. Robert added halved tomatoes to the baking sheet and a few tired mushrooms—the boys would never eat these, but Harriet might, if she ever bothered to come home—and put the whole thing in the top of the oven. He longed suddenly for some whisky, but was restrained by its being only twenty to six and more effectively by there being no whisky in the house, as there hadn't been, now, since last Christmas.

Alistair came back in and swept approximately two thirds of the scattered cornflakes into the dustpan, which he then angled into the mouth of the kitchen swing bin in such a way as to drop most of the contents back on to the floor again. He then said, with heavy sarcasm, "Well, Father, I do most earnestly hope that you are now satisfied," and lounged out of the room once more, leaving the door open.

Robert went out of the kitchen into the larder next door—a Victorian larder of great charm with slate shelves and huge hooks for hams—and retrieved a bag of oven chips from the deep freeze, and a separate bag of frozen peas. The peas' bag was already open, its torn plastic loosely tied up with a twist of paper-covered wire, which fell off as Robert picked the bag up and several handfuls of peas pattered gently out and filtered themselves down through three feet of frozen food to the bottom. Robert swore, slammed the freezer lid shut and took what remained back to the kitchen.

In about twenty minutes Lizzie would be home, her arrival coinciding, almost exactly, with the moment the children's supper would be ready. Clearly, Robert could say nothing until the children had eaten, and he reflected that it would be better to delay saying anything still further until they both had a glass of supermarket Bulgarian Country Wine inside them. There had been a period, a brief, luxurious period, when Robert had had an account with a wine merchant in Bath, and went to tastings and read serious articles about the oenological promise of New Zealand and Chile. Now, he and Lizzie, during the great, weekly, two-trolley binge of household shopping, allowed themselves three bottles of whatever was on special offer. It was, he told himself severely, three bottles more than plenty of people ever aspired to, let alone got, but he had had a glimpse once of something more carefree and he missed it.

How, he wondered, shaking the chips on to a second baking sheet, was he going to phrase it to Lizzie? Was he going to come at it obliquely, or simply say it, straight out, looking straight at her, wham, bang, there you have it? Once upon a time, he'd have opted without thinking for the second method; it was what she'd liked, how she'd operated herself. She never flinched, when she was younger; it was one of the first things Robert had loved in her, this direct, sturdy taking of whatever you told her, asked of her. But not only was this thing a worse thing to have to say than any previous thing, but Lizzie had changed. Of course, being older, she was both tireder and less optimistic, more disillusioned, but she had also been, since Frances brought her Spaniard down, more withdrawn. She seemed preoccupied, as if she was turning over a lot of deep and important things in her mind, reassessing them. If he was honest, Lizzie's recent abstraction was driving Robert mad. He was used—after all, there'd been twenty years of it— to Lizzie having Frances in her thoughts frequently and absorbingly, but this was different. He got the distinct impression that Lizzie was prowling round and round the idea of Frances and Luis in a way that could only be described as fixated. How, frankly, dare she, Robert now thought, tipping the few remaining peas into a pan of boiling water, how *dare* she absent herself, even for a moment, from him and their problems in such a time of need?

The outer kitchen door opened and Harriet banged in, hurling her school bag on the floor and kicking the door shut with a foot clad like a navvy's.

"Hello, darling."

"Hi," Harriet said. She had plainly been crying and her eyes, carefully mascaraed for school and/or Jason Purdy, were smudged, like a sad panda.

"You all right?"

"What does it look like?" Harriet said.

Robert put down the tongs he was using to turn the sausages and went across the kitchen. He put an arm round Harriet.

"Boys?"

"Among other shitty things—"

"Don't say shitty. What things?"

"Oh," she said, wrestling herself free. "School, history, Miss crappy Phelps, that bitch Heather Morgan—"

"Do you want to tell me about it?"

"I can't," Harriet said. "I can't tell anybody. What's for supper?"

"Sausages."

"Again?"

"Again."

"I'm going to watch telly—"

"No," Robert said. "You're going to lay the table."

Across the hall, the door of the playroom opened. Davy emerged, tunelessly singing the words of a television commercial for a multi-surface kitchen cleaner.

"Shut up!" Sam yelled after him.

Davy appeared in the kitchen doorway, still singing.

"When I want you to sing, man," Sam yelled again in an American gangster accent, "I'll stick a nickel up your ass!"

Davy stopped singing.

"What's a nickel?"

Robert looked at Harriet. She was grinning.

"It's an American coin," he said, grinning too, thankful to grin. "It's a piece of American money."

Davy felt the corduroy seat of his trousers anxiously.

"Ow," he said.

When the children had eaten and at least roughly stacked their plates in the dishwasher, and Lizzie, who had returned home very tired with two card-index boxes she said she wanted to sort out before she went to bed, was over halfway down her glass of wine, Robert suddenly told her, with no preamble, and against all his intentions and plans, about his visit to the bank. Then he waited for her reaction.

For at least a minute, there wasn't one. Lizzie simply sat there, in the armchair she had so carefully covered three years earlier in a pretty checked fabric imported from Sweden, and gazed down into the dark-red liquid in her glass, in silence. Then, equally quietly, she began to cry, still looking down, so that her tears, which seemed unnaturally large to Robert, slid down her cheeks and fell on to her hands and lap and into her glass. It was a profoundly upsetting sight. Lizzie never cried. She disapproved of crying for any reason except that of deep and genuine grief. She always said that to cry over anything less than the loss or pain of another human being was sheer self-indulgence, yet here she was, weeping and weeping, the tears coming more and more heavily, pouring out from under the curtains of hair swinging forward either side of her bowed head.

"Lizzie," Robert said in terror and anguish. He came and knelt by her side and tried to take her glass away, because she had begun to tremble, but she gripped it tightly.

"No—"

"Lizzie, darling, my darling Lizzie—"

"No!" Lizzie said between sobs. "No!"

"We have to," Robert said. He put his own hands awkwardly over hers around the wine glass. "We have to, Lizzie. But it isn't the end of the world. We'll pick up again in a year or two and then we can buy it back—"

"I can't bear it, I can't, I can't—"

"Lizzie, it's only a house—"

"No!" she wailed. She flung his hands off, spilling wine across her skirt. "It's everything that's going, simply melting!"

"Nonsense," he said, trying to smile, trying to peer in under her hair and see her face. "Don't get this out of proportion. Come on, darling. We're all right, the children are all right, and that's what matters."

Lizzie raised her head. Her face was flushed and shining with tears, glistening with them as Davy's sometimes did when in a paroxysm of Sam-induced grief.

"I can't face any more," she said, dragging the back of one hand uselessly across her cheeks. "I just can't. I can't go on."

Robert handed her his handkerchief.

"Come on," he said, half facetiously, half reprovingly. "Don't overdo it. It isn't the end of the world."

"It's the end of *mine*," Lizzie said, blowing.

"Thanks a million—"

She turned on him.

"Why can't I say I've had enough? *Why* can't I? Why can't I speak the truth and say I'm at the end of my tether and that I haven't the heart to go on with this stupid, pointless, miserable pretence that we are waving when in fact we're drowning?"

"We are not drowning."

"Oh yes we are!" she shouted, her voice rising. "We're giving up everything we've made, we haven't even got a home now, it belongs to the bloody bank, it always has, everything has, we've just lived a lie because everything's been built on sand, nothing's real, nothing's solid"—her voice rose to a scream—"and none of it's been worth it, has it, none of it, it's all just been a stupid, self-deluding charade!"

She was glaring at him, swollen-faced, open-mouthed. Before he knew what he was doing, and immediately full of sheer horror at himself, Robert lifted his right hand and slapped her.

Alone in the left-hand spare-room bed, Lizzie lay awake and stared into the not-quite-darkness, at the line of bluish light from the street lamp outside that fell in between the imperfectly drawn curtains, and at the yellow glow that came in under the door from the light on the landing that Davy could always sense being turned off, even from the depths of slumber.

It was her choice to sleep apart from Robert. It had never happened before, in all their married life, unless one of them had influenza, and Robert had assumed—indeed had said—that she was sleeping apart from him because she simply couldn't bear, any more, to sleep with him. That was true, but not in the way he supposed, and for some reason she couldn't seem able to explain to herself and thus reassure him. She couldn't, somehow, say that she couldn't bear to sleep with him, not because she felt he had failed her nor because he had slapped her, but because she was full of shame.

She had never, she thought, staring dry-eyed into nothingness, felt so full of shame. Those tears downstairs, those terrible, Niagara-like tears were not—or only partly, at best—at the prospect of losing the Grange, but mostly because of self-pity and because of Frances. She had, recently, been quite obsessed with Frances, obsessed with her flowering and her happiness and the exact nature of this most powerful and intimate relationship she was having, until she felt that she was behaving quite insanely. She wanted to stop thinking like this, but she didn't seem able to, it had become a drug-like habit, so that when Robert broke the news to her about the Grange, her first piercing thought had been that there was Frances climbing blithely up a rainbow into ever stronger sunlight while she, Lizzie, fell down into a black hole with something horrible roaring at the bottom. And what was worse was that Frances, climbing and singing, wasn't even looking at her, she wasn't looking anywhere but at Luis.

It was at this point of self-knowledge that the shame had begun, and the shame had made her tears flow faster than ever. How *could* she begrudge Frances her happiness? How *could* she let Rob think he had let her down and that she both couldn't and wouldn't go on supporting him and helping him in this crisis which was, after all, their crisis and not just his? How could she wail and scream like a spoiled child because something—all right, something loved and precious, but still only a *thing*—was being taken away from her? How could she fail herself and Rob and all she believed in and had always staunchly said she believed in? She couldn't think how she had behaved like that, but she had, and the thought of lying beside patient, worried, innocent, loving Robert while being herself quite polluted with all these horrible thoughts was intolerable.

So, to the spare room she had come, the spare room which would soon be someone else's spare room, or their children's room, or their old mother's. Lizzie gripped the edge of the sheet—could she even be the same person who had so optimistically, carelessly, bought those very sheets in Bath's antique market?—and stared and stared as if, out of the darkness, would come some image of calm and comfort, of forgiveness. But there was nothing. The darkness was remorseless and blank. Lizzie turned on her side and closed her eyes and felt the hot tears begin again, rising painfully behind her eyelids.

"Oh," she said to herself between clenched teeth. "Oh, I really am the lowest of the low."

FOURTEEN

Juliet Jones seldom went to London. Long ago, she had loved London, had felt a stir of anticipation as the West Country trains approached Paddington, but those enthusiastic days were long past. In her view London was not only now dirty and shabby but also un-English, her very institutions degenerated into sideshows for gawpers as if true personality had given way to cliché and caricature. But after she had seen William, and then Barbara, and after a visit from Lizzie, it seemed to Juliet that she must go to London and see Frances.

The visit from Lizzie had been very confusing. She had looked terrible, her hair lank, her eyes shadowed, and she had, while ostensibly coming up to the cottage to break the news about the sale of the Grange, plainly come to say a whole lot of other things about herself and Rob, and herself and Frances, which she could neither stop trying to say nor succeed in saying. She had sat by Juliet's fire, in the wickerwork chair Juliet kept filled with Paisley-patterned cushions, and talked and talked, nursing a mug of tea. But none of the talk had made much sense to Juliet, or, at least, not until later.

Lizzie kept saying that they would have to rent somewhere to live.

"I don't see," Juliet said, "that that is really so very terrible. As long as you are all together under the same roof—"

But Lizzie wasn't listening. She said she had put her heart and soul into the Grange, with which Juliet had gently agreed, and then she said she was letting Rob down so badly.

"Why are you? In what way? You never have before—"

"By being so angry," Lizzie said.

"About the Grange?"

"No," Lizzie said confusingly.

"Then—"

"I can't make Frances listen," Lizzie burst out.

"But, Lizzie, this isn't Frances's problem—"

"I know, I know. I *know*."

"Well, then—"

"I can't focus on things," Lizzie said, turning her mug round and round.

"Perhaps that's shock."

"I don't know. It might be everything, worry, money, shame, fear. It doesn't really matter what it is, it just matters that I'm not *coping*."

"You're very hard on yourself," Juliet said. "You've always carried so much. You're not to be blamed if you can't cope for a little while."

"But I don't know if I can't," Lizzie said, still turning. "Perhaps I just won't."

"I think you must make plans," Juliet said sturdily. "It's the only way. You must look for somewhere else to live and make plans about it."

"I can't," Lizzie said.

"Why can't you?"

"I told you, I can't focus."

"Give yourself time."

"I don't want time," Lizzie said, "I want a break, I want to be free of all this, I want something new."

Juliet looked at her.

"Don't talk like that," she said sharply.

Lizzie raised her head.

"Why can't I?"

Because, Juliet wanted to say, that's exactly how your father used to talk, and he never did anything about it so I grew to despise him saying it. It seemed to me nothing but selfishness.

"Because it isn't true," Juliet said instead.

"It feels true to me."

Juliet had had enough. She stood up.

"I think you should go home."

"Yes," Lizzie said. "It's where I belong, isn't it, after all?"

"Don't be sarcastic."

Lizzie stood up too and put her mug down on the table half covered, as usual, by the profusion of Juliet's sewing. She touched the nearest piece of fabric, a fold of rough blue-and-white cotton which made her think, abruptly and poignantly, of Greece and a holiday she and Rob had once had, as students, chugging among the islands on a series of boats that had smelled disappointingly of diesel oil and fish and not, as they had envisaged, of olive oil and lemons.

"I become sole school secretary at Westondale next week—"

"Oh good," Juliet said. "Promotion?"

"No. But at least no more Freda Mason." She looked across at Juliet. "Frances brought her man down."

"Really?" said Juliet, who knew already, from William. "Nice?"

"Yes."

"She seems so happy—"

"Yes," Lizzie said furiously, and then added, even more furiously, "there is nothing to be said for me just now, *nothing*," and she fled from the cottage as if Juliet were chasing her out with a broom.

William, coming up to the cottage soon after, said Lizzie and Robert's nerves were on edge, most understandably, and this caused Lizzie to make very little sense. Barbara, met by Juliet in the dry cleaners' in Langworth, said that

everybody, including William, was simply behaving hyster-
ically. Juliet, turning all this over in her mind until she was
sick to death of the subject, concluded that Robert and William were seriously worried about Lizzie; that Lizzie and
Barbara were, for different reasons and from different
points of view, jealous of Frances; that Robert and Lizzie
and William and Barbara were all, and again for different
reasons, resentful of each other and were equally determined, or unable, to articulate this resentment and thereby
at least attempt to resolve it. All this inspired in Juliet a
deep thankfulness for not being involved in family life herself, and a simultaneous resolution to go and see Frances.

She had never been to the office of Shore to Shore before,
though she had heard plenty about it from both Lizzie and
William. It turned out to be in a narrow building in an
undistinguished street which appeared to be otherwise entirely lined with a succession of fast-food outlets of different
nationalities, all clustering together for comfort. There was
a horrible amount of litter, and a miasma of frying and soy
sauce hung in the air. Between the shabby plastic facias
advertising kebabs and satays and fish and chips, the façade
of Shore to Shore shone with a quiet sobriety, its windows
full of plants framing a poster of the Roman amphitheatre
at Lucca, now an oval Italian piazza, russet and ochre and
in perfect crumbling taste. Juliet pushed open the door and
was greeted by the smell of coffee.

Frances, across the room, was on the telephone. She
waved at Juliet and mouthed that she would only be a
moment. Another girl, with long, smooth nymph's hair,
rose immediately from behind a desk, and came over, saying she was Nicky.

"And I'm Juliet."

"Frances is expecting you. Shall I take your coat? Would
you like some coffee?"

Juliet surrendered her coat gratefully. It was, as it always
was and as she always forgot it would be until it was too
late, ten degrees warmer in London at least than it was on
her own windy heights. She looked round approvingly.

"This is charming."

"Lizzie did most of it," Nicky said. She put Juliet's coat respectfully on a hanger.

"Please don't bother. It's not that kind of coat, it doesn't expect such treatment."

"It's no bother," Nicky said, putting the coat away in a cupboard. "Nor would coffee be, if you would like it."

"I would. I would indeed. London always gives me a raging thirst."

Frances put down the telephone and stood up. She wore a fawn wool trouser suit of a distinctly glamorous cut. She held her hands out to Juliet, smiling.

"Juliet, I'm so pleased."

They kissed across the desk. Nicky put a cup of *cappuccino* coffee down in front of Juliet. Juliet began dimly to feel that she was an unpaid extra in a television series about a modern businesswoman.

"I'm taking you out to lunch," Frances said. "Just round the corner."

The telephone rang again, and then a second one began.

"Juliet, would you forgive me—"

Juliet nodded, picked up her cup of coffee and took it over to a small sofa by the window.

"I'm so sorry," Nicky was saying into the telephone, "but I'm afraid the first Spanish holidays for next spring are already fully booked. Miss Shore is trying to organise more at this moment, and of course, if this comes off, we will let you know at once—"

Juliet's gaze roved round the room. It was charming indeed, with the kind of cool charm that she supposed was necessary in order to convey an air of efficiency. It wouldn't do to have an office that looked too homey, after all, just as it wouldn't do to be dealing with people whose appearance was in any way amateurish. Frances certainly didn't look amateurish. She looked—well, Juliet thought, I last saw her at Christmas standing below my bedroom window in a boringly standard fawn mackintosh, and although she is now in fawn again, she looks neither standard nor boring. She looks interesting and almost stylish and decidedly female. I wonder if her Mr. Moreno takes her shopping for clothes in that possessive way some European men have ("No, no, *chérie*, it cannot be the black, it must be the red, I adore the red"), and so forth. I wonder if she has started looking at herself differently to please him or because he has made her, so screamingly evidently, pleased with herself. I see she is wearing a ring, too, though I can't from this distance see what sort of ring it is. How curious it is that at the early stages in a relationship, people violently want to advertise their belonging to one another, and so often, later on, equally violently wish to obliterate any visible evidence of mutual dependence. Presumably Mr. Moreno is still wearing the wedding ring he put on in order to pledge himself to Mrs. Moreno and therefore has no extra badge of belonging to Frances, while Frances, the mistress . . .

"Juliet," Frances said, "shall we go now? Nicky will hold the fort."

Nicky, smooth-haired and serene, smiled at them from behind her computers and her telephones.

"Wonderful Nicky," Juliet said politely. Nicky, she thought, had a face like an egg, perfect, bland and featureless. What would happen to a face like Nicky's when it got into a rage?

Frances led Juliet back down past the kebab houses and the Chinese take-aways and the baked-potato place outside which a huge, smiling plastic potato stood on a stand and held out a fillings menu towards them in grotesque little plastic hands, and round several windy corners to an Italian restaurant called the Trattoria Antica. It was small and pretty, with pink tablecloths and rustic rush-seated chairs and Frances, being plainly well known there, was given a table in the window.

"I never go out to lunch," Juliet said pleasedly. "At least, sometimes I take one of my poor lonely hearts lot from the village to a pub, but there is something about a country pub at lunchtime that is very disheartening. I've eaten more microwaved steak and kidney pie without enough seasoning in it than I care to contemplate."

"What are you going to eat now?"

Juliet rather thought mixed salamis and then the three-coloured tagliatelle and a salad. Frances said she loved people who could make up their minds about menus.

"Talking of love," Juliet said, "you look wonderful."

Frances looked up at her with a dead-straight gaze that had, she thought, always been one of the twins' chief charms.

"I feel it."

"So your Mr. Moreno has satisfactorily filled up your inner spaces and there is presently no need for stories?"

Frances blushed faintly and nodded.

"Well, I'm glad," Juliet said. "There's nothing like love for giving the emotions a really good gallop."

"It's more than that, it's better—"

"Of course it is. I'm teasing you, really. And I'm delighted for you, delighted, and luckily everybody seems to like him."

A waiter put down two plates of pink and white and red salamis in front of them, studded with shining black olives.

"Actually," Frances said, "it wouldn't make me change my mind for one second, even if they didn't."

"I know."

"Of course, Lizzie thinks it's estranged us—" She stopped.

Juliet rolled a disc of salami into a neat parcel with her fork, and ate it.

"Lizzie is why I've come."

"Yes."

The waiter leaned between them and poured white wine into their glasses.

"Lizzie is in a bad way."

"The house—"

"And Robert."

"Rob?" said Frances, startled.

"Yes," Juliet said. She ate an olive. "It is a common and absolutely mistaken supposition that trouble brings two people closer together. It doesn't, of course, it makes them snarl and snap at one another because they are worried and frightened. It's only when trouble is safely past that people feel devoted to one another out of sheer relief that they've weathered the storm. Lizzie and Robert haven't got to that stage yet. The storm is still raging."

Frances picked up her wine glass and took a slow sip.

"I've tried to help, you know. I've offered them money and I've offered them a holiday. Lizzie doesn't want either. At least, she doesn't want them from me."

"She is terribly ashamed of herself," Juliet said.

"For what?"

"For being frightened and worried, for blaming Robert when she knows it isn't his fault, for being hysterical about putting the Grange on the market, for envying you your love affair and for resenting your closeness to Mr. Moreno, which last emotion is complicated by both liking him and finding him, I suspect, rather attractive."

Frances went on eating, not hurriedly, but with a kind of determination that suddenly looked to Juliet almost stubborn.

"She desperately wanted your happiness, Frances, but she never bargained for how she might react when you got it."

"I'm sorry," Frances said.

"Sorry about what?"

"I'm sorry that Lizzie is in this tangle. I'm sorry that you had to come all the way to London to say things to me that I can't help feeling she might have said herself. I'm truly sorry about the house and the loss of all their profits and success."

"But?"

"But," said Frances, eating a piece of bread, "beyond loving Lizzie and offering her such help as I can give her, there isn't any more I can do. I can't," she said with sudden fierceness, "adjust my life any more in order for it to be something that Lizzie can live with."

Juliet was amazed.

"My dear Frances—"

"No," Frances said, "just listen a moment. I may be a twin, as Lizzie is, and we may, largely at her instigation and by my acquiescence, have divided life somehow between us up to now, but none of that means that I am not whole, independent and separate any more than it means she isn't. I am not responsible for her choices. She isn't for mine. I'd do anything in my power to help her but she doesn't want me to. She wants help on her terms just as she wants my happiness on her terms too. I think her current situation is horrible for her, but it's no less horrible for Rob and it isn't the end of the world. If I was her, I mean them, I'd turn the café and the exhibition floor of the Gallery into a flat and move in there. It would halve the administration and the work and the expenses. And I also would leave me alone to develop my life as I want and need to, just as I have always left her alone to do. I don't think I've ever criticised Lizzie. I once asked her quite mildly why she was having Davy christened when she and Rob were once full of such high-minded ideas about not imposing spirituality on the older children, and I truthfully think that was the closest I've got to seriously questioning *any* of her decisions. Well, I've had enough. I'm not a sort of honey pot she can just stick a finger in for a lick when she fancies it. I'm me and I'm free and when she can honestly respect that and, what's more, put it into practice, then we'll be getting somewhere. In the meantime, I may ache with sympathy for her but I don't, any more, ache with guilt. Right?"

Juliet gave her a long, astounded look.

"Right," she said faintly.

"Good," Frances said. She picked the wine bottle out of its perspex cooler. "Drink up, then."

Later, driving out to the airport to meet Luis on an early-evening flight from Madrid, Frances waited out of habit to feel a twinge of remorse. She didn't. As she had said to Juliet, it wasn't that she didn't feel sorry for Lizzie, but it was rather that she had stopped feeling tied to her by some primordial cord of responsibility, largely because her perceptions of responsibility were now deflected in quite another direction; that direction which was presently, with any luck, beginning its descent in an aeroplane over Heathrow. There was also the added element, Frances told herself, of having her own preoccupations now, preoccupations which were of enormous importance to her, and which it was as much in her nature to keep private as it was in Lizzie's to make public.

All of these preoccupations centred inevitably round Luis. Their love affair, carried on in snatches between their business lives in two countries, might have looked to the outside eye the epitome of glamour—the travel, the infrequency of meeting and frequency of telephoning, the emotional partings and reunions, the consequent novelty sustained at an intoxicating and high-octane level—but Frances had discovered, quite early on, that the organic nature of the relationship had set its own inevitable time clock ticking the moment Luis had said to her, with such urgency, that they must understand each other's national natures if they were to become lovers. You could not, she had learned, stop that time clock. You could not, whatever tricks you attempted to play on it by getting on aeroplanes and flying off or by not being available for telephone calls, halt the steady, relentless tread of a love affair's development. Whatever you did, however you disciplined yourself, it *would* progress, it *would* change and in the process, it would force you to progress and change with it. And the stark measure of that, Frances told herself, beating the palm of one hand lightly on the steering wheel, is that in May I would have sold my soul to be his mistress, and now that I've been his mistress for six months, I want to be something more.

She had said this to him, outright, and the consequences had been two extremely thunderous weekends. Luis said he did not consider himself married to José's mother any more, he considered himself wholly committed to Frances, but he did not wish to raise the storm of seeking a divorce since, even if he were free, he wouldn't marry Frances, he wouldn't marry anybody again, ever, he wasn't a married kind of man. He said he hadn't told his mother about Frances, and he wasn't going to because he knew exactly what her reaction would be, which would distress Frances deeply even if she was prepared for it, and no, Frances couldn't meet her, ever.

"But you have met my parents, I have taken you to my family, I have been open and honest and generous with you—"

"Yes."

"So why can't you, even out of mere decency and courtesy, reciprocate with a little honesty and generosity with me?"

"Because I am different from you. I am a man, I am a Spaniard, I was born and reared a Catholic. *Querida*, we have been over and over this. My father is a deeply traditional, right-wing ex-soldier. My mother is a devout Catholic with a will of iron and a fondness for anger and scenes. They would probably refuse even to meet you, and if they met you, they would be, at best, cold and hard. There is no *point*, Frances. You would be badly hurt, and nothing would be gained."

"So I have to stay a secret? You tell me I'm the most important person in your life and I have to stay a *secret*?"

"José knows you, so does Ana and my brother-in-law—"

"But I'm a secret for them, too!"

"Listen," Luis said, taking her by the shoulders and putting his face close to hers, "there is no other way. Do you understand me? There is *no other way*."

She hadn't gone on pleading. She didn't want to whine, she didn't want to lose any of that life-enhancing self-esteem he had given her by whining and pleading, so she had stopped. Not particularly gracefully, she now thought, but at least she had stopped. In any case, she had growing inside her, more strongly with every day that passed, a far greater preoccupation even than the one of being somehow miraculously accepted into Luis's family and his public life. Of course she wanted to be his wife because she wanted him to acknowledge before the world what she meant to him, and she wanted them to live together so that the lows of life were woven into their every days as well as the highs, so that they could build upon the foundations they had so splendidly laid within the security of marriage and so that, most of all—Frances stopped herself. The stream of traffic swirling round the roundabouts before the airport was demanding all her attention, and in any case, the conversation that had arisen only last weekend from the voicing of this, the most powerful of her desires, took a great deal of courage to recall. But then, Frances had recently grown rather used to courage, both of the stoical kind that accepts and bears the unacceptable and the unbearable, and also of the adventurous kind that goes out either to seek or to defend. Frances had definitely been seeking when she had said to Luis, in his flat in Madrid last weekend, that she would be thirty-nine on her next birthday, and that because of meeting him, she now badly wanted to have a baby before she was forty.

He was making a salad. He was both deft and competent domestically, and he was standing at the island unit in the centre of his tiny, urban kitchen, slicing vegetables. She was sitting the other side of the unit on a stool, wearing a bathrobe of his because she had just had a shower and because they both liked her to wear his bathrobe, his shirts, his jerseys. When she had spoken, she sat and waited, her elbows on the unit close to his chopping board, and her face in her hands. He went on slicing. She watched the fine wafers of peppers and tomato and cucumber fall brightly on to the board, and the flash of the knife blade. He stopped every so often, and scooped up the slices in his cupped hands and dropped them into the deep pottery bowl they had bought together in Córdoba, blue and white and butter-yellow, with a single scarlet rose painted in the bottom.

Then Luis said, "If you have a child, Frances, then I must tell you that that will be the end of everything."

She had got off the stool then, and gone into the small, darkish bedroom, with its wide bed and its view down into an ordinary Madrid street lined with blocks of flats and news vendors. She sat on the bed and folded her hands together, back very straight. She knew he meant it. She knew that if she pointed out how fond he was (however occasionally exasperatedly) of José, how sweet he had been with Lizzie's Davy, how much they loved one another, how natural and right a baby would now be as the fruit of their sexual harmony and passion, it would be like trying to shout at somebody with the wind snatching your words away as you uttered them. He simply wouldn't hear her. Nothing would change him, nothing, even though she used every weapon in her armoury, emotional, moral, rational. There was no point in battering on the closed door of his mind until her knuckles were raw, because he would never admit her. Assault, in this vital matter of a baby, would achieve nothing but an estrangement which would, she knew, simply break her heart. So she got up from the bed, dressed herself in the blue jeans and oversized white shirt he liked to see her in, went back to the kitchen and said in a friendly voice that after they had eaten, she would like to go out to the cinema. He had looked at her. He had looked at her for a long, steady time, and then he had stopped what he was doing and had taken her straight back to the bedroom.

Last Saturday, that was, Frances thought, and last Sunday was the last time I drove down the airport tunnel, except that I was coming the other way, away from Spain and Luis and not, as now, towards him. She felt extremely happy, not just with the still undiminishing anticipation of seeing him, but with a deeper happiness borne of certainty, of accomplishment. When she had reached home the Sunday before there had been a message from Luis waiting for her on the telephone answering machine, a message that wasn't exactly an apology in words, but was, because of its warmth and intimacy, a tacit one. He hadn't crowed in victory over her, he had rather implied his profound appreciation of her reaction. He had ended the message in Spanish. Spanish, as she grew better at it, was becoming the private language of their love.

When she had played the message several times, Frances went through the necessary discipline of swift, immediate unpacking. She had found that if she didn't unpack the moment she got home, her bag lay, partly rummaged through, on the floor until the next frantic, joyful Friday night forced her either to repack it or finally empty it before Luis arrived. She hung up her skirts and jacket, lined up her shoes in the way that Luis, meticulous about his personal possessions, lined up his, and took her sponge bag into the bathroom. She tipped it out, as she always did—a habit Luis hated—into the washbasin, toothpaste, face creams, hairbrush, lotions, and began to pick out individual things and line them up on the glass shelf below the shaving mirror. She picked up the flat foil envelope that held her contraceptive pills, and slid them out into her hand. They were arranged round the edge of a small plasticised card, each one neatly in its own sealing bubble, each one helpfully labelled with a day of the week. Frances counted. Ten days left to go of this cycle. She flicked the card once or twice with her thumbnail, then slid it back into the envelope and dropped it into the bin under the basin.

That was five days ago, Frances now thought, emerging from the tunnel into the floodlit glare of the various terminal approaches, five days and I've swallowed nothing but food and drink. Above her, the signs for Terminal Two hung huge, clear and kindly instructive. With any luck, Luis's plane would be touching down this very moment, and with even more luck, he would, with the skill of long practice, be one of the first off the plane and one of the first through those impenetrable sliding doors from the customs hall and into her waiting arms.

PART
FOUR

APRIL

FIFTEEN

The children, like domestic animals transported from one side of the country to another, strayed endlessly back to the Grange. Robert said consolingly that this was only because the house's new occupants had a teenage son with even more cool than Jason Purdy, an ice-cream machine and a half-sized snooker table. But Lizzie thought that they were more like poor Cornflakes, torn from their familiar dresser drawer and poignantly trying to find it again. Cornflakes wouldn't use the same dresser drawer in the new kitchen, nor would he adapt, because of being in a flat, to an earth tray. He cowered under tables and chairs and glared at Lizzie with a mixture of deep reproach and malevolence. He made messes beneath beds and behind the sofa. He also learned, in order to revenge himself upon her for the loss of the Grange's garden and its game reserve of voles and shrews, how to open the door of the fridge and help himself to the contents.

It was a nice flat; everybody said so. No one quite knew where the suggestion had come from that the top two floors of the Gallery building should cease to be uneconomic café and exhibition space and become the Middletons' home instead, but it had arrived somehow, like the slow onset of a new season, and quietly enlarged itself from a notion to an actuality. Robert had worked on the conversion with his own hands all winter, doing almost everything himself except the plumbing and some necessary rewiring, and they now had a kitchen and a family living room and three bedrooms and a bathroom, and views of Langworth High Street in front and the decayed small industrial muddle at the back, and really, the change wasn't that bad and the sun came in morning and evening and it was, wasn't it, wonderful just to nip downstairs to work rather than race, late, through the town, and everybody would, of course, get accustomed to living in a quarter of the space they were used to, and it was a relief, surely, not to have the tyranny of a garden, particularly when Langworth had a perfectly good recreation ground, and it must be such a boon to have shops so close and everybody got used to sleeping through traffic after a week or two, didn't they?

Lizzie hated it. Her beloved possessions, the lovingly collected furniture and objects, seemed to huddle miserably in the new featureless rooms, wearing expressions similar to Cornflakes'. The noise, the inevitable chaos of the children's crammed bedrooms—how long, for heaven's sake, could Harriet and Davy share a room?—the fact that a large proportion of their furniture had to be expensively stored, the lack of privacy, the endless domestic difficulties of finding somewhere to hang the washing, or eat in peace with Robert while sharing the same space with the television and Alistair and Harriet breathing elaborately and heavily over their homework, combined to make her feel that she was like a hamster on a wheel, doomed to go round and round without ever advancing one iota. It wasn't, either, as if she and Robert had reached a point where they could raise their glasses of Bulgarian wine to each other in mutual congratulation at being out of debt. They weren't yet. They had had, in order to achieve the quick sale the bank had demanded, to sell the Grange for considerably less than they had paid for it, or than it had once been worth. It had also cost a frightening amount to do the necessary work on the flat, and move into it, and the money spent that way aroused in Lizzie exactly the same feelings of repugnance that paying interest on the overdraft did.

The new people at the Grange were very nice, too, she heard. For herself, she had tried to meet them as seldom as possible over the sale, not because she disliked them as people but because she disliked them intensely for being able to live in her house when she couldn't. They were called Michael and Bridie Pringle. He was tall and thin with a fringe-like beard and owned a small, specialised factory that made drill bits for deep-water oil wells. She was Irish and very active in the Green Movement. Harriet reported that she had really improved the Grange.

"It's all white, it's really cool, and the floors are all pale and shiny and the curtains are huge and have checked bow things tying them back and they have this brilliant myna bird and they don't eat anything that isn't organic and they have this list in the kitchen about recycling things. Why don't you recycle things?"

"I do, I do, I always go to the bottle bank, I have for ages—"

"But not paper and plastic and tins and cardboard. And we always have bought ice cream. Bridie says if we knew what manufacturers put into bought ice cream, we wouldn't give it to our worst enemy. You should see the kitchen. It's superb."

"It was superb before—"

"It was not," Harriet said crushingly. "It was a pretentious mess."

"You don't know what pretentious means—"

"I do," Harriet said. "Alistair told me. It means pretending to be grander than you are."

Robert said Harriet was just winding Lizzie up. He said she loved being in the middle of town and that she only seeped back endlessly to the Grange because of the welcome she got there, the faint superiority she could feel for having lived there first, and the boy, Fraser. He said, with the slight edge of sharpness his voice had lately developed when speaking to Lizzie, that this was just a new beginning, that it was imperative to see it as such and that what they had done once, from nothing, they could do again.

But Lizzie was disorientated. She found she was even longing for the new term to start at Westondale—her third term, unbelievably—because at least Westondale gave a structure to her days and a focus for her thoughts. She was a good school secretary. Even Mrs. Drysdale, who had feared the possible consequences of Lizzie's independence of mind, was moved to say, with many meaningful nods and becks, that it was amazing, wasn't it, how never a door shut (Mrs. Mason) but another and better one opened (Lizzie). The school office, cleared of its craft-sale artefacts (except for the red-and-yellow papier-mâché lump, for which Lizzie found she had an arcane affection, doubtless because the thing seemed to have a strong and poignant personality without managing or needing to have an identity) and with the Parents' Association computer in working order, was a very different place. The card-index boxes were dwindling, the orange-and-brown folk-weave curtains had been bundled up and hidden at the back of the Lost Property cupboard, the telephone, though still busy, did not utter quite the same steady stream of complaint that had so fuelled Mrs. Mason's conviction that parents had been, as a breed, sent only to try her. Lizzie's competence was unquestionably Westondale's gain even if it was, Robert often now felt, the Gallery's loss.

She wouldn't consider the autumn stock.

"Please," Robert said.

They were in the office of the Gallery, now piled with boxes as it had to do duty as a stock room as well. Lizzie was doing household accounts. She had always done them, in a broad-brush kind of way, ever since she had learned how, but now she did them with the sort of manic meticulousness Robert remembered his mother applying to her own household accounts book in the fifties: "Four half-penny stamps, two haddock fillets at nine pence each, a sixpennyworth of old potatoes."

"Do you have to do that?"

"You know I do," Lizzie said, tapping her calculator.

"Do you realise that it cost sixteen quid to get your shoes resoled and heeled?"

"I'll wear espadrilles, then."

"Don't be silly."

"Lizzie—"

Lizzie wrote on, industriously, down her long, long column. Robert watched her bent tawny head, her face, as usual, hidden from him by her swinging hair. She wore jeans and a dark-blue sweatshirt with the sleeves pushed up and a spotted snuff handkerchief knotted round her neck. She was thinner. Quite a lot thinner, now he came to look at her. How terrifyingly easy it was to live closely with someone and look at them without actually seeing what you were looking at for months on end.

"Lizzie, I want you to come to the gift fair at Birmingham with me, as usual, like we always do."

She stopped writing and turned in her chair. She looked at him for several seconds.

"Robert, I don't want to come."

"Why?"

She said in a low voice, casting her eyes down, "I don't like the Gallery just now."

"What?"

"I don't like it. It feels like our millstone."

Robert put his hands over his face. Then he took them away and said, with evident self-control, "It isn't our millstone, Lizzie, it's our lifeline. It's keeping us going."

Lizzie sighed and turned back to her accounts book.

"Then I can't explain it."

"You can't mean you'd *prefer* to work at Westondale than in the Gallery—"

"Yes, I can."

"Lizzie!"

"I don't have to think at Westondale, I just *do*. For a few hours every day I can sink myself in other people's lives, in problems I love solving because they are so remote and impersonal. It's a kind of freedom."

Robert leaned across and slammed the accounts book shut.

"May I remind you, Lizzie," he said angrily, "that that is a freedom I never have?"

She looked up at him for a fleeting second, and then down again.

"Sorry—"

He seized her wrist.

"Come with me."

"Where are we going?"

"Into the Gallery, *our* Gallery, our invention and our livelihood."

"But I know it—"

"I want you to look at it as if you didn't," Robert said, opening the office door and pulling her through. "I want you to look at it with new eyes and see it not just for what it is but for the potential it still has. I want you to look at it properly because it's bloody well time that you remembered it's *ours*."

"There'll be customers—"

"Only a few," Robert said, opening the door into the shop. "It's nearly five-thirty."

There were two, a woman instructing Jenny to roll, not fold, her two sheets of giftwrap, and a boy of twelve or so, presumably her son, lovingly stroking a fleet of Indian wooden ducks with beaks and eyes of inlaid brass. Jenny glanced up as they came in and then returned to her customer.

"A pound, please."

"A pound!"

"I'm afraid the paper you chose is fifty pence a sheet."

"Have you nothing cheaper?"

"The lower rack has paper at thirty-five pence—"

"Wait," the woman said. She darted back to the giftwrap stand. Patiently, Jenny began to unroll the original roll.

"But it isn't as pretty."

"No."

"What am I to do?"

Robert drew Lizzie away to the far end of the shop floor. It was much more crowded now, the kelims hanging layered on the walls, the cushions piled in soft, steep mountains, the display tables stacked densely with lamps and pottery bowls and wicker baskets.

"There's no room for more stock," Lizzie said.

"There will be by the autumn. Sales were better last month."

Lizzie looked hopelessly at the lithographs Luis had admired.

"Were they?"

"Lizzie," Robert said, "I *told* you." He took her by the shoulders and turned her to face him. "I think we should look for cheap, pretty things for the autumn, cotton cushions, Indian brass candlesticks, some of the Shaker tinware, things that people can buy to give their houses a quick face-lift without breaking the bank."

"But we were always so adamant about quality—"

"I don't mean as a permanent policy, I just mean as a short-term measure, to cheer the shop up, to make it look as if nothing in it has actually been sitting here for months. I thought we might try some little room settings, to show people what they could do with not much outlay, a Kelim on a table rather than the floor, you know the kind of thing, you're brilliant at it—" He stopped.

"Well?"

"The thing is," she said slowly, "that I just don't want to do it."

He dropped his hands.

"Lizzie, are you ill?"

"No."

"Then—"

"I know I'm failing you," Lizzie burst out desperately. "I know I'm not being dependable, competent, capable Lizzie, I know I'm hopeless just now but I feel—I feel that in order to survive, just *survive*, all I can do at the moment is crawl."

There was a silence between them. Robert knew that his face wore his feelings as clearly as if they had been printed there in capital letters, feelings of frustration and bewilderment and, try as he might to quell it, a dangerous cocktail of exasperation and resentment.

"Is it your blasted sister still?"

Lizzie moved her head so slightly it could have been either a nod or a shake. She lifted one hand and hooked her hair behind her left ear.

"Take Jenny."

"What?"

"Take Jenny to Birmingham. She's so experienced now and she'd love to go with you."

Robert opened his mouth to say, as a reflex action, that he didn't want to take Jenny, he wanted to take his wife and said instead, "I can't. There'd be no one to mind the shop."

"I'll do it," Lizzie said in the maddening voice of some-one offering to do a kind deed which is in fact their re-sponsibility in the first place. "Term doesn't start until next week, after all."

Robert stared at her. If she was insisting on playing this daft game, then he'd play it too, for the moment. He thought about the idea of taking Jenny to the vast gift fair at Birmingham. It wouldn't be exciting to take her, but it might be quite soothing, and in his present mood, there was a strong allure in being soothed. He shrugged his shoulders.

"OK then."

"Good," Lizzie said. She sounded relieved. She leaned forward and kissed him, on the cheek.

"Money troubles are not ennobling, are they—"

"No," he said crossly. "No. But they needn't be golden opportunities for self-pity either."

"Rob! I never—"

"I don't want to talk about it any more," he said, inter-rupting. "You go back to Westondale and I'll take Jenny to Birmingham."

Then he turned on his heel and went back across the shop floor to the cash desk, where Jenny was checking the till for the night.

"Do you know," Lizzie heard her say, "that in the end, after all that fuss, that woman bought both the expensive *and* the cheap paper. Aren't people weird?"

"Yes," Robert said with loud and meaningful emphasis. "Yes. Some of them certainly are."

"Is this meat?" Sam said. He poked a suspicious finger at his plate.

"Of course it is," Barbara said. "What does it look like?"

Privately Sam thought it looked like cat sick, but some warning bell in his head rang in time to prevent his saying so. His grandmother, whom he liked because she was so completely unsoppy, had to be treated, he had learned, with a certain circumspection. You could be entirely blunt about some things with her, but not about others, and one of those others was her cooking. That she couldn't cook had never occurred to Sam; he simply thought she didn't try. After all, all women could cook, couldn't they? It was what they did. Some fathers did it too. In Sam's view, Robert was a better cook than Lizzie because he didn't keep wanting you to eat salad. Salad was death to Sam, so was cabbage and, worst of all, broccoli. Broccoli was death times a squillion. Sam couldn't even think about broccoli. He looked at Davy. Davy was regarding his grey meat with apprehension.

"Davy gets very nervous about lunch," Sam said.

Davy immediately looked close to panic.

"He'll have reason to be nervous," Barbara said coolly, "if he doesn't eat it."

She eyed them both. She had offered to look after them for the two days that Lizzie had sole charge of the Gallery while Robert was away in Birmingham. She liked having them, not least because it gave her a chance to rectify various things she thought wrong about the way they were brought up by Lizzie and Robert, like too much television, not enough time in bed and careless table manners. She gave them jobs to do, weeding and shoe cleaning and dusting between the banisters with a miraculous object that was just a mad bunch of feathers on the end of a bamboo that Davy, for some reason, adored, and sent them out into the field behind the house with a list of things to find—various leaves and flowers, pebbles, bird eggshells, wormcasts—to prove to her that they had actually looked at things and not just dawdled about slashing at the hedges with sticks. In the evening, William played draughts and dominoes with them and read to Davy out of something called *The Yellow Fairy Book*, which was dated 1894, so practically out of the Ark, which Sam affected to despise but always loitered just within listening-distance of. If you didn't pull the lavatory plug properly in Granny's house, she made you come back and do it again and then wash your hands and let her smell the soap on them. Her lavatory was terribly cold but it had an interesting chain hanging from an iron tank near the ceiling and a box of sort of tracing paper as well as the usual kind. Davy wouldn't go into it on his own.

"Eat up," Barbara said.

Davy whispered, "Ketchup."

"What?"

"He said could he have some ketchup," Sam said.

"Why?"

Davy whispered, "To take the taste away."

Barbara's mouth trembled. If he hadn't known her better, Sam would have said she was about to smile.

"Grandpa and I don't have ketchup."

Sam looked at Davy. Pimlott had said Davy was a wimp three days before when Davy wouldn't go down the recreation-ground slide head first, and to his considerable surprise, Sam had found himself kicking Pimlott. Pimlott had been amazed. He had stared at Sam with his light eyes as huge and round and spooky as moons, and then he had taken to his heels. Sam hadn't seen him since. After he'd gone, Davy, without further urging, had crept down the slide head first, determined and petrified, clinging to the metal sides with little rigid hands, and on the way home, Sam gave him a piece of chewing gum and a sticker which said, "Be Alert. Britain needs lerts," which Davy was wearing now, stuck on his jersey. He leaned towards Davy.

"Eat it with your potato."

"Why not," Barbara said. She sounded quite friendly.

She was looking at them in quite a friendly way too, as if she almost approved of them.

Davy took a bite and chewed with resolution.

"Well done," Sam said encouragingly.

Davy took another. This one was harder. Swallowing it made his eyes water.

"Where's Grandpa?"

"Out," Barbara said shortly. Out meant that he had gone to get petrol and some grass seed, and probably a pint of stout, and more than probably he would squeeze in a visit to Juliet. Juliet was reputed to be very anxious about Lizzie, according to William, which showed, Barbara thought, the most astounding nerve on Juliet's part. She had no business of any kind to be anxious about Barbara's daughter. Barbara had her own views about Lizzie. They were not unaffectionate views, but they were strongly tinged, also, with disapproval. She looked at her grandsons. Sam was helping Davy load his fork in such a way as almost to conceal the meat under a small cliff of mashed potato. Odd, really, but the twins had always objected to her ground beef too, all those years ago. Odd too, though perhaps less surprising, that the fact of Lizzie's maternal eye being evidently, and one did hope and pray, only temporarily, off the ball was making the children at last take a little responsibility for one another.

"There now," said Sam in cosy tones to Davy, "that wasn't so bad, was it?"

"It wasn't so bad," said Davy bravely, but nonetheless seizing his chance, "as when I cracked my jaw."

Robert gave Jenny lunch in one of the cafés at the Exhibition Centre. He bought her a glass of wine although she protested she never drank at lunchtime, and they ate disappointing slices of quiche full of chunks of potato, and salad, and then surprisingly good coffee, with which they shared a piece of carrot cake. They were having a successful time. Jenny had been very quick in taking in both their budget and the principle of giving the shop an inexpensive, stylish face-lift. Robert had always supposed her taste would run to very traditional things, flowered china and chintzes and slightly teashop ornaments, but she turned out to have a very good eye. She said, eating a morsel of carrot cake, that she had learned what to look for from Lizzie.

Robert said, "Lizzie is a really good sculptor, you know. It was what she was doing at art school when we met."

"Why doesn't she do it now?"

Robert stirred his coffee.

"Why do you think?"

Jenny didn't reply. She was enjoying herself but she didn't feel, at bottom, that it was quite right for her to be here with Robert while Lizzie minded the shop. She had said this, tentatively—it was not in her nature to say anything very forcefully—and had been given to understand that Lizzie had not wanted to go to Birmingham and had suggested that she, Jenny, go instead. She didn't feel quite certain that Robert wanted her there and had said, rather than point this out openly, that surely it was best that he go on his own. No, he had said, it wouldn't be; it was always best to have two tastes and two pairs of eyes because of understanding all the different appetites of the Gallery's customers. Jenny, understanding him to mean that she, being conventional and mildly sentimental, represented a large proportion of the customers, then agreed. She had no illusions about herself, and was proud of the fact that she was a good saleswoman because she was intuitive about what people wanted, and frightened nobody. So she put most of her apprehensions about propriety to the back of her mind, arranged for Toby to spend the night with her next-door neighbour and allowed herself to be taken to Birmingham. When there, she also allowed herself to voice some quite strong opinions, to make some decided choices and to take pleasure in being with Robert, who was, after all, charming, good company and extremely attractive. There were, however, some things she wouldn't allow.

"I don't think we ought to talk about Lizzie. Not when she isn't here."

"But I was only saying, admiringly, what a good sculptor she was—"

"And that would lead to saying other things. Wouldn't it?"

"Are you," Robert said, smiling at her, "just a tiny bit priggish?"

She was unoffended.

"I expect so. My father, who was very colourful, used to say that I was a good girl but that nobody ever climbed a mountain out of goodness."

"Was Mick good?" Robert asked.

Jenny blushed faintly.

"Not very."

"Do you miss him still?"

"Of course. He's—" She hesitated.

"What?"

"He's easier to miss than he was to live with."

"Oh Jenny—"

"But I don't like not being married," Jenny said quickly. "I'm designed to be a wife, I think. If it wasn't for Toby and the Gallery, I'd be miserable. I like being necessary. I like being depended on."

"We do depend on you."

Jenny blushed again. She finished her coffee quickly, and put the cup down.

"Is it very impertinent to ask if things are getting better? Money things, I mean?"

"Not impertinent at all. After all, I told you before I told anyone. I think they perhaps are getting a little better in the sense that they aren't getting worse anymore. We're bumping along the bottom but we aren't still falling."

"I'm so glad."

"It's been so ghastly. Terrible for Lizzie."

"Robert—"

"I have to talk about her," he said firmly. "I have to talk to someone about her and I can't talk to her parents or to Frances and so it has to be you. I just have to say to somebody that I can't take very much more of Lizzie behaving like this, absenting herself in spirit from me and the chil-

dren and the business. I know the money situation has been
a nightmare but we aren't out on the streets, we've got our
home and our business still, the children haven't really suffered. And I know it's tough, when she's been used to
having Frances almost as an extra child, another dependent,
to have her so wrapped up in Luis she hardly even telephones just now, but it's not that tough. Frances is her
sister, not her husband or children. And she's always gone
on about how she wants to see Frances settled and happy,
and now that she's happy she's gone all to pieces, as if *she*
was involved in the love affair. Frankly, it's driving me
crackers, and I also don't see why I should try and put the
Gallery back on its feet single-handed because she doesn't
happen to feel like committing herself to it just now. It
isn't that I'm not trying to understand but I get more baf-
fled every day. I begin to think I've married into a family
of absolute nutters. I always thought the others were a bit
suspect, but I never, until the last year, thought that Lizzie
might be. I'm going to get some more coffee. Would you
like some?"

Jenny shook her head. She was full of sympathy, dangerous, luxurious sympathy. She watched Robert go back
to the self-service counter, shoulders square in his corduroy
jacket. He always wore corduroy jackets, they were his
trademark and they made him, Jenny thought, look both
distinctive and very faintly raffish. Poor man. Poor Robert.
Yet poor Lizzie, too, so unhappy and burdened. Families
could be so terribly oppressive, she could see that, even
though she was herself an only child and mother of—so
far, she always said privately—another one. Jenny hardly
knew Frances, she only knew her as a quieter, dimmer
version of Lizzie, sometimes, in the past, in the shop on
Saturdays, but never now. This was because of her love
affair. Jenny said the words over to herself again: love affair. She hadn't had a love affair with Mick; it had been
more of a courtship, starting at a tennis-club dance and
ending on a Saturday afternoon at Langworth Parish
Church in a frightfully outmoded white lace crinoline chosen by her mother and now lying folded up in a box in

Jenny's attic, never even to be glanced at again. Love affairs
were by all accounts very different to the tidy ritual Jenny
and Mick had followed, like people going through their
allotted paces in a square dance. In love affairs, Jenny suspected, you took your clothes off emotionally and psychologically as well as literally, you let yourself go, you flung
yourself in. In their case, Jenny had to confess, she had
never really let herself go, and when Mick began to, after
their wedding, she didn't really like it. She didn't seem to
recognise him when he wasn't controlling himself. She
looked up. Robert was coming back holding a coffee cup.
You could tell, just by looking at him, that he was sensitive.
Mick had been sensitive too, in his way, but more about
himself than about other people. Robert put the coffee cup
on the table amidst the debris of their lunch and sat down.

"I am very sorry," he said, "to have blown like that. But
if it's any kind of consolation, I feel better for having done
it."

She smiled at him. She wanted to say something to express the sympathy she felt, but at the same time was afraid
to dip her toe in the boiling waters that presently seethed
about Robert and Lizzie. "You're a good girl," she heard
her father's voice say, in despair.

"What are we looking at this afternoon?" she said instead.

He got out his catalogue and spread it open on the edge
of the table. He had ringed various stands on the map of
the exhibition with red biro circles.

"Tinware," he said. "Posters and cotton rugs. For starters
at least."

He smiled at her. She smiled back. He held his hand to
her.

"Come on, Mrs. Hardacre," he said. "What are you sitting there for? It's time you earned your lunch."

SIXTEEN

Frances sat in the neglected gardens of the Alcázar in Seville. It was warm. The clear spring sun shone down out of a bright spring sky. She sat on a tiled seat in one of the brick walks and gazed at the sprouting ungainly palms and the orange trees, already dusty, even in April.

Luis had first brought her to the Alcázar the summer before, on a day of such blinding heat that she had felt she was in a dream. He had led her through the colonnaded courts and tiled rooms of the Palace, the Moorish arches and domes and arabesques so strangely muddled up with the Renaissance columns and galleries. Luis had said the place seethed with stories. One of them concerned King Pedro the Cruel, who had murdered a guest from Granada, one Abu Said, for the sake of his jewels, among which was an uncut ruby that Pedro then presented to the Black Prince at a Court ball given in his honour, in 1350. It was firmly believed that the ruby had gone back to England and that Henry V had then worn it during the battle of Agincourt.

"And where is it now?"

"Where do you think? In the crown of your Queen Elizabeth!"

Frances thought about it and pictured the Queen wearing Abu Said's ruby together with her bifocal spectacles as she was wont to do on State occasions. She told Luis about it. He loved the idea. They had been out in the gardens by a great still tank of water and Frances had looked down and seen the reflection of Luis laughing and laughing about the Queen. Pedro the Cruel had kept two queens at the Alcázar, first, a Bourbon princess, whom he had rejected in favour of María de Padilla, his beloved second wife, so beloved that the gallants of his court were reputed to have queued up to drink her bathwater. One of them had refused, Luis said. He'd claimed that if he tasted the sauce, he might covet the partridge afterwards. Frances had gone down into the vaulted basement to look at the place where María's famous baths had been and then climbed to the upper floor of the palace to inspect the bedroom King Pedro had made for her because, he said, the winter coldness of the ground floor might damage her. It was, six centuries later, a weird bedroom. It had Moorish arches and panels and very bad nineteenth-century ceiling paintings and a terrible silver table that had belonged to Queen Isabel II. Over the door lintel was painted a row of five skulls. It made you wonder, Frances thought, about the private life of Pedro the Cruel and María de Padilla; it made you wonder too, as she so often did now, about the essential, ancient and utterly different nature of Spanishness.

Frances had flown to Málaga three days before to escort her first party to the *posada* at Mojas. It had been a huge success. Her clients were charmed with the hotel, with the countryside, with Juan and the smiling waiters, with the look of the dinner menu, with the new yellow deckchairs waiting for them in welcome under the acacia trees. There had been the usual tiny hitches—a dripping shower, not enough coat hangers, a jammed window—but nothing serious. Frances had stayed two nights, overseen the first walks and meals, collected her congratulations and left them plotting the best route to Gerald Brenan's village and the order of priority for the glories of Granada. She had

then driven back to Málaga and caught an internal flight
to Seville for the weekend.

Luis's flat in Seville was in reality a small suite of rooms
at the back of the *Posada* de los Naranjos. They were cool,
dim rooms—cold in winter, Frances had found; Andalucía
seemed, like Tuscany, to have no idea of how to comfort
itself in cold weather—that looked down into an alley
Frances loved, whitewashed as usual, but with whitewash
that was peeling a little. The walls were all of different
heights, and some were pierced by windows, and some, the
lower ones, had russet-tiled tops and the stiff, shiny-leaved
branches of orange trees thrust themselves over them.
There were balconies in the alley too, and lamps on brack-
ets, and a lot of rather shabby back doors through which
people went with shopping and ladders and bicycles, and
on all the balconies and ledges there were flowerpots, held
in place by loops of wire, and already cascading starry
geraniums, scarlet and white and pink. At night, in summer, a man in the opposite house, in a room with a balcony
on which no one ever sat, played a guitar and sang the
long, plangent, melancholy strains of the *cante jondo*. Those
summer nights had introduced Frances to the spirit of the
south.

Luis had a bedroom and a sitting room looking down
into this alley, and a bathroom with no window except a
skylight which made you, Frances thought, think about the
weather in a way that no ordinary window ever did. In
that bathroom, as in the even smaller bathroom in Madrid
and in the slightly larger one in Fulham, Frances now kept
a toothbrush and a bottle of cleansing lotion and a pot of
moisturising cream. Every time she came, she added something. Luis liked that; he wanted her to add more, he
wanted her to keep shoes and shirts and pairs of jeans in
both his flats. He said they gave him comfort during the
long and frequent times when she was at home in London.
He said that if he felt particularly melancholy without her,
he would sometimes brush his teeth with her toothbrush,
and there was certainly something piquant, even piercing,
to think of him standing in that bathroom with a square

of huge Sevillian stars shining down through the skylight above his head, with her toothbrush in his mouth.

Bathrooms were a preoccupation with Frances that afternoon in the gardens of the Alcázar. Ten days before, on two successive mornings, Frances had gone through a little private ritual in her London bathroom with two home-testing pregnancy kits, bought from two different chemists. She had done this twice quite deliberately, out of a most enormous need to be entirely sure, a need which seemed to rise out of her like a physical reflex she couldn't possibly control.

The ritual had taken place as such rituals commonly have to do, first thing in the morning, one involving two separate plastic phials, and one a kind of plastic dropper, whose tip, said the accompanying leaflet, would turn blue if the result were positive. In the first kit, a circle would form, a blue or purplish circle, and hang there, signifying the beginning of the world or the end of it, depending upon your circumstances. The leaflets were written in chatty nursy prose, using the kind of language in which Frances half-expected any mention of a foetus to be described as "a little stranger." The assumption, in both, was that the blue dropper tip and the blue circle would be greeted with relief and delight, the result, naturally, of careful, rational, adult planning.

Precisely what her own feelings were, she could have described to nobody; chiefly, she was conscious of the sheer strength of them. Above everything, she knew, as she had known for months that she wanted—no, *desired*—Luis's baby, not just *a* baby because the time clock was ticking on towards forty, but his baby. Every hour with him, even if they were quarrelling, confirmed this, notwithstanding his having said that if she were to become pregnant, it would be the end of everything between them. He could not, from the point of view of his circumstances, have been a more wrong-headed choice, but that seemed to Frances to weigh as nothing against the rightness of him as a human being; as a man, for both her and for a potential baby. Yet besides all this surging conviction and instinct, there was fear. Sitting on the edge of the bath in Fulham and looking at the two little phials of urine side by side on the closed lid of the lavatory, Frances would have said that her feeling was actually closer to terror than to fear, and a very complex terror at that, composing, as it did, an equal desire to see and not to see the blue circle. As she sat there, during the interminable five minutes the instructions had told her the chemicals would take to react, she had, it felt, all the unwanted time in the world to reflect upon the size of the gamble she had taken.

It did not seem to her possible that Luis could, in any way, simply switch off loving her, like turning off an electric current, if she were pregnant. They were too deep in for that, too involved, too twined about one another. He would be furious and then he would relent. He might even consider at last divorcing José's mother and marrying her, and they would, all three, be a family in a flat in Madrid and she would push the baby out for walks in the Botanical Gardens near the Prado—stop this, Frances told herself sternly, stop this, it's absurd and *will not happen*. Or—will it? And, besides Luis, there will be Lizzie to tell, and Mum and Dad, and Nicky. And the business! What will happen to the business? And what will Lizzie say to hearing that I am pregnant? If I am ... She stared at the two phials. She was cold now, still only in her nightgown and bathrobe, her feet bare on the bathroom floor. She sat up straight, pushing her hair off her face, then holding her hands together in front of her, almost in an instinctive attitude of prayer.

It was there. In the right-hand phial a blue circle was suspended, clear and symmetrical. The blue circle. The test was positive. She, Frances Shore, was pregnant by Luis Gómez Moreno. She had longed for it to happen and now it had and she was filled first with disgust that this huge event should be represented by a cold blue ring in a horrible little test tube, and then, in a deluge, with panic and rapture and misery and relief. She stared and stared at the phial. Then she unlocked her hands and laid one of them, with a kind of enquiring amazement, on her belly under the bathrobe. She looked out of the bathroom window. The April sky was an undecided mixture of blue and grey and white, but it seemed, suddenly, to have enormous significance for Frances, as confused and full of conflict as she felt herself.

"I am pregnant," she said out loud to the empty bathroom. "And nobody knows but me."

The second morning she performed the second test and was unsurprised to see the tip of the dropper turn blue and very surprised to feel all the enormous engulfing emotions she had felt the previous day all over again. The second day, the joy seemed slightly less and the fear slightly more, as were a whole tide of wretched, unavoidable preoccupations with advancing practicalities—what to do, who to tell, when to tell whom, how to phrase it. She was terribly tired that day, and had a headache, and Nicky, thinking it must be about the time for Frances's period, suggested she go up to the flat in the afternoon and lie down. Frances shook her head. She did not, that second day, wish to think. The prospect of being shut up alone with her thoughts reminded her too much and too wretchedly of those long wastes of solitary life before Luis, and this was because, for the first time in their relationship, there was a secret between them, and a potentially explosive secret at that.

It was not difficult for Frances not to tell anybody, but it was extremely difficult to speak to Luis on the telephone when he rang, as he did, every evening, for a long and comfortable conversation. Of course he felt no constraint, but she felt absolutely trussed up by it, and she also felt, unhappily, as if she were, for the first time since they met, a long and chilly way away from him. He asked, on a couple of evenings, if she was feeling all right.

"Fine. Just a bit tired. There's so much work always as the season begins. You'd think you'd done all the work, all winter, and all you'd got to do now was pop the people neatly on to aeroplanes, but it doesn't seem to happen like that—"

"You must look after yourself, *querida*."

Her heart leapt. That was what contented, proud, protective fathers-to-be said to their pregnant beloveds in romantic novels. Could he . . . ?

"In one week you will be here, and I will look after you. I think it is time you came to the bull fight."

"No! Luis, you promised—"

He was laughing. He loved to startle her, ruffle her feathers.

"You are so satisfactory to tease."

"I know," she said, mortified.

"I love you."

"I know that, too."

"Good," he said. "You ought to, by now. Go to bed early. Take care of yourself."

"I will. I am—"

Bed was the one place she wanted to be until she got there. She wasn't physically tired, only emotionally so, which was confusing and landed her flat on her back by nine o'clock with her brain whirling like a windmill. It was the prospect of radical change that had begun to haunt her, a change that would involve coping with almost nothing at present known to her. Falling in love with Luis had been a change, of course, from her reticent and single life, but that had been a change that was all too easy to accommodate because it brought nothing that wasn't enriching and expanding, did nothing to curtail her freedom, nothing to increase her vulnerability or decrease her independence. But this change was of another order altogether; she had brought it about of her own free will, and now that it had happened it was going to take a lot of that free will straight back again. Those first few nights after the ritual in the bathroom had been, to say the least, profoundly unnerving.

It had been a relief to get on the plane to Málaga. In an airport crowd, talking to several of her clients who had, by now, become friends and were apt to send her Christmas cards enclosing photographs of themselves on a Shore to Shore holiday, or of their grandchildren, Frances began to feel real again. The ordinariness of what was going on— people asleep wretchedly, half on seats, half on their luggage, people glazedly eating and drinking, people mooning through the duty-free shops stupefied by artificial decisions about alcohol and tobacco, watches and chocolate—was an effective restorative for her sense of proportion. Barbara, she reflected, had always flung herself into whirlwind domestic activity the moment there was an emotional crisis. Perhaps this was not only instinctive, but an excellent instinct at that. It reminded you that, at bottom, life was quite literally a matter of survival, of making sure that you were still there, living and breathing, at the dawn of a new day. It was no bad thing to remember that sometimes. It put all the sweaty struggles of achievement firmly in their proper place.

The moment the plane had touched down in Málaga, Frances had felt better still. There was the sun, there was Spain, there, in three days, would be Luis. There was also the *posada* at Mojas, which Frances thought she could probably never visit without emotion, and would be disappointed if she did. She had elected, in order to spare the room of her first visit for two of her clients, to take a much smaller single room without a view, whose door opened into one of the irregular internal courtyards. She couldn't help reflecting, while unpacking in it, how miraculous it would have been if this baby had been conceived in Mojas, even, best of all, in the very bed where Luis had first become her lover and in which Mr. and Mrs. Ballantyne from Amersham now lay, no doubt, as trimly and separately side by side as figures on a tomb. But it hadn't been conceived in Mojas, it had been, almost certainly, conceived on a Saturday afternoon in Fulham after a morning spent buying Luis some English shoes ("Brogues? What is this word 'brogues'? Irish? These are *Irish* shoes?") and a bottle of wine with lunch. It had been good lovemaking, but not remarkable. Looking back, it seemed wrong, somehow, that the making of a baby such as this baby should have been good but unremarkable.

Whatever it had been, it had been done more than a month ago now. Everything in these shabby Spanish gardens, the palm trees, the myrtles, the leggy box hedges, the oleanders with drifts of litter underneath them, had all been standing there then as they were now, and as they would be in the coming darkness of the evening when she, Frances, would tell Luis that she was, without question, going to have a child.

José came up to the flat for dinner. They had ordered, as they often did, from the restaurant of the hotel, and José, as he often did, came up to eat at least one course with them. He preferred doing this while Frances was in Seville, because if she wasn't there, his father was not so restrained with him and was likely to tell him that he was over-indulged, incompetent, and only kept on as manager of the hotel because of blood ties, which he, Luis, was beginning to feel was the worst reason in the world for employing anybody. If Frances was there, Luis was more moderate, and made something of a joke of his exasperation. José liked Frances. He thought her an incomprehensible choice for a mistress strictly on physical grounds—his taste ran currently in the direction of golden-skinned, golden-haired Californian dreams—but he could see why his father liked her company. He liked her company himself, he liked her straightforwardness, her strange sense of humour, her lack of melodrama. He thought she'd had a good effect on his father, made him happy, relaxed him, given him other things to think about than scaffolding and hotels and boots and shoes. One of José's friends, a young woman who was rising rapidly through the civil service ranks of the Andalusian health service, asked if José thought his father would marry his English girlfriend. José had been horrified.

"*Marry* her? Of course not, it's absolutely out of the question. You must be mad even to ask me such a thing!"

It had quite disturbed him. He was perfectly used, now, to his mother's relentless vendetta against his father, and his grandmothers' lamentations and recriminations about the separation between his parents—after all, plenty of his friends had parents in the same situation and divorce was becoming as common as marriage—but for his father to marry Frances was quite another matter altogether, a matter not to be thought of without indignation amounting to outrage. The next time they met, after this suggestion had been made to José, he had looked at Frances quite differently, with suspicion and disapproval. But she not only hadn't seemed to notice his cold and furious glances, she had also behaved with exactly the same unpossessive collectedness in his father's presence as she had always shown. It struck José suddenly that perhaps she might not *want* to marry his father, her choice not his, and this thought threw him into quite a reverse turmoil of angry feelings. He also had a dreadful apprehension that if Frances wasn't actually laughing at him, she was certainly smiling a little. He began to avoid Frances in case this was indeed true, and he wouldn't go up to the flat when she was there. Nobody commented on this and nothing, emotionally, seemed to change. José began to miss both his dinners in the flat and Frances, who, even by her silent presence, seemed to defend him from his father. He told himself he had rightly made a stand in defence of the honour of his family; he began to appear again at the Friday and Saturday night dinner table. In time, as with every other crisis in José's life, he ceased even to think about what had troubled him. He brought Frances flowers occasionally and took, as a pretty Austrian student at Seville University, and on whom he had his eye, had taught him to do, to kissing Frances's hand.

"Oh, fol-de-rol," Frances said to him.

"Why do you say this?"

"Because it makes me think of the way people behave in operettas. Oh fie, sir, and la, sir, and I shall tap you playfully in reproof with my fan."

"I do not understand you."

"No," Frances said. "You wouldn't."

"Why would I not?"

"Because you're Spanish."

"It is magnificent to be Spanish!"

"José," Frances said affectionately, "you are an ass."

He grinned at her. She looked tired, he thought, even a little transparent, as if her skin was about to bruise, out of fatigue, of its own accord. It was probably overwork, he decided. He himself did not know the meaning of overwork—he took enormous care not to—but he knew that it could easily afflict people who weren't constantly on their guard against it.

"Where is my father?"

"In the shower."

"Did you order the *ajo blanco* tonight? It is excellent. And also the *salmonetes*, what is it—"

"Mullet," Frances said. "Red mullet. I don't know. Luis has ordered it all. I spent the afternoon at the Alcázar."

"The Alcázar?" José said in amazement. "But what were you doing there?"

"Thinking."

"You are a most extraordinary person. I think you also are a little tired."

"Yes."

"Then you should be sitting and I shall bring you a glass of wine."

"Yes please," Frances said. She stepped out of her shoes and folded herself up on the sofa by the window, open to the darkening alley.

Luis came out of the bedroom running his hands over his still damp hair. José went up to him and they embraced, easily, without words. Frances thought of how naturally Davy and Sam kissed their father but how Alistair would now stand a little at a distance, stiffly, shackled by the onset of self-consciousness.

"English men, I mean fathers and adult sons, hardly ever kiss each other."

Luis cast himself down on the sofa beside her.

"Often I do not want to kiss José, I want to smack him."

"Used you to?"

"Often," José said, bringing wine in thick, pale-green glasses with bubbles of air trapped in them. "My childhood was terrible. He beat me with sticks and shut me in cupboards." He winked.

"Poor you," Frances said. She could feel Luis lying against her, heavy and clean.

"And now he kisses me but he shouts."

"I don't shout," Luis said. "I never raise my voice. I

merely say things you do not want to hear so you imagine
that I am shouting."

Frances looked at him.

"Do you imagine that, too? What do you do when people
say things you don't want to hear?"

He turned his head. Their eyes were only inches apart.

"Why do you ask me that?"

There was a tiny beat and then she said, "Oh, idle curiosity. To see if things run in families—"

"Oh?" he said.

José went to the telephone.

"I am going to check on your order for dinner. You must
eat the mullet—"

"I don't want it," Luis said. "I want the crayfish."

"But—"

"In a minute, I *will* shout," Luis said. "I own this hotel,
I want the crayfish; you may be my son but you are also
my manager."

José's hand hovered over the telephone.

"Why don't you," Frances suggested, "go down to the
kitchen and see what looks best and we will eat that, even
if it's neither mullet nor crayfish?"

Luis laid his cheek on her shoulder.

"How diplomatic."

"Or practical. I'm hungry."

"I shall bring *tapas* also," José said, moving towards the
door. "You want the little mussels?"

"Yes."

"Anything—"

"The little mussels and the big olives—"

"José," Luis said in Spanish, "get lost."

The door opened, and closed.

"An exasperating boy."

"Just rather young for his age perhaps—"

Luis took his cheek away from Frances's shoulder and
picked up her free hand, the one not holding the wine glass.

"Frances?"

"Yes—"

"What do you wish to say to me that I will not want to hear?"

She gave a tiny, involuntary gasp. This was not in her plan. Her plan had been to wait until Luis was replete with wine and food, and José had taken himself back downstairs to his end-of-the-day managerial duties; and then to say, by way of many gentle introductory sentiments and expressions of love and personal happiness, what she had been planning how to say all the long afternoon in the gardens of the Alcázar. But Luis, with that powerful human instinct that he had used like a sword to cut through to the heart of her, had, at a stroke, wrecked her plan. She panicked.

"Not now—"

"Yes. Now."

"No, later, when we're alone—"

"We are alone now," he said. His hold on her hand had become a grip.

She swallowed. She leaned forward and put her wine glass on a little lamp table near by.

"It's very important. I don't want to tell you badly, or in a hurry—"

"Now," Luis insisted.

She turned her head. She said, looking at him, "You don't want to hear this. It's the one thing you don't want to hear."

"Tell me!"

"Let go of my hand. You're hurting."

He dropped her hand abruptly, as if it were an impersonal object not in any way attached to her.

"Now, then. Tell me."

"I am pregnant, Luis," Frances said, and her voice seemed to echo in the small room, as if she were speaking in a church. "I am going to have a baby."

He shouted, "No!"

"Yes," she said.

"How dare you?" he shouted. "How could you? How dare you deceive me?"

She got up and moved away from him, behind the table already laid for the three of them with spoons for the white *gazpacho* and knives and forks for the fish, and glasses, glimmering in the fading light.

"I wanted to," she said. "I needed to. I wanted your baby with a want I can't really describe to you because it's more like a need, a craving. I decided to risk it. To risk—" She paused, took a breath and added, "You."

He stood up too. He was almost incoherent with fury.

"You know what I said to you!"

"Yes—"

"You will become a mother, you will change, it is too horrible to think of! Is this a trap? Do you suppose you will force me to marry you this way?"

"No."

"Then you are right! I will never marry you! Do you hear me? You have deceived me, betrayed me, *deliberately* you have done this, you even admit it! You were the one woman I have ever known who I thought was honest and now you are not honest, you are like all the rest, you play tricks, you cheat, you break our trust and our faith!"

She held on to a chair back. She was shaking and her heart was thudding.

"And," he yelled in Spanish, "you don't even care! You think you have won! You think you have tamed me! But you will see, I will show you, you will see what it is to betray me."

"You're quite right," she said in English. "I'm not sorry. I meant to do it and I'm glad."

He went over to the open window and held the bottom of the frame, gripping it, his shoulders shaking as if he were weeping.

"You don't know what you have done, you stupid Frances—"

"I do—"

"No," he said, turning round. "No. You think you know, and perhaps you may know for yourself but you don't know for *me*."

She said, idiotically, "Well, I've clearly made you very angry."

He gave a little snort of exasperation.

"Not that—"

From the alley outside rose the sudden broken strains of someone strumming on a guitar, a strolling someone, tuning up, humming a little. Luis gave a shuddering sigh.

"I will lose you now," he said more gently. "That is what you don't understand."

"Never!"

"Yes," he said. "You can't help it, nor can I. But there is not room for a child and a man with a woman who is a mother."

"What utter nonsense!"

"No," he said, shaking his head. "You will see. You will see what you have done."

She held hard to the chair back.

"Oh don't be so theatrical, so *Spanish*—"

"Enough!"

"Children *add* to relationships, they are a development of relationships, they're part of the nature of being together—growing together."

He said softly, interrupting, "I don't think so. I don't believe it."

"Luis—"

He let go of the window and came over to her. He put his arm around her shoulders, a kindly arm. He said, "I am going out now."

She was horrified.

"Oh no!"

"Yes," he said. "What's done is done. You must take care of yourself and I must help you to do it. But not now, not tonight. I will be back later but for now I must go out."

She nodded. Desolation flooded through her in a cold, heavy wave.

"As you wish."

He kissed her. He leaned forward and kissed her cheek, not her mouth, and then he took his arm away from her shoulders, and went into the bedroom. When he came out, he had added a tie and a jacket to his previous shirt and trousers. He paused for a second and looked at her, and then, without speaking, he went across the room and

opened the door and went out. Frances didn't move. She
stood there, still leaning on the chair back, and longed and
longed for him. The longing made her feel quite faint.
After several minutes, she managed to feel her way round
the table and back to the sofa. She took a gulp of her hardly
tasted wine, and sat there, holding the glass in one hand
with the other laid across her stomach. There was no thinking to be done. She simply had to sit there and keep
breathing and wait for these first moments to be over, to
become the past, that was done with, and not the present,
that still had to be endured.

There were feet on the stairs, and José's customary tact-
ful tap on the door.

"Come—"

"Look," he said. "The little eggs of the *codorniz*, what is
the *codorniz*?"

"The quail," Frances said.

José looked round.

"Where is my father?"

"Gone out."

"Out? But—"

"José," Frances said, "I think you had better leave me.
We won't be eating dinner tonight." She glanced at him.
"You see, I'm afraid that your father and I have had a
quarrel."

SEVENTEEN

Alistair caught chicken-pox. He felt rotten but his feelings of rottenness were outweighed by the mortification of having a spot-ravaged face. He could bear nobody to see him, not even his parents, and lay wretchedly in the hot little bedroom he shared with Sam with an old silk scarf of Lizzie's draped across his face. When the spots spread downward into his armpits and across his chest and finally into his groin, he was almost in despair. Consumed by self-disgust and a terror of being seen, he crept to the bathroom wrapped in a sheet like a ghoul, and would only let the doctor examine him if there was no one else in the room, and the door was shut.

"It's only chicken-pox," Lizzie said in exasperation.

"Not to him," Robert argued. "He thinks he's decaying—"

"Rubbish."

Robert glared at her. How could she be so unsympathetic?

"It's not rubbish. He's about to become an adolescent and you know what that means. He's really suffering."

Lizzie pulled a face. She had made Alistair a jug of

homemade lemonade but he had refused to lift his scarf even to look at it, let alone drink it. She was extremely sorry for him, she told herself, but she also thought he was being hysterical lying there in the dark, shrouded and self-pitying. It was only chicken-pox, for heaven's sake, common, or garden, old childhood chicken-pox.

"I don't really want to take time off work," Lizzie said. "As long as you and Jenny can cope. After all, he won't let me do anything for him, he won't even let me stay in the room with him, so there doesn't seem any point in being here rather than at work, does there?"

"You're his mother," Robert said.

She shot him a defiant glance.

"And you're his father!"

"With work to do—"

"I've got work to do!" Lizzie shouted. "Don't give me that! Who's paying the interest on the rest of the overdraft if it isn't me? Who's—"

"Shut up," Robert said. He closed his eyes. "Shut up. This isn't a competition, you know, about who's tireder or who's working harder—"

"You started it!" Lizzie shouted again. "You started it by implying it was more my job to look after Alistair than yours!"

Robert glared at her.

"Don't tell me I don't do my fair share with the children—"

"When it suits you."

"That's monstrous," Robert said furiously, "monstrous and untrue. I asked you whether you'd like it to be me or you who took an outside job, and you chose yourself, so of course, being here all the time, I've been responsible for the children far more than you have. Hell, when I went to Birmingham, you couldn't even cope with them all for two days and had to send the little ones to your mother—"

"But you took Jenny!" Lizzie screeched. "You had Jenny!"

"Leave Jenny out of this!"

"Why? Why should I? You have Jenny here and I don't have anyone—"

"Please," a voice said.

They both turned. In the doorway of the sitting room stood a medium-sized figure draped in a pink sheet with a yellow-and-white-striped towel over its head and face. At the bottom, two grey wool feet protruded gloomily.

"You're making my room shake," Alistair said. "I really can't see what there is to shout about. You haven't got chicken-pox."

"Sorry," Lizzie said, "sorry—"

"I don't want to be looked after," Alistair said. "I just want to be better. And I certainly don't want you two yelling all over the place."

Robert went over and put his arm around Alistair's pink-sheeted shoulders. Alistair flinched.

"Don't *touch* me!"

"Sorry, old son. Come back to bed now—"

"I'll take you," Lizzie said, rushing forward.

"No!" Alistair said. "Neither of you will and if you touch me again I shall probably bite you."

"Darling—"

"Go to work," Robert said to Lizzie. "Just go to work, would you?"

She hesitated. Alistair suddenly appeared neither melo-dramatic nor comical to her but full of real pathos.

"I won't go in today, I'll ring—"

"No," Robert said.

"But—"

"You can't do anything here," Robert said. "Can you? I mean, you said so yourself."

Alistair turned and began to shuffle back down the short corridor to his bedroom, trailing his pink-cotton train.

"OK," Lizzie said, almost in a whisper.

Alistair's bedroom door banged shut.

"I'll come up every hour," Robert said, "as I've done since he got ill. As I've done all the time you were away at work."

"I'm not at work for fun!" Lizzie cried resentfully.

Robert said nothing. He didn't even look at her. He merely picked up the keys for the Gallery office and went out of the room and down the communal stairs and left her standing there, in a turmoil. After a few minutes, she went along to Alistair's room and knocked.

"Ally?"

"Go away!"

"I just want to make sure you're all right before I go—"

"I'm fine," Alistair said flatly, his voice muffled by the scarf.

"I'll see you tonight—"

"OK."

"Is there anything you'd like, anything you really like to eat—"

"No."

"Ice-cream? That American one? Melon?"

"No."

Lizzie put her forehead against the flat, painted surface of the door.

"See you tonight, then."

"OK."

"Keep drinking, drink as much as you can—"

"OK."

"I'm not being heartless, going to work, Ally, really I'm not, I have to go, you know that, don't you?"

Silence.

"Because of money. You do know that, don't you? It's so that we can go on living, so that—"

She stopped. She straightened up.

"Bye, darling."

"Bye," Alistair said in a voice loud with relief.

After he had seen Lizzie leave the Gallery, Robert came out of the office and went down to the shop floor to see Jenny. She was cleaning pictures with some emerald-green liquid in a spray bottle. She looked up as he approached but she didn't stop polishing.

"I don't think customers ever consider that most of shop keeping is housework, do you?"

"Did you see Lizzie?"

"Only briefly," Jenny said. "Because she was late, poor thing, she came through like the wind so we only had time to say hello and good-bye in the same breath. How's Alistair?"

"Spotty and miserable."

"Poor boy," Jenny said. She squirted glass cleaner onto another picture. "I had chicken-pox about his age and it was awful. I suppose the others will get it now."

Robert groaned. "Don't say such things—"

"They might as well," Jenny said comfortably. "Get it all over with at once."

"But how would we manage?"

She looked at him.

"Manage?"

"Yes. If the little ones get it too, how on earth would we cope with them and the Gallery?"

Jenny stepped back from the picture, squinting to see if she had left any smears on the glass.

"Well, I don't suppose many pictures would get polished for a bit, but there'd be no problem with two of us. One down here, one up there, take it in turns. And if Toby gets it, I'll just bung him in with the others."

She sounded so sensible and ordinary that Robert suddenly felt she was both an angel and a genius.

He said, "Don't you ever lose your cool?"

She looked away from him.

"I try not to. I'm rather frightened of not being in control."

"I think everybody feels that—"

"Maybe they do," Jenny said, "but I think I'm worse than most."

"I think you're wonderful," Robert said.

Jenny blushed, a slow, steady, glowing blush.

"You mustn't talk like that."

"Because?"

"Because it isn't true," Jenny said. "I'm practical and reliable and useful, but that's all."

Robert smiled at her.

"Just now," he said, "being useful and reliable and practical is my definition of wonderful. No tantrums, no screams and shrieks—"

"No problems either," Jenny said crisply, moving away towards the next picture.

"Jenny—"

"No," she said, "go and get started. I'm not a fool, I know what you're trying to say and you shouldn't talk about it, not when she isn't here, I've *told* you."

"Sorry," Robert said. His heart ached suddenly, as if there was a headache in it. "You're quite right. I'll be in the office if you need me."

She nodded, her grey hair swinging neatly. She didn't dare look at him.

"See you later—"

As he opened the office door, the private telephone line was ringing, the line whose number was only known to the children's schools, to Barbara and William, to Frances, to a few very favoured suppliers and customers.

"Robert Middleton," he said into the receiver.

"Mr. Middleton? Oh Mr. Middleton, it's Mrs. Cairns here, from Langworth Junior. I'm afraid I have to ask you to come and collect Sam at once, if you would. He's a mass of spots, looks like chicken-pox to me. He says his older brother has it."

"Yes," Robert said.

"Mr. Middleton, you know the quarantine rules—"

"Yes."

"It means that every other child Sam has been in contact with—"

"I know, Mrs. Cairns. I'm so sorry."

"Then you'll be here at once?"

"As soon as I can—"

"And I think you'd better take Davy home with you too."

Robert put his hand over his face.

"Yes, Mrs. Cairns," he said.

Lizzie came home to find Alistair still shrouded like a mummy, and Sam spreadeagled stark naked on the sofa. He said if he put his pyjamas on, or even a T-shirt, the itching was unbearable, and he couldn't even put his legs together or his arms by his sides because then the itches touched each other and he had to scream. He screamed anyway, just to show her. In the kitchen Harriet was eating a raw carrot and reading a teen magazine, with dark glasses on because, she said, she had a headache and chicken-pox started with headaches, didn't they. In the bathroom, Robert was bathing Davy, who was perfectly certain he had found a spot on his knee and was begging not to have to lie in the dark wound up in sheets and towels and scarves.

Lizzie sat down on the closed lid of the lavatory and took her shoes off.

"What are we to do?"

"Carry on," Robert said grimly, soaping Davy's back.

"I'll do that," Lizzie said. "You start supper."

"No."

"Then I'll start supper. What is there?"

"What you've brought home."

"I haven't brought anything home. I worked until five-thirty today, remember? Everything shuts at five-thirty."

"Then there's nothing."

"No food?" Davy whispered. He peered at his knee. "It really tickles—"

"You haven't got chicken-pox," Robert said patiently.

Davy looked up, eyes like saucers.

"Suppose they come in the night?"

"You come and tell us," Lizzie said.

"Suppose—"

"There must be some pasta," Lizzie said, standing up, interrupting.

"If you say so."

"Why are you in such a foul mood?"

Robert said nothing. He lifted Davy up to wash his bottom.

"I've done termly bill reminders all day," Lizzie said. "All damn day, nothing else. It was charming, one phone call after another to parents who don't answer or are in permanent meetings." She stepped over Rob's legs. She was suddenly so tired she could hardly stand. "It's not my fault," she said, her voice shaking, "that they've all got chicken-pox—"

"I never said it was."

"But you're implying—"

"Go and start supper," Robert said. He lifted Davy out of the bath as if he were a baby and not, Davy thought, a boy. Davy squirmed free of his father's hands and seized the towel.

"I'll do it—"

"As you wish."

"Robert," Lizzie said, looking down at them both, "why do we keep bickering like this?"

He looked back up at her with a look quite devoid of sympathy. Then he turned back to Davy and began to dry his feet with a trailing corner of the towel.

"What a bloody stupid question," Robert said. "Why the hell do you think?"

The following day, Lizzie rang Westondale to say she would not be in since two of her children now had chicken-pox and one of the remaining ones, if not both, was bound to succumb any minute. Mrs. Drysdale, who had answered the telephone, sounded insincerely sympathetic and said she would ask Freda Mason to come in and hold the secretarial fort for a few days. Lizzie could have wept. She imagined Freda Mason remorselessly undoing in three days all that Lizzie had accomplished in three terms, rehanging the terrible curtains and string holders for spider plants, deliberately feeding stapled paper into the computer's printer, reraising the parental hackles it had taken Lizzie a year to persuade to lie down.

"Couldn't you get a temp from an agency?" Lizzie said. "Isn't it a bit unfair to ask Freda, now that she's retired?"

"Not unfair at all," Mrs. Drysdale said firmly. "Once part of the Westondale family, always a part of it. She'll be only too pleased."

You bet, Lizzie told herself, you absolutely bet she will be. She shouted to the empty kitchen, "She'll be in her blasted element!"

"What elephant?" Davy said, coming in wearing only the bottom half of his pyjamas. "Could these be kung fu trousers?"

"What?"

Davy stuck out one foot at an angle and clenched his fist.

"Like this. To go pow, *pow* in."

"I expect so." She looked down at him. "If you're going to get chicken-pox, could you try and hurry up?"

By lunchtime, he had obliged. It was a hot day, one of those freakish hot days of early summer, and when Lizzie opened the windows of the flat, traffic noise and fumes seemed to swirl into the room like brown smoke. Sam had the television on, far louder than necessary because he said chicken-pox had made him deaf, and anyway he couldn't hear above the noise of the cars. He pulled the curtains because Alistair told him he would go blind as well as deaf if he didn't, and he and Davy lounged in the gloom in front of an old Greta Garbo movie, complaining and scratching. Behind one closed door, Alistair lay as usual even though, as Harriet had pointed out, his spots were fast fading, and behind the other Harriet painted her toenails alternately red and black and fantasised that Fraser Pringle would one day look at her with the look he was now bestowing on her once best friend and now worst enemy, Heather Weston. Lizzie made a careful invalids' lunch of thinly sliced ham and new potatoes and tiny frozen peas and everybody groaned and refused it and said why couldn't they have hamburgers. Then Pimlott came sliding in like a shadow, sent by his mother to catch chicken-pox and get it over with, and immediately, at the sight of Sam, took all his clothes off too, revealing a pale, greenish body that reminded Lizzie of the subterranean roots of bind-weed. It also made her panic. She did not, she found, want a naked Pimlott anywhere near Sam or Davy, so she lost her temper out of a primitive apprehension and shouted at Pimlott and ordered him into his clothes and out of the flat. He went, slithering and muttering, his moonish eyes fixed malevolently on her face, and when he had disap-peared, Lizzie sat on the stairs out of a pointless but in-stinctive need to prevent his coming back, and burst into tears of strain and fatigue and disappointment and confu-sion, which is where Jenny found her half an hour later, coming up during a lull in the shop to see what she could do to help.

Jenny took over. For the next few days, she said, Robert must mind the Gallery, she would mind the children and Lizzie must go to Westondale.

Lizzie said, "But I can't have you nursing my children!"

"Why not?"

"Because it isn't fair, it isn't your problem—"

"That's why it's easier for me to do," Jenny said.

She got Alistair out of his sheet and his bed and into clothes, she got Sam and Davy into at least T-shirts and she made regular, unremarkable meals which the children ate with stunned docility. At lunchtime, Robert came up to the flat for an hour, and she went down to the shop in his place, and at three-thirty each afternoon she went off to collect Toby, and returned until Lizzie came home. Robert and Lizzie almost fawned over her in their gratitude, but she wouldn't accept thanks.

"I like this. Everybody likes to be needed, don't they? There's something rather exciting about an emergency, anyway. Just let me get on with it."

So they let her. They let her nurse their children and wash their kitchen floor and iron their shirts and sheets and leave, in the fridge, for their supper, bowls of soup and salad. They let her, so that Lizzie could drive off to Wes-

tondale without leaving in her wake a clamour of complaint and recrimination, and so that she could then work
all day without guilt pressing upon her like a migraine.
They let her, so that Robert could devote himself to the
shop without feeling the fractious pressure of domestic life
nagging at him and the accompanying resentment it in-
duced building up in him like a gathering thunderstorm.
They let her, because it was so easy to do so and they were
so tired, deep down, after all the months of stress, that
anything remotely easy seemed to them like unexpected
water in a desert.

And then Robert came up from the shop at closing time,
on one of Lizzie's late days, and found, to his astonished
admiration, all five children, Toby Hardacre and his own
four, peacefully in the sitting room, without the television
on.

"Where's Jenny?"

"Cleaning the bathroom," Harriet said.

"Why aren't you helping her?"

"I offered but she said no as long as I copied this recipe
out for her, so I am."

Robert went into the bathroom. Jenny was standing
shoeless in the bath polishing the tiled wall behind it.

"Jenny, stop that, *really* stop that—"

"No," she said, smiling, "I'm nearly done."

He leaned forward.

"I'm not having it," he said. "You're not to become our
slave," and then he put his arms around her and lifted her
out of the bath.

She gasped.

"Stop it!"

"Stop what—"

She looked at him, eyes wide. She put her hands down,
one still holding the polishing cloth, to push his arms away,
but he was too quick for her and pulled her to him and
kissed her on the mouth.

Then Lizzie called from the door to the staircase, "I'm
home!"

. . .

"I never kissed her before," Robert said tiredly, in the resigned manner of someone repeating something for the umpteenth time, "I shan't kiss her again. I don't love her, I'm not in love with her, I love you, I just felt full of gratitude to her because she reassured me."

Lizzie was standing by the window of their bedroom looking down into the wrecked factory yards behind the building. The western sun shone down on the piles of broken bricks and the rotting fences and the clumps of bright new weeds. She held the windowsill and stared out.

"What do you mean, reassured you?"

Robert sat on the edge of their bed with his head in his hands.

"By being," he said wearily, "just so bloody ordinary, so soothingly, wonderfully normal."

"What do you mean?" Lizzie said again.

"You know exactly what I mean."

"Not like me—"

"Not like you just now."

Lizzie stepped out of her shoes and kicked them behind her.

"How long had you been planning to kiss her?"

Robert flung himself back on the bed and closed his eyes.

"I didn't plan it!"

"Don't shout."

"You make me shout. I didn't plan it, it had never crossed my mind, it was an impulse, an impulse born of shame, and gratitude, to see her ungrudgingly cleaning our bloody *bathroom* for God's sake. I wish I hadn't. You'll never know how much I wish I hadn't. I've upset her and you and myself and all for nothing."

"Nothing?"

"I didn't kiss her for sex, Lizzie!" Robert yelled, sitting bolt upright and glaring. "I kissed her because I was grateful and ashamed, just as you ought to be!"

There was a long pause, while Lizzie went on staring out of the window. Then she turned round and collapsed

on to the bed beside him. He waited for her to be angry
or sad but all she said was, "I know."

"What?"

"I am grateful. I am ashamed."

Robert groaned and rolled away from her.

"Don't start that, the mortifying of the flesh—"

"Mum!" Harriet yelled from behind the closed door.

"What?"

"Phone! Frances on the phone!"

Lizzie sprang up.

"Frances! From where, where's she ringing from—"

"I dunno," Harriet said, her voice receding as she moved
away.

"I'll be back," Lizzie said, running from the room. Robert grunted. He shut his eyes. He could have kicked himself. He couldn't imagine what had led him to be so clumsy,
so *ludicrous*, as to kiss Jenny. It had been such a funny little
kiss too, an almost childish kiss with Jenny's cool dry mouth
closed beneath his and her eyes above it wide with amazed
disapproval. Hell, he thought now, punching a pillow, am
I really that unattractive? Is being kissed by me so revolting
that my victim has to bolt home as if she'd been raped?
Jenny had bolted all right. She had been distraught. She
had gathered up Toby and her bag and Toby's plastic car-
rier of sports kit and fled from the flat, almost whimpering.
Robert was left with the distinct impression that he had
offended her. But offended what exactly? Her person? Her
principles? Her self-esteem? Her self-image? She had said
almost nothing as she fled, only a few incoherent words of
apology to Lizzie and the phrase, "There's nothing, nothing, I couldn't ever—" Lizzie had said, stunned herself,
"Don't worry—" Don't worry about what? Don't worry
that I shall blame you? Don't worry that my husband is
such a lousy kisser? Jesus, Robert thought, isn't there
enough to bear just now without feeling a perfect fucking
fool into the bargain?

The door opened again. Lizzie came in quietly and shut
it behind her equally quietly. She sat down on the very

edge of the bed, as far away from Robert as possible, and folded her hands.

"I'm going to ring Frances again later, when all the children are in bed, when I'm not having to compete with all of them telling me how awful they feel—"

Robert sat up. He glanced at her. She was white as a sheet.

"Lizzie?"

"I'm all right," she said. She put her hand to her head, as if to reassure herself that it was still there. "It's just that Frances is pregnant, you see."

"Pregnant!"

"Yes," Lizzie said. "Pregnant." She looked at him with a straight, blank gaze. "That's rather taken the wind out of our sails, hasn't it?"

Later; much later, Lizzie sat at the kitchen table nursing the third mug of tea she had made but had not seemed able to drink. Robert had gone to bed. She had been in to see him and he was asleep, on his back, with, as was his wont, one arm flung up across the pillow. He looked exhausted, even though he was asleep; it was as if sleep wasn't enough for that kind of exhaustion, as if it would only provide a temporary, partial remedy. Lizzie had gazed at him enviously. How marvellously men managed to sleep as a refuge, seeming to switch oblivion on as easily as turning off a light. She'd seen it in William, all her life, snoozing off the effects of Barbara's attacks and discontents; she saw it in Alistair, seizing the fusty cavern of his duvet as a place of sanctuary from the pain of being himself, of being, now, thirteen. I'm not sure I'll ever sleep again, Lizzie thought, gazing at Robert, I feel that I'm quite beyond it, every nerve cracking but grimly, eternally awake. She went back to the kitchen and plugged the kettle in. It was a completely automatic action, she thought dazedly as she did it, she might as well have turned the washing machine on, or the iron. Why do people always make tea when their wits are scattered like a burst pillow? What did they do in a crisis before there was tea? There, there, they said to each other, no doubt, there's a nice mug of mead to set you right. What is mead made of anyway? Honey? Barley? And what, precisely, does it matter what it's perishing well made of while Frances has been pregnant for three months and told nobody, and particularly not me?

"I meant to get pregnant," Frances had said during their second call. "I wanted to be. I want Luis's baby. Best of all, I want Luis and his baby, but it doesn't look as if I shall get both."

"But you *knew*," Lizzie cried. "You knew what he felt! You knew how he'd react! I mean, I can't quite think how you can really love a man who thinks like that, but you seem to, and he never made any bones about it, did he?"

"No. He didn't. And the thing about love, you see, real love, is that when you love someone as I love him, you have to learn to accommodate yourself to qualities in your loved one that you would really detest in someone you didn't love. That's the nature of the beast, that's *it*—"

"Yes," Lizzie said, chastened. She sat on the sitting-room floor, in her dressing-gown, with the telephone on the sofa beside her. Frances said she was sitting on the floor too, in Fulham, but that she was wearing Luis's dressing-gown, because that was what she always did now, what she liked to do.

"Did—" Lizzie began, and then stopped.

"Did what?"

"Did he—ask you for an abortion?"

"No," Frances said sharply.

"Have you got views on abortion? Odd, but we've never talked about it—"

"If I had an abortion," Frances said loudly, "I'd be denying everything Luis and I've had, everything we've been to each other—"

"Been? Aren't you seeing him? Oh Frances—"

"Yes, I'm seeing him. As much as before. He's very loving to me."

"Then—"

"Lizzie," Frances said, "I knew his mind and my mind,

and I knew what I was doing and I've done it and I'm thrilled and I'm terrified and I think I'm right and I think I'm wrong. Got it?"

"Yes," Lizzie whispered. She gripped the telephone. "Can—can I help you now?"

"What do you mean?"

"I—I don't know, specifically," Lizzie said, flailing about in her instinctive thoughts. "I mean, I suppose, about being pregnant, about having the baby. Where will you have it? Will you have it in Bath?"

"I don't think so—"

"But London would be so bleak—"

"Not London, either."

"Then—"

"I shall probably have the baby in Spain," Frances said, "in Seville."

Lizzie gave a little scream.

"But why? You're mad!"

"Don't be idiotic. Spain has wonderful hospitals, people have babies in Spain all the time."

"I don't mean that!" Lizzie cried. She was crouching on the floor, holding the receiver with it and her face almost touching the carpet. "I mean far away, from all of us, from your family."

"But it isn't your baby," Frances said calmly. "It's my and Luis's baby."

"But he doesn't *want* it!"

There was a little pause and then Frances said carefully, "He doesn't want me to have it, but that isn't quite the same thing."

"Oh Frances," Lizzie moaned, worn out, beyond being able to make much sense. "Oh Frances, are you all right?"

"I don't know," Frances said. Her voice sounded tight, as if she were restraining tears or feelings. "I really don't know." She paused and then she said, "I just love him, you see. All the time. I just love him," and then she put the receiver down.

Robert had wanted, yawning and swaying with fatigue but still concerned and conscientious, to know what Frances

had said. Lizzie could hardly tell him. She said Frances
wasn't even considering an abortion and that she was probably going to have the baby in Spain and then her voice
died away. Robert waited for a little while and then said,
with a kind of diffident politeness that he thought, if it was
all right, that he'd go to bed. Lizzie nodded and automatically held her face up for a kiss which he gave her, too
quickly, on the cheekbone. Then he had left her, making
tea and not drinking it, going over and over what Frances
had said as a way, among other things, of blotting out a
horrible little voice that said, deep inside her and with pip-
ing insistency: But *I'm* the one who has babies!

EIGHTEEN

It was desperately hot. Even in the dark, cavernous hallway of the block of flats, the heat was like a muffling blanket. Out on the July streets, where there was no wind except perverse little gusts whose sole aim seemed to be to blow dust in your eyes, it had really been quite difficult to breathe.

The lift that served the flats lived inside a huge black-and-gilded cage ornamented with grotesque metal lilies and acanthus leaves. It was, Frances thought, a thoroughly Spanish piece of ironwork, heavy, ornate, grandiose, ridiculous and undeniably impressive. On a panel beside the portcullis-like folding lift-gates was a row of illuminated bells next to a row of neat white cards with names engraved on them; Dr. Lurdes Piza, Señor e Señora J. S. Lorenzo, María Luisa Fernández Preciosa, Professor J. and Dr. A. María de Mena. Frances counted to three and pressed the bell.

A faint crackling sound emerged from a small nearby grille, like the sound of an old-fashioned tannoy system at an English village fête, then a woman's voice said, *"¡Diga!"*

"Is Dr. de Mena there?" Frances asked. "Dr. Ana de Mena?"

The voice thought a little.

"*¿Quién habla?*"

"Frances. Frances Shore."

"I will enquire."

Frances waited in the dark vestibule by the little grille. At one end of the vestibule, half-glazed doors led back to the baking streets, and at the other end an archway framed the shabby little door to the apartment where the building's concierge lived an apparently lightless existence. The door had been left propped open by a plastic bucket, presumably for a gasp of air, and out of the bucket rose, in slow enquiry, the face of a tabby cat, who regarded Frances for some seconds, without approval, and then subsided again.

The grille crackled again.

"Frances? Frances, I am sending the lift down. Come up."

"Thank you, oh thank you—"

A vast structure wreathed in cables and pulleys clanked ponderously downwards inside the iron cage. It shuddered to a halt, level with Frances, and allowed her to open and shut two sets of gates and to enter its gleaming mahogany interior, offset with bevelled looking-glasses and gilded sconces holding light bulbs like candle flames. Then it gathered up all its mighty strength and bore her heavily upwards to the de Menas' apartment on the second floor.

Ana did not kiss Frances. She took her hand, held it for a moment quite firmly, and then dropped it. She was wearing a short-sleeved summer suit of saffron-yellow linen with gold buttons, and her hair, as sleek as if it were painted to her head, was held back by a black silk scarf spotted in white.

She led Frances into the salon. It was shrouded against the sun so that the furniture appeared to be a series of huge humped beasts crouched on the carpet. Only by the windows had a single slice of sunlight managed to sneak in under the blinds and lie there in defiance, no doubt bleaching the rug on which it had alighted.

"It is too hot," Ana said. "Sevilla is terrible in July and

August. I would never stay here in the summer if I didn't have to. Would you like a *granizado*?"

"Oh yes," Frances said gratefully. She sank down on the sofa she had sat on when Luis had brought her here to dinner, a ceremonial great sofa upholstered in tapestry. "It's very kind of you to see me. I should have telephoned, I know, and I don't quite know why I didn't. I knew perfectly well, you see, that you aren't in the hospital on Wednesdays, so I suppose I was trying to kid myself that it was an impulse."

"An impulse? To see me?"

"To talk to you. To ask you something. That is, when I have told you something else."

Ana went over to the door of the salon and called out for drinks to be brought. The voice that had first answered Frances replied that it would oblige when it had finished doing what it was currently busy with.

"It's María," Ana said. "She was like a nursemaid to Luis and me, and she came to me when I got married. She is more obstinate than a mule." She came back into the room and sat down at the opposite end of the sofa to Frances. "If she hasn't appeared in five minutes, I will get the juice myself, even if it means ten minutes' scolding for going into the kitchen, which is her kingdom."

"Ana—" Frances said.

"Yes?"

"Ana, I think I just have to plunge in and tell you why I've come—"

"I think so too."

Frances took a breath. This business of telling people she was pregnant ought to be getting easier with practice, but it didn't seem to be. Each time she felt like a terrified child on the edge of a diving board above an icy and fathomless pool, holding her nose, closing her eyes, and leaping simply because the path of retreat was blocked.

"I am pregnant," Frances said. "I am going to have a baby."

There was a short pause in which neither of them moved, and then Ana said, "This is serious."

"I know."

"I will get this juice—"

"I don't need it—"

"You do," Ana said, rising to her feet. "We do. We need something to occupy us while we talk about this."

She went rapidly out of the room. Frances sat on the uncomfortable sofa and heard her calling to old María, and then old María's voice rising in a squawk of protest. That squawk was what Frances had expected from Barbara when she had told her about the pregnancy but, to her amazement, it hadn't come.

"I see," Barbara had said, down the telephone.

"What d'you mean, you see?"

"I mean," Barbara said, "that I have heard and taken in what you have just said, but that I haven't yet got a reaction. At least, not over the telephone."

"I have to go to Spain next week," Frances said.

"Do you?"

"Yes. But when I'm back, I'm coming down to see you and Dad."

"I see."

"Mum, please don't keep saying 'I see' like this!"

"You may find," Barbara said unexpectedly, "that I see more than you think. Are you all right?"

"Not particularly—"

"No," Barbara said, "how could you be? But it was brave to ring. Better than writing—"

"Writing!"

"Letters," Barbara said witheringly. "Letters. The last refuge of the coward. You aren't a coward—"

"Oh Mum—"

"Go to Spain," Barbara said. "Go to Spain and then come home and see us."

And here she was in Spain, in Ana's salon, being given a tall glass of translucent, whitish liquid, clattering with ice.

"Now," Ana said, sitting down again, "does Luis know?"

"Of course."

"And he is angry?"

"Yes."

"You knew his views."

"Yes."

"It was an accident, of course."

"No," Frances said. "I meant to. I wanted a baby. I want Luis's baby."

Ana took a neat swallow of her drink. She sat bolt upright, raising the glass high with one smooth, olive-skinned arm, the other lying, in a controlled manner, in her lap. Frances bowed her head.

"This, Frances, is a very bad situation."

Frances waited.

"It isn't just the facts," Ana said, "though these are quite bad enough, but the complications. There are many moralities here in Spain, you have seen that with your own eyes, you have seen that the old conservative view and the new liberal view do not live easily together, that there is still so much—too much, you will think, no doubt—that is allowed for a man and not for a woman. May I advise you a little?"

"I wish you would," Frances said.

"You know Luis's and my family situation. You know about our mother, about José's mother. You know about all the secrecy, the feuds. This—this pregnancy—cannot be known. You do understand that?"

"You tell me so," Frances said. "Frankly, coming from England, it sounds perfectly extraordinary, so archaic, so melodramatic—"

"I don't know," Ana said firmly, interrupting. "I don't know about English ways, I just know about my family here in Sevilla, in Spain. We are different, OK, so you must accept that." She leaned forward and pointed a forefinger at Frances, as if she were chastising her. "You must also, Frances, give up all claims now, on Luis, on his family. You must go home now and have this baby in England. I will talk to Luis about the money."

Frances gazed at her.

"Oh no."

"What?"

"Oh no, Ana," Frances said. "I didn't come for that. I didn't come to be told like some nineteenth-century servant girl to take my shameful bundle out into the streets and never to darken these respectable doors again. I came for help."

"I gave it. I told you the best thing for you."

"You didn't. You told me the best thing, or at least, the most convenient thing, for the de Menas and the Gómez Morenos. Spain *is* old-fashioned in lots of ways, it *is* stuffed with pride and family honour and Catholic guilt, but it is partly my country now too because I am carrying a half-Spanish baby."

"Half-English, too."

"Of course. But if I go to England, this baby will never see its father."

"Would that not be best?"

"For whom?" Frances cried indignantly. "For whom? For your mother?"

Ana looked away.

"I am afraid that in some ways my mother is impossible."

"You will find," Frances said, "that if you don't help me, I will become impossible too."

Ana turned back.

"But what can you do? Luis is married, and even if he weren't, he would not marry again. He doesn't want this child—" She stopped suddenly. She leaned forward. "Did he ask you to have an abortion?"

Frances flinched. She did not want to remember hating him so much.

"Yes."

"And you refused?"

"Of course I refused! How dare he? How *dare* he? I made this choice, I am not asking for anything, never mind what I hope and long for, except that he doesn't abandon me just yet and that he never abandons the child! I wanted to kill him, I was so angry."

Ana's face was briefly shaken by some strong emotion.

Then she said, not quite steadily, "It is a tragedy, this life of ours. Men want women, but women want children."

"Yes," Frances said harshly, not caring if she were being tactless. "Didn't you?"

"Oh, I can't remember."

"Of course you can!"

"You train yourself," Ana said. "You train your desires—"

"And your instincts?"

Ana looked at her.

"Not so easy."

Frances finished her *granizado* and set the empty glass down on a table beside her.

"I told a lie to my sister. I told her Luis had *not* asked for an abortion. That was instinctive, to protect Luis. I will tell her so much and no more and I can't quite explain, even to myself, why I do this. But I know exactly why I've come to you."

"Yes," Ana said.

"I've come because you are a doctor and I need your help in getting a bed in a hospital here to have my baby in December. I could, I suppose, have asked Luis, but I didn't want to. I prefer to ask you. I want to have the baby here because it is our baby, not just my baby, and also because I want to have it in the country where I have been happier than I've ever been anywhere else and which is also the country of the man I love. These aren't very rational reasons, I know, but they are quite tremendously powerful ones, and if anyone in my life told me to stop listening to reason and to listen to my feelings instead, it was your brother, and if it's all led to my downfall, it's led to my *bliss* as well and I shan't forget that ever, *ever* as long as I live. Do you understand me?"

Ana sighed.

"I don't know. This is like some waterfall—"

"I mean it to be, I mean you to feel some of my urgency, some of my intensity, I mean to *make* you help me."

Ana got up. She walked about the room for a few steps, between the tables and the heavy chairs with their ball-

and-claw feet, their strips of inlaid brass, their smooth, un-
yielding damask seats.

"Does Luis know you have come?"

"No. I will tell him if you agree. If you won't, then I
shan't bother, I'll simply ask him to pull strings instead."

"You are very determined."

"Or desperate," Frances said shortly.

Ana turned to look at her.

"Where will you have your prenatal care?"

"Wherever I happen to be, here or London—"

"I will talk to a colleague."

Frances gripped the arm of the sofa.

"Will you?"

"Yes," Ana said, "I will. But don't ask me why."

Luis turned back the sheet on Frances's side of the bed and
piled up the pillows. From behind the closed door to the
bathroom came the sound of the shower, splashing down
into the bathtub, pattering like rain against the panel of
frosted glass that prevented the water from flooding the
floor. Usually, Frances left the bathroom door open while
she bathed or showered and Luis was obscurely and faintly
troubled that tonight she had shut it. If there were going
to be decisions taken about shutting each other out in any
way just now, he wanted them to be his decisions. He
wanted that not because he wished to dominate Frances,
but because such decisions seemed to be the only tiny relief
he could find just now from being so helplessly, ragingly
angry with someone in whom he had come to both believe
and trust, and in whom he was now so disappointed.

He sat down on the edge of the bed and spread one
hand out on the space of sheet where she would lie. She
astonished him. No, "astonished" was far too feeble a word,
she astounded him, appalled him, terrified him, she took
his breath away, she stunned him by her outrageous, bare-
faced *audacity* in making herself pregnant by him against
his clearly expressed wishes. He didn't think he had ever
felt so betrayed or so furious or so utterly uncomprehending

in his entire life. She had left him not so much gasping for words as gasping for thoughts, and whenever he felt too furiously bewildered to be able to articulate even a simple remark to her, he would then be further confused by a rush of love for her, by a most peculiar tenderness. He sprang off the bed as if he had been burned. What in God's name was he doing, smoothing sheets and patting pillows? Why did he keep finding cushions for her back, telephoning her in London to see if she was resting, looking at her thickening body with a most complicated mixture of interest, protectiveness and desire? Why did he? Because he couldn't help himself, that's why. Because he, Luis Fernando María Gómez Moreno, despite all the social and religious tenets of his rigid upbringing, simply couldn't help himself, and it was driving him *mad*.

And now she had enlisted Ana! She had gone to Ana's flat and asked her, outright, for help and been promised it! And when he, Luis, had demanded, over supper, to know how she had dared to do such a thing without consulting him, she had said that he couldn't have his cake and eat it, which was a typically evasive English saying which seemed to mean *"No puedes tenerlo todo,"* or "You can't have everything," which in its turn was an outrageous thing to say because it seemed to him, at the moment, that he had nothing. Nothing! He had nothing and yet he was still involved. He had protested, as he had once previously protested to her in Granada, that he was a civilised man, not a wild beast, and that of *course* he was concerned for her welfare!

"Mine perhaps," Frances said, "but not the baby's."

"I don't know!" he'd shouted. "I don't think about this baby, I can't because I know it means the end and I cannot *stand* that this doesn't break your heart like it is breaking mine!"

"Yours is only breaking because you are breaking it yourself. You are *determined* that this baby shall be the end and not the beginning!"

"I don't want it," he said more quietly. "I am not determined, I just *know*. I hate this knowledge, but I know."

It was then, looking at her, he'd seen how tired she was,

worn-out tired, bleached by fatigue. Have a shower, he'd said, go to bed, you must rest, Frances, really you must, how foolish you are to drive yourself like this.

"But I *have* to, because you won't help me—"

"I do help you, I do, I look after you—"

"That's not what I mean. It's this relentless fatalism of yours that I have to fight all the time."

He'd looked at her across the remains of their supper, the plates strewn with grains of yellow rice, fragments of sweet red peppers, little piles of blue-black mussel shells. He said, "I'm not like this because I want to be like this, I'm like this because this is what I am."

She'd sighed, a huge deep sigh from the very depths of her.

"And I am what I am too."

"In Spain, we are not very good at compromise—"

"In England, we look as if we're very good at it, but deep down, we're as bad as anyone else. We just harbour resentments."

"Come," he said, holding his hand out, "bedtime."

She took his hand, and let him lead her across the room towards the bathroom. The man in the house across the alley had started mournfully on his guitar, the long, lamenting strains mixing with the muted chatter of people drifting past below. Luis opened the bathroom door.

"Have a shower, and I will make the bed ready."

She turned and gave him a small, tired smile. "Thank you," she said and then she closed the door on him.

She was, she discovered later in the tremendously hot night, too tired to sleep. She had climbed into bed almost fainting with relief and had then expected to fall heavily and smoothly into sleep like a stone dropped over a cliff. Luis had waited until she was comfortable and then he had said he would go down to the hotel's dining room and bar, just for an hour, and give José a bit of a fright. Would she be all right? Yes, she said, nodding slightly on the pillows, eyes already closed, yes, I'll be fine, I'm nearly asleep already, thank you for looking after me so kindly. But she had then waited and waited in vain for sleep to come, listening to the sounds of Seville from the alley below, remembering Ana in the shadowy room that afternoon, remembering the quiveringly hot streets on the walk home, remembering the odd little look of hurt on Luis's face when she came out of the bathroom at last, having cried her heart out in the muffling cascade of water from the shower.

She had shut him out deliberately, not because she wanted to, but because she felt she had to, she had to begin to acclimatise herself to not turning to him. Something had frightened her on the walk back from Ana's apartment to the *posada* that afternoon, something had made her realise how vulnerable she was now that she was pregnant and how very vulnerable she would become when there was a baby to be cared for before herself. She had been coming along past the walls of the Convent of the Mother of God when she had caught her foot clumsily in a broken piece of pavement and fallen with a cry, not just of surprise, but of sudden panic. She had fallen on her side, not particularly hard or heavily, and had then lain there on the dusty stones, in a most paralysing, disconcerting state of fear, until a man and a woman came hurrying across the street from a building opposite and, with much clucking and soothing, had helped her to her feet. She had felt dizzy. The street and the sky seemed to swoop about her in the most sickening way, and she had leaned on the man, who was small and square and in his fifties, as if he were the only thing that prevented her from spinning off into a void.

"I am pregnant," she heard herself say in a remote, precise voice to the woman. "I must not fall, if I am pregnant."

They had assisted her across the street and on to a wooden chair in a slice of black shadow cast by a house wall. They brought her water, they asked if she would like a doctor. No, she said, I just frightened myself by falling. The woman had then shrieked for her daughter, and between them, they had accompanied Frances through the few streets home, telling her, as they went, unencouraging and dramatic accounts of their own pregnancies and childbirths. They were truly kind, truly sympathetic. They left Frances in the shady green courtyard of the hotel, with many injunctions to take care of herself, and it was only when they had gone that she realised with rising alarm that it was always going to be like this now, that she would always, in some part of herself, be defenceless and in need of other people. In defending this baby of hers, she would not, any longer, always be able to defend herself.

It was this glimpse of a new, and disquieting, state of affairs that had led her, out of a childish feeling that she must start *now* as she had to go on, to shut the door on Luis. She must get used to being alone again, she told herself, even if this was a very different kind of aloneness. He insisted upon it, after all, it was he who was determined that their love for one another couldn't survive Frances's becoming a mother. She might find it incomprehensible, intolerable, *mad*, but as the weeks wore on, she couldn't any longer tell herself that she was imagining it. Nor could she tell herself she hadn't known what she was doing, or been misled into thinking Luis might turn out to be different from what he said he was.

He still said, though less angrily now, that she had deceived him. Of course she had. She had been the one to take contraceptive responsibility, had indeed offered to be the one since Luis was not of a generation of men to whom such responsibility came at all naturally, and then she had been the one to drop that responsibility in the bathroom bin, and not confess to what she had done. In the crudest, simplest terms, she had tried to use him to get what she wanted, which was a baby, a baby by him, the baby that had come to mean, for her, the rich, natural outcome of everything they were to one another.

Had she done that, she now wondered, sliding her feet round the too-warm sheets in search of a cool place, because she believed she knew what was good for him better than he knew himself? Had she done it because she felt she was right and he was wrong and therefore her desires took precedence over his objections? Was she therefore being patronising as well as dishonest? What in the end, Frances demanded of herself in the hot darkness lit by gleams of lamplight from the alley, is the truth? What is true about a person, and is truth the same as worth? I am honest with myself, I do believe I am, and however hard it is, I am not trying to pretend I don't long for this baby *and* for Luis. Whether this makes me a less worthy person, I don't know, I can't tell. If you're honest with yourself, then you have to live with the horrible truths about yourself, whatever happens, but surely self-delusion of any kind is only a slow death in the end? I've surrendered to myself, to the truth, the instinctive truth of myself, and now look where I am . . .

The door opened quietly.

"Luis?"

"I didn't want to wake you—"

"I wasn't asleep. It's so hot—"

"Would you like some water?"

"Oh please."

He crossed the room to the bathroom and turned the light on and then she heard him humming and the sound of water pouring into a glass. The tiny domesticity of it was suddenly almost more than she could bear.

NINETEEN

William waited by the gate. It was a heavy, thundery, windless day and a queer, grey-gold light lay on the fields opposite, and the poplars in the hedgerow and the distant scattered roofs of the village. While he waited, he tied up wayward fronds of the climbing rose that grew over the wall by the drive gate. He couldn't remember the name. It was a dreary little rose, pinkish fading to no colour as it opened, with flat, fragile petals which fell off at the first draught of wind. Perhaps it didn't have a name, didn't deserve to.

He had come out to watch for Frances, partly because Barbara had made it plain that if he went on fidgeting round her in the house for one more minute, she might murder him. He knew he was being annoying, restless and aimless, picking things up and putting them down, starting sentences he didn't finish, wandering about, but that was the sort of thing that happened when you were upset, and William didn't think he had ever felt more wretchedly upset in his life.

It had never crossed his mind that Frances might start a baby, simply never entered his head as a possibility. He had thought only how lovely it was to see Frances so free and so fulfilled, to see her doing something that took her out of the lifelong controlling habits of her existence. It had occurred to him once or twice that the love affair might very well end, and that Frances would then be desolated and yet still enriched, and Barbara could say I told you so, over and over, but it had simply never struck him that this enormous complication might arise and change everything in Frances's life, for ever. And then—and here his hands began to shake as if they had a crazy life of their own—change everything in everyone else's, too.

"It wouldn't strike you," Barbara said. "Things never do. You never think through problems, you never have, you just amble past them as if they were no concern of yours."

Frances must be my concern, William thought now, pricking an unsteady finger sharply on a rose thorn. She is my concern because she will now go straight back to where she came from, all the growth of the last eighteen months will be wasted, and the awful thing is that I find I *want* her to come back. I want her to be where everything is safe and conventional and we—I—can look after her. He glanced at his finger. A bead of blood sat on it, bright and neat. William put his finger in his mouth. He remembered, with sudden acuteness, standing in his tidy kitchen all those years ago rejoicing that the twins were on their way to him. Now Frances was on her way to him again, but oh, in such different circumstances, without that beautiful clean sheet of paper ahead of her which was one of the chief charms of babyhood, of innocence, and without the certainty of a secured future.

A horn sounded. William dropped his roll of garden twine and hurried out into the lane, waving and gesturing. Frances slowed her car until the window of the driver's door was level with him. He peered in at her.

"Darling—"

She wore a dark-blue overshirt and white trousers and sunglasses.

"Dad. Were you watching for me?"

"Of course—"

She tried a smile. It wasn't very successful and William realised that he was wearing an expression of consummate anxiety. He changed it at once. Poor girl. What help to her was it to look as if the end of the world was nigh? He reached into the car and patted her hand.

"Drive on in," he said. "I'll close the gate behind you."

Barbara said they would sit in the garden, under the tulip tree. She said it was absolutely airless indoors, and she led Frances firmly outside and made her sit in the most comfortable chair, a huge old wooden structure that had belonged to William's father, with a footrest and a bookrest and a shelf with holes in it, for drinks.

"I'm not ill," Frances protested.

"No. But probably tired. There is nothing to be said for being pregnant, it's a frightful state. Do you feel sick?"

"I'm beginning not to—"

"Oh Frances," William said suddenly, tremulously. "Oh Frances!"

They both looked at him.

"I never thought—"

"Dad," Frances said pleadingly, "please don't, please don't make things worse—"

"It's the sight of you," William said, hunting furiously for a handkerchief. "It's seeing you there, and knowing."

"Knowing what?"

"That you can't get away now," William said, blowing into his handkerchief. "That you're trapped now!"

Barbara said calmly, amazingly, "She doesn't want to get away."

Frances stared at her. Barbara stared back.

"Do you?"

"No, I—"

"You want this baby, don't you? You told me you meant to have it and I imagine I may believe you?"

"Oh yes—"

"Then don't talk bilge," Barbara said to William. "Don't talk sentimental *bilge*."

"But—"

"But what?" Barbara said, standing up. "But she'll be an unmarried mother? Is that it? Does that upset your cosy notions of how life should be organised—adultery is absolutely fine but babies should always have a mummy and a daddy living in a state of married tidiness even if it's also a state of purgatory, rather than of bliss?"

"Stop it!" Frances shrieked. "Stop it!"

"He makes me so angry," Barbara said less heatedly. "He's so idle and hypocritical. He's so—"

"I didn't come for this! I didn't come to umpire one of your quarrels!"

"Sorry," William whispered.

Barbara said, "I shall go and get tea."

Frances put her head back against the chair and watched her mother move briskly and stiffly away across the grass.

"I want you to come home now, you see," William said the moment Barbara was out of earshot. "I want you to come home now and have the baby here and let us help you and look after you."

Frances rolled her head so that she could look at him.

"So does Lizzie."

"Ah. Yes."

"What does Mum want? She wouldn't say on the telephone. You might as well tell me, everyone else is telling me what they want, after all."

"She wants you—to do what you want."

"Nonsense!" Frances cried. "Nonsense! She's never wanted that in my entire life!"

"Well, she does now."

Frances looked intently at him. He looked not so much shrunken as collapsed, his sweet, worn face quite devitalised.

"Dad?"

"She thinks," William said slowly, "that if you feel you should have this baby in Spain, then you should. I feel quite the opposite. I feel you must be where there are people to support you. I usen't to feel this, I used to feel you should be away from all of us, all the guy ropes cut, but now I

feel you must be where there is some security because—
because—"

Frances leaned forward.

"Because what?"

"Because there is so little security in the end, in anything, so that we must seize what we can, like love—"

"Dad," Frances said, "are you talking about me, or you?"

He looked at her. She noticed that his eyes, for the first time, had a milky, elderly film to them.

"You," he said, and then, after a pause, "me."

"What—"

"We have quarrelled all our lives, Mum and I, you know that. But we have quarrelled so badly over this baby of yours, we have quarrelled from the depths of ourselves, from our instincts, we have really been quarrelling about the most primitive thing of all, about our sense of survival. And they are so different, our senses of survival, so very different. I want to cherish, to cling to things, she wants self-sufficiency. She says that's what you are doing. She says that Lizzie and I are passive in the end because we are terrified of our own thoughts and that you and she, though possessed of equally alarming thoughts, aren't afraid to confront them. She admires you. She has said so over and over."

Frances climbed out of the huge chair and came to kneel by William. She put her hands on his, which were gripping his handkerchief as if it were the last branch hanging out over a ravine.

"Dad—"

"I expect she'll say all this to you herself, only more forcefully. But she may not say—" He stopped, swallowed, and then hurried on. "She may not say that it's you who have brought everything to a head, by having this affair and now by having this baby, and you should know that, not because I blame you, I don't, I couldn't blame you for anything, ever, but because it will explain things for you, you see. You will understand why it's happened."

"What things?" Frances demanded. "What things?

What's happened? What are you *talking* about?"

William took his hands away from Frances, and blew his nose and sat up straighter.

"Your mother—"

"Yes!"

"Your mother wants us to sell this house and divide the proceeds so that she can go and live in Bath, in a little flat, on her own."

Frances stared at him.

"She's leaving you—"

"Yes. That's what she wants."

"Oh *Dad*—"

"I suppose—I suppose she's had perfect reason to leave for thirty years—"

"But she loves you, in her way, needs you. She's—she—"

"No," William said. He seemed to be a little calmer. He managed a small, faint smile. "No. That's where we've all been so wrong. It's always been assumed by her and by me that I never really loved her, which is why I fell in love with Juliet, and that she always loved me, in a curious way, which is why she never left me, despite Juliet. But it seems, my darling Frances, that it has always, in fact, been the other way about. I am the loving, she the loved. Or perhaps love has nothing to do with it, and it's merely habit and we've got so used to it we can't tell the difference any more. She said—she said she felt she had done me an injustice, letting me go on like this all these years, clinging to me. She said she always wanted me to love her, even though she didn't love me in return. She is remarkably honest, remarkably."

Frances got up, bemusedly, from her knees.

"I don't see where this baby comes in—"

William leaned back in his chair. He flapped a hand at Frances.

"Go and ask her. Ask her yourself."

"Dad?"

"Yes—"

"Dad, do you want me to come back here because you think it will make Mum stay?"

"No," William said.

Frances looked at him but he would not meet her gaze.

"I see," she said.

"I've mismanaged the whole of my emotional life," Barbara said, slicing cucumber. "I've dissipated all my energies, I've never let myself go. I've had fads, as substitutes for emotions. You know that."

Frances said nothing. She sat by the kitchen table and buttered bread.

"I think I'm rather an unpleasant woman," Barbara said. "I say dreadful things and sometimes I get a little shaft of pleasure out of saying them. I'm all the wrong generation too, too young to accept being just a dutiful, dependent wife; too old to be independent of marriage. But I mean to have a go."

"Isn't it—a bit late?" Frances said. She laid the buttered slices out on the table top. "I mean, what's the point of creating such an upheaval after all these years?"

"There's always a point! There's never a moment when it's too late! What makes you think that life is of more value to you at thirty-nine than to me at sixty-nine? If anything, it's more valuable to me because there's less of it left." She glared at Frances. "I've worried about you all your life."

Frances sighed.

"I know. You've always thought me incompetent and weak—"

"No," Barbara said, "no, not exactly that. It's more that I've always thought you such an unsuitable person to be a twin. Just as I am an unsuitable person to be a wife."

"Oh Mum—"

Barbara began to arrange the cucumber in overlapping rows on the bread.

"You really want this man, don't you?"

"Yes."

"You're lucky. I've never really wanted anyone except, I suppose, to stop someone else having them. Will you go and live in Spain?"

Frances looked up.

"I might—"

"I can't advise you. I can't advise anyone, I'm not fit for it. But I'll support you."

"Will you? Oh, will you?"

"I was in such a temper when you started this affair. I thought: How could you be so stupid, when it couldn't possibly have a future, how could you lay the foundations so carefully for pain? Then I thought: What's pain, for heaven's sake, and what's life if all you do is try and avoid it? I considered your love affair. I asked myself: If you hadn't done that, what would you have done? Married one of those feeble young men who always found you so attractive or just gone trailing on sending tidy tourists to Tuscany and ended up just like me, in essence, frustrated and futile. But then you started this baby and I thought: She's done it! Frances has damn well gone and done it! I hadn't felt that exhilarated since I decided to go to Marrakesh, which was, incidentally, not at all what it was cracked up to be and full of extremely second-rate dropouts who were mostly too stoned to make sense. And I thought: Hurray, at last William and I will see eye to eye about something, and I found that, instead of rejoicing, he was shaking with respectable anxiety. I told him, I've had enough of the only permitted unorthodoxies being for William. What would you have done, I said to him, if Juliet had had a baby?"

"And?" Frances said, amazed.

Barbara slapped top slices of bread on the sandwiches.

"He hadn't an answer. I don't think he'd ever thought about it. I know he's a dear, you needn't leap to his defence, but he's also intolerable in some ways. I'm tired of him and I'm even more tired of the sort of person that living with him makes me be."

Frances put her hands over her face.

"Will you divorce?"

"Shouldn't think so. What would be the point?"

"Have you told Lizzie?"

Barbara stopped slicing off crusts.

"Not yet."

"Then I will," Frances said. "I'd like to. Please let it be me that tells her this!"

"All right. If you want to. It would probably be best anyway—"

"Why?"

"Because," Barbara said carefully, "Lizzie and I had a bit of a quarrel last week. They'd had the chicken-pox and then some upset about that girl who works in the shop and she'd flounced out, and then your news came, and Lizzie started creating, so I went over and I said, Now look here, Lizzie, you're jealous and that's a problem you have to confront because it's poisoning you and you keep calling it by other names that are easier to live with and you've got to *stop*. I probably shouldn't have said it in front of the children."

"No, you shouldn't—"

"But it had to be said."

"Did it?"

"If she wants any future relationship with her husband or sister, yes, it did."

Frances crossed her arms flat on the table, and laid her face down on them. The thought of Lizzie suddenly made her feel deeply sad, troubled sad, as it had done that long ago lovely morning in Mojas with the curtains swishing on the tiles and the woman in the alley below calling for her little hiding boy.

"I shall go and see Lizzie," Frances said. "I shall go and see her tomorrow. I ought to anyway, I haven't seen her for so long. Mum—"

"Yes?" Barbara said.

"What will happen to Dad if you go and live in Bath?"

Barbara paused. She arranged the sandwiches on a plate in a little block.

"He can do," she said, "what he probably should have done twenty-five years ago. He can go and live with Juliet."

• • •

Lizzie said she didn't want to talk in the flat, she said it was too crowded with children because of the school holidays having begun. She didn't look well, Frances thought. The children, on the other hand, despite the last vestiges of chicken-pox, looked in rude health. Harriet was helping Robert in the Gallery because since Jenny had gone, they were very short-handed. Lizzie said Harriet had amazed everyone, and most of all herself, by liking working in the Gallery. Lizzie also said that Frances must speak to Harriet on her own.

"Must I? Why?"

"Because she's hurt."

"Hurt?"

"Yes," Lizzie said, "because you didn't tell her yourself about the baby, you just assumed I would. It didn't matter with the boys. You know boys. I sometimes think they simply don't have the mechanism for receiving information of any human kind, but Harriet is different. Harriet has always thought you and she have something special, that you feel differently about her."

"I do."

"Then you should have told her about this baby."

"It isn't *this* baby," Frances said, "it's *my* baby."

She went down the staircase to the Gallery. There were quite a lot of customers, some of them with the holiday-clothed, questing air of tourists, and Robert was sitting on a rush-seated stool behind the till, smiling and counting out change and putting purchases into the Gallery's new buff-and-dark-blue recycled bags. Frances waved to him and he gave her a returning wave, almost like a salute. Then she went towards the back of the shop and found Harriet holding up Indian rag rugs while a customer colour-tested a scrap of cotton fabric against them.

"Not quite the same beige—"

"Won't it look a bit dull," Harriet suggested, "if it's exactly the same?" She glanced up and saw Frances, and blushed.

The customer sighed. "I'm afraid I'll simply have to think about it."

Harriet laid the rugs down.

"I do like the blue, though," the customer said, "and the green is very pretty. But then, the rust has more character—"

"Yes," Harriet said, scowling with self-control.

"Is Mrs. Hardacre here?" the customer asked. "She has such an eye for colour—"

"I'm afraid she's on holiday just now."

The customer looked as if she thought that this was very inconsiderate. She put the piece of curtain fabric away in a little zipped compartment inside her handbag, and then she glanced at Frances.

"I mustn't keep this lady waiting—"

"Thank you," Frances said, adding, "I *am* in rather a hurry—"

"Are you?" Harriet said when they were alone. She stood behind the piles of rugs, as if to keep a barrier between herself and Frances. "Are you in a hurry?"

"No," Frances said, "I just wanted to get rid of her. I came to say sorry."

Harriet said stonily, "I expect Mummy sent you."

"She did say that I had been thoughtless and that I'd offended you and I wanted to say I am truly sorry about that."

Harriet lifted a foot as if to kick the rug pile and then remembered her position as shop assistant, and desisted.

"Doesn't matter. It's your baby—"

"Yes, but you're my niece and we've always been particular friends."

"Until—" Harriet said, and stopped.

"Yes," Frances said, "until."

"I think," Harriet said, too loudly, "I think you're being unfair."

"To you?"

"No. To this baby. Mum says you aren't getting married."

There was a beat and then Frances said as lightly as she could, "No, it doesn't look like it."

"That's not fair on the baby. People can talk and talk and say it doesn't matter if kids don't have a mum and a dad, but it does matter, it does, otherwise it's just grown-ups doing what they want, as per usual, it's just one more poor kid having to explain why their name isn't the same as their mum's name or their dad's name, it's just some awful battle you've started that your kid will have to do the fighting in, not you!" She tossed her head so that her hair flew up in a plume before it fell back again across her face. "You should have thought of that, you should have thought of all that before you started!"

"Harriet—"

"I don't want to talk to you," Harriet said. "I don't care whether you told Mum first or me first, I don't *care*. I'm just pissed off you turned out to be like all the others, all the other grown-ups with their secrets and their lies. I've got to help Dad now, anyway."

"Yes," Frances said. She put a steadying hand out against a sturdy pine dresser filled with pottery plates painted with hens. "I hope—I hope that, when your cousin is born, you won't take your anger with me out on it."

" 'Course not," Harriet said scornfully. "What do you take me for?"

Lizzie and Frances lay on a rug under an enormous horse-chestnut tree on the edge of Langworth recreation ground. At some distance away, a group of boys were being given net practice for cricket by a ginger-headed man with un-naturally long arms, like a chimpanzee, and Sam and Davy had drifted enviously towards the group, full of shy long-ing. Sam adored cricket, as he adored all games; Davy was trying to accustom himself to not being afraid of the ball.

Lizzie lay on her stomach, plucking at grasses at the edge of the rug. Frances sat beside her, legs outstretched, propped on her arms. She had told Lizzie about Harriet's angry reaction and Lizzie had said, Well, you know how conventional teenagers are.

"But she has a point."

"Maybe. But we all have points. That's the trouble, all

of us having points and wanting them heard."

Frances looked at her sister, took a deep breath and said, "And now Mum wants hers heard."

She waited for Lizzie to spin round, but Lizzie went on weaving three stiff grasses into a little rigid plait.

Then she said, "You mean this plan to go and live in Bath?"

"You know about it!"

"Mum has dropped so many heavy hints, I couldn't fail to. I suppose we ought to try and stop her, but frankly, I can't take on another single emotional thing just now, I simply can't. They're our parents, I know, but it's their marriage, if you can *call* it a marriage."

"I think they think it is. Anyway, it appears to be my fault."

"Does it?"

"Dad said my pregnancy had brought everything to a head and made them quarrel so badly that Mum can't stay any more."

Lizzie said dully, "It isn't you."

"Oh?"

"Well, it's only partly you, it's really Luis."

"Luis?" Frances demanded.

"He's made you behave so differently, he's taken you away from us and now he's going to abandon you."

Frances said furiously, "If you ever say anything remotely like that again—"

"Sorry!" Lizzie shrieked. "I didn't mean it, I didn't mean—"

"I thought we were beyond all this, we'd done with this kind of rubbish—"

"We have, we have, I'm sorry, I'm sorry—"

"Lizzie—"

"Listen," Lizzie said, speaking rapidly, her head bent low over her plaiting fingers, "I've got rather a lot to say to you and I'm not quite sure what order it will come out in. Perhaps I'll do Jenny first, shall I? Poor Jenny. I caught Rob kissing her, or rather, having kissed her, which he said was out of relief and gratitude to her for being so normal

when I've been so bonkers. I don't know if I believe that
or not, but I've decided to try to. I went to see Jenny, who
was behaving as if she and Rob had had a full-blown affair,
and it was perfectly plain she was in agony because she *had*
found Rob very attractive and therefore couldn't disentan-
gle what had happened and what she had fantasised might
happen. She's sacked herself from the Gallery, which is the
worst thing she could possibly do from everybody's point
of view including her own, but I can't persuade her otherwise. And then you. This awful situation you've got yourself into. I mean, you're my sister and I'll help you all I
can, of course I will, but I can't pretend I think you've
done a wonderful thing, because I don't, I think the whole
thing's been a disaster, from that first trip to Spain, an utter
disaster—" Her voice broke a little and then, without
warning, she reared up and said, gazing at Frances, "Oh
Frances, what am I going to do?"

Frances knelt up and put her arms round her.

"Nobody," she said, "can feel very normal when there's
a situation like mine around. *Nobody* can."

Lizzie clung to her.

"Are you going to be all right?"

"I don't know. How can I possibly know?"

"And Luis, I mean, is Luis being kind to you?"

"Very."

"Mightn't he—mightn't he feel differently when the
baby is born?"

"I don't know," Frances said again. "In this situation, it
doesn't seem possible to know anything, for certain."

Lizzie pulled away a little and looked at her.

"Are you afraid?"

"Yes."

"About the baby, about your job, about what will become
of you?"

"Not—so much about those, but those too—"

"Then what?"

Frances sat back on her heels, holding one of Lizzie's
hands.

"It's a more primary fear. I suppose it's the irrational

fear of aloneness that we all have, that goes right back to childhood, but in my case, at the moment, I'm afraid I'll lose access to parts of myself I've only found through— someone else."

"Luis."

"Yes."

"What parts?"

Frances looked away.

"I can't tell you. It's too private. I can just sense that the loss would shake me badly."

Lizzie whispered, "What can you do about it?"

"Nothing."

"You said that—that the loss of Luis would shake you badly—"

"Yes."

"Well, you see," Lizzie said, putting Frances's hand down carefully as if it were something fragile, "I feel just as destabilised by the loss of you." She looked up, half-waiting, half-hoping that Frances would say, But you haven't lost me! You couldn't! I wouldn't let you! but Frances said quietly instead, "I know."

"Just that? Just 'I know'?"

"Yes."

"Frances—"

"No," Frances said, scrambling suddenly to her feet, "no more talking, I'm sick of talking. I'm sick of going round and round everyone's bloody *feelings*!"

"But what else do you expect?"

"I don't know what I expect, but I know what I like just now, I like plans. I prefer Mum's plans to Dad's feelings. I prefer Ana's plans—"

"Who is Ana?"

"Luis's sister."

"You never told me—"

"Well, I have now," Frances said, almost shouting, "I have now. Ana is a doctor and she is finding me a colleague with whom I can register in Seville and a hospital bed in which I can have this baby. I'm going to join the boys." She looked down at Lizzie, and then she said fiercely, "If you don't start counting your blessings, Lizzie, you won't have any left to bloody *count*," and then she set off, half-running, across the grass, before Lizzie could say, as she could see she was just about to say, You sound just like Mum.

"What will happen to Shore to Shore?" Robert said.

"I expect it will go on. There's Nicky, after all. Anyway, it'll have to. What else can she live on?"

Robert squeezed toothpaste on to his brush and wedged it into his mouth while he screwed the cap back on the tube.

"But if she decides to live in Spain—"

"I don't know. Perhaps Nicky will run London and Italy and Frances will run Spain. Or Spain and Italy. I don't know and she doesn't seem much interested."

"But it's her company."

"Rob," Lizzie said, lying back in the bath, "I don't know what's happening. I only know she is having the baby in a hospital in Seville because that's what she wants. And what Frances wants, she does."

"Lizzie!"

"It's true. Why shouldn't she?"

Robert stared, his mouth full of foam. Then he spat.

"Why indeed—"

"I'm not thinking about it any more anyway," Lizzie said.

"Aren't you?"

"No," Lizzie said. "There's no point. It's not my life any more, it's hers. I mightn't like that, but that's how it is, so—" She put the back of her hand to her mouth and stopped.

Robert put his toothbrush down and then he knelt by the bath.

"Thank God for that," he said.

TWENTY

When William had at last gone, Juliet was filled with a
sudden energy, a violent, unnatural, purging energy. It led
her to pile all the small pieces of furniture that she could
lift on to the big central table where her sewing machine
stood, and brush fiercely at the rush matting that covered
the floor, raising clouds of dust and legions of aggrieved
woodlice. She brushed until her arms ached, then she put
the furniture back and stripped all the covers off the cushions to wash, and cleaned the windows and lifted the sewing machine and all the heaps of attendant fabric off the
table prior to spreading on the latter, with half an old pair
of pyjama bottoms, a thin, nourishing layer of beeswax polish made by a retired dentist in the village, who kept bees.

Then she suddenly couldn't do any more. She stood for
a moment by the table, holding the rag and the jar and felt
that she hadn't even the energy to unscrew the lid. She put
both down on the table, and leaned there for a moment,
then, like somebody fainting, groped her way across the
room, holding on to things as she went, and half-fell into
the wicker chair where the poor denuded cushions lay like
a heap of plucked chickens. As she collapsed among them,

a few tiny dusty feathers rose into the air and settled gently on her clothes.

"There's no change without sacrifice," Juliet said out loud, wearily, to the dishevelled room, "and it seems that there is no continuity without it either." She put her hands over her face. They were rough from cleaning, and smelled of dusters. Was life, in the end, just a series of losses, a manifest reflecting image of those hundreds of thousands of brain cells that one was reputed to lose, impotently, every day from the age of fifteen onwards? I must get a dog, Juliet thought, or a cat or a canary. I must have someone to say these things to, otherwise I shall turn into a muttering old loony up here on my hill, it's what happens to people who live alone and that's what I shall do for ever now, it's what I have just, finally, chosen to do.

"I'm so sorry," she had said to William.

He had smiled, a sad, stiff little smile.

"I expect I'm just being pathetic."

"It is frightening, getting older," Juliet said. "It is frightening, wondering how one will cope, but I'm not at all sure, except for limited and mechanical purposes, that the presence of another human being actually makes any difference. Unless, of course, you're ill."

William was holding a glass of cider, the flat, potent, amber-coloured cider that came from a local farm.

"I wonder if I just left it too late—"

"No," Juliet said, hating herself for being honest but feeling equally that honesty was the least she owed him, after all these years, "I never wanted to live with you, I never wanted to live with anyone. Except perhaps—if I'd had one—with a child."

William looked at her.

"Barbara asked me what I would have done if you had had a baby—"

"I tried to," Juliet said. "I tried and failed exactly as Frances has tried and succeeded. I'm glad, now."

William tried not to feel aggrieved.

"Are you?"

"Yes," Juliet said. "Frances is only just beginning—"

"Please don't talk about it," William said quickly. "Please don't tell me what awful things lie ahead for her, please don't tell me you're glad now that you didn't have a child by me, please don't be so self-contained and separate and realistic and female and unreachable, please—" He stopped and took an unsteady swallow of cider.

"Are you sure," Juliet said, watching him, "that you didn't come up here because you really just couldn't think what to do next?"

"No," William said more confidently, "I came because—" He stopped. He couldn't, he found, say that he had come to ease the pain of losing Barbara, that Juliet had always been his bolt hole, the person and place he turned to when troubled or unhappy. He looked up. Juliet was wearing the sort of expression that made him wonder, uneasily, if she knew exactly what he was thinking anyway.

She said more gently, "Did you really, truly, think that we could live together now? Can you honestly imagine it?"

"I'm quite easy, you know—"

"I didn't mean that."

"I don't want to know what you meant," he said. He drained his glass. "I expect I'll find a flat in Langworth, near Lizzie, and then I can toddle to the library and the bowling club and the post office on pension days, can't I, in a manner appropriate to a dear old thing—"

"You aren't a dear old thing," Juliet said sharply, "you're a self-pitying one. It's no good blaming life, William Shore, it's no good blaming anything, you're not a leaf on the wind, you're a person!"

He sighed.

"That's what Barbara says."

"You're like a Ping-Pong ball," Juliet went on energetically. "You've just let yourself be batted back and forth between Barbara and me all these years, saying 'Oh help' to yourself in mild astonishment every so often, but never *doing* anything. I did love you, I do, you're one of the most lovable people I've ever known, but I couldn't live with you in a million years. Who could I bat you away to when I needed my own space and time?"

He gazed at her. She waited, in sudden apprehension, for him to say something exasperating like, Am I really that impossible? but he didn't. He simply gazed as if he were both looking at and thinking a lot of things for the first time, and then he said, unexpectedly, "The trouble with me is that my life has just been too easy, and if ever it shows signs of getting difficult, I make absolutely sure it stops any nonsense of that kind at once. I'm the original oyster. Always have been. I'd have made a whacking great pearl out of every grain of sand they shoved in faster than any other oyster on record." He smiled at her. "Would you give the oyster a goodbye kiss?"

She was startled.

"Goodbye? Why, won't we be seeing each other again?"

"Oh, we'll *see* each other," William said, "of course we will, but this is—the end of this bit. Isn't it?"

She nodded slowly. She thought to herself, in some astonishment: Yes, he is right, this is the end of this bit, but I wonder what else it will be the end of? They both stood up. She stayed where she was, and William came over and put his arms round her and kissed her on her forehead and then, more firmly, on her closed mouth. She felt, he thought, a little more solid than usual; to her, he felt more frail.

Then he stepped back and said, "I probably will join the bowling club, you know. To meet lots of nice ladies in white cardigans."

Then he went. Juliet stood in the open doorway and, as she had done countless times before, watched his car bounce down the track—he was not a natural driver and it had never occurred to him to try and avoid the ruts—sending up plumes of smoky summer dust and showers of little stones.

And now she was sitting here with the sewing machine on the floor and a pile of cushion covers in the doorway to the kitchen and the air full of dust and flecks of feather. A chapter had closed. It had closed so that she could go on with life as it had always been, except that in actuality she couldn't, because the closing of the chapter meant, perversely, that her life would never be quite the same again. She had chosen to stay put while the humans in the landscape around her all changed places, and by so choosing she had kept something and lost something and how would she ever know if she had chosen to keep and to lose the right things? All you could do in these matters was trust your instincts, obey your inner voice. She had done it for years, so had William, and it sounded even as if at last inconsistent, caustic, three-cornered Barbara was doing it. And of course, Frances was, *par excellence*. Juliet looked at her sewing machine. She thought, automatically, of the baby clothes it might make and as she thought that she felt a rush of pure alarm for Frances followed, almost immediately, by a rush of even purer envy.

Harriet had earned thirty-three pounds and four pence. Robert had paid her in cash. He had said he would pay her the current under-eighteen basic wage for every hour she worked in the shop in the holidays, with fifty pence per hour extra for any overtime she did outside shop-opening times, unpacking or pricing or cleaning. Harriet could hardly believe it. She knelt on her bedroom floor and spread the notes and coins out on Davy's Rupert Bear rug. He was, in a way, too old for such a rug now, but he still liked it. He had told Harriet one night, when he was still awake when she came to bed, that he didn't much want to be bigger.

Harriet had never possessed so much money, had never, in her life before, seen the point, the possibility even, of the choice that it offered. She laid her hands on the money, pressing it to the rug, as if it were dough, as if she wanted to leave some mark on it, as hers. She felt a bit odd, a bit emotional, as if a lot of things that she had taken for granted in her life as forming the necessary, but apparently irrational, background for childhood in fact had had a pattern and a reason all along. She gathered up the money, put it back neatly into the envelope in which Robert had given it to her, and slid it between the mattress and the divan base of her bed, pushing it right across against the wall.

In the sitting room, Alistair was making a swear-words chart. It had everyone's names across the top, and down the side, a list of swear words with, at Lizzie's request, most of the vowels replaced by asterisks. Alistair had concocted a system of fines and said the proceeds were going to charity. He had made a charity box, which he had hidden in his cupboard and which Harriet had looked for, and found, when he was out. He had covered it in left-over Christmas paper and stuck on neat transfer letters which read, "Save the Alistair Fund." Harriet could read his mind like a book. He had done this because he was jealous of her working in the shop and Robert had said he would have to wait until he too was fourteen and nearly fifteen to work there as well. Harriet was waiting until the appropriate moment to expose the fraud of the charity box.

Alistair looked up as she came in.

"How much did he give you?"

She went over to the sofa and draped herself across an arm.

"None of your business."

"I can guess, anyway," Alistair said. "I can easily work it out. He gave you thirty-three pounds, and four p."

"No he didn't."

"Yes," Alistair said calmly, drawing neat lines under "b*gg*r" and "b*st*rd." "He did. He really is a fool. You aren't worth half that."

Harriet picked her nails.

"You're jealous."

Alistair said nothing.

"You are," Harriet insisted. "You're jealous because you're no bloody use to anyone." She bit off a hangnail. "You're just a drone, a dead weight on the family, you're like the little ones, you just take and take and you don't give anything back, you're useless."

Alistair drooped his head lower and lower over his chart. Harriet peered at him.

"Ally?"

He snuffled. Harriet got off the sofa.

"You're crying!"

"No!" Alistair yelled. He snatched his glasses off and hurled them across the room, where they fell, with a small clatter, behind the television. His face was scarlet.

"I don't want to live here any more!" he shouted. "I don't want to live with all these awful people, I don't want it to be so confusing!"

Harriet waited a bit, and then she said, "Where will you go?"

Alistair banged his fist down on the swear chart.

"I'm not useless, I'm not, I'm not! I can work Dad's computer better than he can!"

"Ally—"

"I want to kill them!" Alistair screamed. "Mum and Dad and Granny and Grandpa all fighting and quarrelling!" He swung round on Harriet. "What about *us*?"

She regarded him soberly.

"They don't ask us, they didn't ask us about the Grange—"

"Do you want to go back there?"

Harriet thought.

"No."

"I don't know what I want," Alistair said drearily. "I just don't want all this to go on."

Harriet took a huge breath. She said, "I'll lend you ten pounds."

Alistair looked at her. His face was paler now, blotched red in all the wrong places, and his hair stood up in unkempt tufts at one side of his head.

"Why?"

She shrugged.

"I just will."

He sighed and began to rummage behind the television for his spectacles.

"It—"

"Yes?"

"It'd better be my money," Alistair said, retrieving them.

"What?"

"It's better if it's my money. I mean, it's nice of you but I'd rather—"

"I can't *give* it to you—"

"No," Alistair said. He put his spectacles on and rubbed at the lenses clumsily with his sweatshirt sleeve.

"Why don't you ask Dad?"

"Ask him?"

"Why don't you ask if you can help on the computer?"

"He'll only say no."

"He won't," Harriet said, "he won't."

Alistair trailed back to the table, picked up his swear chart and crumpled it up in his hands.

"Why won't he?"

"Because everything's different," Harriet said.

"Yes," Alistair said. He nodded. "You're telling me."

The Gallery was empty. It was Friday night, after closing time, and the shop was dusky, except for the carefully angled spotlights in the window, timed to turn themselves off at eleven o'clock. Lizzie sat at the back of the shop in an Italian garden chair made of enough natural canvas slung on a polished teak frame. It was an extremely handsome chair, but Robert and Jenny had bought it.

She had taken her shoes off. She sat very still in the Italian chair, with her hands in her lap and her bare feet resting on the harsh fibre matting on the floor, and looked out through the silhouetted shapes of all the things in the Gallery, past the brightly lighted stage of the window, into the High Street. There weren't many people about but then, it was after seven o'clock, and after seven, in Langworth, people were either firmly at home or firmly in the pub or firmly at Bingo in the old cinema where Lizzie and Frances had once gone, illegally, because they were then way underage, to see Anthony Perkins in *Desire Under the Elms*. It was the word "desire," coupled with Anthony Perkins, that had made them want to go. When they came out, Lizzie had been full of things to say but Frances had said, "Shh, *shh*, I'm thinking."

I'm thinking now, Lizzie thought. I don't much like it, I'd rather *do*, but when it becomes apparent that almost everything you do is at best clumsy and at worst wrong, you have to stop and think, even I have to. She unfolded her hands and laid them on the arms of the chair. It was a lovely chair, a really good piece of design, a really good buy, too, since Robert had ordered six and this was the last one left. Lizzie couldn't wait for it to go. It was evidence—and evidence was the last thing she wanted just now—of areas of life she had not controlled recently, areas that had plainly got on with themselves more than adequately without her.

But it was no good thinking, however much she wanted to, that she could simply take back the control now that she was ready to, because she couldn't. Most of those people—Robert, the children, her parents, Frances—whom Lizzie felt to be like spokes of a wheel of which she was the hub had, somehow, detached themselves and gone bowling off on their own. It was no use, Lizzie told herself, thinking that she could just snap her fingers now and bring them all to heel, because she couldn't. They wouldn't come, for one thing. When people used that phrase about resuming life after an upset, they didn't really mean that, they didn't mean you could go on where you had left off as if nothing had happened, they meant looking at what you had now, which was never exactly what you used to have, and going on from there. Technically, Lizzie still had one husband and four children and two parents and one twin sister and a home and a business and a job, but only technically. The essence of her old life, that busy, authoritative life at the Grange, was now gone for ever. The essence of her new life was something she had to look at very seriously, because everybody, including Robert, or perhaps particularly Robert, had made it abundantly plain that they weren't going to look at it for her.

"My marriage," Barbara had said to her, not especially kindly, "is none of your business. Certainly I'm your mother, certainly we have the natural concern for one another of mother and daughter, but my marriage is mine, good or bad. It was there long before you came along, and you only know as much about it as you can see. You can't affect it, you can't tell your father and me what to do about it, just because you're younger, just because you think you know."

The trouble is, Lizzie thought, lifting her feet up on to the chair and wrapping her arms round her knees, I did think I knew. In a way, I suppose I still do, but I've got to learn not to *say* what I think I know all the time. Rob hasn't said that but I know he's thinking it, like he's thinking he's absolutely sick with relief that Frances is going to Spain, because even though he's fond of her, he really can't bear her and me any more. Or, let's be completely truthful, please, Lizzie, he can't bear the way I behave about her. Well, I can't behave about her in any way at all any more because she won't let me. Mum says she should never have been a twin, which may be right and all very well for Frances, but what about me? I think I'm a natural twin, I feel one, but it seems I have to stop thinking like that or else, if they're all right, I'll find I'm not a wife or a mother either, and I'll just end up the kind of useless neurotic mess I've always despised.

She stood up and began to pad softly round the shop in her bare feet. Robert said Harriet was properly useful, not just apparently so in order to earn this coveted money. He also said that he was going to explain the stock-taking and marking-up systems to Alistair. Alistair had asked him. Lizzie had opened her mouth to say that Alistair was too young to be of any real use and shut it again without uttering. There had been something distinctly unhelpful in Rob's expression, something that had been there a lot lately, a patient, wary, weary something. She had found herself, most uncharacteristically, on the verge of asking him if he was tired of her and had only refrained because she had discovered she was terrified of risking the answer being "yes." He made it eloquently, mutely plain just now that he didn't want to talk any more, that he was sick of talking, that it was his opinion that talking could very easily become a substitute for living. And loving.

"I don't have to *say* I love you!" he'd shouted at her not long ago. "I don't have to *say* another word! Why don't you look at what I *do*? What I do for you, for us, for the children? Why don't you just look at that?"

So now she was looking at some of it, looking at this thoughtfully, ingeniously stocked shop, at the steadiness it represented, at the hours and hours of lonely minding it had taken over the last two years, grimly holding on, while too few people came, and even fewer bought. But they were coming now. Harriet had told her, Harriet had said this week had been a better week. Alistair had worked out that it was about seventeen per cent better. Lizzie stopped by a display table. On it was a pile of turned wooden boxes with latticed lids for filling with potpourri, boxes that Lizzie remembered ordering from that strange young man who said that he was a Buddhist and that he could also make her spinning wheels if she wanted them. The boxes wouldn't do there, in a pile. Nobody could see the point of them in a pile, how they fitted in. They ought to be next to a lamp, singly, near a pile of books and a vase, they ought to be placed in such a way as to suggest the effect of them, the use of them. Lizzie reached out, picked up the nearest two boxes and began on a little purposeful re-arrangement.

Later, over supper, they talked about the children. It was the sort of conversation they used to have, long ago, and had not had for ages, because of what Lizzie called, well—other things. They discussed Alistair's solitariness and Davy's babyishness with mild anxiety and discreetly congratulated themselves on a dawning sense of responsibility they perceived in both Harriet and Sam. They said at intervals, "Of course, he or she is terribly young yet," and Sam came drifting in, in search of something to eat, and said what were they talking about but please don't tell him actually, because it was bound to be boring. They said, "You," and he was enchanted. He lay down on the kitchen floor in one of the narrow spaces between the table and the cupboards, to eat his Marmite sandwich, and listen in case they talked about him a bit more. When they didn't, he began a chant, muffled by chewing, of "Bor-ing, bor-ing, bor-ing," until Robert threw him out. They heard him go banging cheerfully along the passage, singing the theme tune for the World Cup, and this made them smile at one another, and the smiling suddenly made Lizzie feel rather vulnerable.

"Lizzie—"

"Yes?"

"I've got something to ask you," Robert said.

"If it's about Westondale—"

"It isn't, though it might be, later. It's about William."

She pushed a few last pasta shells that she didn't want to eat round her plate with her fork.

"Juliet turned him down."

"I know that."

"I suppose we could all have seen it coming, I mean, if she'd ever really wanted him or he her, they'd have done something about it sooner—"

"Exactly," Robert said, "a William-style cop-out. William never wanted to lose what he had; Juliet never wanted all the clutter and rows of family life. Just as I always said."

Lizzie nodded.

"Yes, you did. I suppose we just got used to it, like we got used to Mum complaining about it and not doing anything. Frances and I were at school once with a girl called Beverley Lane-Smith. Her parents lived together but they weren't married, her father was called something Lane and her mother was called something Smith, and we didn't think anything of it and nor did she until suddenly, at about twenty-two, she got frightfully indignant about her parents never considering her and her brother in the matter, and she changed her name to Burton, to spite them, because she had a crush on the actor."

"Yes," Robert said patiently, "but what has that got to do with William?"

"Only as an illustration of waking up to something you've always unthinkingly gone along with—"

"Lizzie," Robert said, "where is William going to live when the house is sold?"

Lizzie put her fork down.

"He's going to buy a flat, he says. He's thinking of buying a flat here, in Langworth. There are some new ones, behind the police station—"

"Those are for people on walkers."

"Well, he'll be on a walker one day—"

"Not for years."

"No, but I suppose—"

"Lizzie," Robert said, "I think he ought to come and live with us."

Her mouth fell open.

"Us!"

"Yes."

"But—but you'd go mad, he drives you mad, bumbling about, forgetting things! And there isn't room, there isn't an inch, how could we have any privacy at all, it's bad enough with the children, but how could there be any privacy at all with Dad here?"

"Not here," Robert said. He leaned forward. "We'd buy another house. William could use his half of the proceeds of his house to put down on a house for all of us, and we would let this flat and use the rent to service the mortgage on the remainder."

"But you didn't want help from him! You refused help from him!"

"That was then," Robert said. "This is now. I couldn't bear help while we were going down. I can bear this kind of structured help now that I think we are going slowly up."

"Are we?"

He looked at her.

"What do you think?"

"Why do you ask me?"

"Because the answer really depends on you."

Lizzie looked down at the wooden table top, at the burns and scars and rings lurking under its shiny surface like fish in a pool.

"We might have him for twenty years—"

"Yes."

"Rob," she said, "don't you mind that?"

"I mind it less than a lot of other things. He could help in the shop."

Lizzie thought.

"*Could* he?"

"Yes; for the odd hour. When neither of us can be there."

"Neither of us?"

"Yes. Do you really intend to go on at Westondale?"

"I have to."

"You don't."

"I do!" Lizzie cried. "The interest on the bloody loan!"

"I could get a job," Robert said. "My turn."

Fear clutched her.

"But why, when I've got one already—"

"I need a change. We all do. We need to have a kind of life now where we feel we're building, not just standing around in a panic with our fingers in the hole in the dyke. You can get as stuck in panic as you can in boredom. I want to make things happen now, I want to move things."

She said, controlling herself, "But what might you do?"

"Teach."

"Teach!"

"Yes. Picture framing, furniture restoration, that sort of thing. There's a vacancy, in Bath, on a course for retraining people who've been made redundant—"

"Not students, then—"

"No," Robert said, grinning faintly at her tone. "Why should you be frightened of students?"

Lizzie wanted to say she seemed to feel frightened of most things at the moment and said instead, untruthfully, "I'm not. But surely that wouldn't pay very well?"

"Slightly more than Westondale pays you, for fewer hours."

"Because you're a man!"

"I'm not a *sculptor*," Robert said deliberately. "Why don't you think of starting that again?"

"Nobody wants that—"

"People always want that. What about starting with children, our children even, for practice?"

"Where would I do it?"

"Lizzie! What's the matter with you? You'll do it, if that's the only thing holding you back, in a special studio in the new house we will buy with your father when he has sold his present one! You'll do it in the holidays when I'm not teaching and at weekends when the children or part-timers can help in the shop! You'll do it so that you have something creative to do that will take the pressure off all of us."

Lizzie swallowed. He suddenly seemed so necessary to her that she could hardly look at him.

"I'd like that."

"Good," Robert said. "About bloody time." He stood up. "Right, now. Will you ring your father or shall I?"

"I will."

"Good."

"It's all—really nice of you—"

"And self-interested too. Self-interested for us."

"I know."

"*Us*," Robert said emphatically.

Lizzie got up and went round the table to lean against him.

"Frances's baby is going to be like Beverley Lane-Smith, isn't it?"

Robert kissed her hair.

"Shore–Gómez Moreno—"

"Oh Rob, it's so sad, it's so lonely, poor baby—"

Robert put his hands on her shoulders and pushed her away from him, shaking her a little.

"Won't you ever learn?"

She turned her face away, smiling faintly.

"I'm so tired of learning—"

"Listen," Robert said fiercely, "listen to me. It's our parents' shortcomings that make us, they made you, they made me; *our* shortcomings will make *our* children, you see if they don't. How do you learn to swim along otherwise? How do you learn about a wider world if you have everything you could ever need at home? Endless happiness isn't formative, it only makes you vulnerable, or else it makes you smug. And another thing. Wearing a wedding ring doesn't mean you're automatically a better mother! And one good parent is a lot more than most people get!" He stopped and drew a breath. "OK?"

"OK," Lizzie said. She was really smiling now.

"Then go and ring your father," Robert said, "and I shall go and do a little formative shouting at the children."

"Rob—"

"Yes?"

"I wasn't jealous on purpose," Lizzie said. "I didn't ask to be, I didn't mean to be. It's terrible being jealous, it's like being chained to someone else, who's completely mad. And it's so destructive—"

"I know all this," he said politely, "really I do. Remember, I was the one with a seat in the stalls."

Lizzie pushed her fringe off her forehead.

"I'm trying to say sorry."

"You don't have to."

"But I need to somehow, I—" She paused and then she said, "I know I went absolutely over the top about Frances, I know that, and I don't blame her for wanting to have her baby miles away from me, but it does haunt me that I may have damaged something between us that won't ever be mended."

Robert gave a little bark of laughter.

"Oh no."

"No?"

"Not you two," he said. He leaned forward and gave her a quick, rough kiss. "As far as you two are concerned, I reckon you'll always feel the twitch upon the thread."

PART
FIVE

DECEMBER

TWENTY-ONE

"It's a saint's day," the taxi driver said. He had had to slow the cab to a crawl.

Ahead of them some local Sevillian *cofradía* swayed along the street in procession, carrying a statue on a primitive litter draped in spangled blue cloth. The statue was draped in spangles too, in a robe of white brocade that glittered like hoar frost edged in what looked like white marabou. When the taxi finally managed to overtake the procession, Frances knew, she would be alarmed and repelled by the statue's face, the highly painted, sentimental, doll-like face of an obscure Catholic saint, or even of one of the myriad versions of the Virgin, the Virgin of the Dews, or the Rosary, or the Holy Blood.

"Can't we overtake them?" Frances asked.

The taxi driver shrugged. "When the street is wider." He glanced at Frances in his driving mirror. "Will two minutes make so much difference?"

"I don't know," Frances said. She held her belly. "I've never done this before."

"I have five—"

"No," Frances said, "your wife had five. You don't know what it feels like."

"True," he said, smiling. He was a little man, like so many Andalusians, and he had helped her into the cab very tenderly, with great solicitude and without any embarrassment. Luis had not been there. He hadn't suggested he should be, and Frances hadn't either.

The members of the brotherhood in the procession wore dark suits and ties. The men were at the front with the glittering saint and behind them the women bunched together, the old ones in black with black mantillas as if for Holy Week, the younger ones in respectful finery and high-heeled shoes. The little boys had ties, like their fathers, the little girls wore bows in their hair. There was about everybody, and even from behind, an air both of formality and of devotion.

"Now," the taxi driver said.

The street had widened by a few feet between the shuttered shop fronts, closed in honour of the day. The driver gave a small polite touch to his horn, and edged the taxi first level with the procession and then slowly past it. The nearest people in the long line turned their heads without any particular curiosity and regarded Frances, both unmistakably pregnant and unmistakably not Spanish, as she slid by, and then turned back again towards the swaying white back of their image.

"It is so easy to feel left out in Sevilla," Ana had said once. "Life here is so much for the people of the city. Strangers come here for the *feria*, expecting to be swept up into a great flamenco carnival, and find that they are asked to nothing. The whole of Sevilla is having a party, but it is not for outsiders."

"It is a very local city," Frances's Spanish doctor had said on another occasion. She came from Galicia and was mildly contemptuous of her southern compatriots. "It isn't even like the the rest of Andalucía, it isn't like anywhere!"

Frances liked her doctor. She was called María Luisa Ramírez, and she had come to Seville with her mother, after her father died, and her mother, a Sevillian, had longed to return home. Dr. Ramírez had been born in the rainy, green Atlantic region of the north, and she said her parents were both spiritually and politically conservative. She told Frances that her childhood had been very happy, orderly and settled, belonging to an almost vanished era whose annual cycles were punctuated by family occasions, schooling, and the frequent festivals of the Catholic Church. At the feast of Corpus Christi, she said, her family's whole town combined to cover the streets with the innumerable petals of flowers painstakingly arranged in complicated patterns, like a carpet, for the holy procession to walk over. They stayed up all night, making these flower carpets, and although Dr. Ramírez said she was now an atheist and a socialist, she still remembered those nights before Corpus Christi as some of the happiest times she had ever spent.

She never asked Frances personal questions that didn't relate either to Frances's or the baby's welfare. They both referred to Luis simply as "the father." Dr. Ramírez had known Ana de Mena for three years, so Frances supposed that she must also make the connection, but if so, she didn't speak of it. She handled Frances, both physically and psychologically, with great sympathy. She loved working as an obstetrician, she said, it gave her both satisfaction and hope. For her first years in Seville, before she had taken a special course in gynaecology and obstetrics, she had worked in the huge hospital that served Triana, the poorer quarter of Seville, on the other side of the river. She had worked mostly in the casualty department there, but had grown afraid of what such work was doing to her.

"If death becomes commonplace," she told Frances, "your sense of morality diminishes."

Frances thought that they were probably about the same age. She tried to imagine Dr. Ramírez's home life with her mother in the flat they shared in the west of the city, behind the Fine Arts Museum. For all Frances knew, Dr. Ramírez simply lived with her mother and worked in the hospital, a steady, uneventful, useful life, undisturbed by the tempest of falling in love or longing for a baby. The thought of the English equivalent—working in a hospital in Bath and living in Barbara's newly acquired flat there—was somehow both ludicrous and impossible, yet the alternative Frances had chosen, she told herself, was hardly less so, in its way.

She had, in the late summer, suggested to Nicky that she become a partner with her in Shore to Shore, with responsibility both for the English end of the business and for the lease on the office and flat in Fulham, an arrangement to take effect on the first of December, a week before the baby was due. Nicky had been serenely pleased about this, just as she had been calmly congratulatory about the baby and reticent on the subject of Luis. Frances had then informed Luis that she would like his help in setting up an office in Seville.

"Hopeless," he had said at once. "Wrong nationality, wrong Spanish city, wrong timing."

"I can't help that," Frances said. "I have to be here. English people do set up businesses in Spain all the time. Look at all those bars and blocks of flats and golf courses all along the Costa del Sol—"

"You need connections," Luis said.

"*You* are my connection!"

"Frances," Luis said, "what is it you intend?"

She had tried not to sound impatient.

"I am trying to stay in the place where our child has the best chance of seeing both parents. And for myself, I am trying to stay in *Spain*."

He had shrugged, but he hadn't argued further. He had simply said in that level, calm, kind voice he now used with her most of the time that she could not just set up a business on her own in Seville, it simply wouldn't work, she would have to buy into one. He told her that the bureaucracy involved would put all that she had already encountered at the hospital in the shade.

"It is very difficult to get residency in Spain. It might involve you in visits to a dozen offices. Are you prepared for that? Also as many visits for bank accounts, for getting the utilities connected to a flat or an office. And your fiscal identity number. Every Spaniard has one. More visits, more bureaucracy, more red tape. It could take you months, very repetitive, very slow. Do you really want to face all that?"

"Yes," Frances said.

He had introduced her, down a labyrinthine chain of business friends, to a man who owned, among other things, a travel company at an excellent address in Seville, just off the Calle Sierpes. There had been several meetings, conducted, on the Spanish side, with perfect courtesy and, at the same time, with a palpable amazement at Frances's proposals, nationality and condition.

"This is most unusual," the owner of the travel company had said, over and over again. "This is not at all common in Spain. How will it be financed? How will it proceed? Is it practical? Is it possible?"

Frances had brought her company accounts out to Seville, proud of the turnover they showed. They were taken from her politely but very gingerly, as if her pregnant state somehow invalidated and made preposterous the pages of satisfactory figures, as if her presence in the office was like a bomb ticking quietly in an airline bag, and she might just explode, without warning, there and then, and make a farce of a sober business meeting. There were many glances at her left hand. On it she wore, as she had now worn for over a year, a silver ring Luis had given her, set with an intaglio of chrysoprase, as green as jade. It was definitely not a wedding ring, was it, the glances said, but on the other hand, it was on the wedding finger. Yet this determined Señorita Shore had been sent by Luis Gómez Moreno, with whom the owner of the travel company had, all those years ago, taken his first communion. And the figures were excellent, the rate of growth of her company steady, her proposals for offering English holidays in small, selected hotels to Spanish people certainly possible ... He smiled at Frances.

"These holidays would have to be most carefully planned. The Spanish, as a race, like to keep moving—"

"I've noticed," Frances said.

Except now, she thought, leaning forward in the taxi. The driver, now well clear of the procession, was still driving with reverent slowness, gazing at the scene behind him in the driving mirror.

"Please," she said urgently, "please, I would like you to hurry—"

His eyes met hers in the mirror. He smiled again, and jerked his right thumb backwards towards the painted idol in her tinsel crown behind them, smiling her vacant red smile.

"You should pray to her," the taxi driver said. "You should pray to the Virgin, to grant you a fine son."

Frances fell back against the seat. Could he mean what he had just said, could he literally mean it? If so, it wasn't just another language he spoke in, it was another world of concepts he inhabited, a world she had elected to join. A contraction seized her. She gave a little gasp.

"It's exactly," she said, "nine months too late for that."

The hospital was new. Half of it was finished and orderly, with lawns and carparks and bossy noticeboards planted in beds of begonias, and half of it was still a building site. Frances had been there once before to register as a future patient and to fill in a thousand forms, some for the Spanish regional health authority, some for the Spanish national health system and some for the relevant department of the European Community, sanctioning Miss Frances Shore to the benefits of the English National Health Service within the boundaries of member states. The staff who had dealt with her had shown no surprise; presumably, to them, to wish to have a baby in Seville was as natural as breathing.

Between them, Ana and Dr. Ramírez had done Frances proud. She was taken into a small single room off the general labour ward, with a view, not of cement mixers and cranes, but of a grove of new young palm trees planted in an equally new lawn of tough Spanish grass, and scattered about with metal seats painted in the colours so beloved by Seville, ochre and white and dusty pink. There were a few round flowerbeds, empty yet of any flowers, whose reddish earth an old man in faded overalls was tenderly sprinkling with water. Beyond the palm grove and the lawn, the blocks of flats of northern Seville began again, festooned with strings of washing, and further away still was a church tower and a bell tower and the dome of something—a convent perhaps—on which a golden crucifix glimmered in the sun.

The room itself was scrupulously new, bare and clean, white walls, white floor, white bed, white bedside cupboard, white basin, pale-green slatted blinds. On the bedside cupboard stood a vase of yellow roses with a tiny card propped beside it. "From Ana," the card said, "with very best wishes." There were no other flowers, no other card. The little room was more impersonal than any room Frances had ever entered, yet it still held an unmistakable air of adventure, a sense that it was a blank sheet waiting to be scribbled on, that it was there, anonymously, noiselessly, just to serve some great purpose.

Frances sat down on the white plastic chair by the window. She would undress when she was told to, get into bed when she was told to, but not before. A nurse had said she would be with her in five minutes, and Frances believed her. For five minutes, she would sit docilely on her chair, timing herself, and peer out through the slats of the blind at the old man in the gardens watering the empty earth. Perhaps he was going to plant something. Should you plant anything in December, even in Seville, even on a soft day like today which might so easily turn into a piercing day, like Frances's first day in Seville almost two years ago, when Luis had followed her fleeing taxi to the airport and had then sat there, for hours, attempting to persuade her to stay?

She hadn't stayed; she'd been adamant about not staying, and now look at her, pregnant by him in a Spanish hospital. The last few months had been so peculiar, so disorientating, that she could hardly remember the feel of that other Frances, the Frances she had always been before. And in a short time, she would be yet another Frances, a mother Frances, and a lifetime's journey would have begun.

The last few weeks, since her arrival in Seville, had been spent in Ana's apartment. Luis had been perfectly happy with the prospect of Frances remaining in his flat in the hotel—he would himself, he made it plain, retreat to Madrid—but there had been a problem in this arrangement in the form of José. José was outraged at Frances's pregnancy. He had liked Frances, trusted her, admired her, and now she had appalled him. For his father to have a girlfriend was fine by José; for his father to have an English girlfriend was initially not so fine by José but he had grown to accept it, but for that girlfriend to become pregnant by his father and then declare she would have the baby in Seville, in the city where José lived, where his mother and grandmothers lived, where the Gómez Morenos were known, were respected, was not only not at all fine, it was intolerable. It was also intolerable, almost to the point beyond bearing, for José to think that his father would soon have another child. Even though that child would initially only be a baby, it would still threaten José's lifelong position as Luis's only child and heir. José could not bring himself to think that this situation was in any way his father's fault. That was out of the question! It was all Frances's fault; she was wholly to blame. José would not see her. He would not speak to her on the telephone. When appealed to by Frances, Luis said that there was nothing he could do.

"You knew all this," he said gravely to Frances. He was never angry with her now, only kind and quiet, telephoning faithfully every day to ask after her health, deflecting all talk of feeling. "You know how my family is, how Spain is. If you make decisions, you must accept the consequences, and you have made the decisions, for you and for me."

"I thought José was my friend—"

"He feels betrayed," Luis said.

"But Ana—"

"Ana is different. Ana is more modern than José, even though she is his aunt. But why am I saying this? Why am I troubling? You *knew* it all, Frances, you knew it, you knew it, I hid nothing from you, I told you everything just as it is. Why do you imagine that just because you have changed, everyone else must change to suit you?"

"Because," Frances said, "what is happening seems to me so utterly natural that I can't—"

"Please, don't go on," he said. "Please stop."

Frances bent now and picked two letters out of her bag, one from Barbara, one from Sam. They were both about houses, about the new places they were living in or about to live in. Frances had read them several times and was amazed at the comfort they gave her, the feeling of support. Barbara said her flat was quite high up, in a tall house off Lansdown, and it had a balcony and a view and plenty of sunshine. She said the stairs were a nuisance, but that the landlord was planning to install a lift, which would be an asset when Frances came to stay with the baby. She said William came to see her a lot, bringing books and flowers and pieces of interesting cheese.

"I think he is still going up to see Juliet too, so I suppose very little has changed for him, in essence, but then, he would be the first to admit he has always fought change tooth and nail. You are about to face a lot of change on the other hand, and I hope you won't be dismayed. It's perfectly possible, in life, to choose something that is absolutely right for you, but not subsequently find the results of the choice either easy or always likeable. But we can't go against our natures, especially if we only discover the truth of them rather late in the day. I think about you."

It was signed, "Love from Mum." Barbara had, long ago, hated being called "Mum," she had wanted to be called "Mother," but Lizzie and Frances called her "Mum" because that was the word everyone else at school used, "my mum," "Lynne's mum," "Sally's mum." It was an odd name, in any case, for Barbara, who would never have sprung to anyone's mind as a shining example of motherliness. But that was a good letter, a heartening letter, a better letter in all sorts of ways than William's more openly loving, anxious, unhappy ones, brimming with his own apprehensions for her. William's letters did not permit Frances the dignity of her own choices, and of living by the consequences of them; they were too full of fear for her, for that.

Sam's, on the other hand, was blithe. He had had to write a letter, he explained, as part of his English homework so he thought he might as well write to her. He said their new house was going to be pretty superb because it backed onto the recreation ground and he could have his bed in a sort of attic thing at the top with a funny roof. Grandpa was going to live in some rooms stuck on the side and Mum was going to have a studio in the garage. He said he had new football boots with red laces (pretty superb also) and that Davy was learning the violin and practised all day and all night and it sounded like a cat being strangled. Harriet had had all her hair cut off, Dad had a cold and Alistair was in love with the new school-dinner lady. Sam hoped Frances knew that oranges came from Seville but that they had a rotten football team, nothing like as brilliant as Madrid or Bilbao. Then he wrote, "Phew, 150 words, end of prep, I can stop. Have a nice baby. Love from Sam."

There was nothing from Lizzie, even though she had addressed the envelope, not even a quick little message at the end of Sam's smudged sheet. It was no good feeling anything about that because to be left alone was what she had asked for. Or rather, demanded. Count your blessings, she'd said to Lizzie, make plans, stop *talking*. Well, now Lizzie had a plan involving one of that row of sturdy semi-detached Edwardian villas Frances remembered along one side of Langworth's recreation ground, villas decorated with patches of half-timbering and stucco. There was a row of lime trees between their back gardens and the football pitches, and their small front gardens had low double-gates with latches, giving on to the road. They could all walk to school from one of those houses, to the Gallery and the bowling club, which William said he had joined, as a joke, to annoy Juliet, and which he had then discovered he liked. "I also discover," he wrote, "that I have a certain aptitude. It is not a heroic sport but it's subtler than you think."

A vision rose before Frances, a domestic, English small-town vision of a front garden strewn with bicycles, of banging doors and running children, of bus routes and neighbourly disapproval of washing hung out on Sundays, of music practice and bowling practice and meals eaten round the kitchen table without a single mouthful of what was being eaten being discussed as a matter of serious concern, of rain and shrub roses and Cornflakes mewing at the window to be let in. It seemed, all at once, to be as familiar as the back of her own hand, and as distant as the moon.

The door of her room opened. A nurse came in, a neat little dark-haired nurse, her white shoes silent on the white floor.

"Señora Shore?"

"Yes," Frances said.

"Are you timing your contractions?"

"About every five minutes," Frances said. She stooped and slid the letters back into her bag. They were England, and then. This was Spain, and now.

"Frances?"

She opened her eyes. Luis was bending over her, dressed in a business suit and holding a long paper cone of flowers.

"Hello."

"Are you all right? Was it all right?"

"Yes," she said, pulling herself up into a sitting position. "It was. It was quite easy. Perhaps it's one of the few things I'll turn out to be good at."

He laid the flowers on the foot of the bed. He did not seem quite composed.

"I came as quickly as I could—"

"Thank you," she said politely.

He looked down at her for a few seconds, and then he bent and kissed her.

"It did not hurt too much?"

"Oh, of course it hurt, it's bound to hurt, but Dr. Ramírez was wonderful and anyway, it's a different kind of pain to any other pain because it's constructive. Aren't you going to look at him?"

Luis took her hand in both of his.

"Yes, yes, of course—"

Frances glanced at the foot of the bed where a clear plastic cradle was neatly parked on its rubber wheels.

"Usually, he's beside me, so I can gaze voluptuously at him, but when I go to sleep, for some reason they always wheel him down there. Go and see."

"Yes," Luis said, not moving. "A boy."

"Yes. A little boy. A little fair-haired, dark-eyed boy. Where could he have come from?"

"You sound so happy!"

"Of *course* I do!" she almost shouted. "I'm ecstatic, I've never achieved anything like this in my life! I'm due to start crying tomorrow, apparently people always do, but today I could rule the world—"

He gave her hand a little squeeze and dropped it. Then he went to the end of the bed and looked down into the cradle, standing almost to attention above it as if apprehensive of what he was about to see.

"Pick him up," Frances said.

He made a helpless kind of gesture, half-laughing.

"Shall I? How shall I?"

"Use your wits, Luis!" Frances cried. "Just do what's natural! Just put your hands under him and pick him up!"

He stooped. He put his hands into the cradle. His face was suffused with a sudden dark colour as it sometimes was when he was furious. Heavens, Frances thought, watching, is he going to cry? Luis slowly lifted the sleeping baby and put him against his shoulder and he instantly curved himself into Luis, relaxed and comfortable. Luis gave Frances a look almost of anguish and then shook his head, as if trying to understand something quite impossible. Then he walked slowly over to the window, and stood there with his back to the bed, holding the baby.

Frances sat upright in bed and waited. She considered saying that she had chosen a name for the baby, and that Ana had been to see her, and that there was a possibility of a nice-sounding flat, near the river, about a quarter of a mile from the Maestranza Bullring. All these were factual things she could say as a substitute, for the time being, for all the nonfactual things she longed to ask, and they might provoke him into saying something in reply instead of just standing there, with his back to her and the baby's head tucked into the side of his neck, thinking thoughts that she would, at this moment, have given her soul to know.

"Luis?"

He didn't reply. He didn't move. He simply stood there and she could see neither of their faces. She leaned sideways in the bed, towards them, gripping the edge of the thin mattress in its clean stiff layers of rubber and cotton.

"Luis? Luis, what are you thinking?"

He turned round. His cheeks were wet with tears, shining as if they had been varnished.

"Luis?"

"I—I don't know what to say to you—"

"Are you happy?" she demanded, joyfully. "Aren't you happy now?"

"Happy," he said scornfully, "such a silly little word—" He turned his head and kissed the baby. Then he moved one hand to hold him more securely, pulled a handkerchief out of his pocket, and blew his nose thunderously. The baby didn't stir. Frances, watching them, thought she might faint. She looked down at the floor past her gripping knuckles. Wasn't this it, wasn't this what she had hoped and hoped for, this moment when all the natural elements came together and she could actually see Luis, unable to help himself, adoringly kissing their baby?

"He is perfect," Luis said. "He is beautiful."

"I know."

"He looks so intelligent—"

"Of course."

"He looks like you."

"And you."

"Yes," he said delightedly, "he does, doesn't he, he looks like me!"

Frances let go of the mattress edge and inched herself backwards across the bed to her pillows.

She said, "He's called Antonio."

"Is he? Why is he? There is no Antonio in my family."

"Nor in mine—"

"Then why?"

"Because I like it, because it's easy to say in English too. Because—" She stopped.

"Because what? Because he can be, you think, Anthony Shore, if he chooses?"

"Yes."

"But—"

"Luis," she said, and looked at him with mock sternness. He kissed the baby again.

"He loves me already, look at him, you can see it!"

"Yes."

"You are wonderful," Luis said, suddenly, passionately. "You are so wonderful to have this baby!"

She held her breath. He stood above her, holding the baby tightly to him, his face full of fervour, of ardour even, but when she looked up, to meet his gaze, she saw—and there could be no mistaking it—that the ardour was no longer for her.

TWENTY-TWO

"My flat is quite high up too," Frances wrote to Barbara, "and it gets the sun in the morning, and there's a balcony just big enough for Antonio's pram. It was terribly difficult to find a pram fit for a boy. Spanish prams are perfectly awful, covered in ruffles, all ready for flamenco. Lizzie would have a fit at my furniture, everything looks like reject props from an amateur production of *Carmen*, but I don't really mind. It's light and it's convenient, and when I start work in earnest next month there's a wonderful crèche for Antonio two streets away, run by nuns."

The nuns wore pale-grey habits over white stockings and sensible black shoes. They were a tiny order, founded by two wealthy and pious sisters in the fifteenth century, with the aim of looking after the orphaned babies of Seville and, more importantly, bringing them up to be devout Catholics. There was even, in the whitewashed wall beside the main entrance, an iron flap, like a huge letterbox, with a metal cage behind it, for the long-ago depositing of unwanted babies. The flap was sealed up now, from behind, with a wooden board, but Sister Rufina—named, she said proudly, after one of Seville's two patron saints—who ran the crèche

for the babies and small children of working mothers, told
Frances that the sisters still, very occasionally, opened the
door in the morning to find a baby, now in a plastic laundry
basket, on the step. Sister Rufina thought that girls came
over the river at night from Triana, where there was a
serious drug problem, because several of the babies, in the
last few years, had been diagnosed as already drug dependent. These babies went straight to hospital because the sisters no longer ran an orphanage, only a clinic for mothers
and babies, in this local quarter, and the crèche. Sister Rufina had been very admiring of Antonio.

"What a beautiful baby!"

"And so happy," Frances said. "A really merry baby."

"Is he a good sleeper?"

"No," Frances said, "he's a true Spaniard. He's an all-
night song-and-dance man."

Sister Rufina would look after Antonio from eight in the
morning, until three in the afternoon, five days a week,
throughout the coming summer. While she did that, Frances would work from the dark suite of offices, where she
was now, after extraordinary patience and persistence, a
partner in a travel company whose new name couldn't
quite be decided upon. Frances favoured "Special Journeys"; her new, and senior, partner Juan Carlos María de
Rivas preferred "The Spanish-English Travel Company."
Frances had already discovered a handful of interesting-
sounding small hotels scattered across the western end of
Andalucía, some of them run by expatriate English on the
broad lines of English country-house hotels, and was at the
same time working up Spanish interest in similar kinds of
hotels in England, suggested by Nicky. She also retained a
business relationship with the *Posadas* of Andalucía. She
received polite, formal letters from José, and one or two,
occasionally, from Luis, signed by a secretary on his behalf.

"Money is a bit of a juggling act," she went on, in her
fortnightly letter to Barbara, "but I think we shall manage.
It's odd how different things are cheap and expensive
abroad and also how differently you seem to spend money.

The doctor who delivered Antonio has become rather a
friend—she wants us to learn to ride together—and I see
something of Luis's sister, Ana. I don't know if I really like
her or not, but she seems to like me which of course I'm
grateful for. I see Luis when he comes to collect Antonio—"

This was most weekends. He hardly missed one. He bore
the baby away as if he were a trophy on Saturdays and
returned him on Sunday nights. It was exactly the kind of
involvement Frances had planned for, but she had not
planned for how difficult it would be, this endless seeing
but not seeing, this sharing, this conflicting, painful tug
between gain and loss. She wouldn't let Luis pay for anything, except for when Antonio was with him, and Luis
had wanted to pay for everything, for a bigger flat for them,
for the best in nursery furniture, for domestic help. It had
taken great strength to hold him off, of course it had, how
could it be otherwise when it was the last thing she wanted
to do?

She put her pen down. Faint crowing noises from the
balcony and the occasional flash of a small, fat brown foot
indicated that Antonio was now awake and would soon
require company. He would be thrilled to see her; he always was, his face brilliant with enchanted smiles at the
sight of her, of shop keepers, of his Aunt Ana, of his father.
There was so much that couldn't be written, so much that
privately coloured Frances's life now, so much that was
more different than even her wildest imaginings had ca-
tered for, from her almost overwhelming passion for this
baby to the startled realisation that although her state of
single motherhood wasn't uncommon, it still didn't have,
plainly and amazingly, the status of having been divorced.

"Señora Shore," Sister Rufina had said firmly.

"I am Señorita—"

"Señora Shore."

"I am not divorced, you see, I have never been married—"

Sister Rufina smiled and made a little gesture towards
the other babies in the crèche, the toddling children, as if
their social sensibilities had to be considered.

"Señora Shore."

And then there was Luis. To nobody did she wish to confide that moment in the hospital when she had seen him fall in love with his son, and out of love with her, and, at the same moment, realise with a kind of awe how much he had loved her. He hadn't said anything, but he hadn't needed to. Frances had understood as plainly as if he had carefully explained himself to her, just as she understood that what now bound them together, as far as he was concerned, was their son. How she was finally going to cope with this, she didn't know, she didn't even, if she could help it, ask herself. William had written to her repeating his lifelong belief that nothing lovely in life was ever, in the final analysis, wasted. At the moment, however, Frances wasn't much interested in waste. Waste seemed quite a trivial thing beside pain. That was why—and this again she would spell out to nobody—she was in Seville. She could not go back, like Lizzie, into the detail, the almost domestic detail, of her old life: only in Spain, for her and for now, lay the continuing vision.

And that is what, Frances told herself, folding up her letter, is what it comes down to. Doesn't it? We follow where the light beckons. A squawk came from the balcony. Frances looked up, waiting lovingly for a glimpse of the kicking feet. She would go on a step at a time, beset, no doubt, by many threatening things but never by regret. Regret was out of the question; regret simply didn't make sense. She might have died the first death, of loss, but she would never, ever—and this she promised herself—die the second death, of forgetting.

Turn the pages for a preview of
Joanna Trollope's newest novel . . .

THE BEST OF FRIENDS

Available in hardcover from Viking,
May 1998

In the badly printed guidebook that the Tourist Information Office in Whittingbourne gave out free, The Bee House was listed under "Buildings of Historical Interest." It wasn't, however, the building that was of interest historically so much as its associations. The building was a ramble, one of those amalgams of styles and constant changes of use that produce a feeling of intense humanity and even greater impracticality. Visitors, stepping cautiously around its odd corners and abrupt switches of floor-level, would murmur about its charm and eccentricity while uttering silent prayers of thankfulness that they were not responsible for either keeping it clean or repairing its roofs. Then they would pick up one of the leaflets that were kept in a wooden rack on the reception desk, and go out into the garden to see the bee boles.

The bee boles were what gave the house its name and its place in the tourist guide. The long garden that stretched away to the north was enclosed, on its east-facing side, by a long and ancient brick wall which supported a number of espaliered fruit trees. It was also pierced a dozen times with neat alcoved recesses, each one wide enough and deep enough to have held a single bee skep made, said the leaflet, of coiled straw and, in medieval times, of wicker. Each skep would have had a wooden alighting board projecting in front of it and the east-facing wall had been chosen in the hope that the morning sun would get the bees working early. Hilary Wood, Gus's mother, had tried to persuade modern bees to take up residence in these ancient dwellings, but they had resolutely rejected them in favour of white-painted chalet-style hives elsewhere and convenient for nearby fields of rape-seed.

In the bar of The Bee House hung several framed copies of historic documents. One was a fragment from the will of Adam Cullinge, in 1407, who bequeathed all his bees and bee boles at The Bee House to the churchwardens of Whittingbourne, "the profit of them to be devoted towards maintaining three wax tapers in the church, ever burning . . ." Another document was an inventory made by a subsequent owner of The Bee House, in the late sixteenth century, which included "8 fattes of bees: 16 shillings." A fatte of bees, said a note typed by Hilary and stuck on the wall below the inventory, was a hive of bees in good condition. An even later occupant of The Bee House, a tenant, had left a memorandum in a strong black hand to the effect that he managed to pay the rent solely from the sale of honey and beeswax. He had added an admonishing postscript to any aspirant bee-keepers: "Let your hives be rather too little than too greate, for such are hurtful to the increase and prosperity of Bees."

It was the bees, really, that had seduced them into deciding to make a home and a hotel business out of The Bee House. There was something about the industry and domesticity of bees which, combined with their appealing appearance and attractive history, made both Laurence and Hilary feel that they hadn't really a choice in accepting this odd bequest, that the choice had eerily been made for them. They'd only been in their early twenties after all, not married yet, and with Laurence full of yearnings about roaming the world before perhaps being an architect. Or maybe a furniture-maker. Something to do with design, anyway.

And then along came this letter from Askew and Payne, Solicitors, of Tower Street, Whittingbourne, to say that Ernest Harrison, who had struggled to teach Laurence and his contemporaries Latin and Greek at grammar school, had left Laurence the dwelling house known as The Bee House, which was in a very poor state of repair but which might fetch a reasonable price on the open market if sold during the summer months.

"I'll sell it," Laurence said, visualizing air tickets to Australia and an open Ford Mustang.

"You can't," Hilary said. "At least, not without thinking. He left it to you."

"I wonder why—"

Hilary let a little pause fall and then she said, "I expect there was no one else."

Laurence remembered his classroom on summer afternoons, packed with adolescent boys who were all, in their turn, packed with exploding hormones, sitting in barely controlled rows enduring old Harrison. He was a stupefyingly dull teacher; most lessons, he'd have been more entertaining and instructive reading from the Whittingbourne telephone directory. Dressed in mouldering garmets of fog-colour and brown, he maundered his way through myths and battles and poems and exhortations to the gods as if they were so many laundry lists. And yet Laurence had felt, in a way he couldn't have explained to himself nor dared to broach his friends, that there was something there, in old Harrison, under the dinge and drab. He remembered two things particularly. One was old Harrison saying that none of them would ever encounter anything in all their lives as truly shocking, in the literal sense, as the *Iliad*. The other was his remark that almost any great work of art is bound to be subversive. Laurence had written that down, covertly, but old Harrison had seen him do it. His eyes had gleamed, faintly, briefly, behind his smeared spectacles. Could it be that, for merely copying down a remark which was almost certainly not an original thought, one could be left a collapsing house with a twelfth-century cellar, miles

of buckling hardboard partitioning and an association with
bees?

"What'd we do with it?" Laurence had said to Hilary.
She was two years into reading medicine at Guy's Hospital
in London and they had met at a New Year's Eve party,
given by a mutual friend in a flat in Fulham. She had been
the only girl there wearing spectacles and when, after midnight, he had tried to take them off her with alcoholic
amorousness, she had said, "Oh you are so *depressing*," and
had left the party in a huff. He'd found her the next day,
after hours of persistent, hungover sleuthing. She had
rented a room in Lambeth and was sitting up in bed, for
warmth, wearing a green bobble hat and studying diagrams
of the ear. It was only a year after that that Ernest Harrison
had left Laurence The Bee House.

"What do we do with it?" Laurence had asked Hilary.

Hilary had looked at him sharply.

"We?"

He hesitated a bit, and coloured. Hilary went on looking
at him for a while, wearing an expression he dared not
analyse, and then she said, quite gently, that she had to get
to the bank before it shut.

It wasn't only the fantasies of the beaches of New South
Wales and a Ford Mustang that caused Laurence to hesi-
tate. It was Hilary, too. He knew, although he hadn't yet
asked her, that he badly wanted to marry her, and he also
knew that, as the daughter and granddaughter of doctors,
she was serious about medicine. He was also in slight awe
of some of her views which she did not express loudly but
with a quiet certainty that was alarmingly impressive. One
of these views (and this made his courage falter just a little
about proposing marriage) was about motherhood.

"We ought," Hilary had said one day, turning her char-
acterful, bespectacled face on its long neck to look past him,
"as a society, to admit that motherhood isn't *everything*. It's
something, for some people, but it isn't everything for everyone. It's a lifelong relationship but then, so is having
brothers or real friends. Mothers shouldn't have a monopoly

on human wonderfulness. After all, babies are only what the machinery is designed for."

"Gulp," said Laurence. Briefly, he imagined Hilary pregnant by him and felt a little faint.

"I don't want," continued Hilary, retrieving her gaze from the distance and bestowing it on Laurence, "to be either some sacred Madonna or some exhausted freak who can't be expected to think a single coherent thought beyond the nappy bucket. Do you see?"

"Yes," said Laurence.

"Some of us should have babies and some shouldn't and those that don't should then be free to get on with something else."

"Yes."

"And not to be told all the time that they are inadequate or incomplete women because of childlessness."

"No."

"If you're a child, you see, it's awful to be mothered all your life. Mothers should know when to stop."

"Yes. Why are you telling me all this?"

"Because it's in my mind."

I can't, Laurence thought later while roaming yet again through the musty, lopsided rooms of The Bee House, ask someone like that to marry me. I want her desperately but I also rather want normal things, like a baby. Some time, anyway. Perhaps I'd better just flog this old heap and go and be a jackaroo for a while and see whether, when I come back, she's missed me.

"I'd miss you, if you went to Australia," Hilary said, two days later.

"Would you?"

"And it's a pretty corny thing to do anyway, going to Australia."

He took her hand and examined it closely as if reading her palm.

"What wouldn't be corny?"

"Doing something that wasn't just an easy adventure. Like—making something of The Bee House."

He pushed his face almost into hers.

"Like what?"

"Like—making a hotel of it? A little hotel?"

He closed his eyes.

"You could do a hotel management course. We—both could."

"But you're going to be a doctor!"

"I was—"

She was smiling, a wide huge smile, and behind her glasses, her eyes were like lamps. Laurence, who hadn't cried for years and thought he had forgotten how, burst into tears. Much, much later, whey they were quite bruised with kissing, Laurence said, "But what about babies?"

She looked up at the sky. He'd taken her glasses off without protest this time and without them, her gaze was vulnerable.

"I wouldn't mind," she said, "at least, not one or two. As long as they're yours."

That was 1970: six years before George, eight years before Adam, ten years before Gus. It was also before Laurence told Hilary about Gina.

"Who's Gina?"

They were in the garden of The Bee House, raking up rubbish for a bonfire.

Laurence said, openly and seriously, "My best friend."

"What sort of best friend?"

"The person I talk to about what we want of life, borrow books from, go to the cinema with."

Hilary leant on her rake. She was wearing a red muffler and her short dark hair was tousled.

"Who is she?"

"What do you mean?"

"I mean how old is she, what does she do, why is she your best friend, what does she look like, why do we know each other for over a year and she never gets mentioned?"

"I didn't mean to," Laurence said simply, "until I knew you'd marry me."

"Are you serious?"

"Of course."

"Were you keeping her as a sort of *reserve*? In case I refused you?"

"No."

"Laurence!" Hilary yelled suddenly, flinging away her rake so that it almost broke against a tree trunk. "Don't you know anything about girls at all except that you are crazy to have one?"

Laurence said nothing. He ran his hands through his hair a few times but the gesture, Hilary noticed, wasn't remotely distracted but, instead, soothing, like someone closing their eyes while they collect their thoughts.

After a long pause he said, "Have you got a best friend?"

Hilary picked up her rake again and examined its tines. "No. Not really."

"But you have two brothers and a sister. I haven't. I met Gina when I was sixteen and she was at the sister school to mine. She was an only child too and she'd never known her father. I'd known my mother but not very well because of her dying when I was six. So I suppose there was sort of a bond. And neither of us liked our home lives very much. We realized we were friends on a joint-school theatre outing to see Paul Scofield play King Lear. We sat next to each other on the coach on the way home."

Hilary began to rake again, vigorously, tugging up wet black roots and clumps of coarse, mud-clogged grass. She wanted to ask Laurence if he loved Gina but felt she couldn't because she had the sensation of being in an emotional landscape she'd had no experience of and where she might commit an ignorant *faux pas*, shaming herself.

Instead, she said crossly, "Why did you choose a girl?"

"I didn't." he said calmly, "I chose a person. She's in Montélimar, at the moment, teaching English and the piano at a *lycée*. She went just after we met. That's why I haven't introduced you."

"That simple?"

"Yes."

"No one else vital it's just slipped your mind to tell me about?"

"No."

"Damn," said Hilary, snatching off her glasses so that she could mop her eyes with her muffler. "Damn you, Laurence Wood, you've terrified me."

When, some time later, she and Gina met, Hilary had recovered herself a little. She was, by then, wearing an antique topaz engagement ring and had embarked upon a hotel-management course. Laurence had attached himself to a firm of architects who specialized in the restoration of old buildings. Both their fathers, who had expected much more traditional professional things of them than hotel-keeping, were deeply disappointed and wore their disappointment like uncovered and grievous wounds. This had the effect of making both Laurence and Hilary very certain indeed of one another and their future. Gina, it turned out, was to be their first firm ally.

Hilary first saw her, by chance, sitting on the steps of the porch of Whittingbourne's great medieval parish church, tipping a stone out of her shoe.

"There's Gina," Laurence said. He sounded pleased, warm, but not ecstatic.

Gina was as dark as Hilary, but smaller. She wore her hair shoulder-length, with a fringe, and her face had a serene look because her eyes were set so widely apart. She greeted them both with affection, as if she'd known Hilary for ages which, in a way, Hilary reflected, she almost had because of the letters she and Laurence wrote each other, every week. "Dear Gina," Laurence's letters began; "With love from Laurence," they ended, absolutely above-board and obscurely unsettling.

"You're so right," Gina had said then, fitting her shoe back on and standing up, "about The Bee House. It's a wonderful idea. It's a *real* thing to do."

She came to help them occasionally with some basic clearance before she went back to Montélimar, for the last year of her contract. At the beginning, Hilary could not help feeling watchful but soon saw there was no need because there was no conspiracy. There was instead an intimate acquaintance, a feeling that, above all else, Laurence and Gina wished each other well.

"We haven't been to bed together," Laurence said.

"Haven't you? Why not?"

"It didn't seem to be an issue. Sometimes it nearly did, especially with me, but that's all. And now, that really is all, because of you."

When Gina went back to France she said to Hilary, "Keep in touch."

"But Laurence—"

"Yes, I know. But you do it. Either as well or instead. And keep an eye on Vi for me now and then. Laurence means to, but he forgets."

After Montélimar, Gina went to Pau. While she was in Pau, The Bee House, courtesy of a mortgage, opened its first cautious doors to bed-and-breakfast guests. It was a mild success and emboldened Laurence to feel that, as well as acquiring the skills of a conservationist builder, he might also learn to cook. Hilary, halfway through a book-keeping course and much involved in plans for the hotel's steady development, asked where he would learn.

"Here," he said. "By myself."

"I'm not at all sure about this," Hilary wrote to Gina. "I'm not sure we really have the time for him to experiment until he knows what he's doing. And anyway, I need him to concentrate on what we already have for a while. I think I'm pregnant."

Gina did not reply. Hilary was upset about that, because her pregnancy ended in a distressing miscarriage and she needed someone to say something quite other to her than all the things her family was saying about working too hard for all the wrong goals and if only she'd stuck to medicine and a proper profession this would never have happened. It was only later that Gina's silence was explained. She had met a man in Pau, an Englishman called Leslie Bedford, rather older than her, and she had gone to Italy for two months. It was an utter impulse, she said, and she had never been so happy. She hadn't known how to look at things before Leslie, nor relish them properly. She said it was an enormous relationship in every way and that she felt absolutely released. Then she brought him to Whittingbourne.

"Well, he's handsome," Vi said. "If you like that sort of thing."

He was handsome, tall and fair, topping Laurence by several inches and making him look, and feel, more flung together than planned. He'd been brought up in European embassies, his father having been a minor diplomat, and he spoke French and German and Spanish and Italian. He seemed charmed by Whittingbourne, so charmed that when Laurence's father, a retired estate agent, mentioned that High Place, one of the town's most interesting houses, was coming up for sale shortly, he announced that he intended to buy it and move his business out of London to the country. It was also about this time that he changed his name. Fergus had been his father's name, he said. Gina looked his father up in *Who's Who*. Fergus had been his father's third name; the one by which he had been known was John.

"Why not John?" Gina demanded.

"Everyone is called John."

"Exactly!" Gina had shouted. "You're just a snob of the worst kind!"

Leslie had gone ahead and changed his name to Fergus. "Fergus Bedford Fine Arts" was printed on the new stationery and business cards above the new High Place address. In the same year that George was born ("This isn't glorious," Hilary said during labour. "I knew it wouldn't be. It hurts like hell") Gina became Mrs. Fergus Bedford and moved into High Place with a piano as a wedding present from her husband.

"Will we all be friends now?" Hilary said, scouring the jobs-wanted column of the *Whittingbourne Standard* for a local girl who might want to help her with George.

"I think so. Don't you?"

"What about Fergus?"

"I think I prefer him since he stopped being Leslie. Maybe we just have to get used to him being smoother than us."

"He's very nice to George. It must be a good sign in a man, being interested in a baby. Farmer's daughter, two O levels, seeks town position with a kind family. Worth a try?"

"Don't like the sound of wanting a *town* position. And she doesn't say she likes children."

"Do you think Gina will have children?"

"Oh yes," Laurence said. "Bound to. She always wanted them. It was one of the things we used to talk about."

Sophy was born a few months after Adam, Laurence and Hilary's second son. They were both born in the newish maternity wing of the Whittingbourne Hospital, within sight of the brown Victorian block where Gina herself had been born and where Vi had lain after her birth for five days without visitors except for a routine priest who kept his gaze severely on her ringless hand. Sophy's birth brought the two families much closer together because they could share so much, like birthday parties and chicken pox and the services of a plump, placid girl who never minded what she was asked to do since she seldom troubled herself to do any of it anyway.

It was also the time when a true friendship began to grow up between Hilary and Gina. It was a friendship based initially on both being in the same trade union of young motherhood, and the daily luxury they both looked forward to—almost, Gina sometimes thought, with a craving—was a long complain to one another, either face to face, or on the telephone. The complaining sessions had several unwritten rules of which one was that neither ever said anything really savagely unpleasant about husband or children and another was that it was a requirement to be as hilariously funny about the day's disasters as possible. Later, looking back on those conversations, Gina knew that she would never have got through the inevitable squalor of Sophy's babyhood and little childhood—from which Fergus required, without question, to be shielded—without being able to rehearse, as she mopped up yet another little accident, as Vi would call them, the version she would later recount to Hilary.

Hilary's sister, Vanessa, a physiotherapist specializing in sports injuries, thought the developing friendship was hardly healthy.

"I mean, she practically *lives* here—"

"I like it. And she's incredibly useful."

"Hasn't she got a job to do?"

"Well, yes, she teaches piano and does some language tuition but not all the time."

"I suppose they have heaps of money. They behave as if they do. I say, don't you think you ought to have that damp patch attended to?"

Hilary looked up. The kitchen ceiling of the flat they had made for the family out of the attics of The Bee House had a long dark stain on it, just the same shape, Laurence pointed out, as a map of Italy except that Sicily was missing.

"We can't," she said, "it's the bar next. It's the most used part of the hotel and the paint's been kicked to pieces."

The map of Italy had stayed on the kitchen ceiling for almost four years, well after Gus had been born. They had tried to decorate the hotel in the bleak winter months after Christmas when demand for bedrooms dwindled to nothing, with one of them on bar duty and the other permanently speckled with emulsion. For their twelfth wedding anniversary, they bought themselves their first proper sofa, and all five of them sat on it, in a row, in ceremonial occupation, as if to demonstrate to whatever powers there were that they had at last achieved something that symbolized stability and a kind of, albeit shaky, success.

It was exasperating, Hilary sometimes thought now, to find herself looking back on those earlier days with nostalgia. She remembered them as noisy, dirty, anxious and achingly exhausting, but only, as it were, technically. Like childbirth, she could remember the anticipation of those years, the sense of adventure and of there being a future where they would all arrive, weary but triumphant, like mariners after a long and stormy voyage. The thing was, she supposed, staring unseeing at her unwanted, inevitable, post-lunch-party task of the weekly books, that she was now *in* the future, they all were, and it wasn't at all as she expected it. It wasn't a golden shore to a promised land but just somehow more of the voyage. The hotel was comfortable enough, successful enough, largely due to Laurence's increasingly admired skills in the kitchen, but Hilary could no longer remember—and was afraid to confess this because it seemed so much like letting other people down—what the whole enterprise was *for*.

She was very tired. The hotel had been full all week and the restaurant was booked out all weekend, including a wedding reception in the room they had converted for such purposes ("We must have been mad," Laurence had said last night) two years ago. On her desk in this tiny office she'd had made out of a beetle-ridden boot hole, lay not only all the accounts and invoices for the week, but a pile of requests for bookings and estimates, a particularly unpleasant letter from a man about an unrefundable deposit, and a seventy-page government directive detailing the new EEC regulations for kitchens in hotels and boarding houses of a certain category (up to 3-star) in urban or semi-urban locations. There was also an in-tray labelled, in Hilary's mind, "Things I Can't Quite Face Today," including Gus's school report (poor) and a number of prospectuses from colleges and universities in which she had so far failed to make Adam take even the slightest interest.

She yawned. She hadn't drunk anything at the party but orange juice—what a disagreeable, metallic, unsatisfactory drink orange juice was, when it was your only option—but still felt soporific from the effect of other people's champagne fumes and cigarette smoke. It had really been rather a grisly party, full of the exaggerated, strained jollity of middle-aged people pretending that they weren't middle-aged, and the poor third wife (whose navy-blue mascara had smudged) listening with bright-eyed anguish to a drunken speech, made by her husband's oldest friend, in which he blithely toasted "Johnnie and Mags, and may they never grow older or wiser." The third wife's name was Marsha. Mags was Johnnie's first wife, a startling, six-foot

brunette, who had left him for a much younger film di-
rector, but who had then taken care never quite to go away.
She had dominated the party, in a scarlet dress, black gloves
and a cigarette holder. It was enough to smudge anyone's
mascara.

And then of course there had been Gina and Fergus, not
speaking. They had spent the party at opposite sides of the
elaborate marquee (pink-and-white-striped canvas complete
with French windows under fibreglass pediments, and
Ionic-topped columns around which flowers and ribbons
had been winsomely wound) being particularly polite to
other people, as if to emphasize their refusal to be even
remotely courteous to one another. Fergus looked frozen;
Gina, haunted.

Stewart Nicholson, a senior member of Whittingbourne's
largest medical practice, said to Hilary, "How long do you
give that one?"

"Years," Hilary had said sharply. "Years. Quarrelling is
as natural to them as breathing."

Stewart Nicholson had taken a huge bite of vol-au-vent,
spraying Hilary with flakes of pastry.

"If you say so." He winked.

Later, in the car going home, with the prospect of her
littered desk and a busy evening ahead of them, and soured
by the party's falsity and too much orange juice, Hilary had
given way to her temper. There had been an elaborate pan-
tomime of who should sit where in the car, and, in the end,
Laurence had, to settle it, climbed in beside his wife and
left Gina and Fergus to sit as widely separated as was possible, in the back. Something about the sight of them,
glimpsed in her driving mirror, staring fixedly out of opposite windows, snapped a frayed cord of self-control in
Hilary.

"If you two," she said, slamming the car into reverse,
"can't behave like civilized beings in public at least, I can't
think why you trouble to stay together one more minute."

There had been, then, a long and awkward silence, during which everyone looked away from Hilary and one another, and Hilary glared at the road. It was broken only,

and finally, by Laurence saying, in a very thoughtful voice and as if Hilary hadn't spoken at all, "What a perfectly godawful party. Why the hell did we think we wanted to go?"

The door behind Hilary opened a crack.

"Mum—"

"Yes," she said, not turning.

"I think you'd better come—"

"Why?"

Adam slid into the narrow space between her desk and the wall. Hilary looked up. His hair, very short at the back, hung over his face in front, and his hands were hidden under long, crumpled, unbuttoned shirt-cuffs. Hilary sighed. She adored, but felt that she was not, in the least, in the mood for him just now.

"Is there a crisis?"

"It's Gina. She's in the flat. She said not to disturb you but she's crying. Gus made her coffee."

"Gina? But I only dropped her home two hours ago—"

Adam shrugged. He lifted his front curtain of hair briefly and revealed his father's face, only young and sadly spotty.

"You'd better come. Shall I get a brandy from the bar?"

"Oh God," Hilary said, "is it that bad—"

Adam shrugged. He screwed up his face in an effort to express himself adequately and then he said, "She looks like someone's died."